C000150100

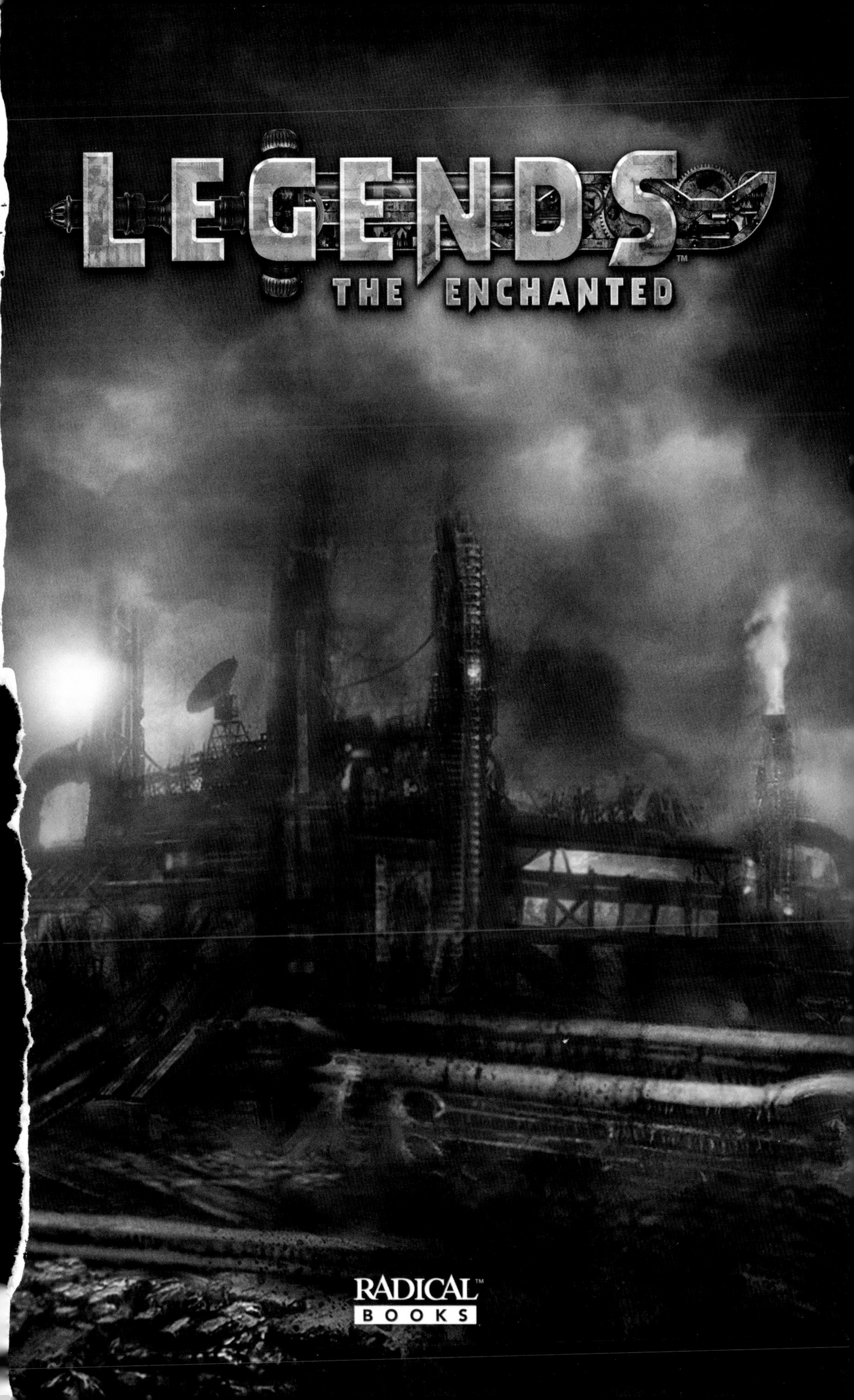
LEGENDS™
THE ENCHANTED
RADICAL™
BOOKS

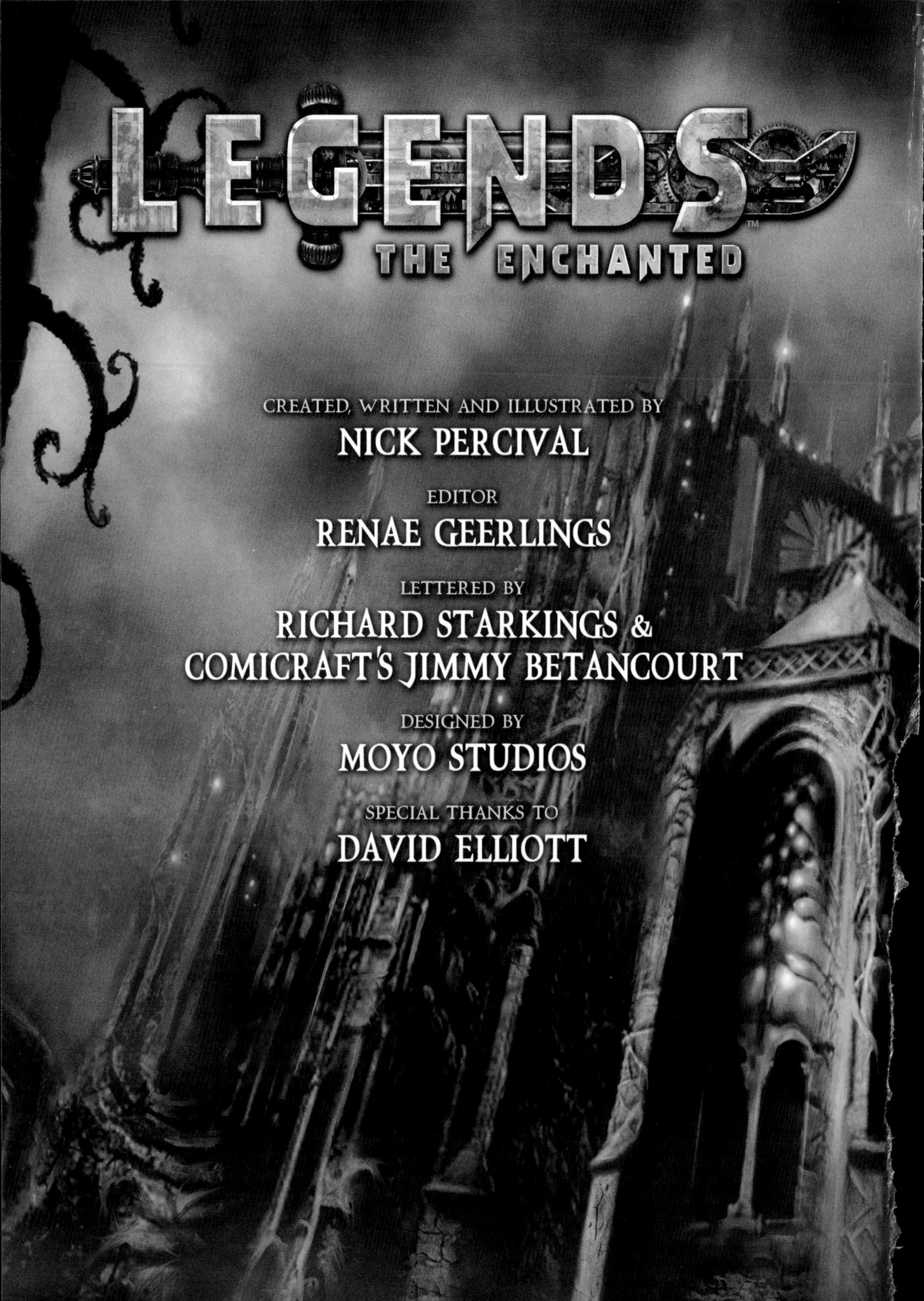

LEGENDS
THE ENCHANTED

CREATED, WRITTEN AND ILLUSTRATED BY
NICK PERCIVAL

EDITOR
RENAE GEERLINGS

LETTERED BY
RICHARD STARKINGS &
COMICRAFT'S JIMMY BETANCOURT

DESIGNED BY
MOYO STUDIOS

SPECIAL THANKS TO
DAVID ELLIOTT

LEGENDS: THE ENCHANTED. Published by Radical Books. Office of publication: 7421 Beverly Blvd., Los Angeles, California 90036. Copyright © 2010 NICK PERCIVAL and RADICAL PUBLISHING. INC. All rights reserved. LEGENDS: THE ENCHANTED ™ (including all prominent characters featured herein). Its logo and all character likenesses are trademarks of NICK PERCIVAL AND RADICAL PUBLISHING. INC., unless otherwise noted. Radical Books ™ is a trademark of Radical Publishing. Inc. All rights reserved. No part of this publication may be reproduced or transmitted, in any form or by any means (except for short excerpts for review purposes) without the express written permission of Radical Publishing. Inc. All names, characters, events and locales in this publication are entirely fictional. Any resemblance to actual persons (living or dead), events or places, without satiric intent, is coincidental.

"For the Percival Tribe: Jake, Lily, Maddie and Izzy - yep,
Dad is finally out of the studio. For my parents who
would always let me buy insane amounts of
comic books and finally for Sarah...she sure knows why."

NICK PERCIVAL

RADICAL PUBLISHING

President & Publisher BARRY LEVINE
Executive Vice President JESSE BERGER
Chief Operating Officer MARK RAFALOWSKI
Chief Financial Officer MARK KAUFMAN
Editor in Chief DAVID WOHL
General Counsel MATTHEW BERGER
Director of Marketing GIANLUCA GLAZER
Director of Production JOHN ZOPFI
Director of Sales TEDDY CABUGOS
Art Director JEREMY BERGER
Director of Operations BARRETT WEISLOW
Designer NICK CABUGOS
Digital Media Manager PAUL KELLER
Art Assistant DAVID MILES
Executive Assistant AMANDA MORTLOCK

LEGENDS
THE ENCHANTED
BY Nick Percival

ONCE UPON A TIME...

ALL THE FAIRYTALES YOU EVER HEARD WERE TRUE.

BUT YOU ONLY HEARD HALF OF THE STORY.

THEIR NAMES ARE SPOKEN IN WHISPERS. THEIR DEEDS
ARE LEGENDARY. THEIR FANTASTIC
TALES ARE KNOWN THROUGHOUT THE LANDS.

THEY ARE THE ENCHANTED.

CHARMED BY MAGIC TO BE FREE FROM HARM, THESE
POWERFUL OUTLAWS ROAM AND PROTECT A STRANGE
WORLD WHERE MEDIEVAL FOLKLORE MEETS MODERN
DAY GRIT...AND DEADLY CREATURES STALK
THE TOWNS BY MOONLIGHT.

BUT SOMEONE WANTS THEM DEAD...

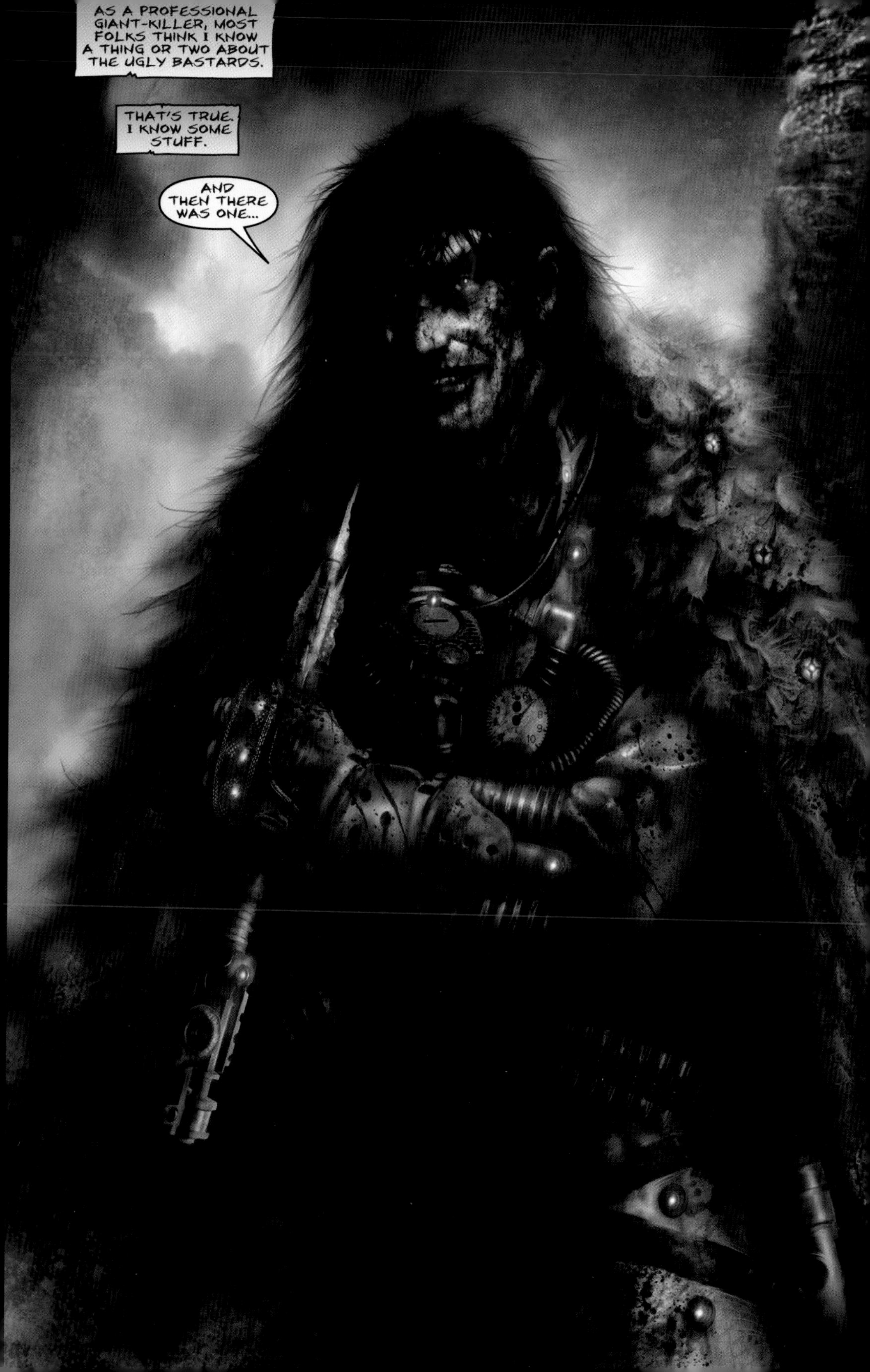
AS A PROFESSIONAL GIANT-KILLER, MOST FOLKS THINK I KNOW A THING OR TWO ABOUT THE UGLY BASTARDS.
THAT'S TRUE. I KNOW SOME STUFF.
AND THEN THERE WAS ONE...

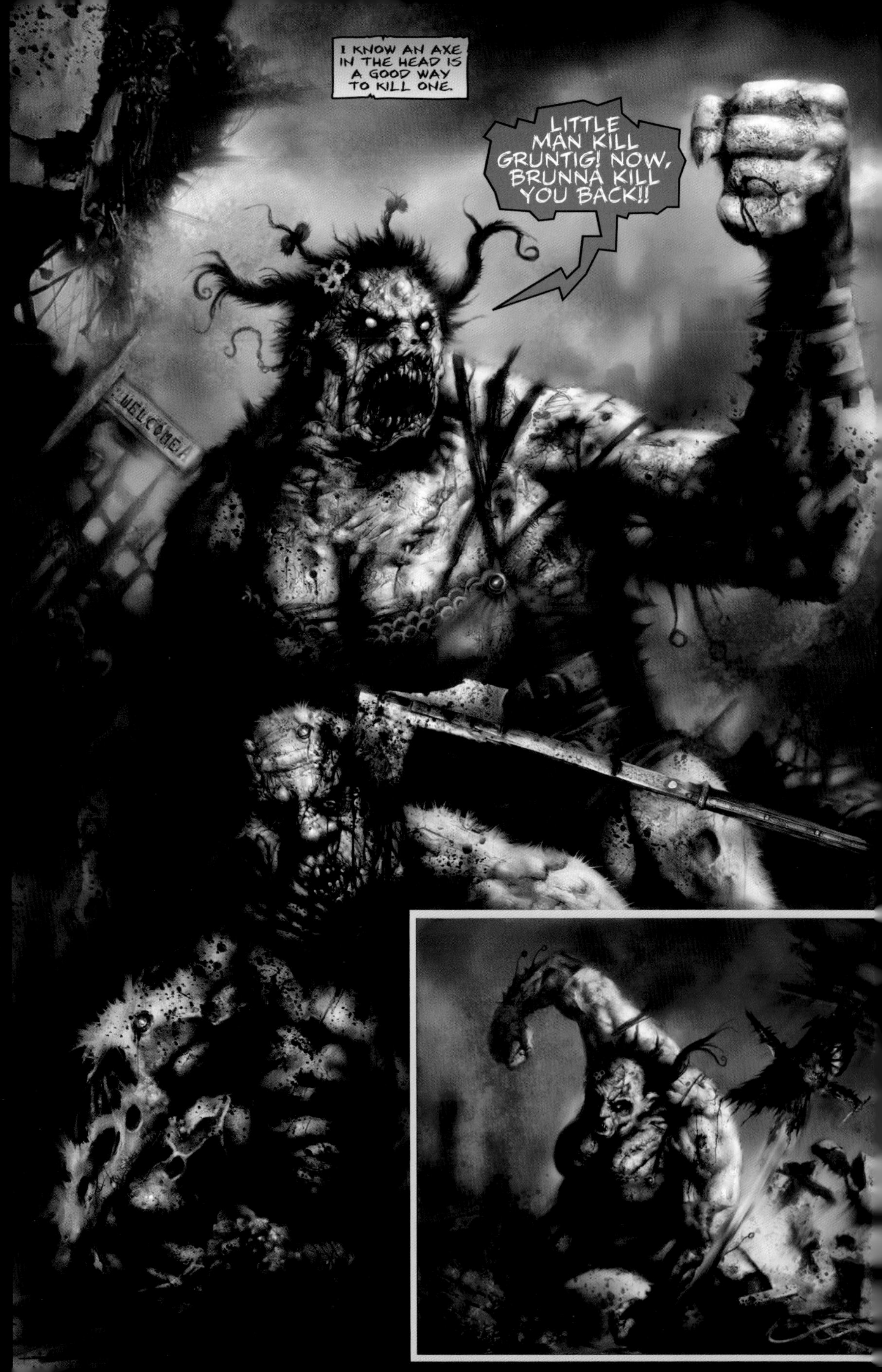
I KNOW AN AXE IN THE HEAD IS A GOOD WAY TO KILL ONE.
LITTLE MAN KILL GRUNTIG! NOW, BRUNNA KILL YOU BACK!!
WELCOME

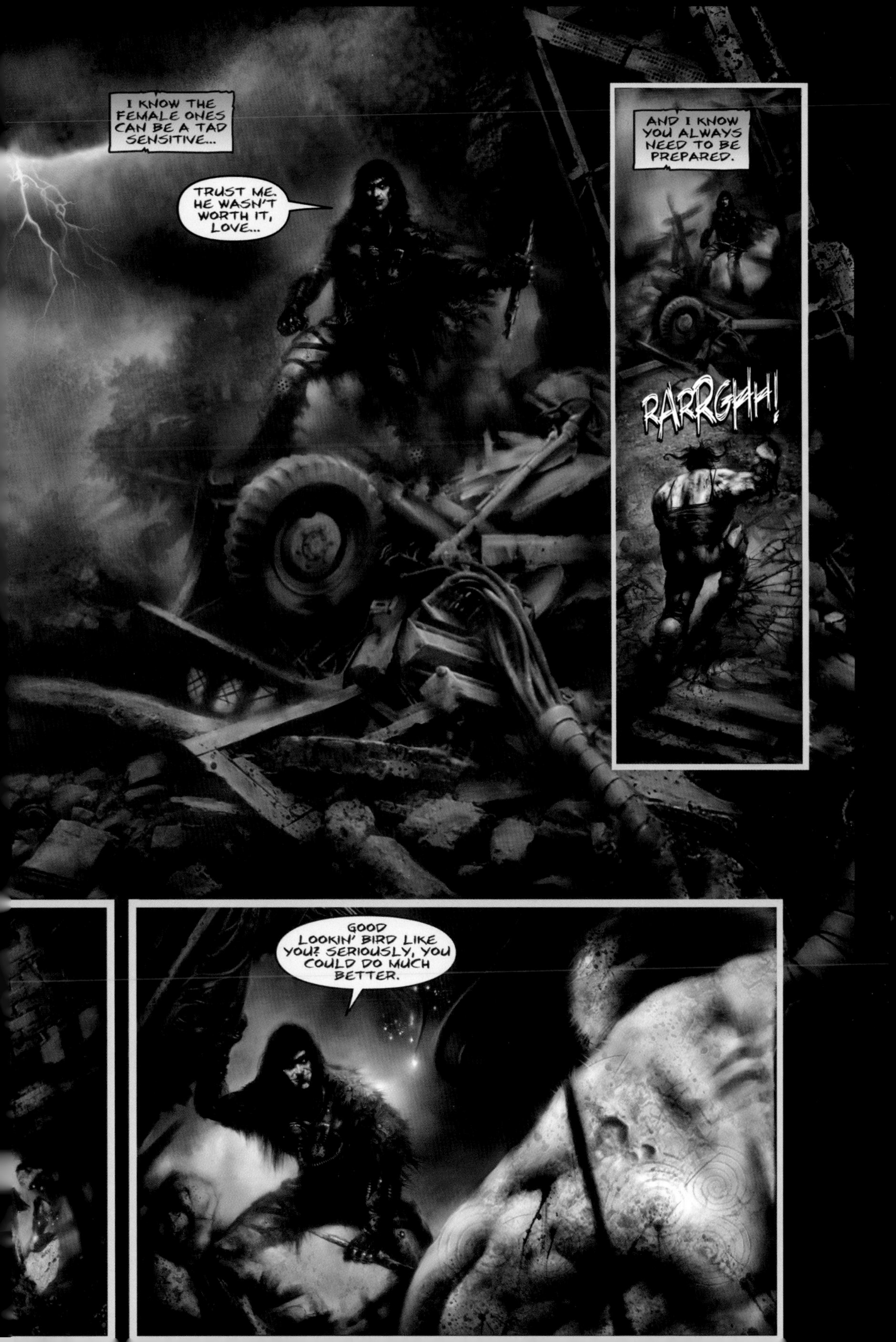
I KNOW THE FEMALE ONES CAN BE A TAD SENSITIVE...
TRUST ME. HE WASN'T WORTH IT, LOVE...
AND I KNOW YOU ALWAYS NEED TO BE PREPARED.
RARRGHH!
GOOD LOOKIN' BIRD LIKE YOU? SERIOUSLY, YOU COULD DO MUCH BETTER.

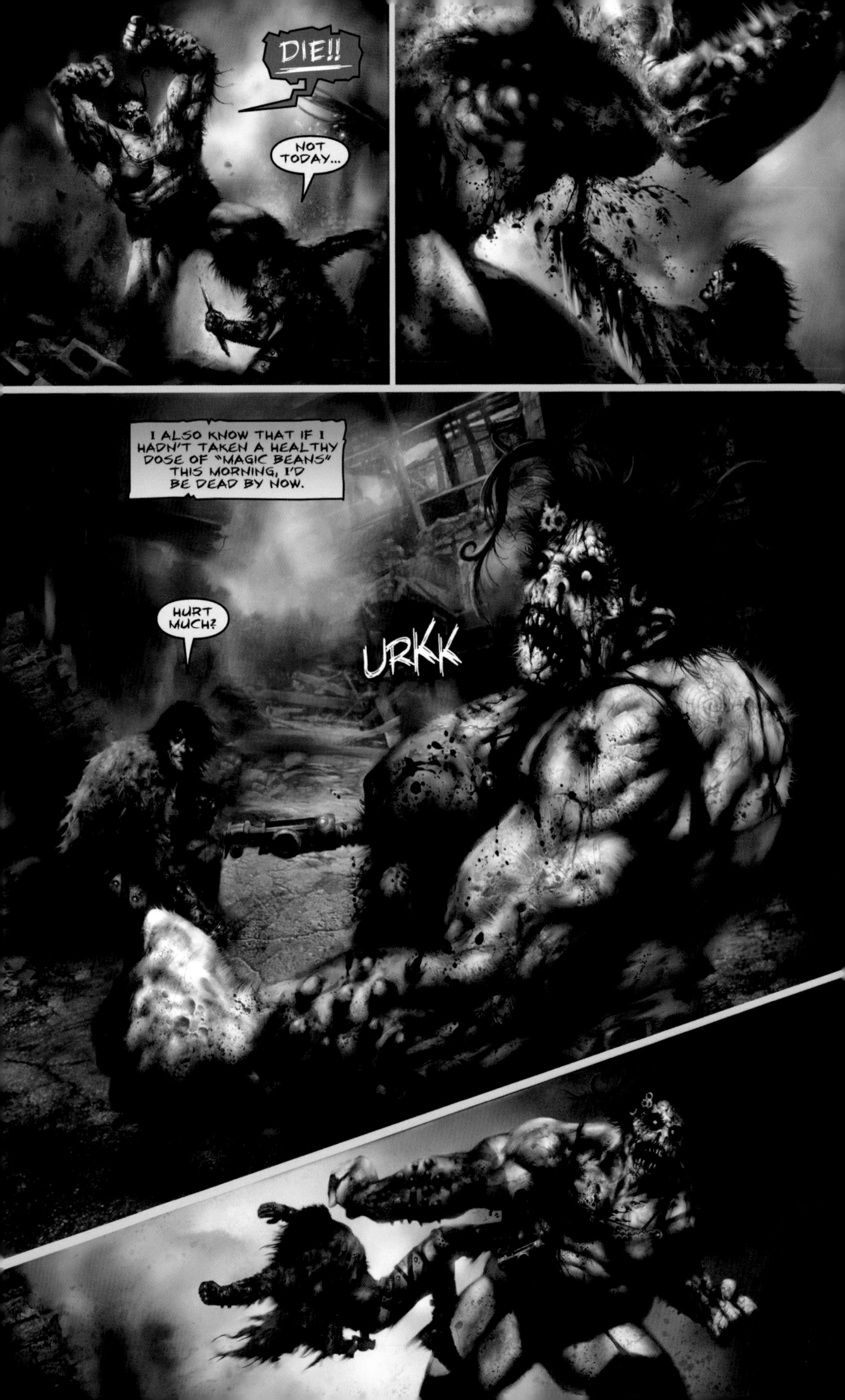
DIE!!
NOT TODAY...
I ALSO KNOW THAT IF I HADN'T TAKEN A HEALTHY DOSE OF "MAGIC BEANS" THIS MORNING, I'D BE DEAD BY NOW.
HURT MUCH?
URKK

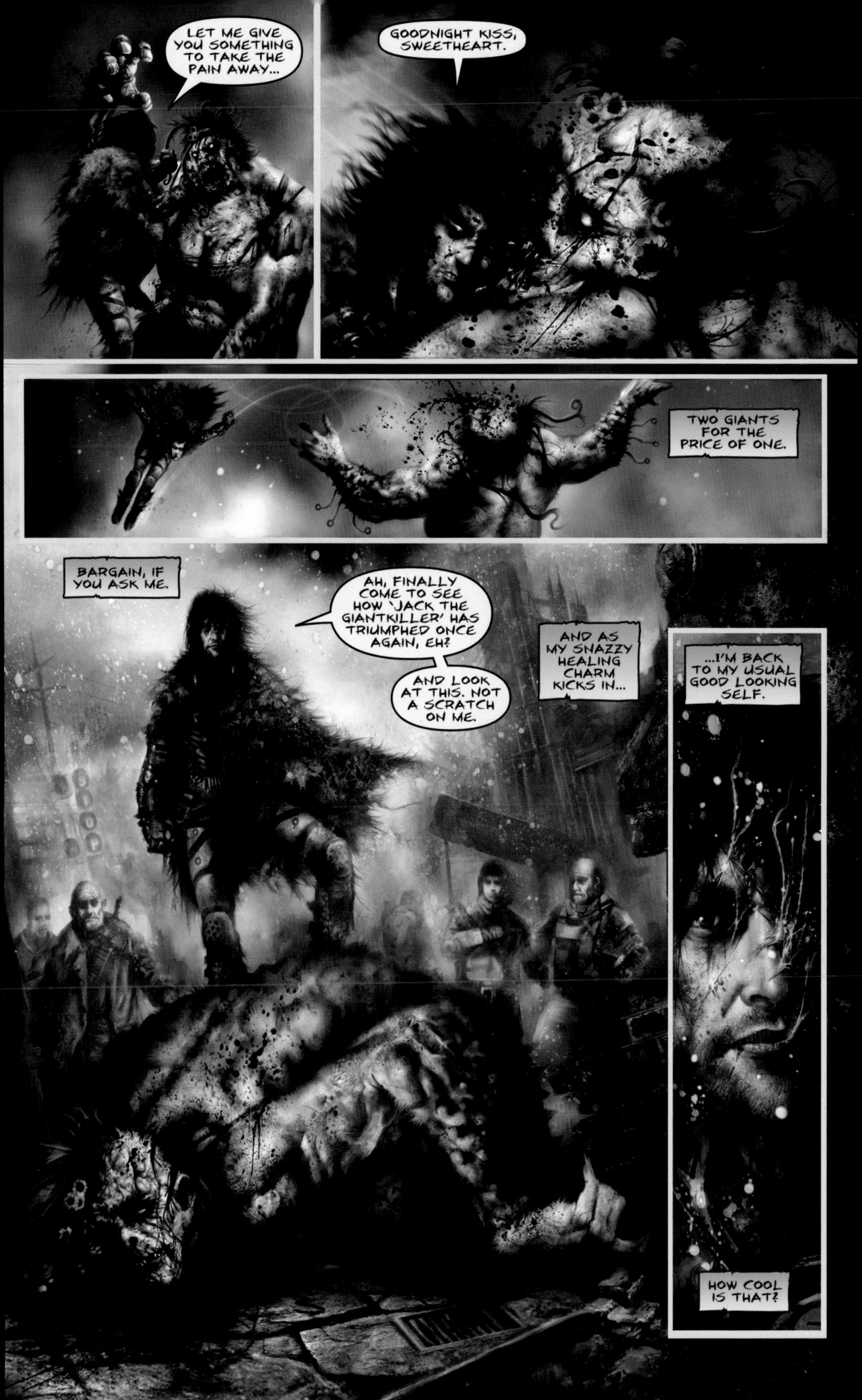
LET ME GIVE YOU SOMETHING TO TAKE THE PAIN AWAY...
GOODNIGHT KISS, SWEETHEART.
TWO GIANTS FOR THE PRICE OF ONE.
BARGAIN, IF YOU ASK ME.
AH, FINALLY COME TO SEE HOW 'JACK THE GIANTKILLER' HAS TRIUMPHED ONCE AGAIN, EH?
AND LOOK AT THIS. NOT A SCRATCH ON ME.
AND AS MY SNAZZY HEALING CHARM KICKS IN...
...I'M BACK TO MY USUAL GOOD LOOKING SELF.
HOW COOL IS THAT?

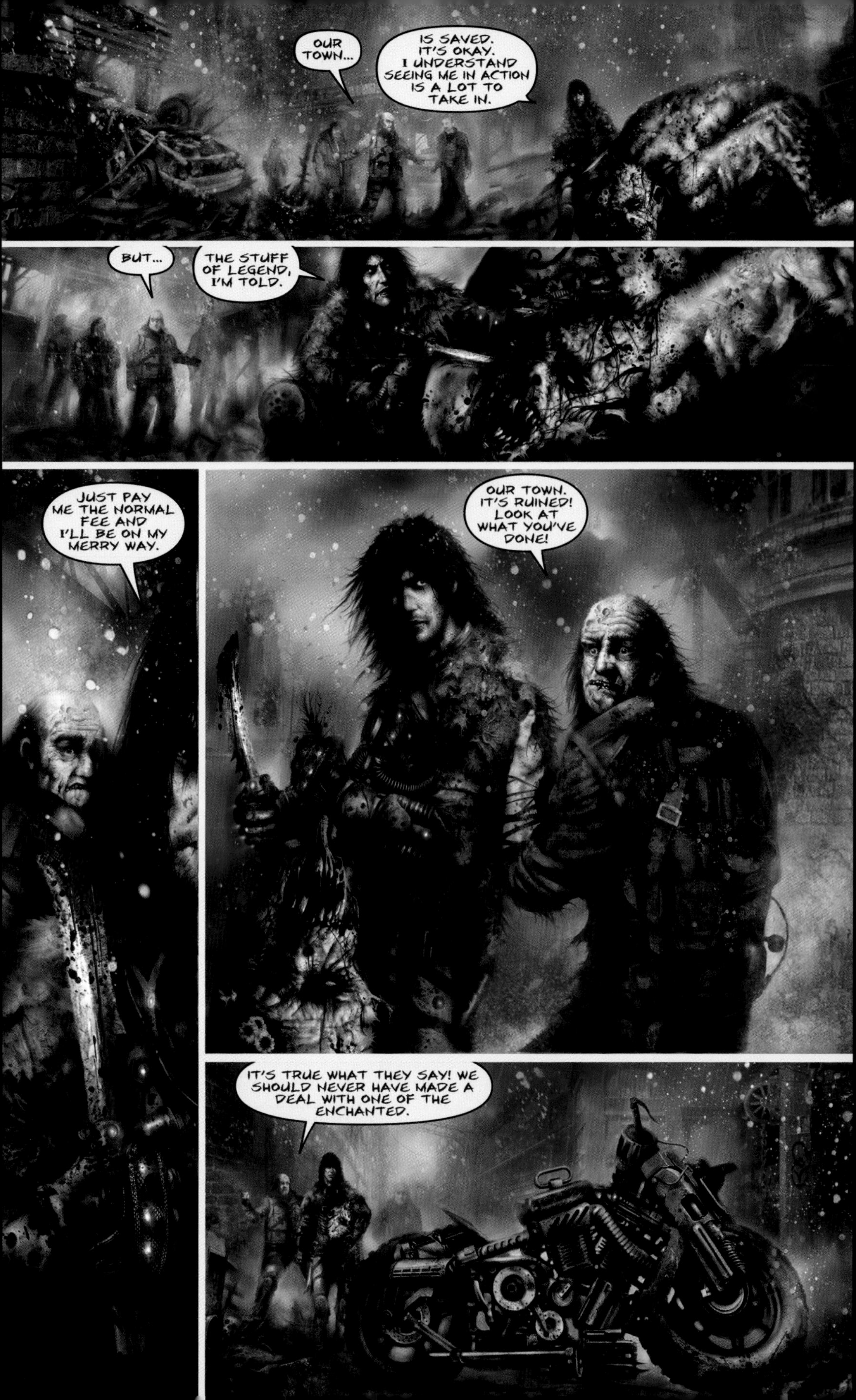
OUR TOWN...
IS SAVED. IT'S OKAY. I UNDERSTAND SEEING ME IN ACTION IS A LOT TO TAKE IN.
BUT...
THE STUFF OF LEGEND, I'M TOLD.
JUST PAY ME THE NORMAL FEE AND I'LL BE ON MY MERRY WAY.
OUR TOWN. IT'S RUINED! LOOK AT WHAT YOU'VE DONE!
IT'S TRUE WHAT THEY SAY! WE SHOULD NEVER HAVE MADE A DEAL WITH ONE OF THE ENCHANTED.

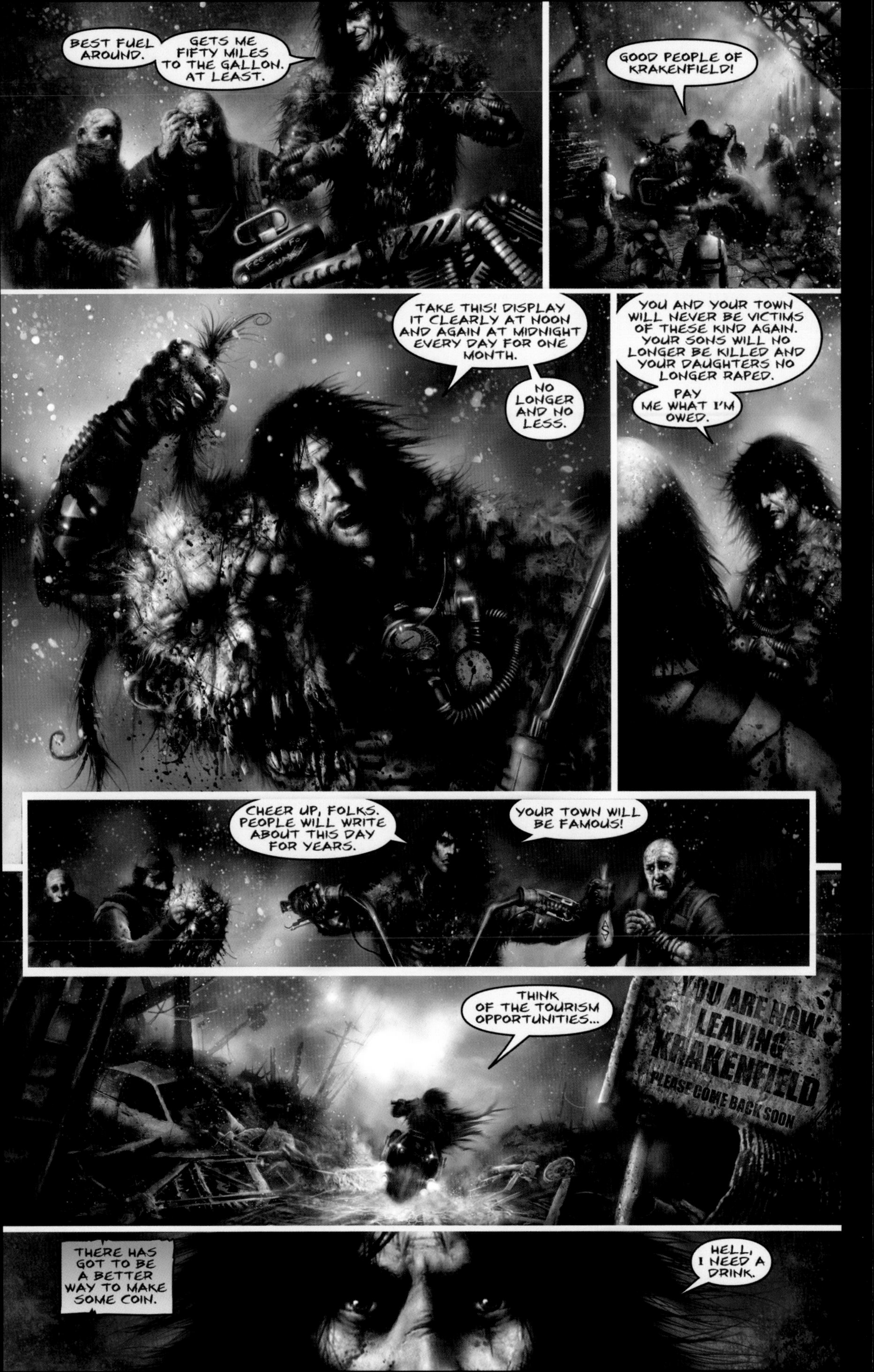
BEST FUEL AROUND.
GETS ME FIFTY MILES TO THE GALLON. AT LEAST.
GOOD PEOPLE OF KRAKENFIELD!
TAKE THIS! DISPLAY IT CLEARLY AT NOON AND AGAIN AT MIDNIGHT EVERY DAY FOR ONE MONTH.
NO LONGER AND NO LESS.
YOU AND YOUR TOWN WILL NEVER BE VICTIMS OF THESE KIND AGAIN. YOUR SONS WILL NO LONGER BE KILLED AND YOUR DAUGHTERS NO LONGER RAPED.
PAY ME WHAT I'M OWED.
CHEER UP, FOLKS. PEOPLE WILL WRITE ABOUT THIS DAY FOR YEARS.
YOUR TOWN WILL BE FAMOUS!
THINK OF THE TOURISM OPPORTUNITIES...
YOU ARE NOW LEAVING KRAKENFIELD
PLEASE COME BACK SOON
THERE HAS GOT TO BE A BETTER WAY TO MAKE SOME COIN.
HELL, I NEED A DRINK.

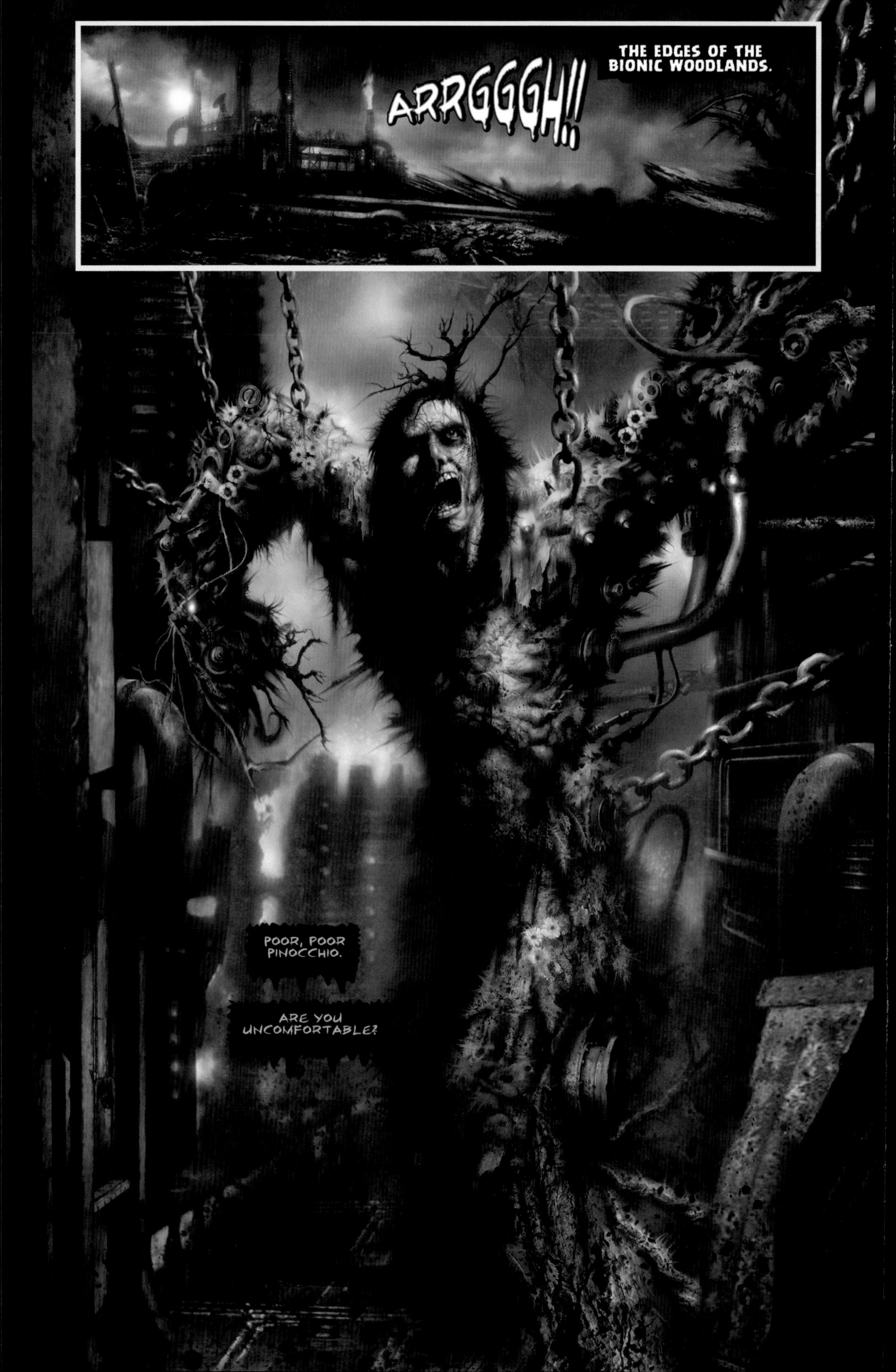

THE EDGES OF THE BIONIC WOODLANDS.
ARRGGGH!!
POOR, POOR PINOCCHIO.
ARE YOU UNCOMFORTABLE?

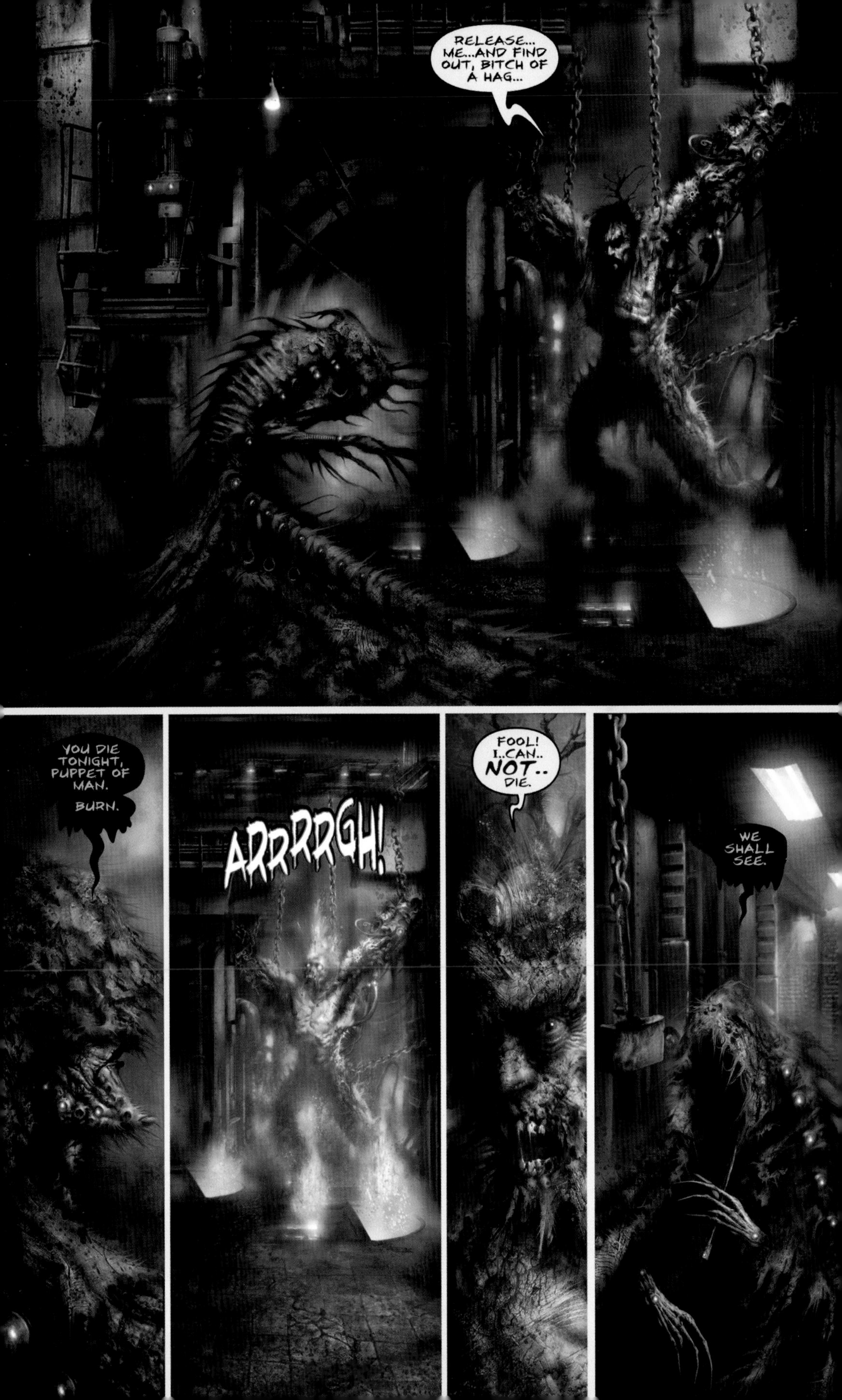
RELEASE... ME...AND FIND OUT, BITCH OF A HAG...
YOU DIE TONIGHT, PUPPET OF MAN.
BURN.
ARRRRGH!
FOOL! I..CAN.. NOT.. DIE.
WE SHALL SEE.

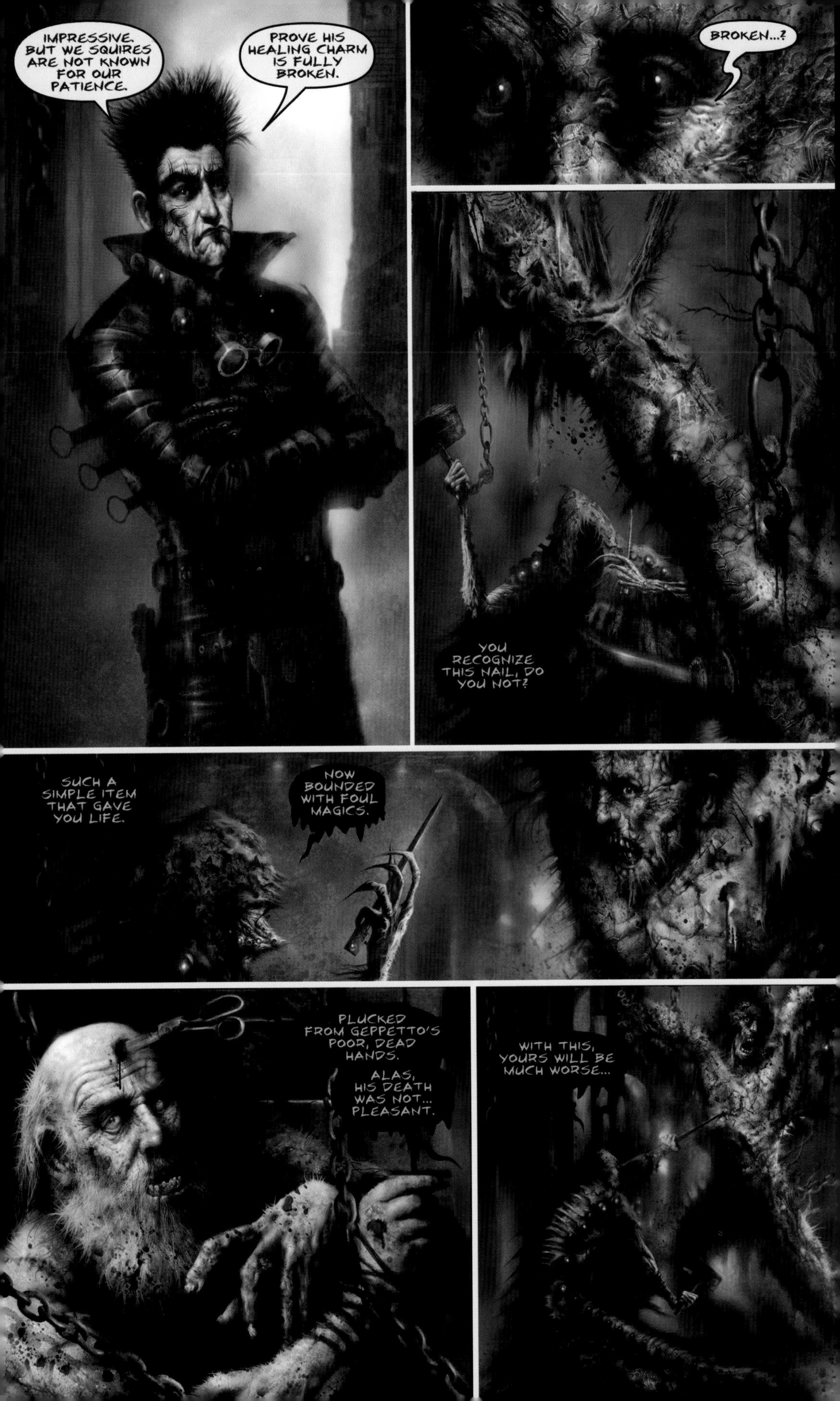
IMPRESSIVE. BUT WE SQUIRES ARE NOT KNOWN FOR OUR PATIENCE.
PROVE HIS HEALING CHARM IS FULLY BROKEN.
BROKEN...?
YOU RECOGNIZE THIS NAIL, DO YOU NOT?
SUCH A SIMPLE ITEM THAT GAVE YOU LIFE.
NOW BOUNDED WITH FOUL MAGICS.
PLUCKED FROM GEPPETTO'S POOR, DEAD HANDS.
ALAS, HIS DEATH WAS NOT... PLEASANT.
WITH THIS, YOURS WILL BE MUCH WORSE...

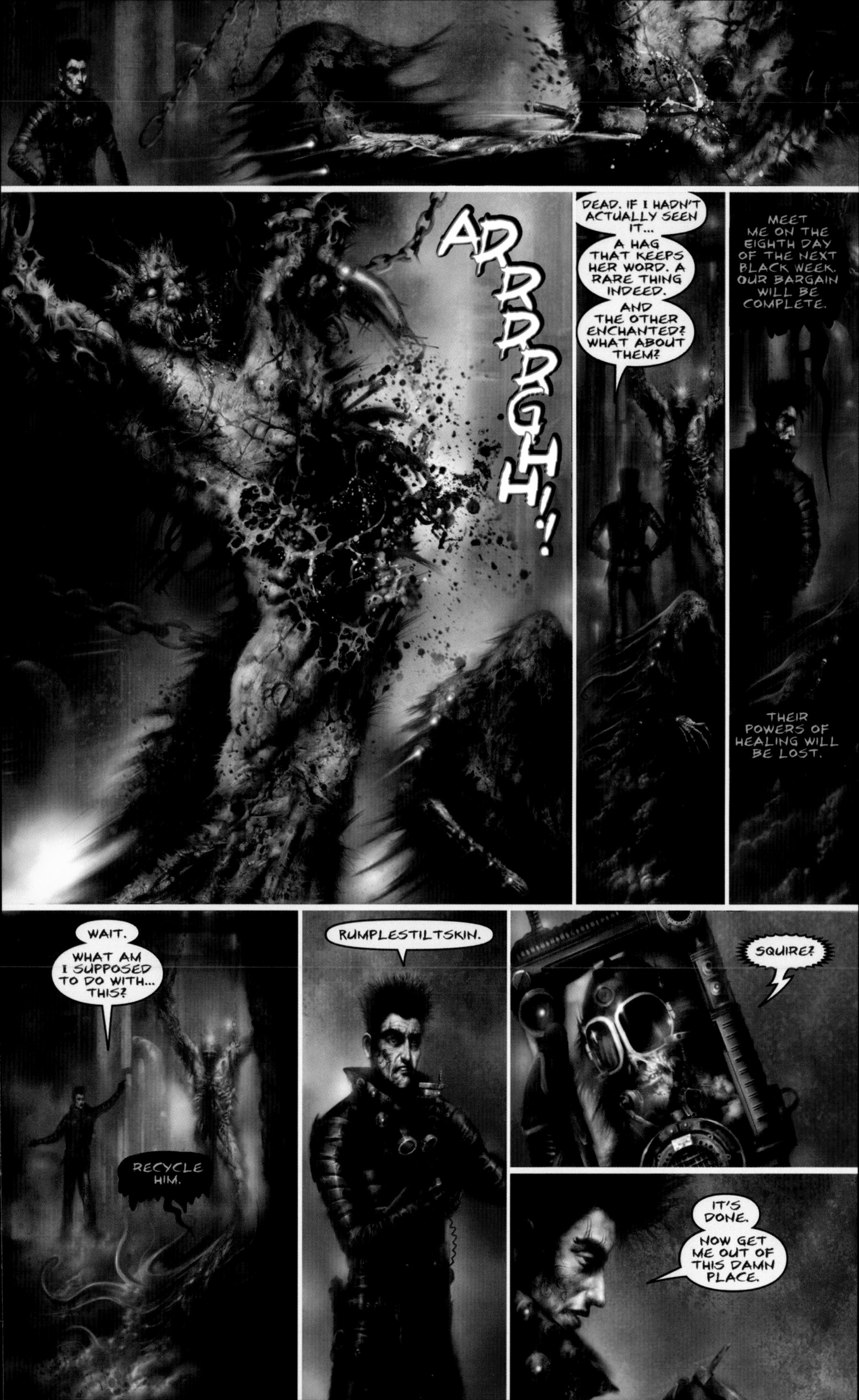
ARRRRGHH!!
DEAD. IF I HADN'T ACTUALLY SEEN IT...
A HAG THAT KEEPS HER WORD. A RARE THING INDEED.
AND THE OTHER ENCHANTED? WHAT ABOUT THEM?
MEET ME ON THE EIGHTH DAY OF THE NEXT BLACK WEEK. OUR BARGAIN WILL BE COMPLETE.
THEIR POWERS OF HEALING WILL BE LOST.
WAIT.
WHAT AM I SUPPOSED TO DO WITH... THIS?
RECYCLE HIM.
RUMPLESTILTSKIN.
SQUIRE?
IT'S DONE.
NOW GET ME OUT OF THIS DAMN PLACE.

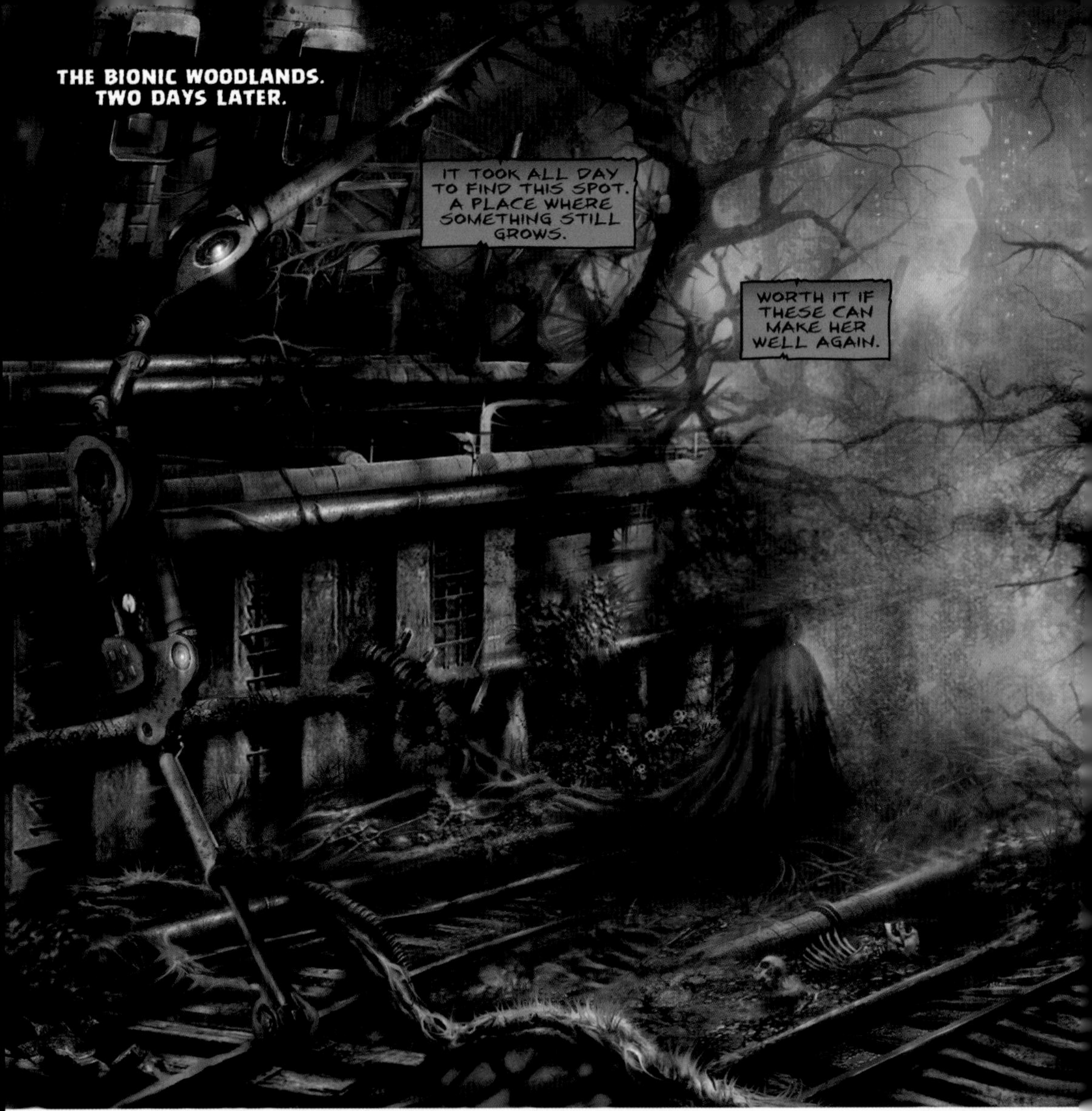
THE BIONIC WOODLANDS. TWO DAYS LATER.
IT TOOK ALL DAY TO FIND THIS SPOT. A PLACE WHERE SOMETHING STILL GROWS.
WORTH IT IF THESE CAN MAKE HER WELL AGAIN.

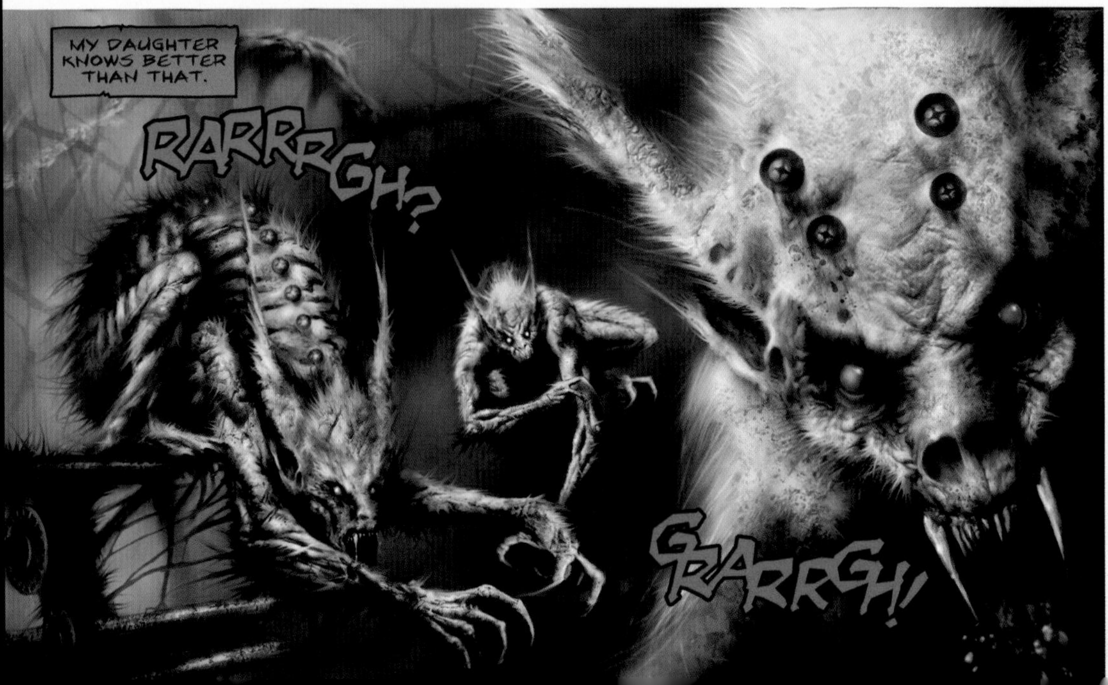
MY DAUGHTER KNOWS BETTER THAN THAT.
RARRRGH?
GRARRGH!

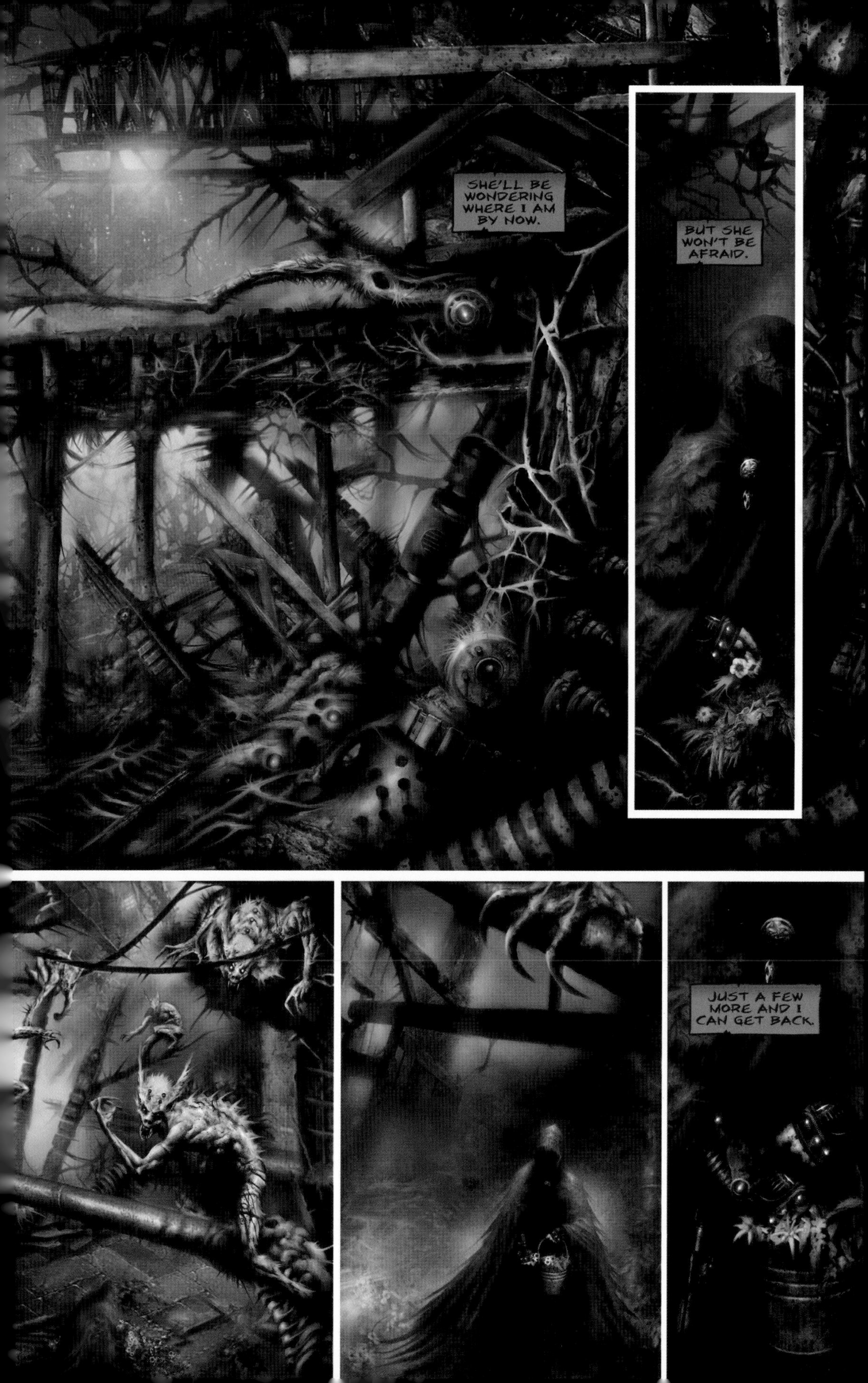
SHE'LL BE WONDERING WHERE I AM BY NOW.
BUT SHE WON'T BE AFRAID.
JUST A FEW MORE AND I CAN GET BACK.

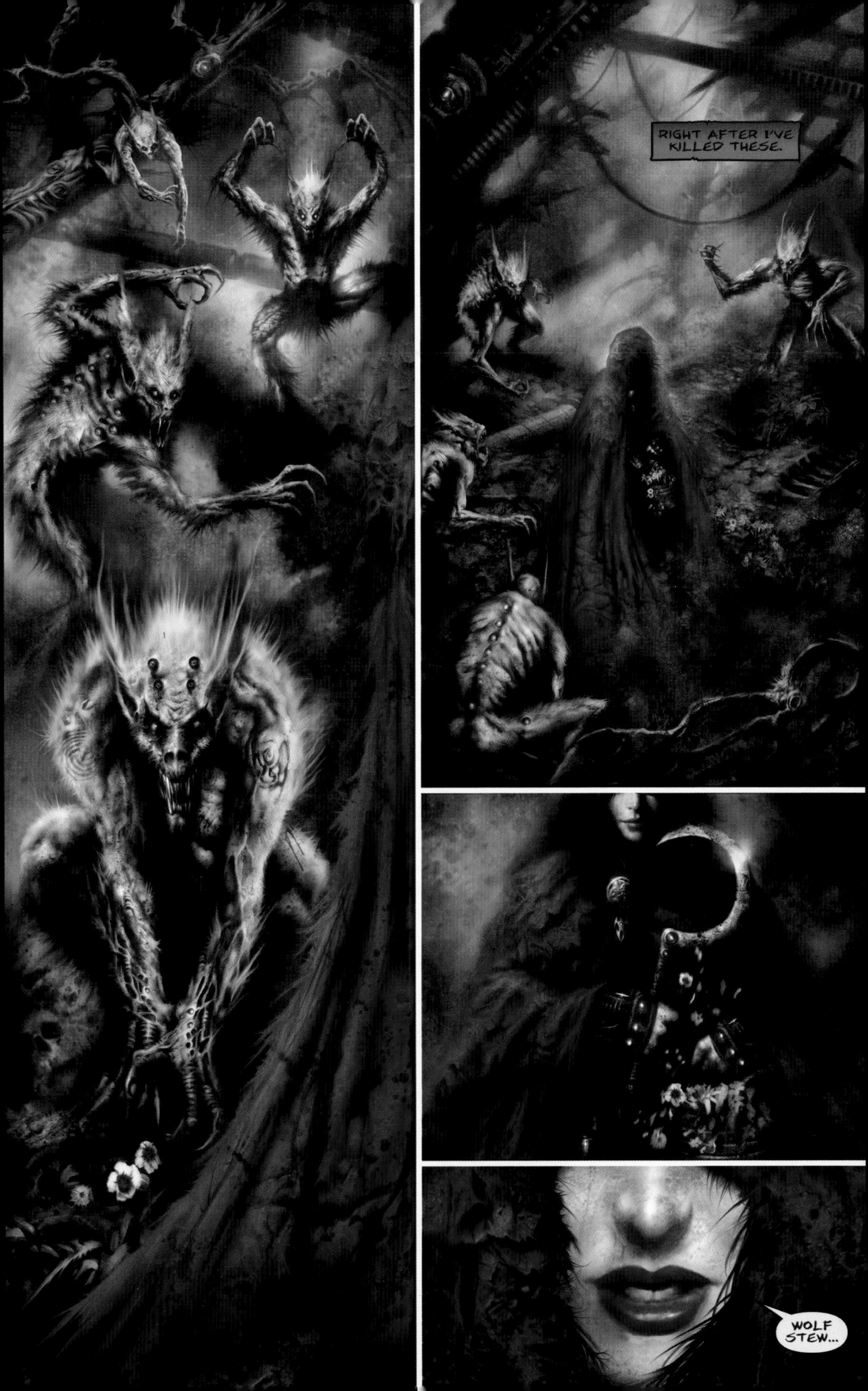
RIGHT AFTER I'VE KILLED THESE.
WOLF STEW...

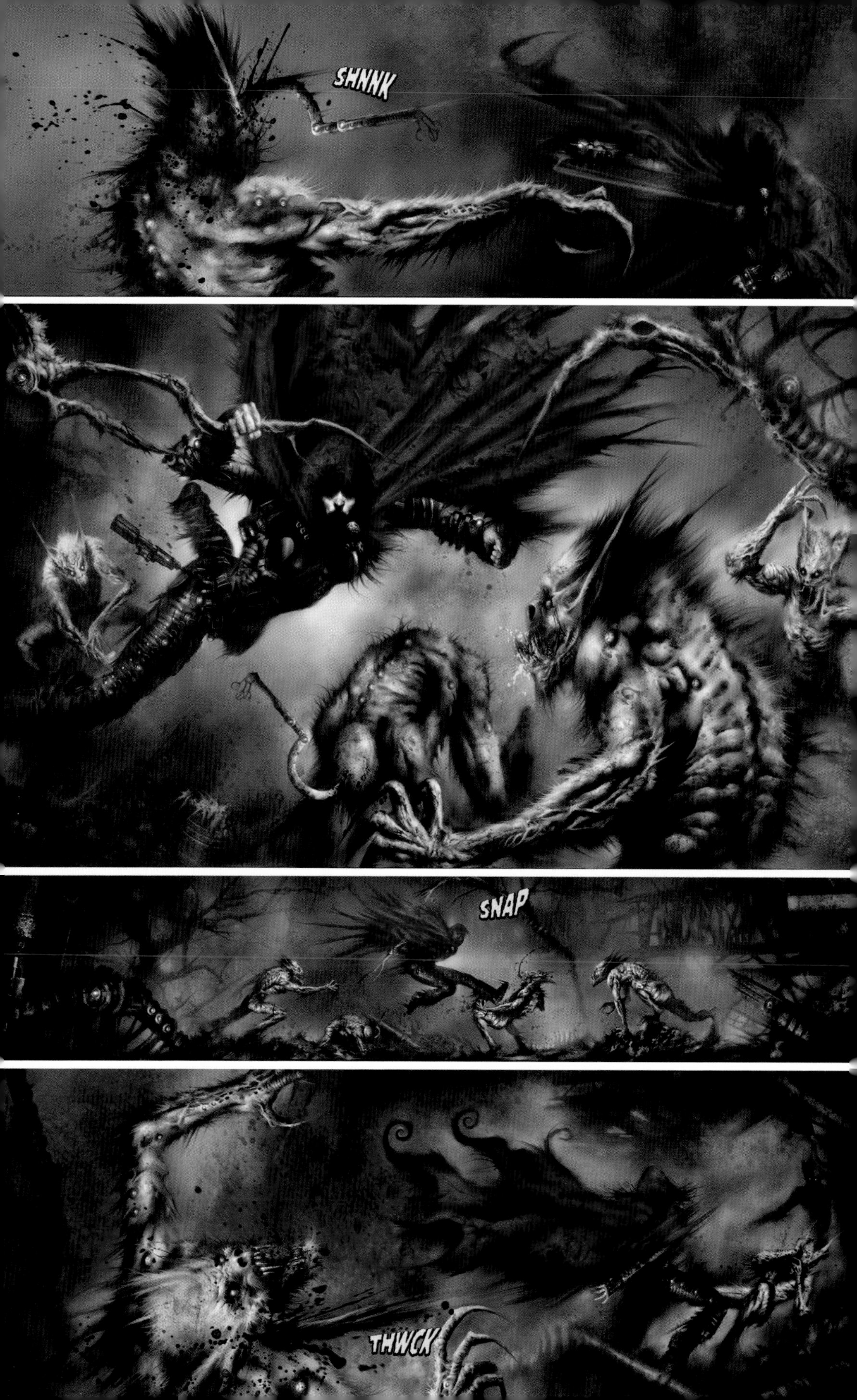
SHNNK
SNAP
THWCK

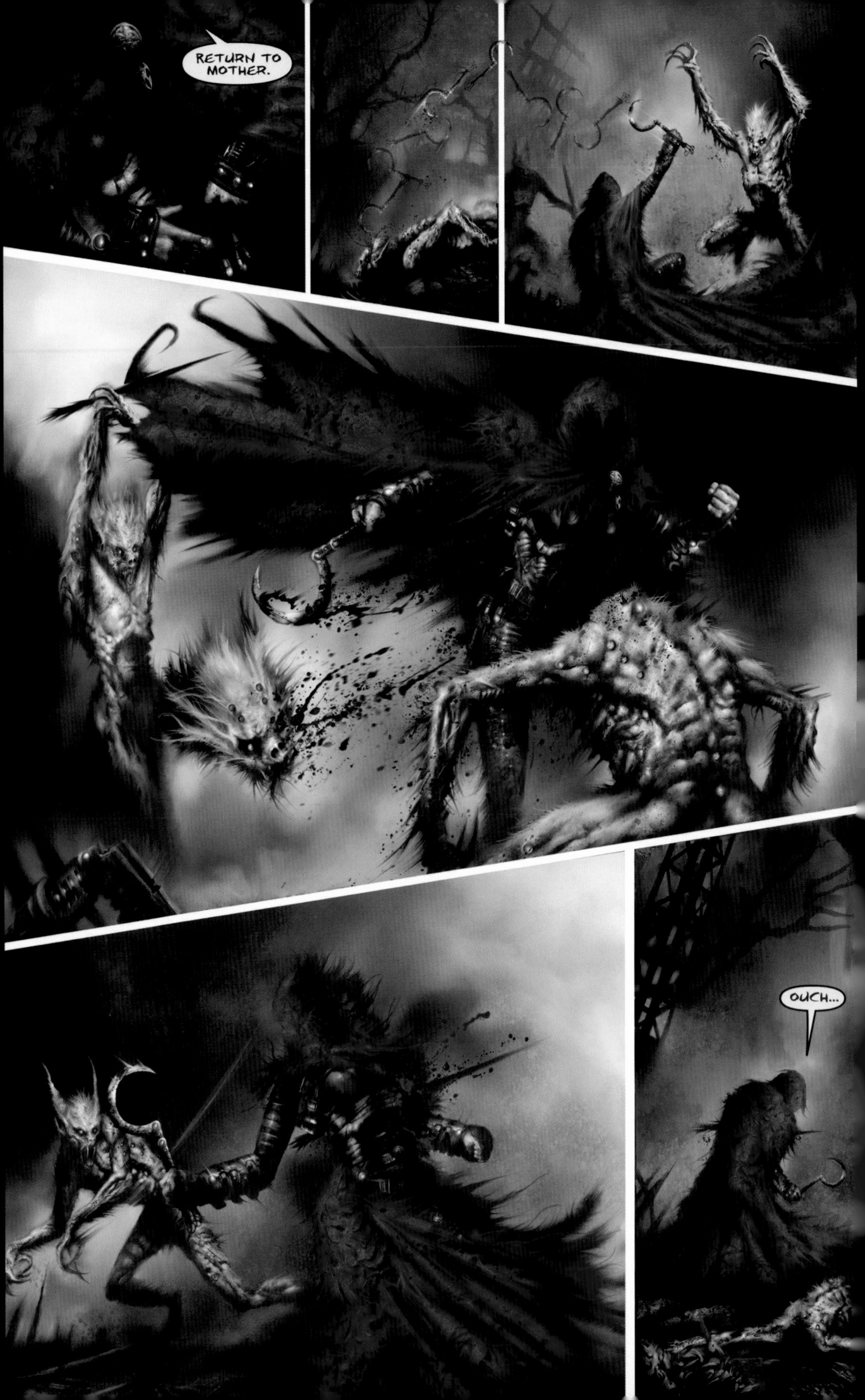
RETURN TO MOTHER.
OUCH...

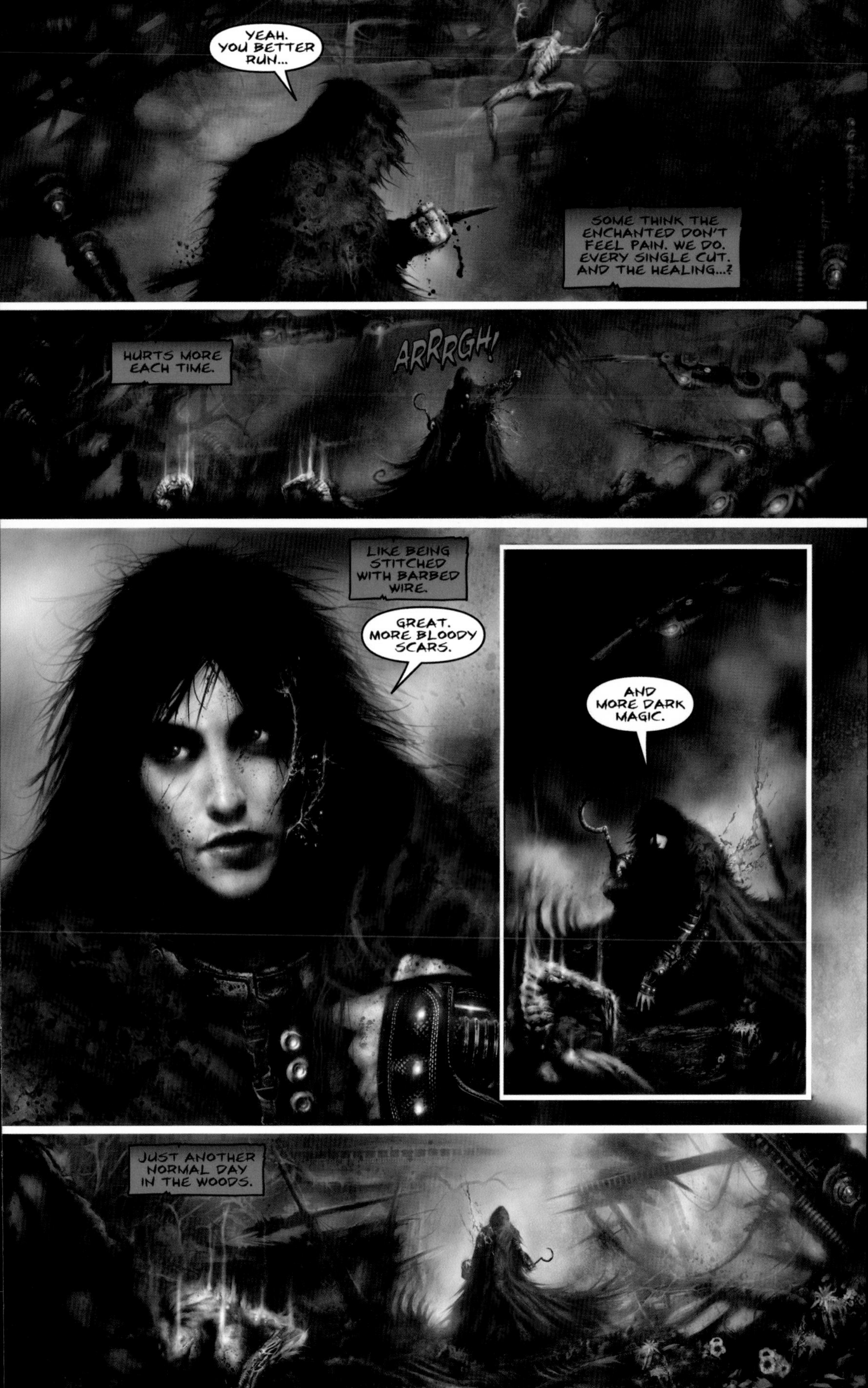
YEAH. YOU BETTER RUN...
SOME THINK THE ENCHANTED DON'T FEEL PAIN. WE DO. EVERY SINGLE CUT. AND THE HEALING...?
HURTS MORE EACH TIME.
ARRRGH!
LIKE BEING STITCHED WITH BARBED WIRE.
GREAT. MORE BLOODY SCARS.
AND MORE DARK MAGIC.
JUST ANOTHER NORMAL DAY IN THE WOODS.

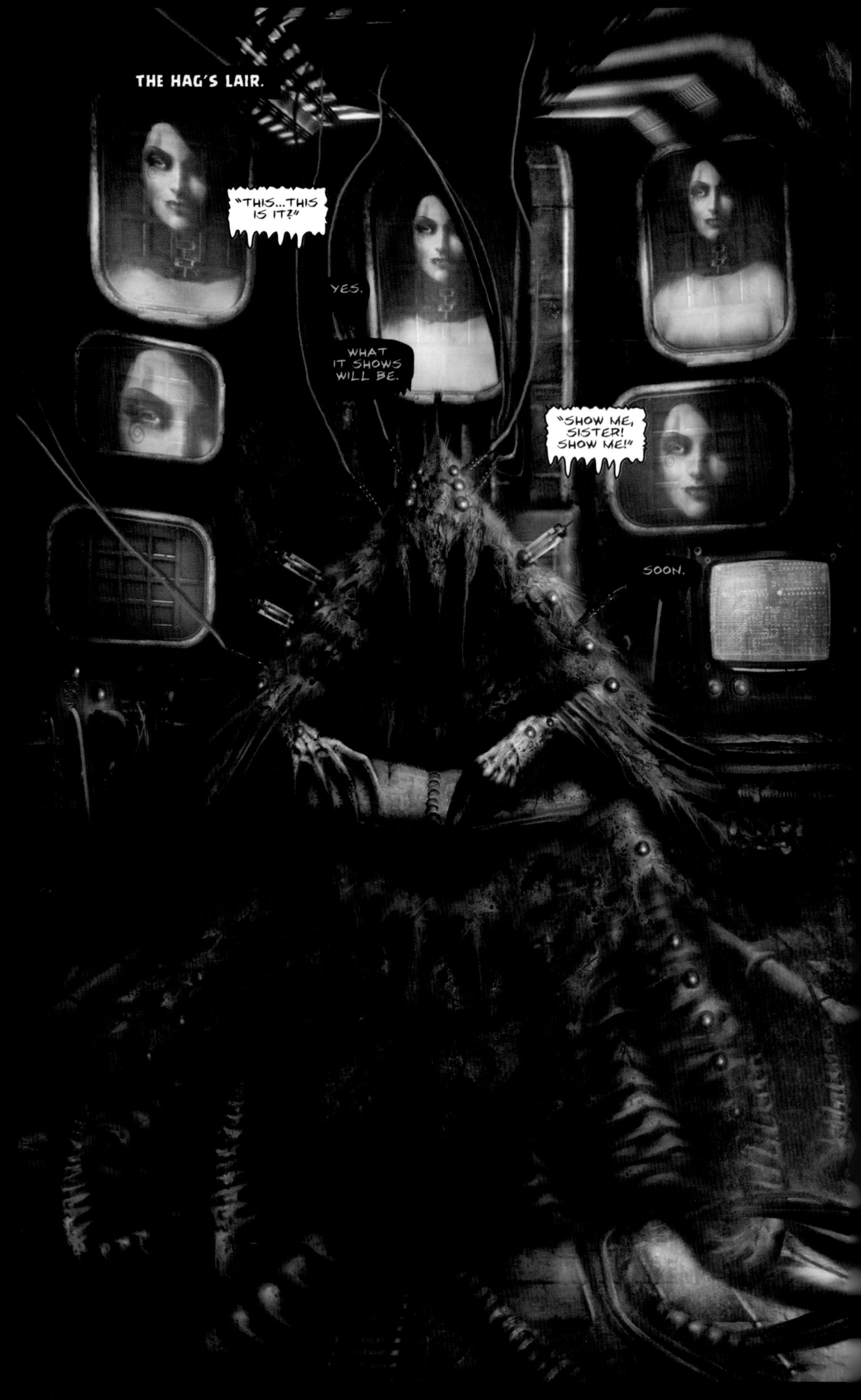
THE HAG'S LAIR.
"THIS...THIS IS IT?"
YES.
WHAT IT SHOWS WILL BE.
"SHOW ME, SISTER! SHOW ME!"
SOON.

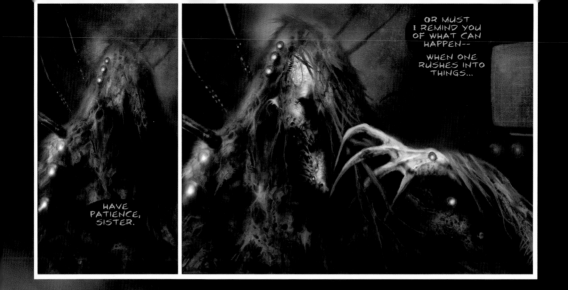

OR MUST I REMIND YOU OF WHAT CAN HAPPEN-- WHEN ONE RUSHES INTO THINGS...

HAVE PATIENCE, SISTER.

OUR TIME WILL COME.

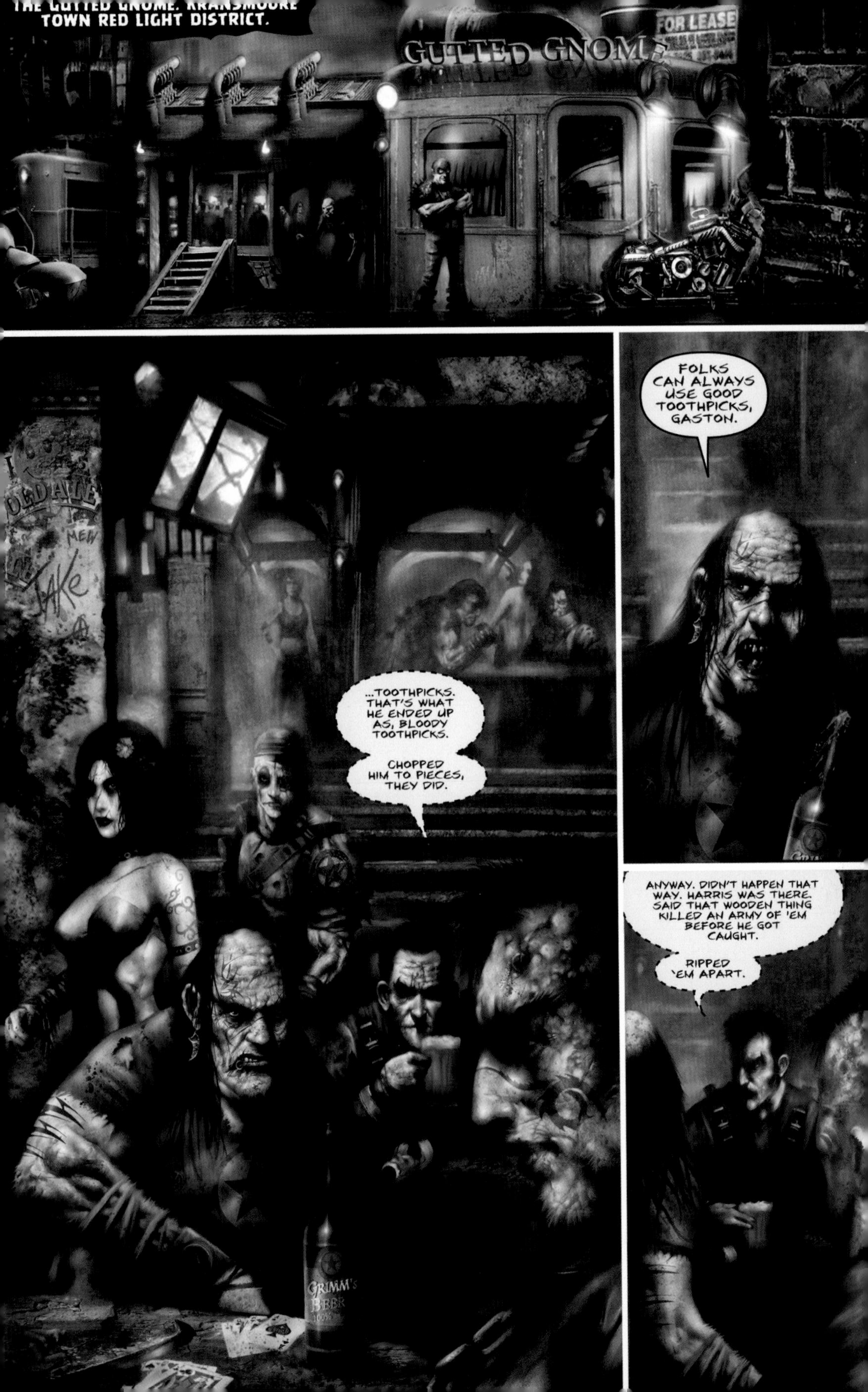
THE GUTTED GNOME. KRANSMOORE TOWN RED LIGHT DISTRICT.
FOR LEASE
GUTTED GNOME
OLD ALE
JAKE
...TOOTHPICKS. THAT'S WHAT HE ENDED UP AS, BLOODY TOOTHPICKS.
CHOPPED HIM TO PIECES, THEY DID.
GRIMM'S BEER
FOLKS CAN ALWAYS USE GOOD TOOTHPICKS, GASTON.
ANYWAY. DIDN'T HAPPEN THAT WAY. HARRIS WAS THERE. SAID THAT WOODEN THING KILLED AN ARMY OF 'EM BEFORE HE GOT CAUGHT.
RIPPED 'EM APART.

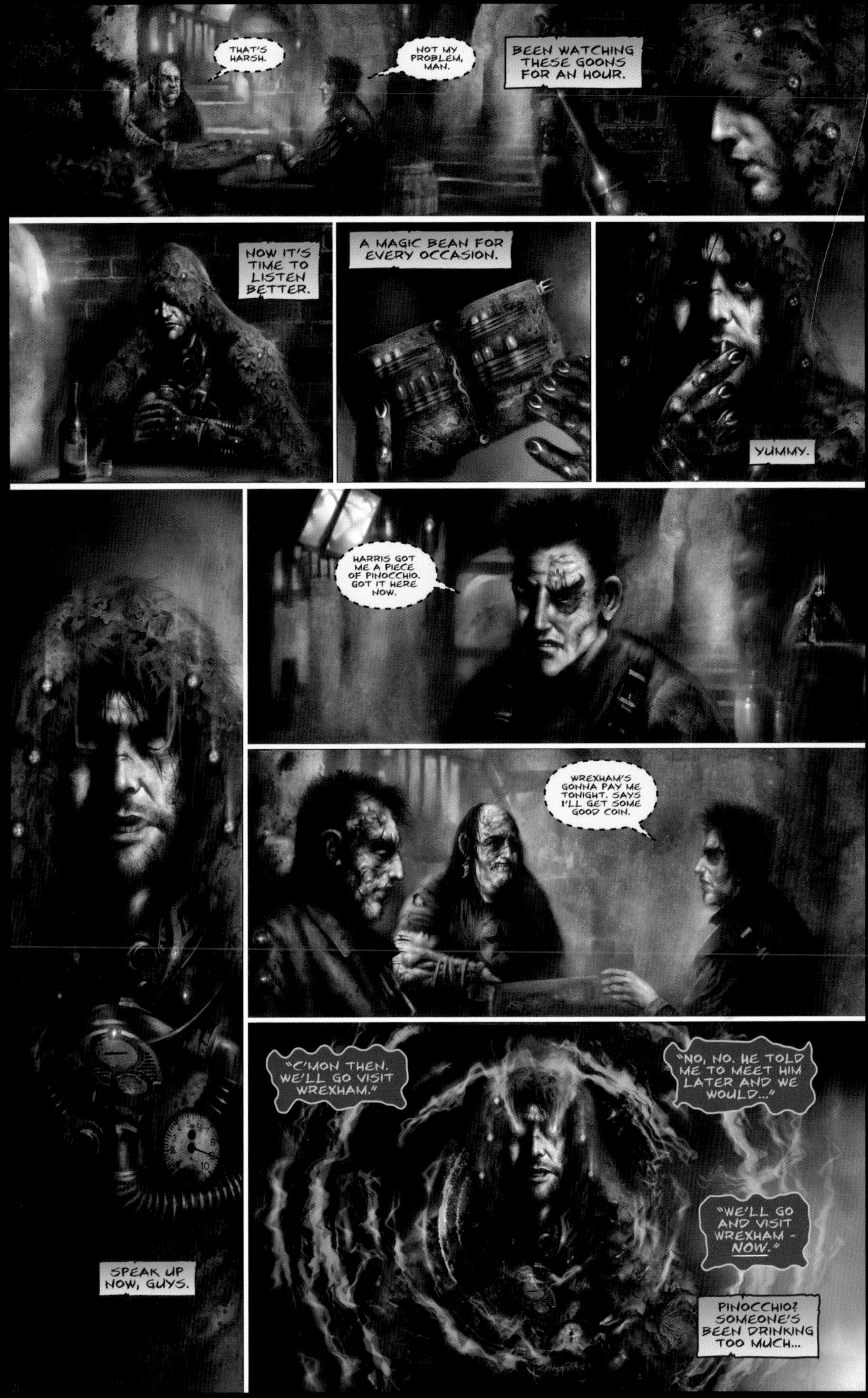
THAT'S HARSH.
NOT MY PROBLEM, MAN.
BEEN WATCHING THESE GOONS FOR AN HOUR.
NOW IT'S TIME TO LISTEN BETTER.
A MAGIC BEAN FOR EVERY OCCASION.
YUMMY.
HARRIS GOT ME A PIECE OF PINOCCHIO. GOT IT HERE NOW.
WREXHAM'S GONNA PAY ME TONIGHT. SAYS I'LL GET SOME GOOD COIN.
SPEAK UP NOW, GUYS.
"C'MON THEN. WE'LL GO VISIT WREXHAM."
"NO, NO. HE TOLD ME TO MEET HIM LATER AND WE WOULD..."
"WE'LL GO AND VISIT WREXHAM - NOW."
PINOCCHIO? SOMEONE'S BEEN DRINKING TOO MUCH...

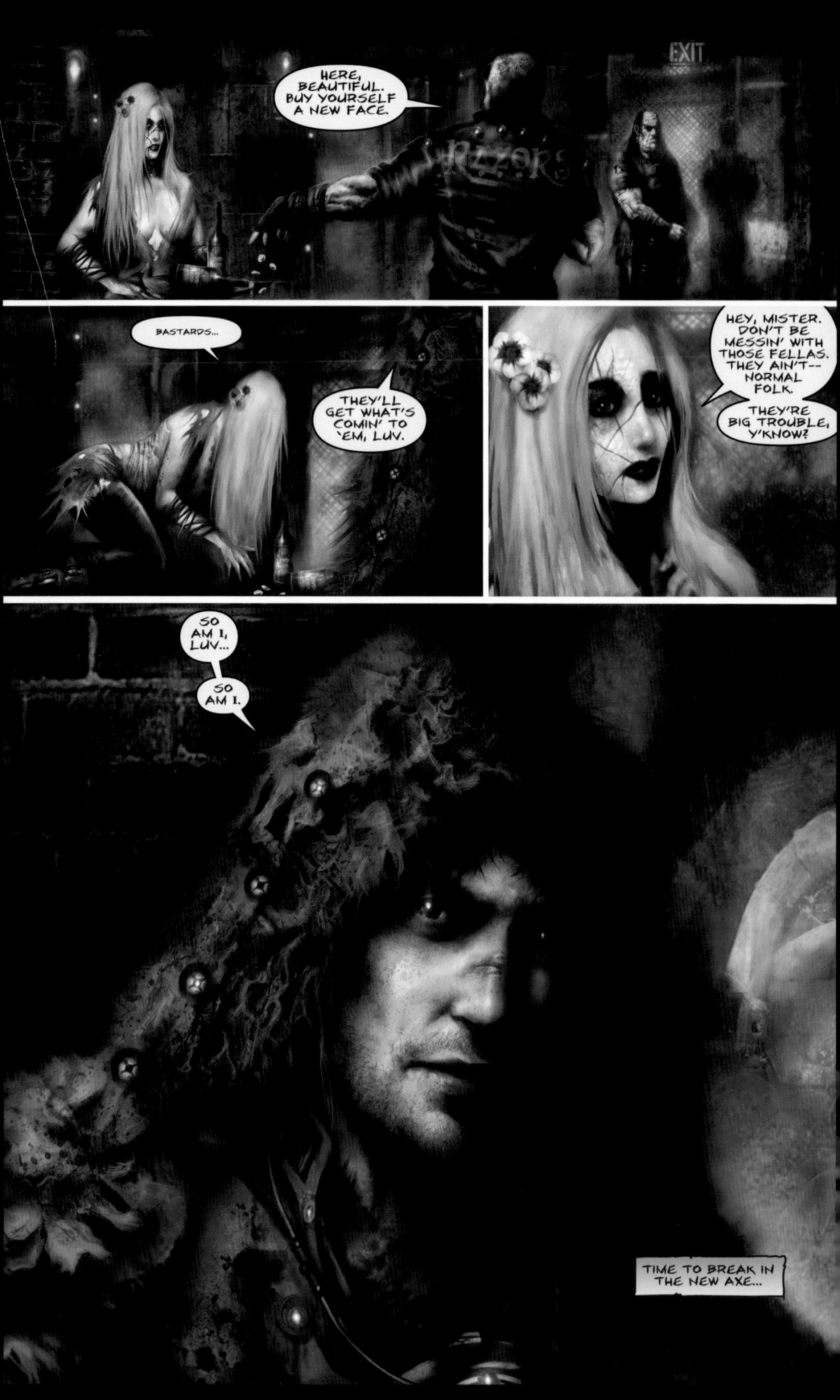
HERE, BEAUTIFUL. BUY YOURSELF A NEW FACE.
EXIT
BASTARDS...
THEY'LL GET WHAT'S COMIN' TO 'EM, LUV.
HEY, MISTER. DON'T BE MESSIN' WITH THOSE FELLAS. THEY AIN'T-- NORMAL FOLK.
THEY'RE BIG TROUBLE, Y'KNOW?
SO AM I, LUV...
SO AM I.
TIME TO BREAK IN THE NEW AXE...

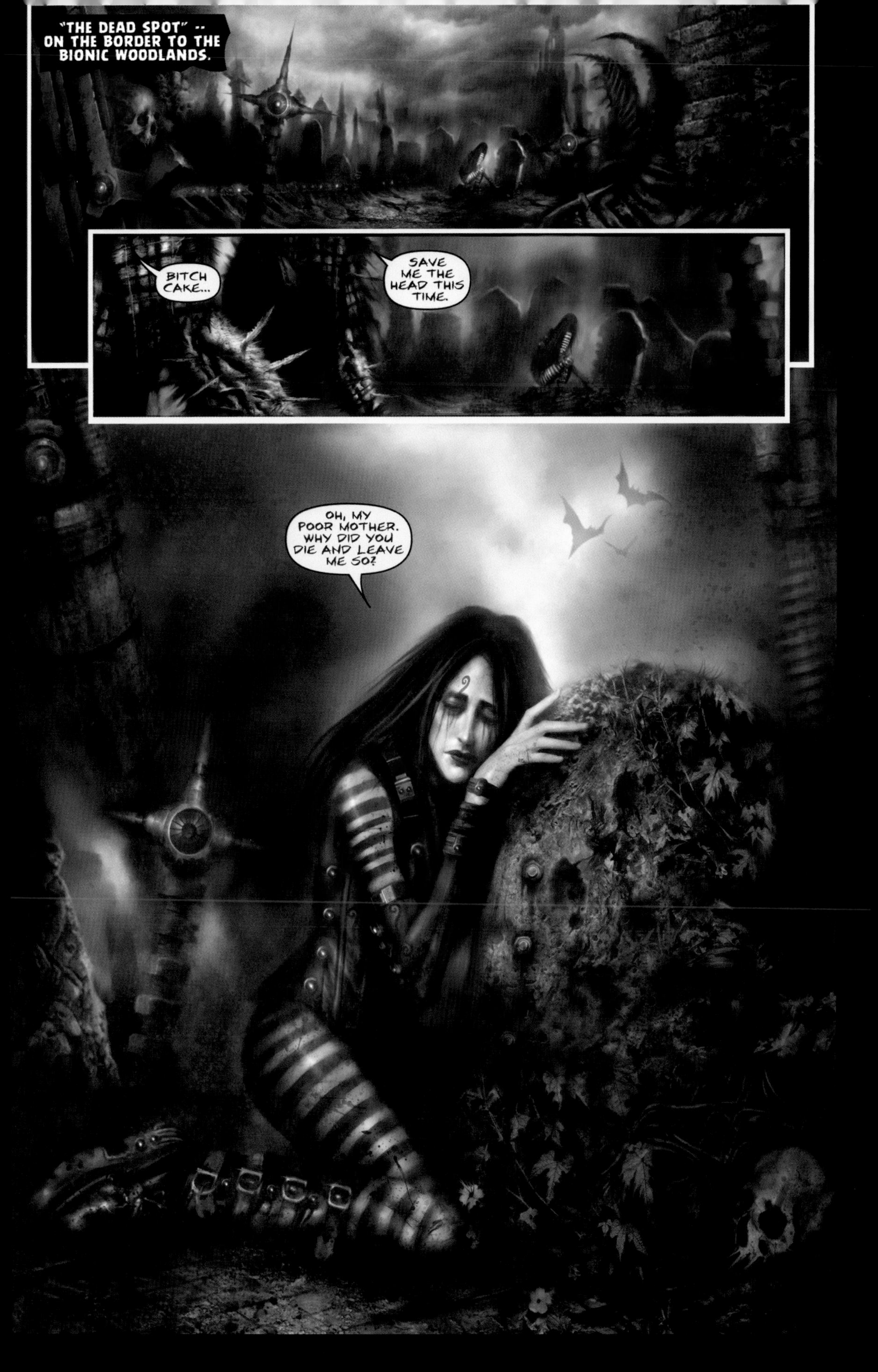
"THE DEAD SPOT" -- ON THE BORDER TO THE BIONIC WOODLANDS.
BITCH CAKE...
SAVE ME THE HEAD THIS TIME.
OH, MY POOR MOTHER. WHY DID YOU DIE AND LEAVE ME SO?

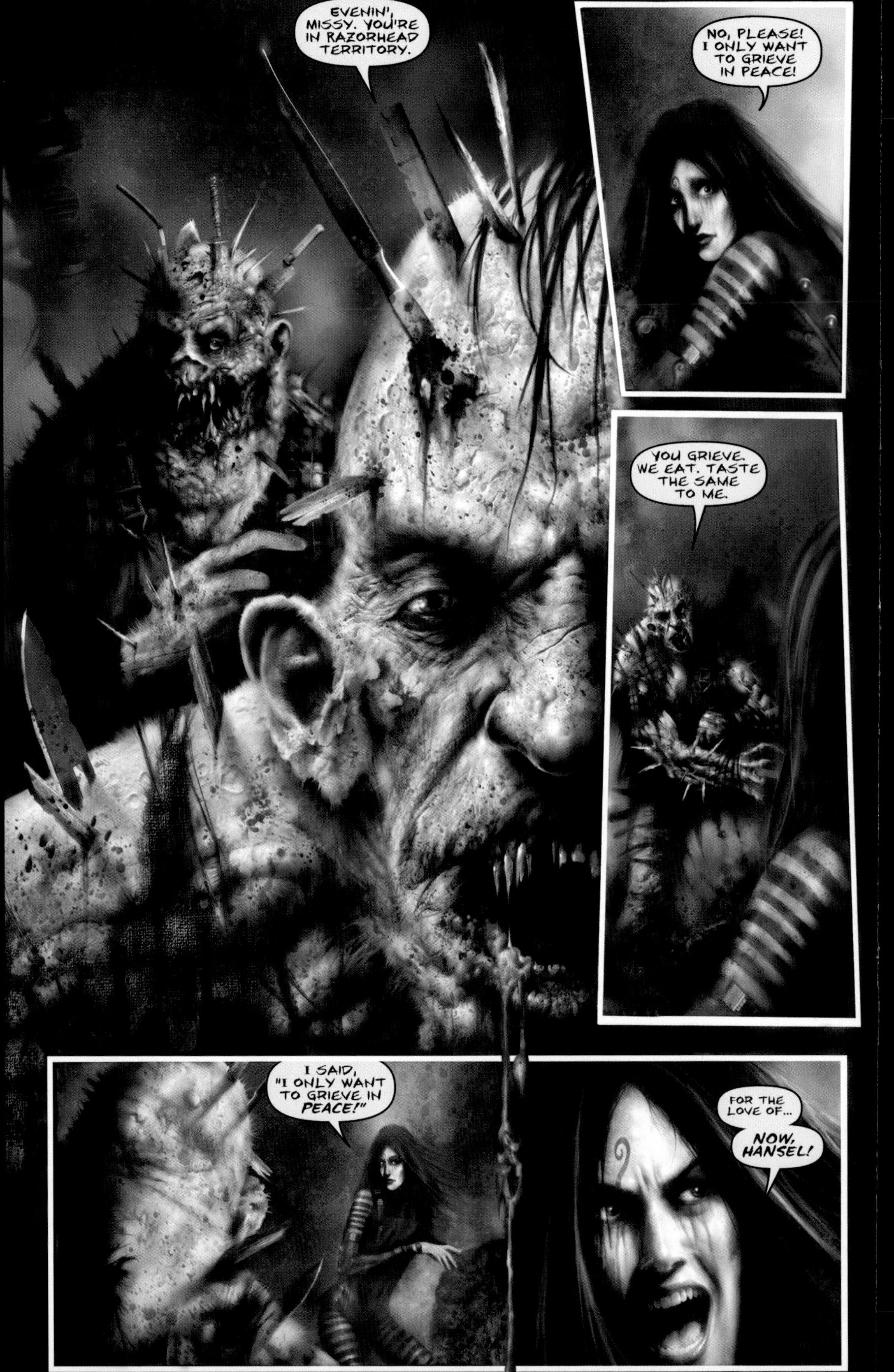
EVENIN', MISSY. YOU'RE IN RAZORHEAD TERRITORY.
NO, PLEASE! I ONLY WANT TO GRIEVE IN PEACE!
YOU GRIEVE. WE EAT. TASTE THE SAME TO ME.
I SAID, "I ONLY WANT TO GRIEVE IN *PEACE!*"
FOR THE LOVE OF...
NOW, HANSEL!

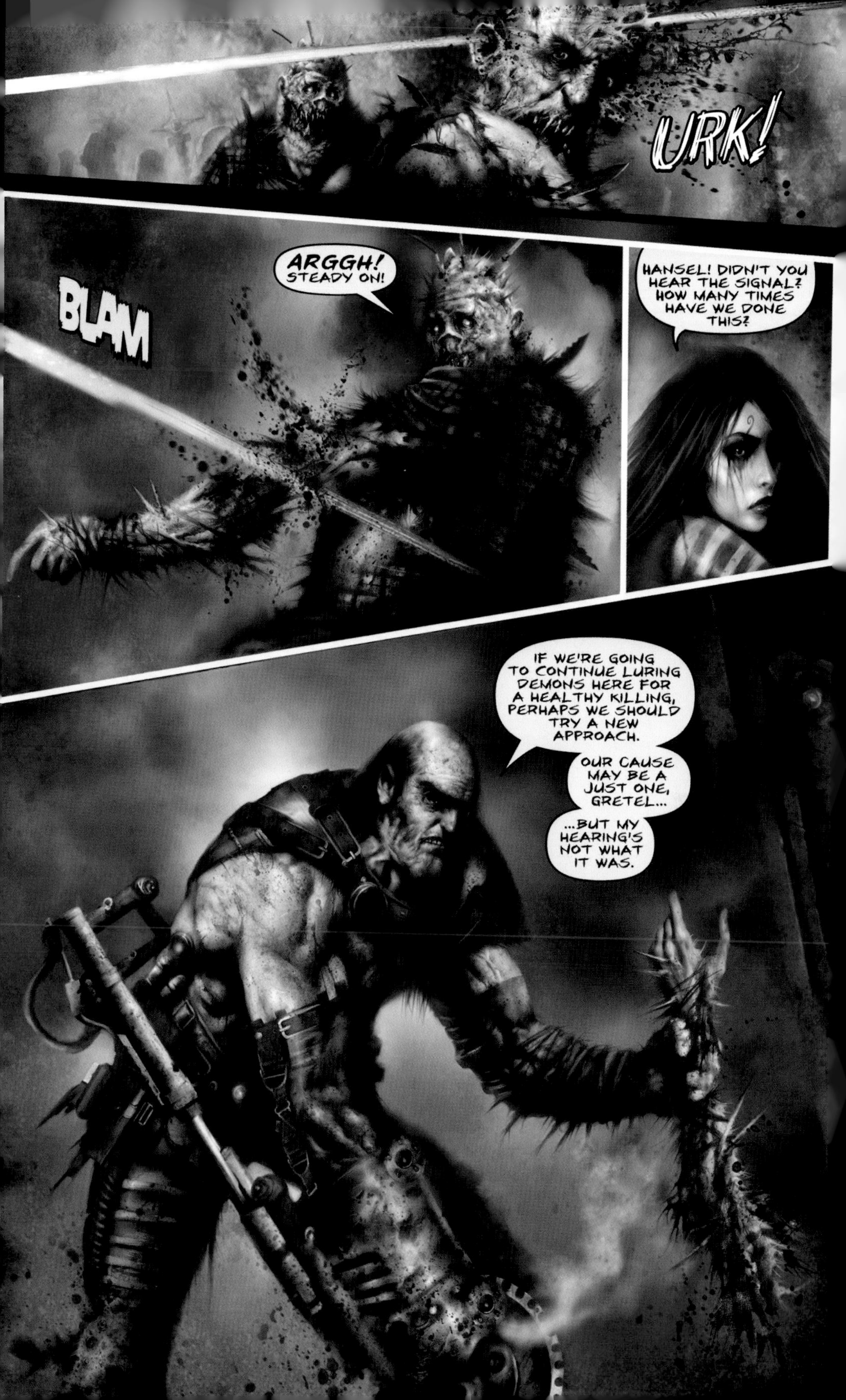
URK!
BLAM
ARGGH! STEADY ON!
HANSEL! DIDN'T YOU HEAR THE SIGNAL? HOW MANY TIMES HAVE WE DONE THIS?
IF WE'RE GOING TO CONTINUE LURING DEMONS HERE FOR A HEALTHY KILLING, PERHAPS WE SHOULD TRY A NEW APPROACH.
OUR CAUSE MAY BE A JUST ONE, GRETEL...
...BUT MY HEARING'S NOT WHAT IT WAS.

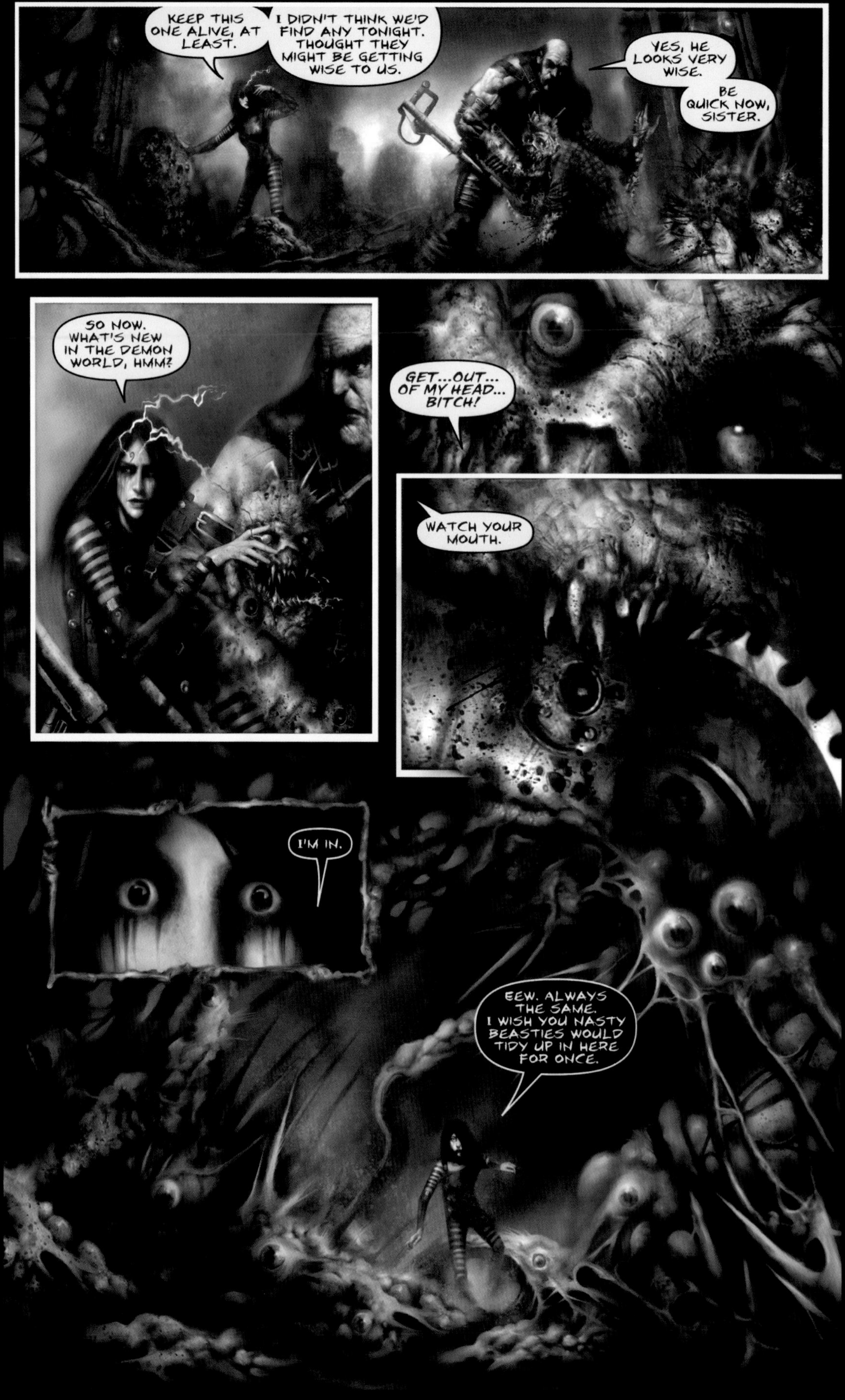
KEEP THIS ONE ALIVE, AT LEAST.
I DIDN'T THINK WE'D FIND ANY TONIGHT. THOUGHT THEY MIGHT BE GETTING WISE TO US.
YES, HE LOOKS VERY WISE.
BE QUICK NOW, SISTER.
SO NOW. WHAT'S NEW IN THE DEMON WORLD, HMM?
GET...OUT... OF MY HEAD... BITCH!
WATCH YOUR MOUTH.
I'M IN.
EEW. ALWAYS THE SAME. I WISH YOU NASTY BEASTIES WOULD TIDY UP IN HERE FOR ONCE.

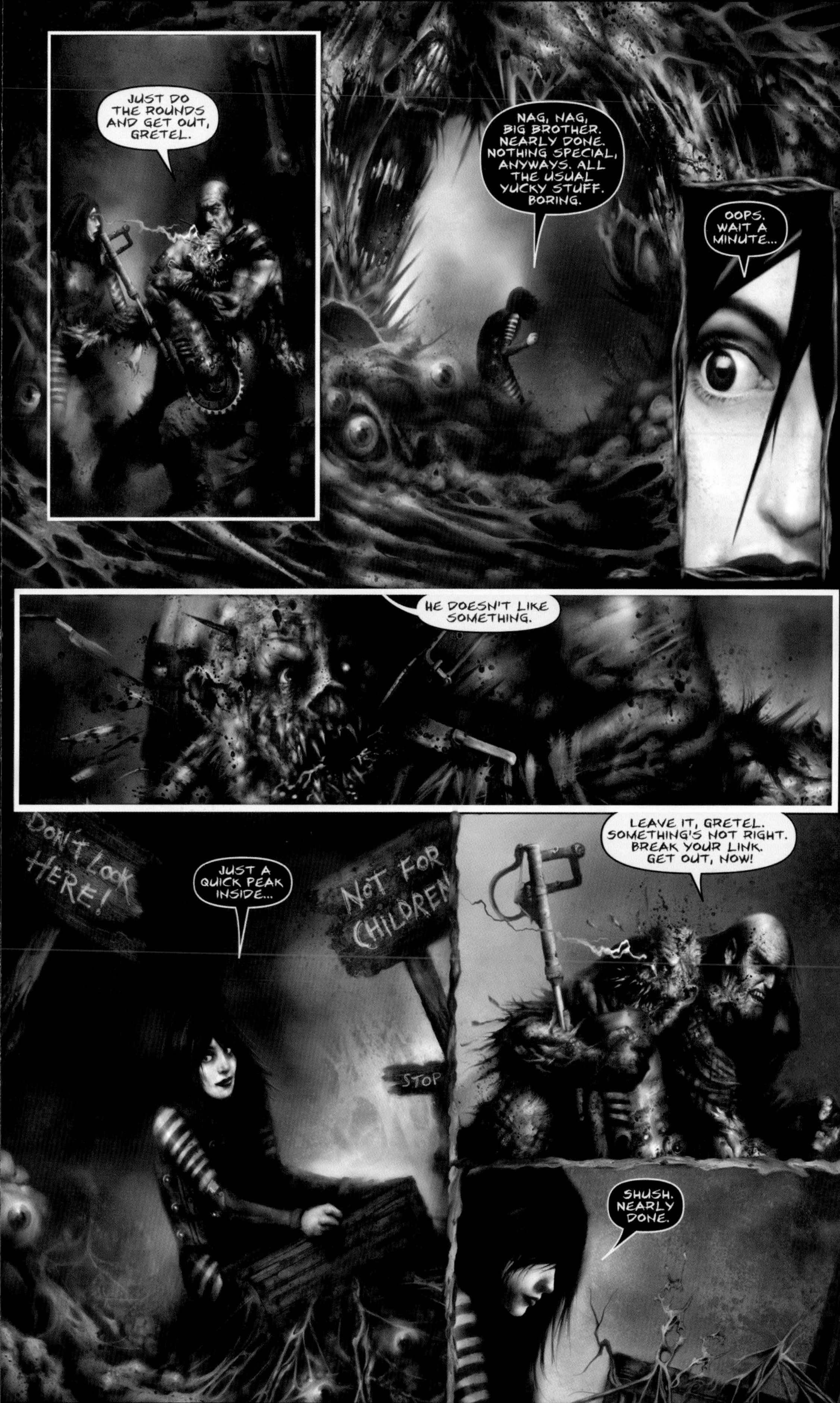
JUST DO THE ROUNDS AND GET OUT, GRETEL.
NAG, NAG, BIG BROTHER. NEARLY DONE. NOTHING SPECIAL, ANYWAYS. ALL THE USUAL YUCKY STUFF. BORING.
OOPS. WAIT A MINUTE...
HE DOESN'T LIKE SOMETHING.
DON'T LOOK HERE!
JUST A QUICK PEAK INSIDE...
NOT FOR CHILDREN
STOP
LEAVE IT, GRETEL. SOMETHING'S NOT RIGHT. BREAK YOUR LINK. GET OUT, NOW!
SHUSH. NEARLY DONE.

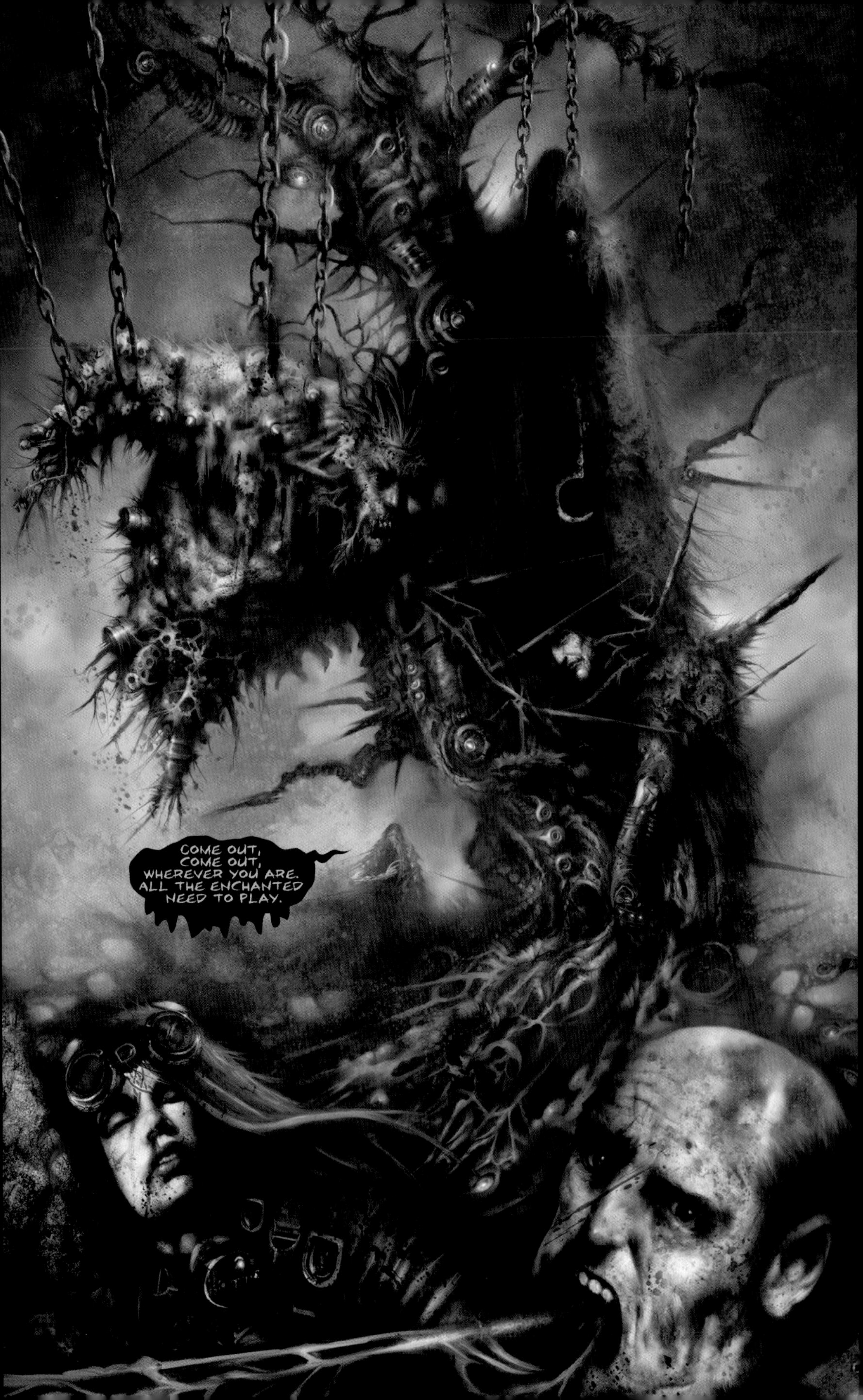
COME OUT, COME OUT, WHEREVER YOU ARE. ALL THE ENCHANTED NEED TO PLAY.

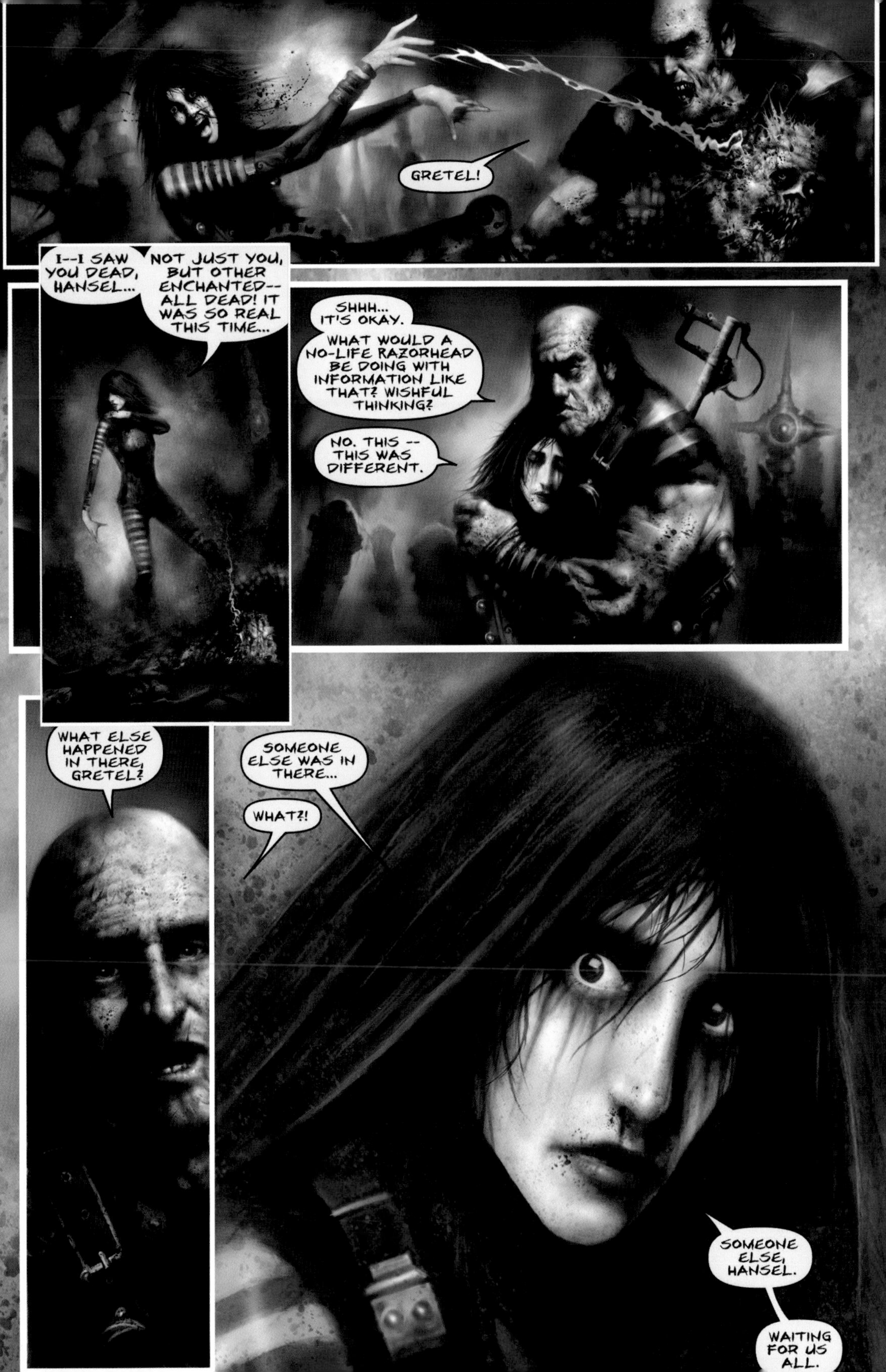
GRETEL!
I--I SAW YOU DEAD, HANSEL...
NOT JUST YOU, BUT OTHER ENCHANTED-- ALL DEAD! IT WAS SO REAL THIS TIME...
SHHH... IT'S OKAY.
WHAT WOULD A NO-LIFE RAZORHEAD BE DOING WITH INFORMATION LIKE THAT? WISHFUL THINKING?
NO. THIS -- THIS WAS DIFFERENT.
WHAT ELSE HAPPENED IN THERE, GRETEL?
SOMEONE ELSE WAS IN THERE...
WHAT?!
SOMEONE ELSE, HANSEL.
WAITING FOR US ALL.

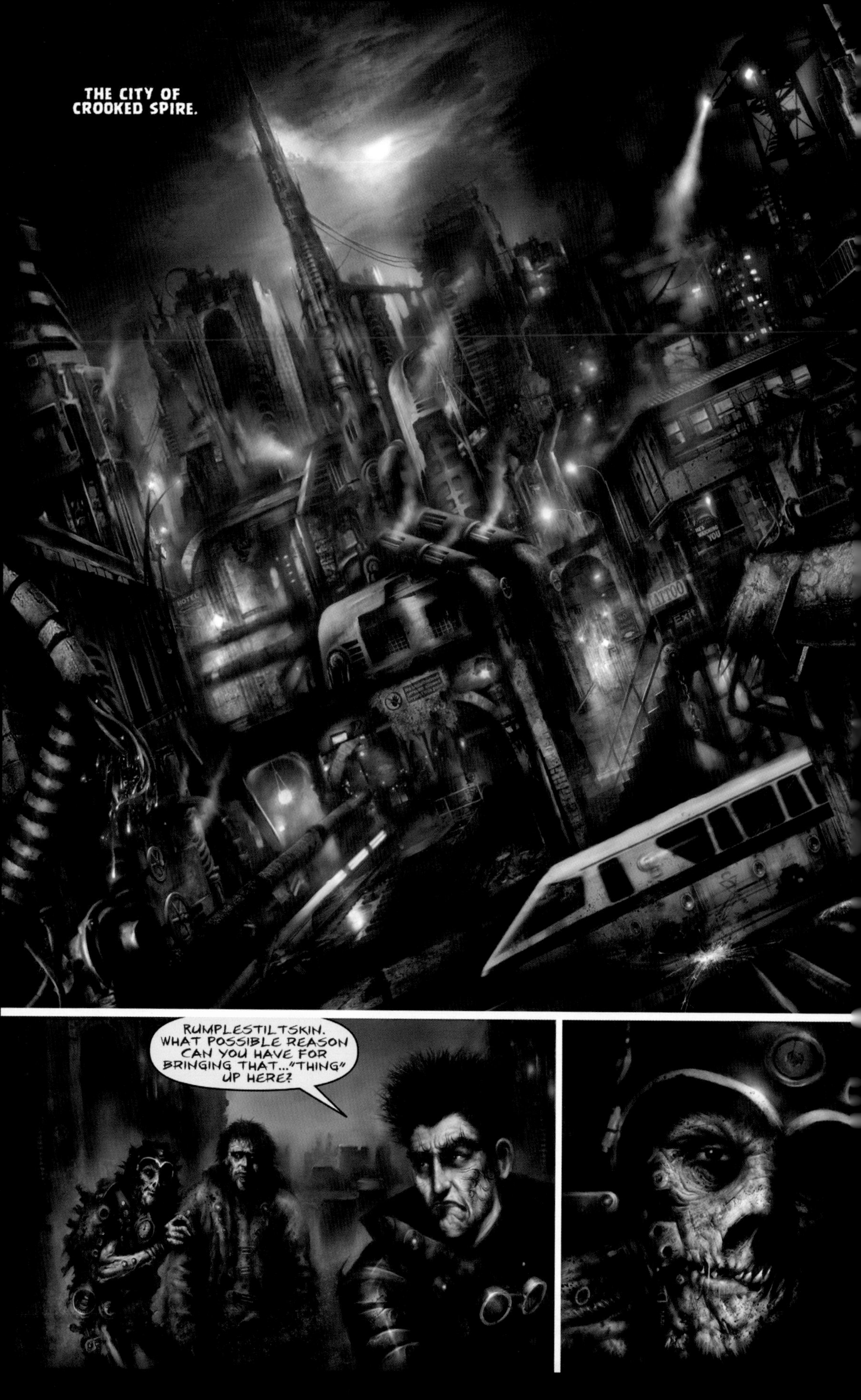
THE CITY OF CROOKED SPIRE.
RUMPLESTILTSKIN. WHAT POSSIBLE REASON CAN YOU HAVE FOR BRINGING THAT..."THING" UP HERE?

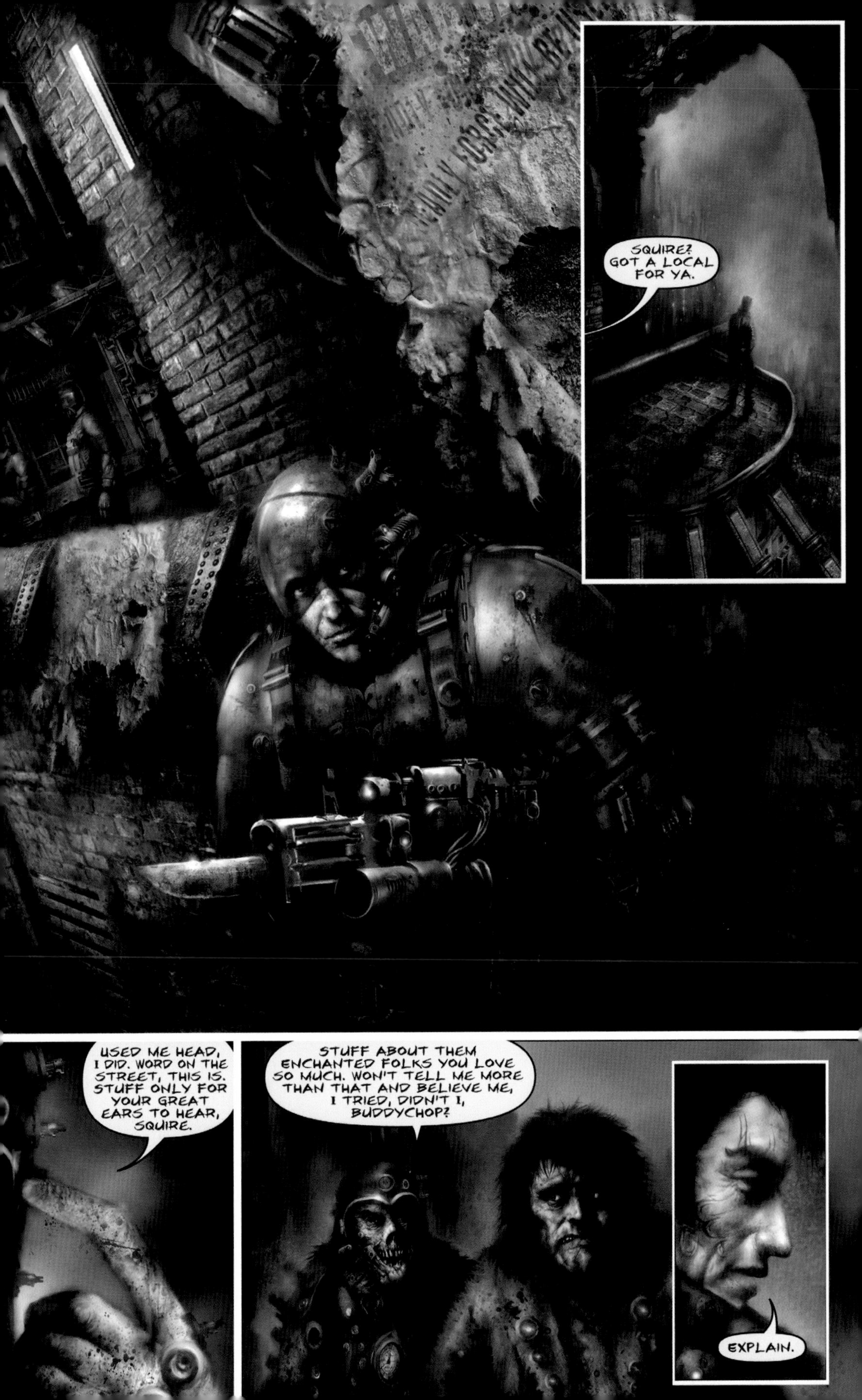
SQUIRE? GOT A LOCAL FOR YA.
USED ME HEAD, I DID. WORD ON THE STREET, THIS IS. STUFF ONLY FOR YOUR GREAT EARS TO HEAR, SQUIRE.
STUFF ABOUT THEM ENCHANTED FOLKS YOU LOVE SO MUCH. WON'T TELL ME MORE THAN THAT AND BELIEVE ME, I TRIED, DIDN'T I, BUDDYCHOP?
EXPLAIN.

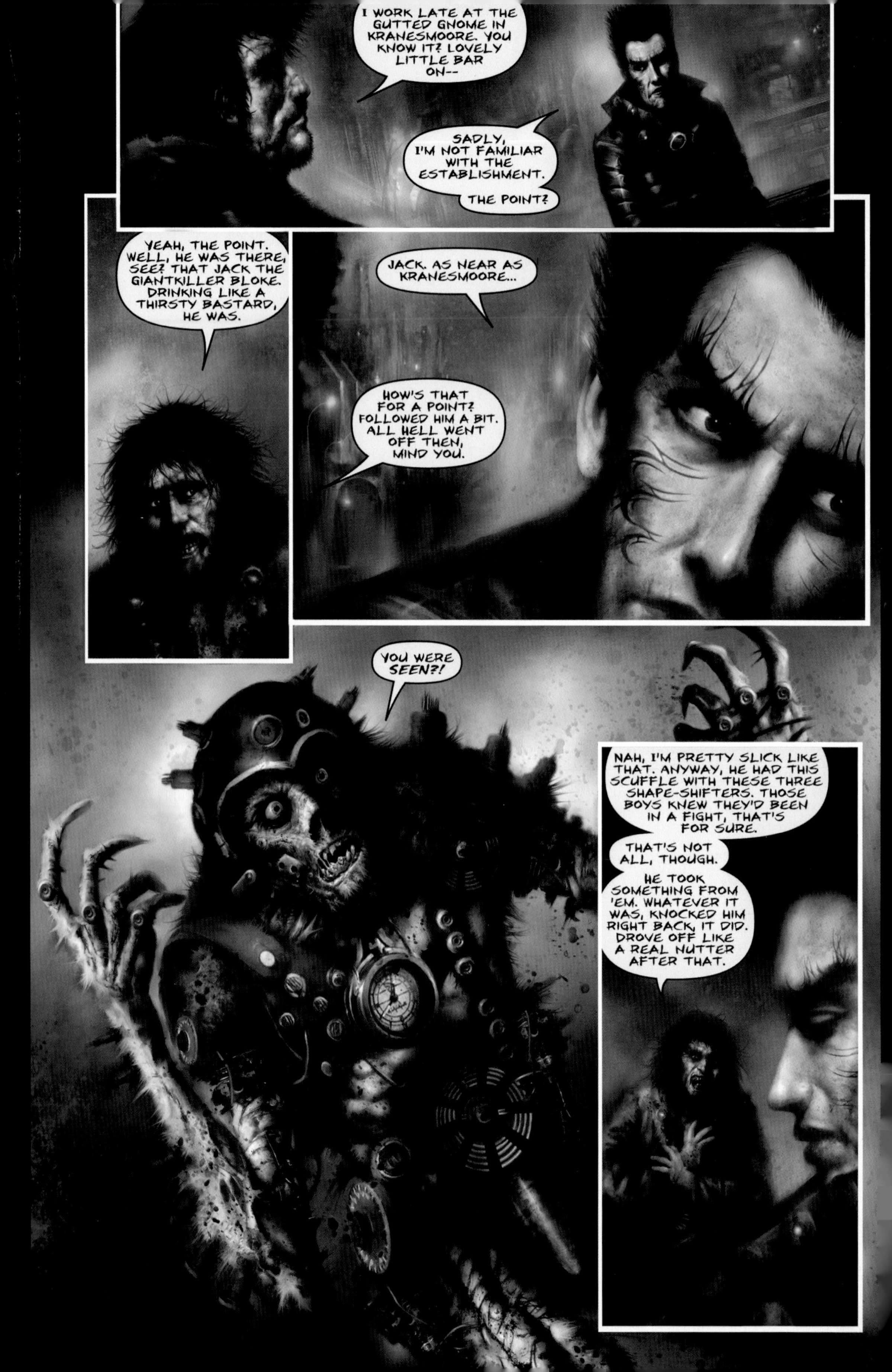
I WORK LATE AT THE GUTTED GNOME IN KRANESMOORE. YOU KNOW IT? LOVELY LITTLE BAR ON--
SADLY, I'M NOT FAMILIAR WITH THE ESTABLISHMENT.
THE POINT?
YEAH, THE POINT. WELL, HE WAS THERE, SEE? THAT JACK THE GIANTKILLER BLOKE. DRINKING LIKE A THIRSTY BASTARD, HE WAS.
JACK. AS NEAR AS KRANESMOORE...
HOW'S THAT FOR A POINT? FOLLOWED HIM A BIT. ALL HELL WENT OFF THEN, MIND YOU.
YOU WERE SEEN?!
NAH, I'M PRETTY SLICK LIKE THAT. ANYWAY, HE HAD THIS SCUFFLE WITH THESE THREE SHAPE-SHIFTERS. THOSE BOYS KNEW THEY'D BEEN IN A FIGHT, THAT'S FOR SURE.
THAT'S NOT ALL, THOUGH.
HE TOOK SOMETHING FROM 'EM. WHATEVER IT WAS, KNOCKED HIM RIGHT BACK, IT DID. DROVE OFF LIKE A REAL NUTTER AFTER THAT.

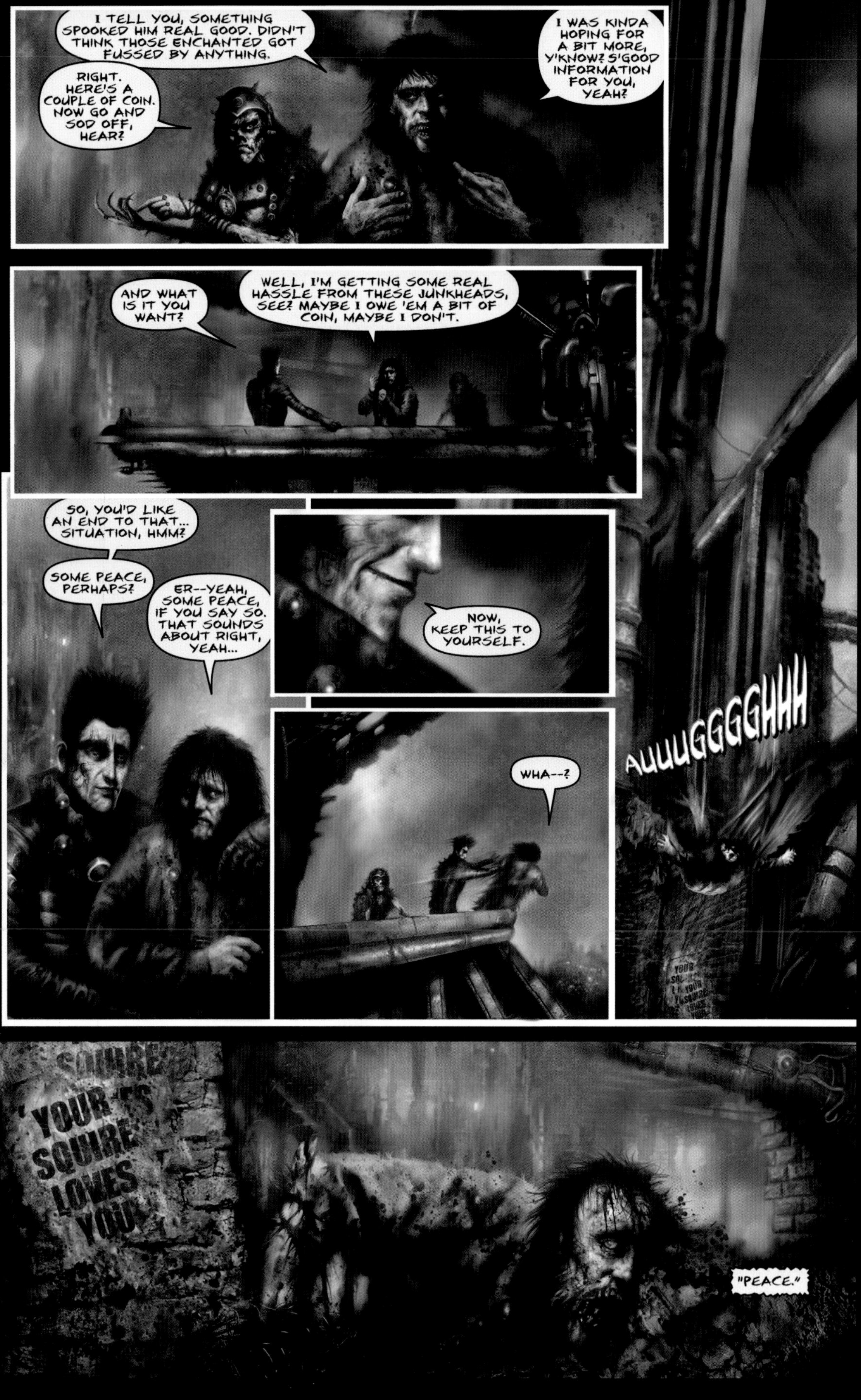
I TELL YOU, SOMETHING SPOOKED HIM REAL GOOD. DIDN'T THINK THOSE ENCHANTED GOT FUSSED BY ANYTHING.
RIGHT. HERE'S A COUPLE OF COIN. NOW GO AND SOD OFF, HEAR?
I WAS KINDA HOPING FOR A BIT MORE, Y'KNOW? S'GOOD INFORMATION FOR YOU, YEAH?
AND WHAT IS IT YOU WANT?
WELL, I'M GETTING SOME REAL HASSLE FROM THESE JUNKHEADS, SEE? MAYBE I OWE 'EM A BIT OF COIN, MAYBE I DON'T.
SO, YOU'D LIKE AN END TO THAT... SITUATION, HMM?
SOME PEACE, PERHAPS?
ER--YEAH, SOME PEACE, IF YOU SAY SO. THAT SOUNDS ABOUT RIGHT, YEAH...
NOW, KEEP THIS TO YOURSELF.
WHA--?
AUUUGGGGHHH
YOUR SQUIRE LOVES YOU
"PEACE."

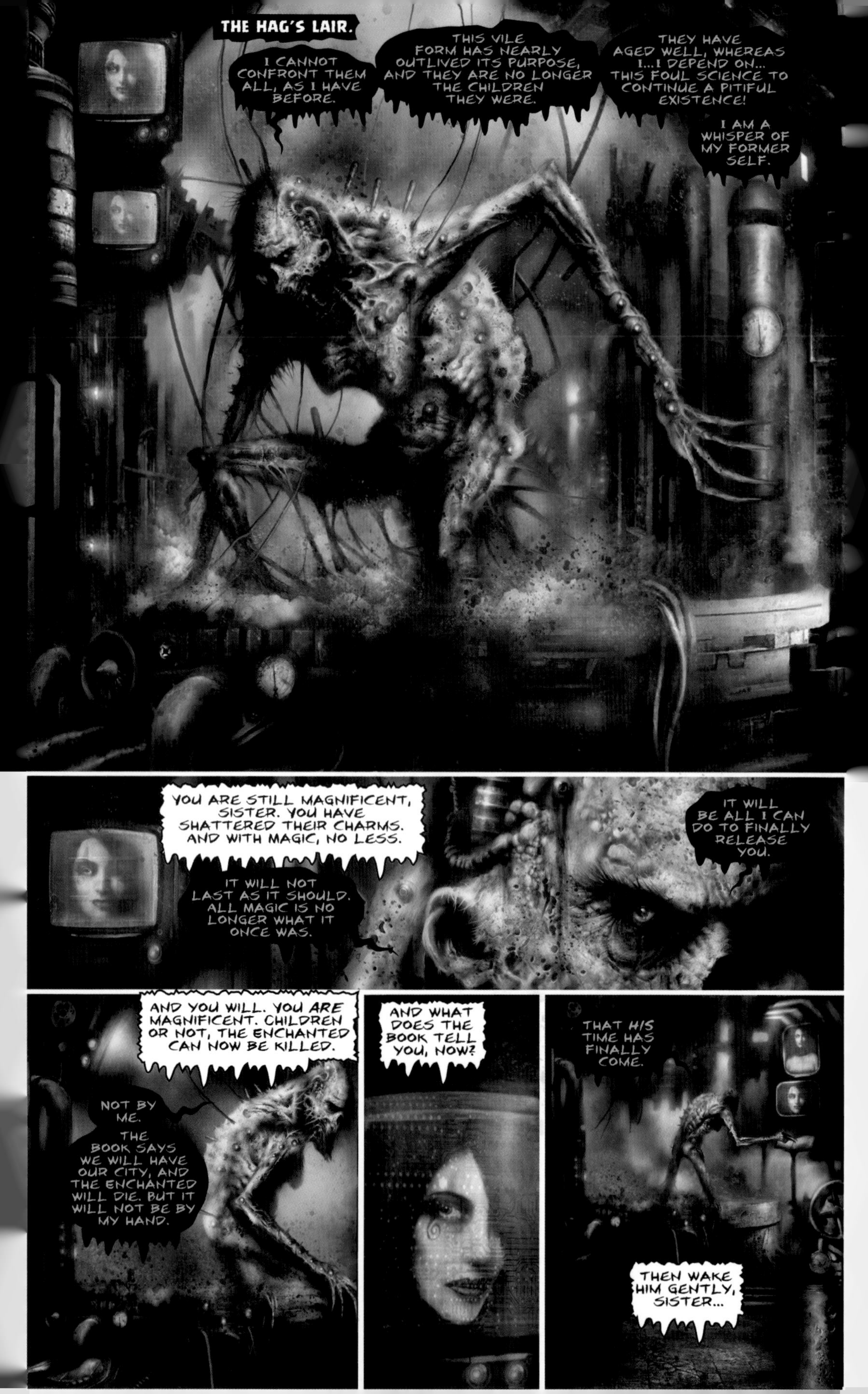
THE HAG'S LAIR.
I CANNOT CONFRONT THEM ALL, AS I HAVE BEFORE.
THIS VILE FORM HAS NEARLY OUTLIVED ITS PURPOSE, AND THEY ARE NO LONGER THE CHILDREN THEY WERE.
THEY HAVE AGED WELL, WHEREAS I...I DEPEND ON... THIS FOUL SCIENCE TO CONTINUE A PITIFUL EXISTENCE!
I AM A WHISPER OF MY FORMER SELF.
YOU ARE STILL MAGNIFICENT, SISTER. YOU HAVE SHATTERED THEIR CHARMS. AND WITH MAGIC, NO LESS.
IT WILL NOT LAST AS IT SHOULD. ALL MAGIC IS NO LONGER WHAT IT ONCE WAS.
IT WILL BE ALL I CAN DO TO FINALLY RELEASE YOU.
AND YOU WILL. YOU ARE MAGNIFICENT. CHILDREN OR NOT, THE ENCHANTED CAN NOW BE KILLED.
NOT BY ME.
THE BOOK SAYS WE WILL HAVE OUR CITY, AND THE ENCHANTED WILL DIE. BUT IT WILL NOT BE BY MY HAND.
AND WHAT DOES THE BOOK TELL YOU, NOW?
THAT HIS TIME HAS FINALLY COME.
THEN WAKE HIM GENTLY, SISTER...

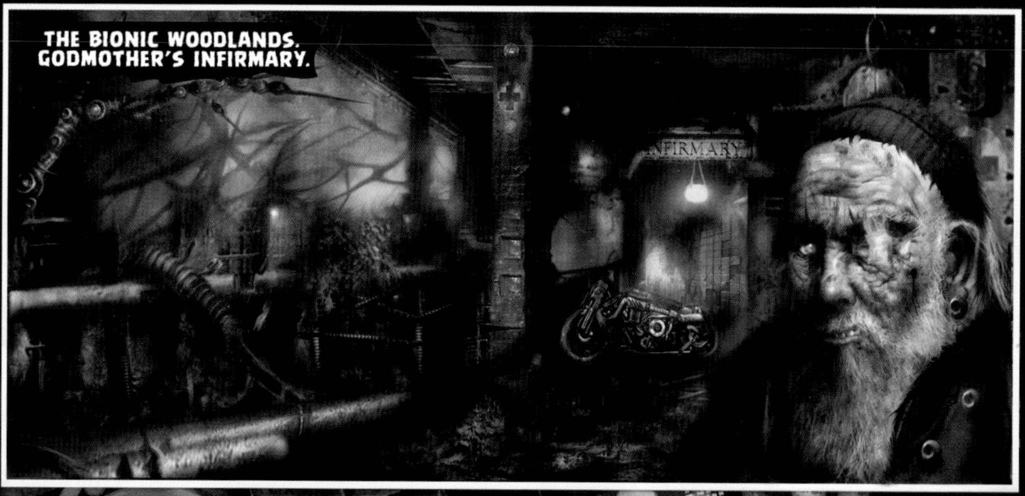
THE BIONIC WOODLANDS. GODMOTHER'S INFIRMARY.
INFIRMARY

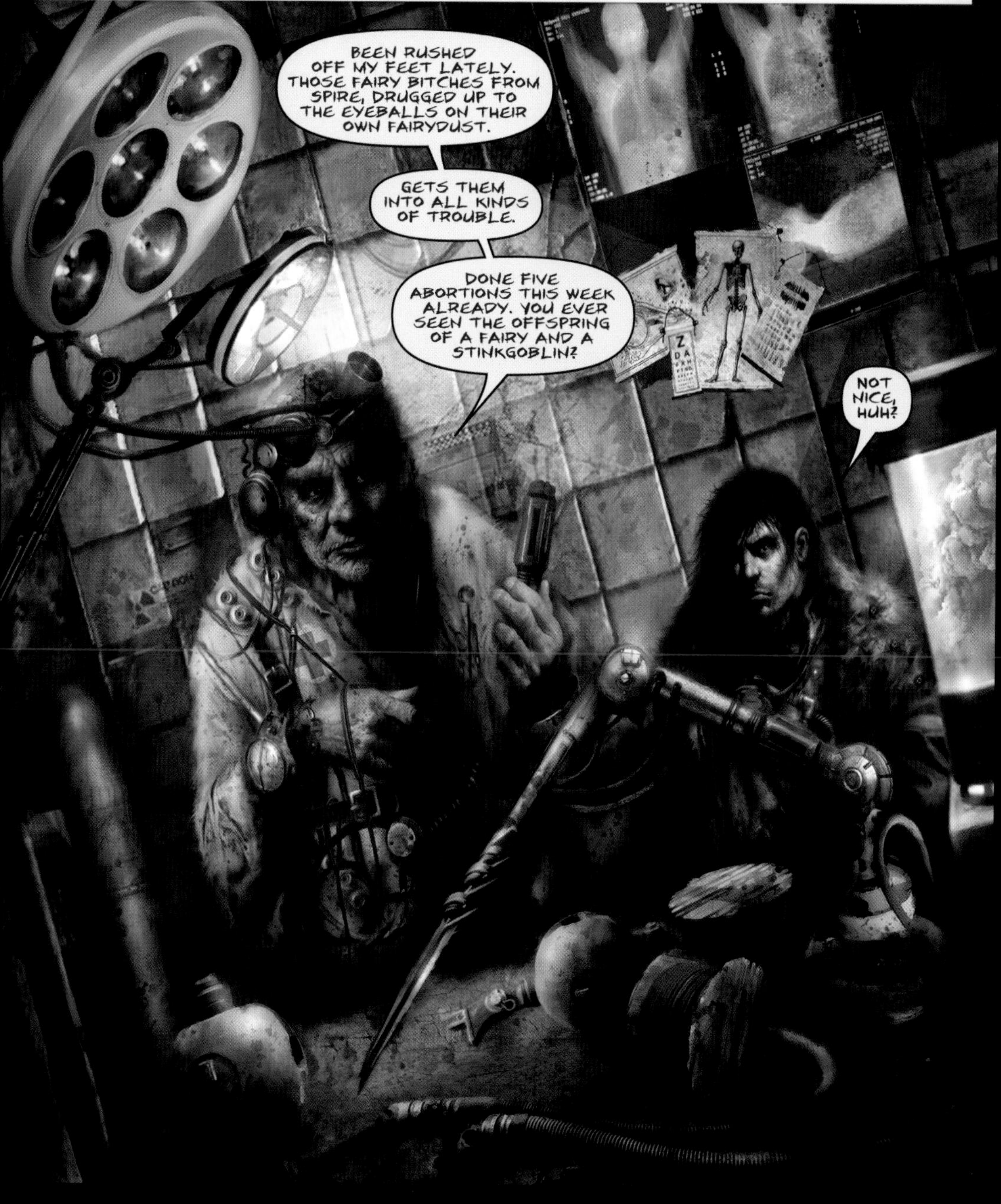
BEEN RUSHED OFF MY FEET LATELY. THOSE FAIRY BITCHES FROM SPIRE, DRUGGED UP TO THE EYEBALLS ON THEIR OWN FAIRYDUST.
GETS THEM INTO ALL KINDS OF TROUBLE.
DONE FIVE ABORTIONS THIS WEEK ALREADY. YOU EVER SEEN THE OFFSPRING OF A FAIRY AND A STINKGOBLIN?
NOT NICE, HUH?

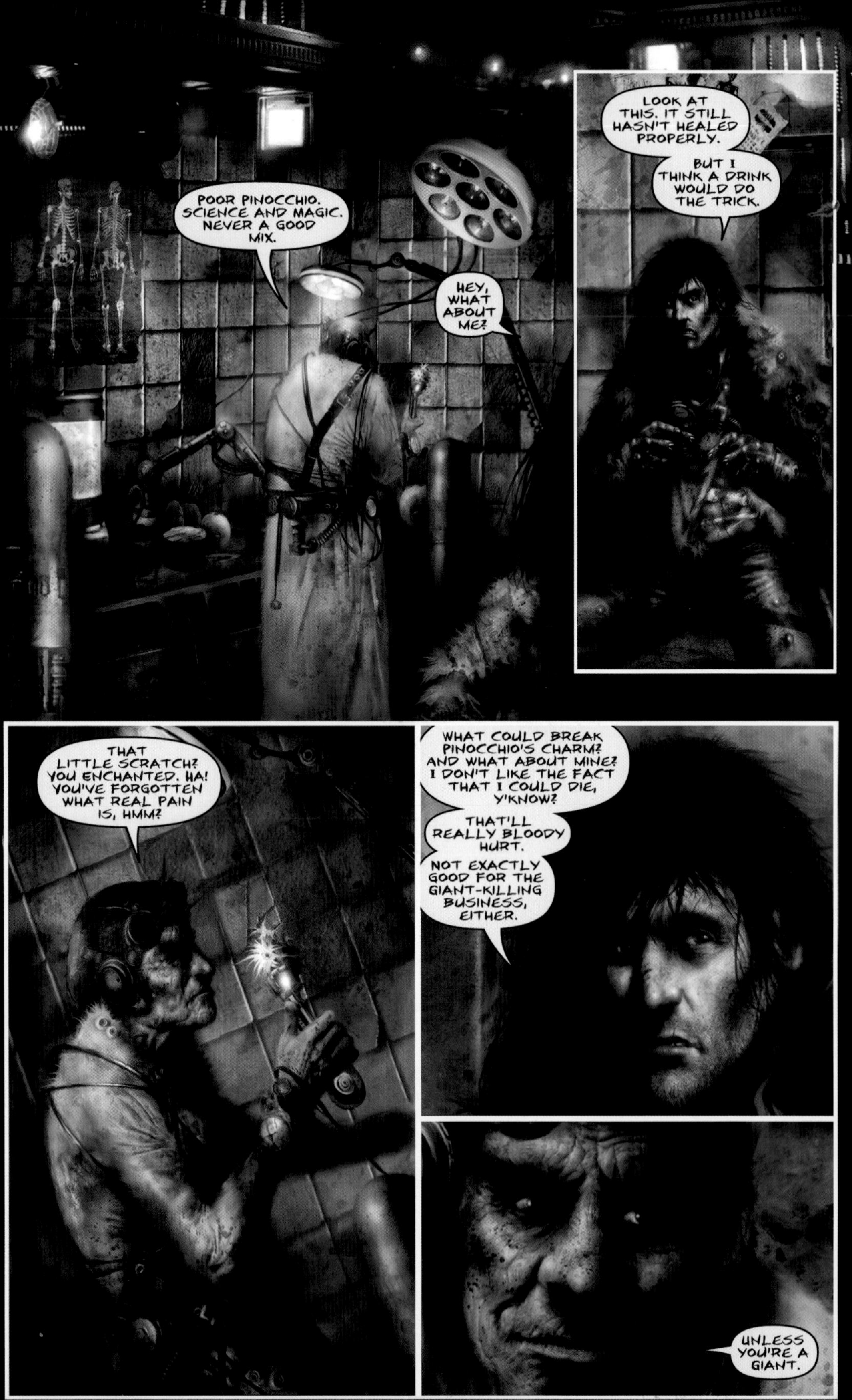
POOR PINOCCHIO. SCIENCE AND MAGIC. NEVER A GOOD MIX.
HEY, WHAT ABOUT ME?
LOOK AT THIS. IT STILL HASN'T HEALED PROPERLY.
BUT I THINK A DRINK WOULD DO THE TRICK.
THAT LITTLE SCRATCH? YOU ENCHANTED. HA! YOU'VE FORGOTTEN WHAT REAL PAIN IS, HMM?
WHAT COULD BREAK PINOCCHIO'S CHARM? AND WHAT ABOUT MINE? I DON'T LIKE THE FACT THAT I COULD DIE, Y'KNOW?
THAT'LL REALLY BLOODY HURT.
NOT EXACTLY GOOD FOR THE GIANT-KILLING BUSINESS, EITHER.
UNLESS YOU'RE A GIANT.

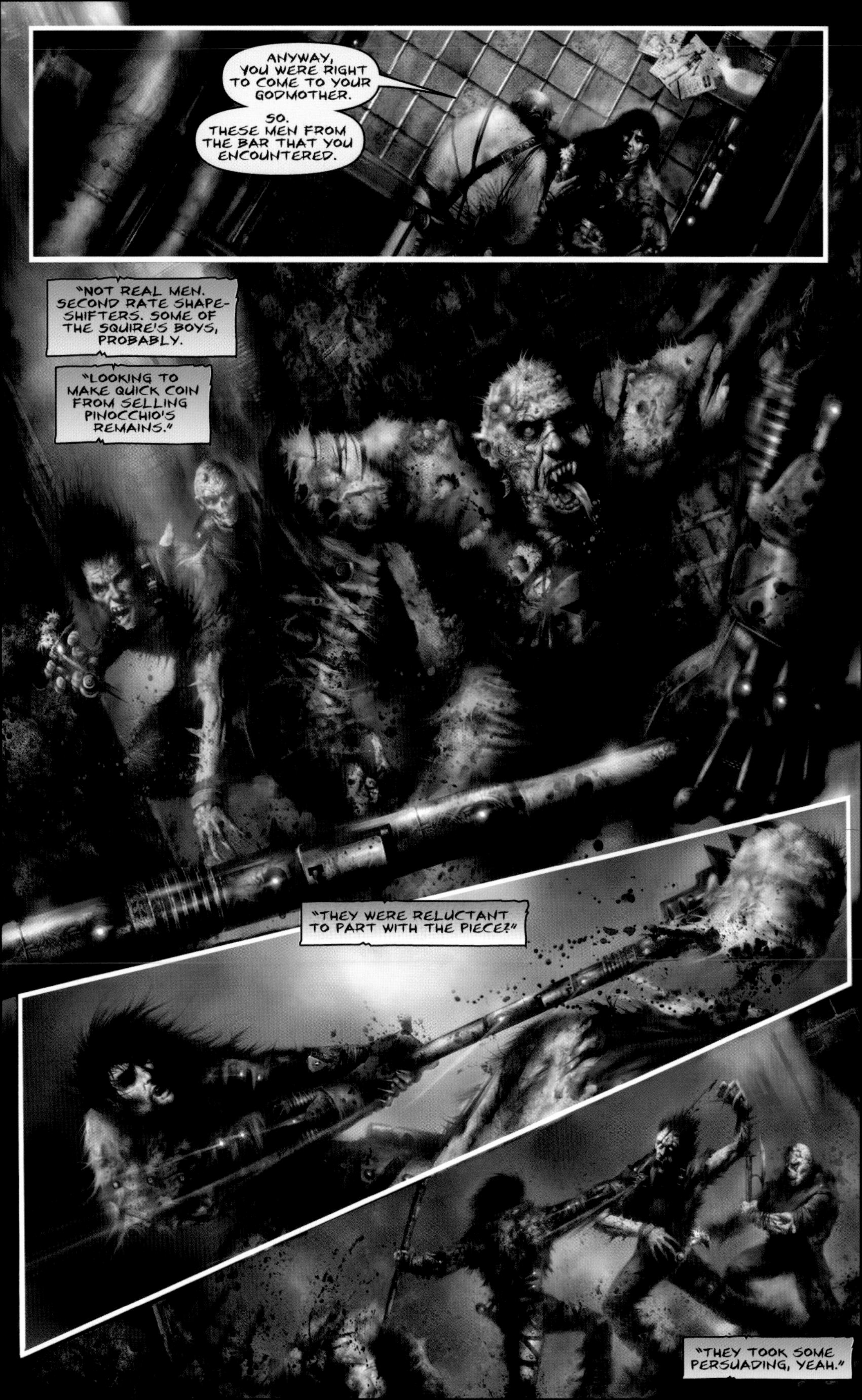
ANYWAY, YOU WERE RIGHT TO COME TO YOUR GODMOTHER.
SO. THESE MEN FROM THE BAR THAT YOU ENCOUNTERED.
"NOT REAL MEN. SECOND RATE SHAPE-SHIFTERS. SOME OF THE SQUIRE'S BOYS, PROBABLY.
"LOOKING TO MAKE QUICK COIN FROM SELLING PINOCCHIO'S REMAINS."
"THEY WERE RELUCTANT TO PART WITH THE PIECE?"
"THEY TOOK SOME PERSUADING, YEAH."

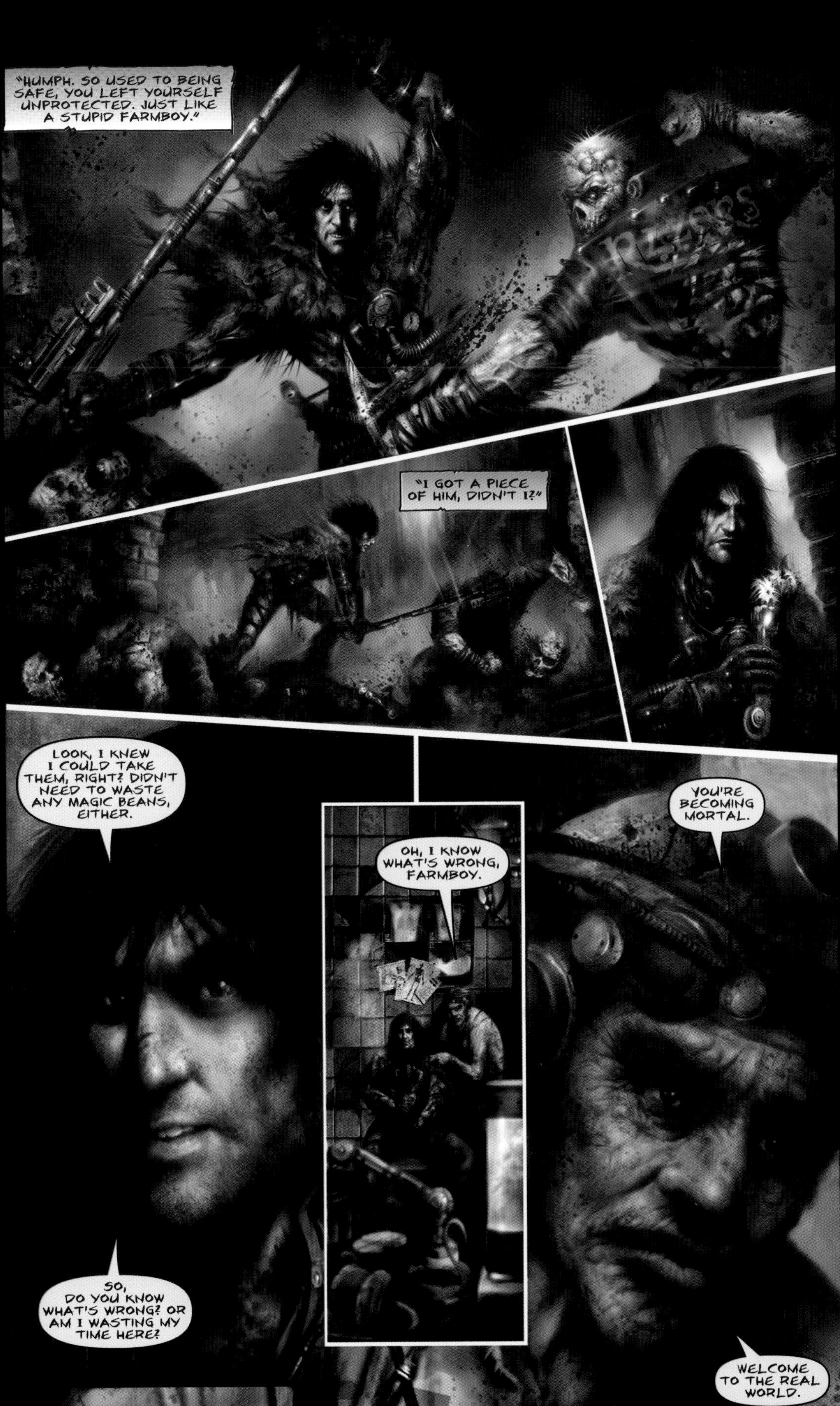
"HUMPH. SO USED TO BEING SAFE, YOU LEFT YOURSELF UNPROTECTED. JUST LIKE A STUPID FARMBOY."
"I GOT A PIECE OF HIM, DIDN'T I?"
LOOK, I KNEW I COULD TAKE THEM, RIGHT? DIDN'T NEED TO WASTE ANY MAGIC BEANS, EITHER.
SO, DO YOU KNOW WHAT'S WRONG? OR AM I WASTING MY TIME HERE?
OH, I KNOW WHAT'S WRONG, FARMBOY.
YOU'RE BECOMING MORTAL.
WELCOME TO THE REAL WORLD.

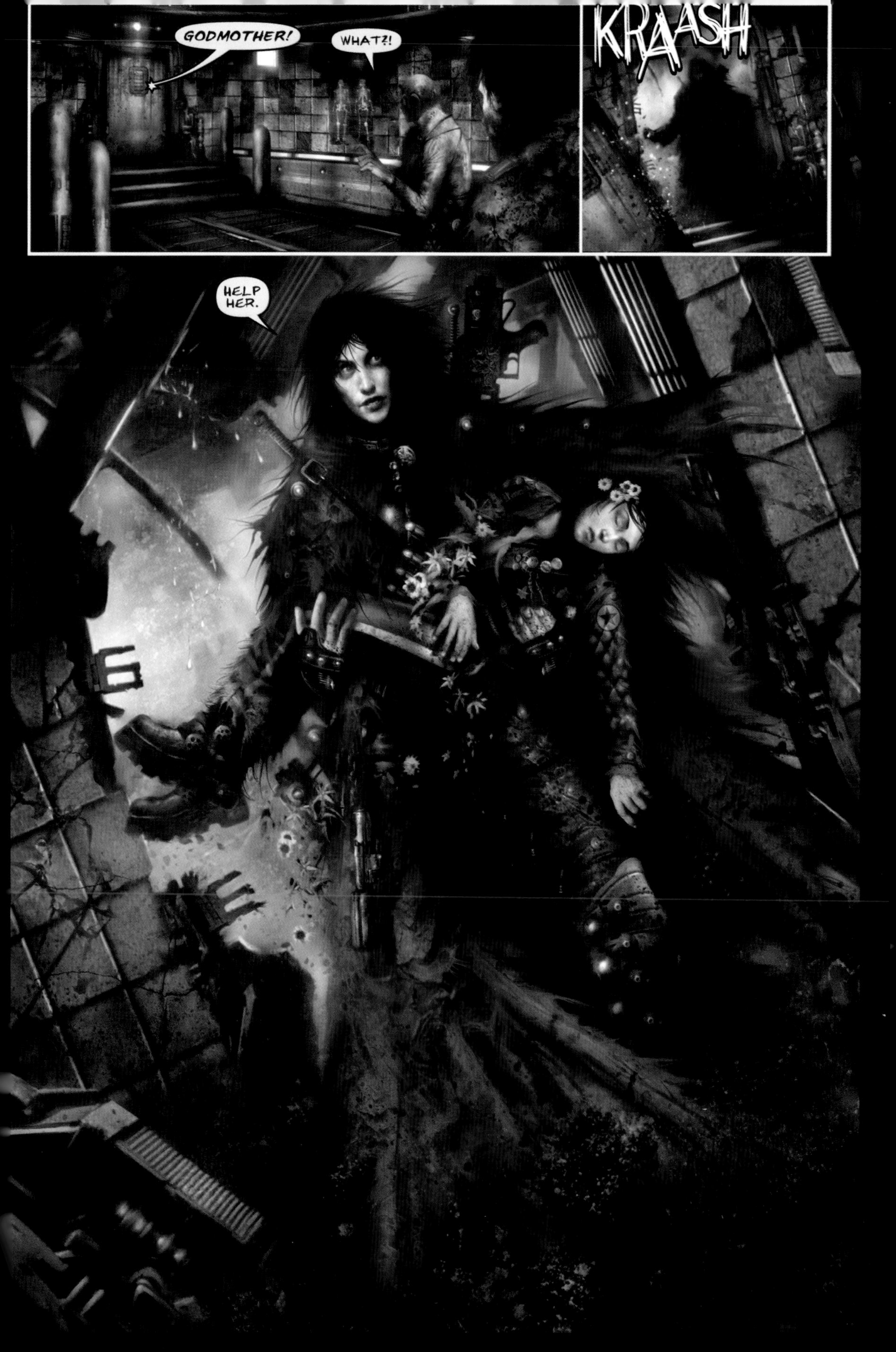
GODMOTHER!
WHAT?!
KRAASH
HELP HER.

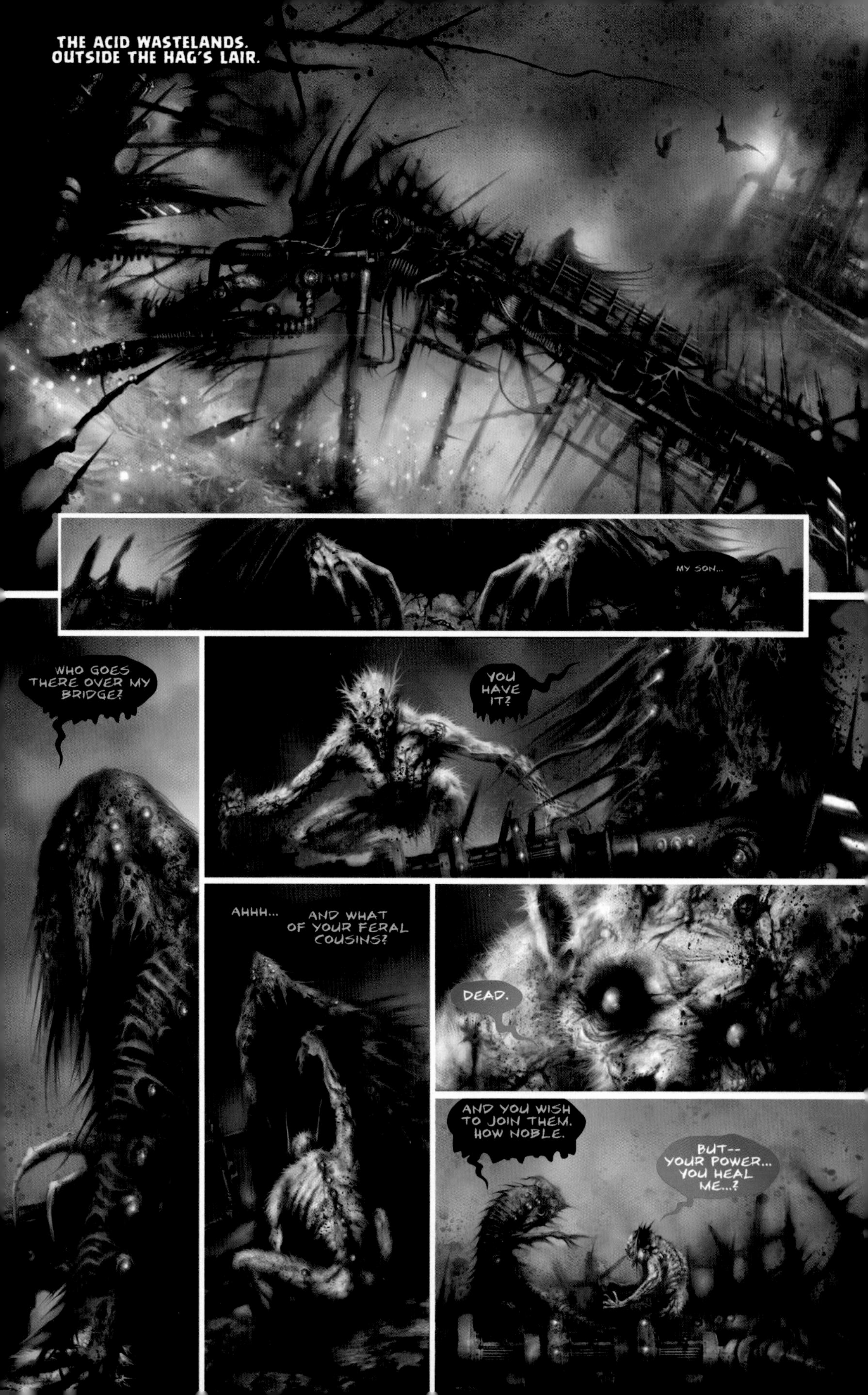
THE ACID WASTELANDS.
OUTSIDE THE HAG'S LAIR.
MY SON...
WHO GOES THERE OVER MY BRIDGE?
YOU HAVE IT?
AHHH...
AND WHAT OF YOUR FERAL COUSINS?
DEAD.
AND YOU WISH TO JOIN THEM. HOW NOBLE.
BUT-- YOUR POWER... YOU HEAL ME...?

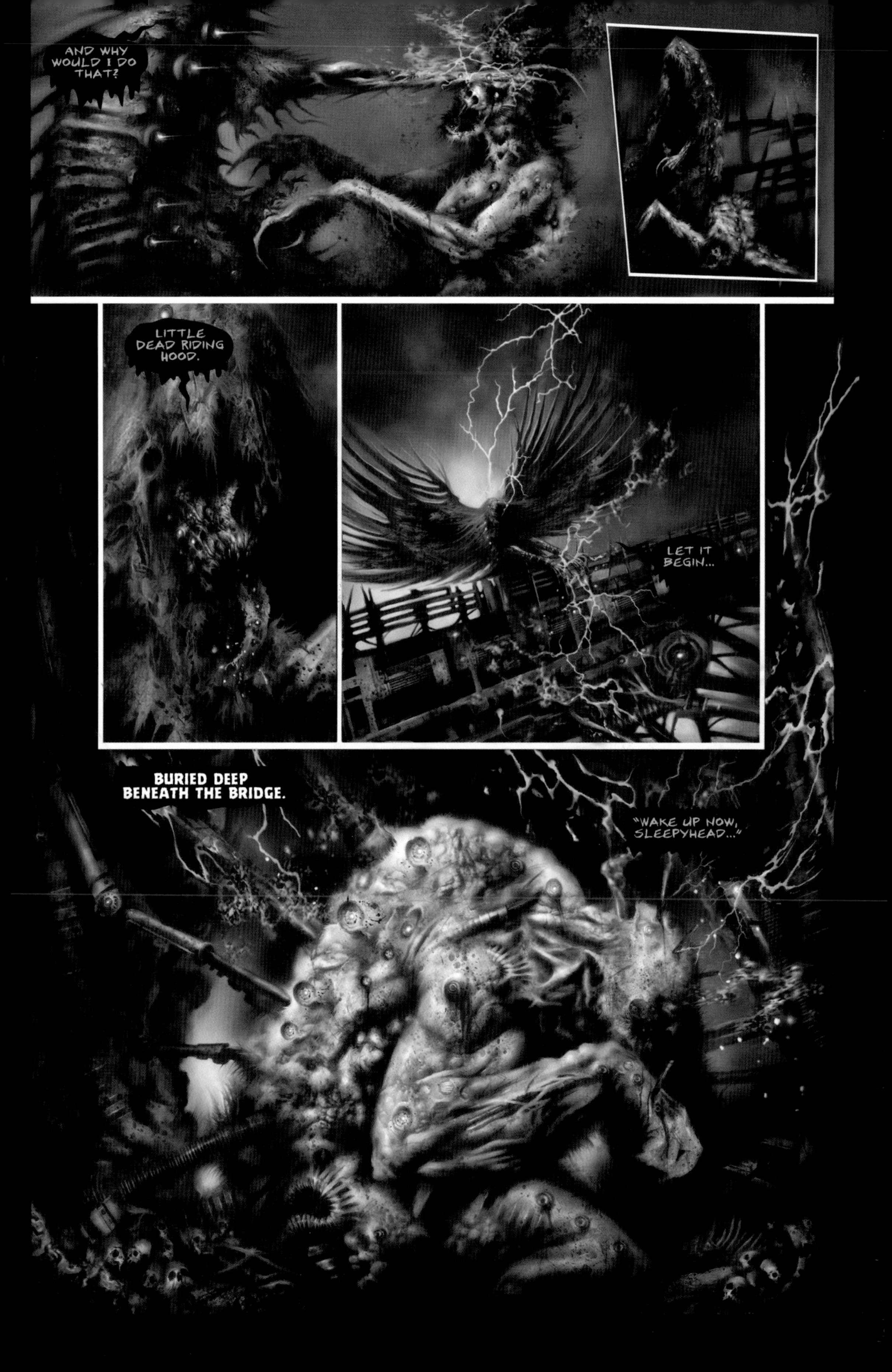
AND WHY WOULD I DO THAT?
LITTLE DEAD RIDING HOOD.
LET IT BEGIN...
BURIED DEEP BENEATH THE BRIDGE.
"WAKE UP NOW, SLEEPYHEAD..."

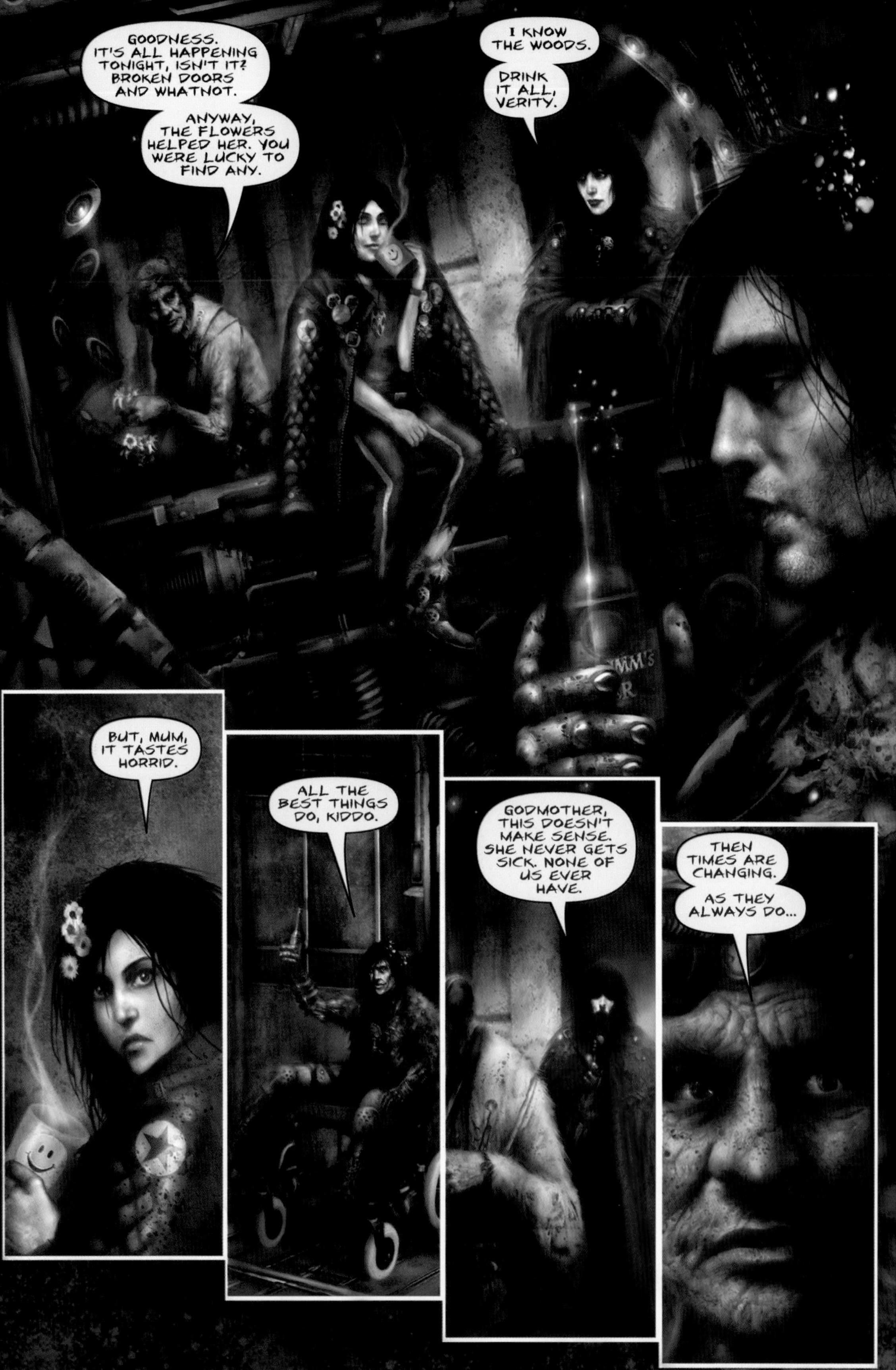

GOODNESS. IT'S ALL HAPPENING TONIGHT, ISN'T IT? BROKEN DOORS AND WHATNOT.
ANYWAY, THE FLOWERS HELPED HER. YOU WERE LUCKY TO FIND ANY.
I KNOW THE WOODS.
DRINK IT ALL, VERITY.
BUT, MUM, IT TASTES HORRID.
ALL THE BEST THINGS DO, KIDDO.
GODMOTHER, THIS DOESN'T MAKE SENSE. SHE NEVER GETS SICK. NONE OF US EVER HAVE.
THEN TIMES ARE CHANGING.
AS THEY ALWAYS DO...

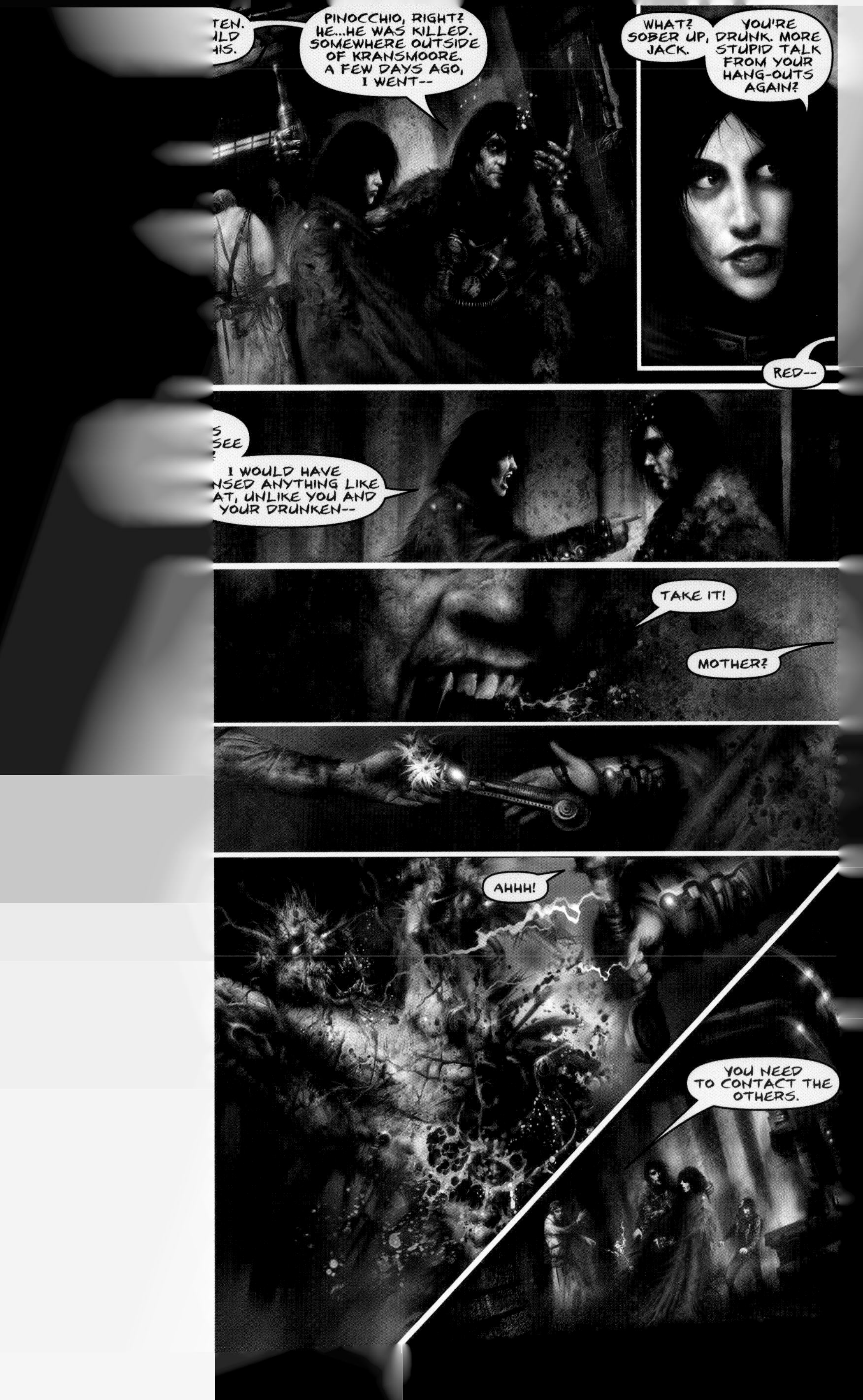
TEN. ...LD ...HIS.
PINOCCHIO, RIGHT? HE...HE WAS KILLED. SOMEWHERE OUTSIDE OF KRANSMOORE. A FEW DAYS AGO, I WENT--
WHAT? SOBER UP, JACK.
YOU'RE DRUNK. MORE STUPID TALK FROM YOUR HANG-OUTS AGAIN?
RED--
S ... SEE
I WOULD HAVE ...NSED ANYTHING LIKE ...AT, UNLIKE YOU AND YOUR DRUNKEN--
TAKE IT!
MOTHER?
AHHH!
YOU NEED TO CONTACT THE OTHERS.

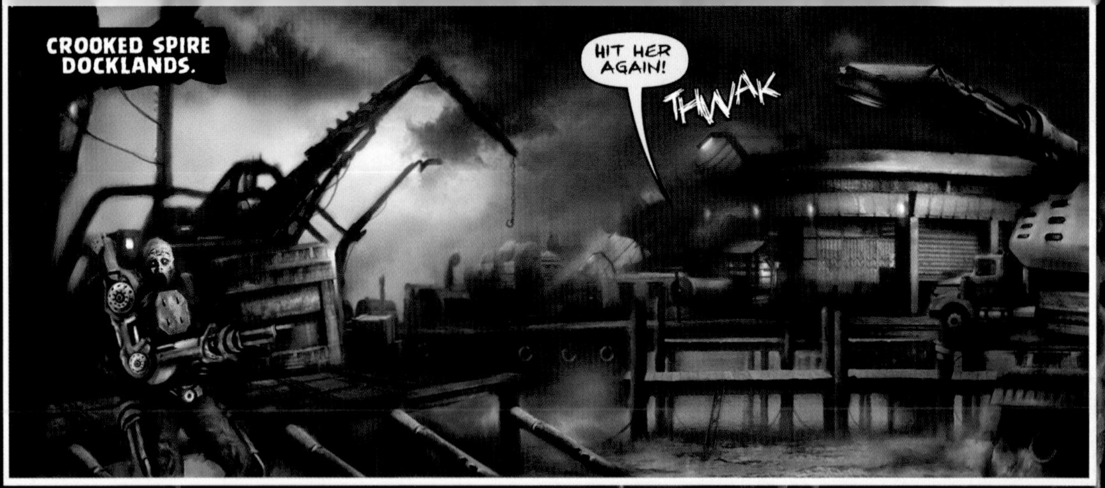
CROOKED SPIRE DOCKLANDS.
HIT HER AGAIN!
THWAK

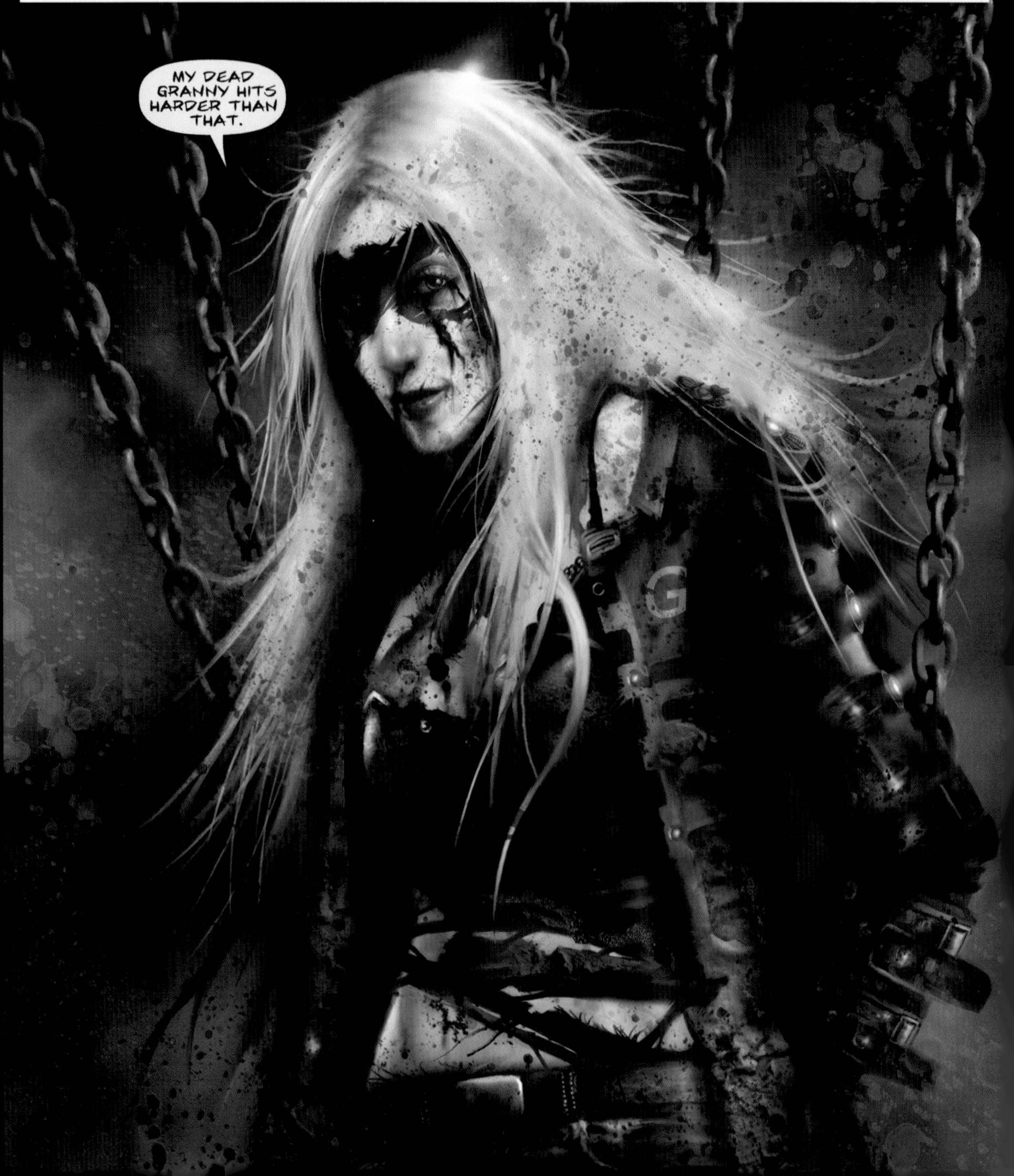
MY DEAD GRANNY HITS HARDER THAN THAT.

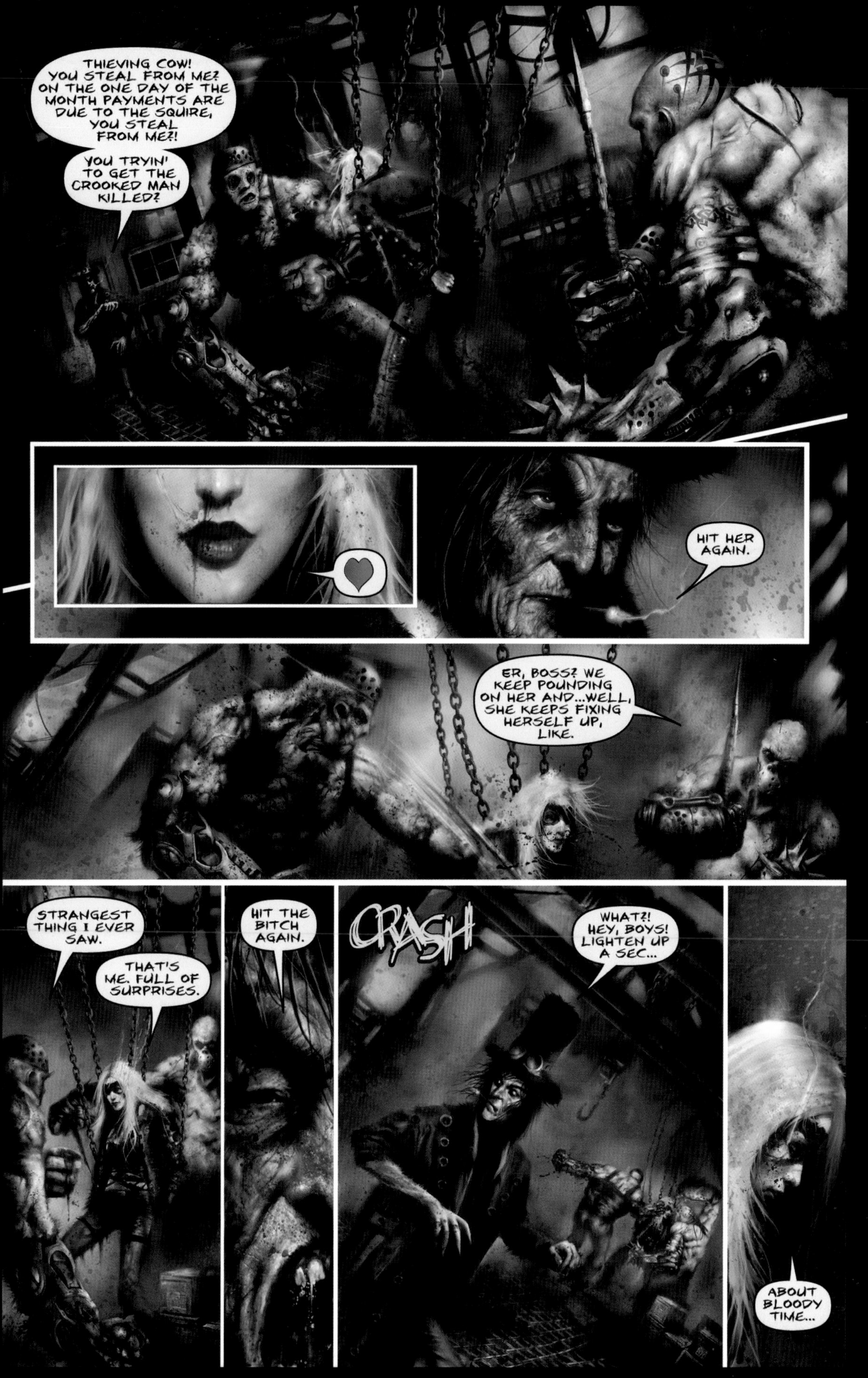
THIEVING COW! YOU STEAL FROM ME? ON THE ONE DAY OF THE MONTH PAYMENTS ARE DUE TO THE SQUIRE, YOU STEAL FROM ME?!
YOU TRYIN' TO GET THE CROOKED MAN KILLED?
HIT HER AGAIN.
ER, BOSS? WE KEEP POUNDING ON HER AND...WELL, SHE KEEPS FIXING HERSELF UP, LIKE.
STRANGEST THING I EVER SAW.
THAT'S ME. FULL OF SURPRISES.
HIT THE BITCH AGAIN.
CRASH
WHAT?! HEY, BOYS! LIGHTEN UP A SEC...
ABOUT BLOODY TIME...

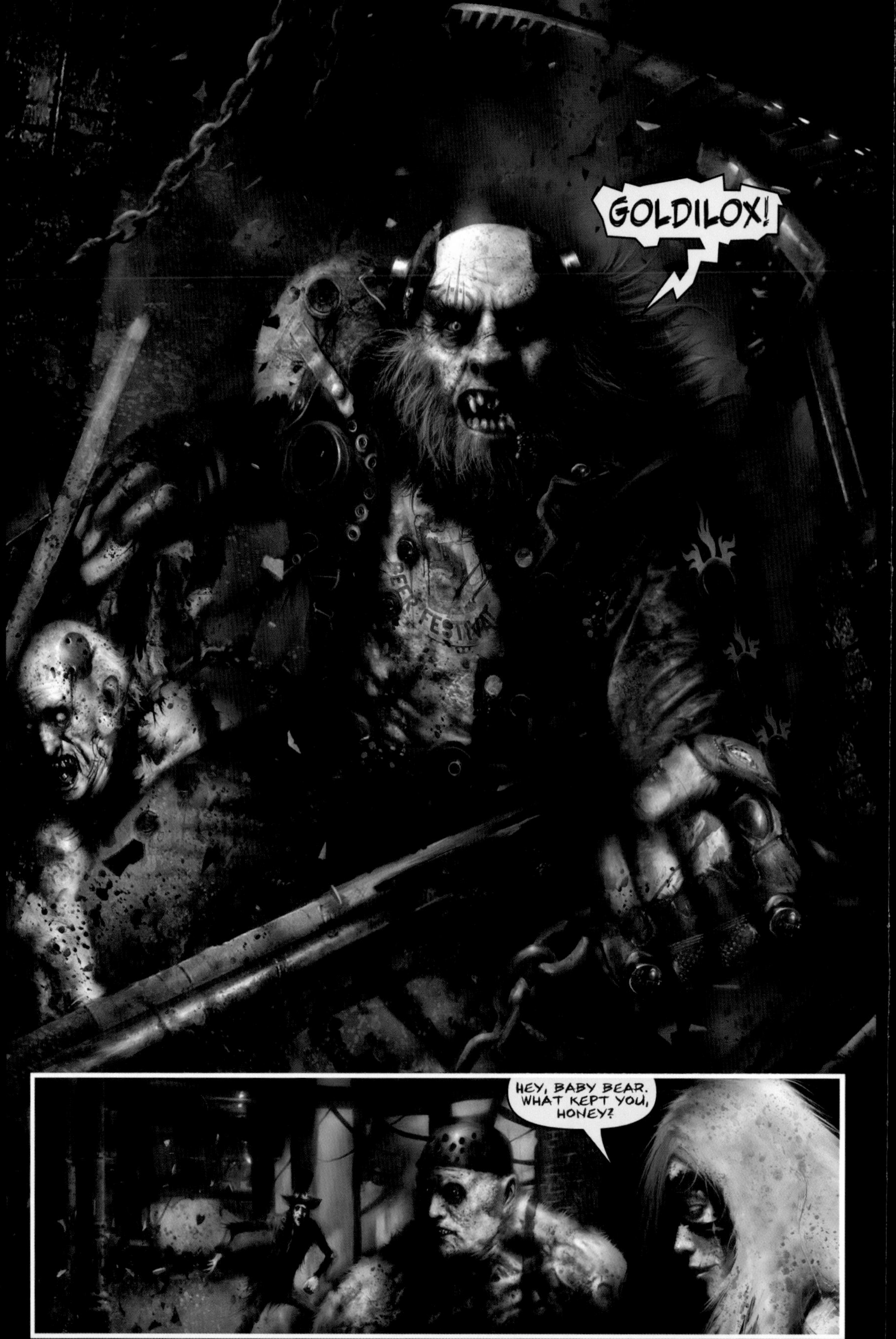
GOLDILOX!
HEY, BABY BEAR. WHAT KEPT YOU, HONEY?

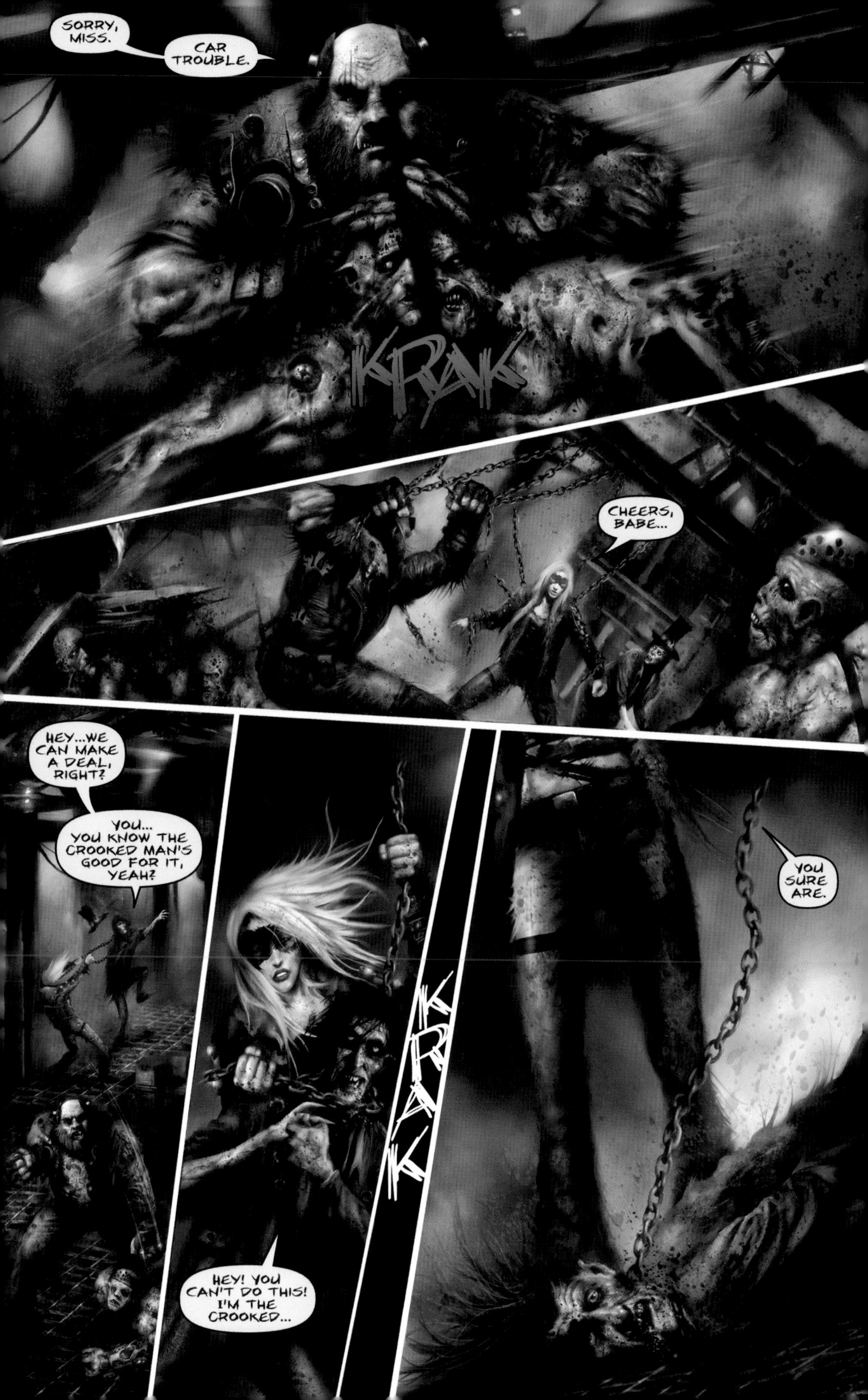
SORRY, MISS.
CAR TROUBLE.
KRAK
CHEERS, BABE...
HEY...WE CAN MAKE A DEAL, RIGHT?
YOU... YOU KNOW THE CROOKED MAN'S GOOD FOR IT, YEAH?
KRAK
HEY! YOU CAN'T DO THIS! I'M THE CROOKED...
YOU SURE ARE.

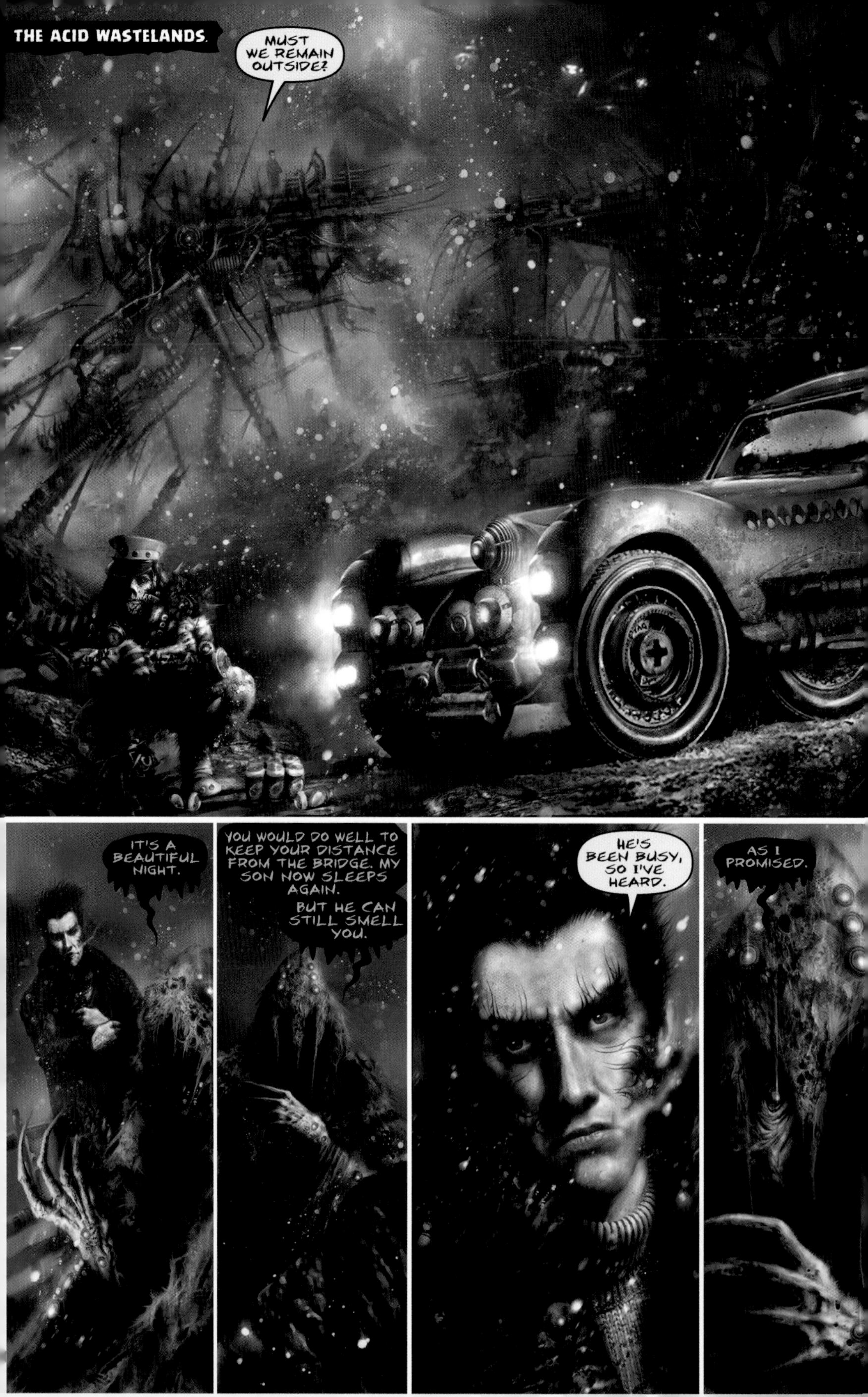
THE ACID WASTELANDS.
MUST WE REMAIN OUTSIDE?
IT'S A BEAUTIFUL NIGHT.
YOU WOULD DO WELL TO KEEP YOUR DISTANCE FROM THE BRIDGE. MY SON NOW SLEEPS AGAIN.
BUT HE CAN STILL SMELL YOU.
HE'S BEEN BUSY, SO I'VE HEARD.
AS I PROMISED.

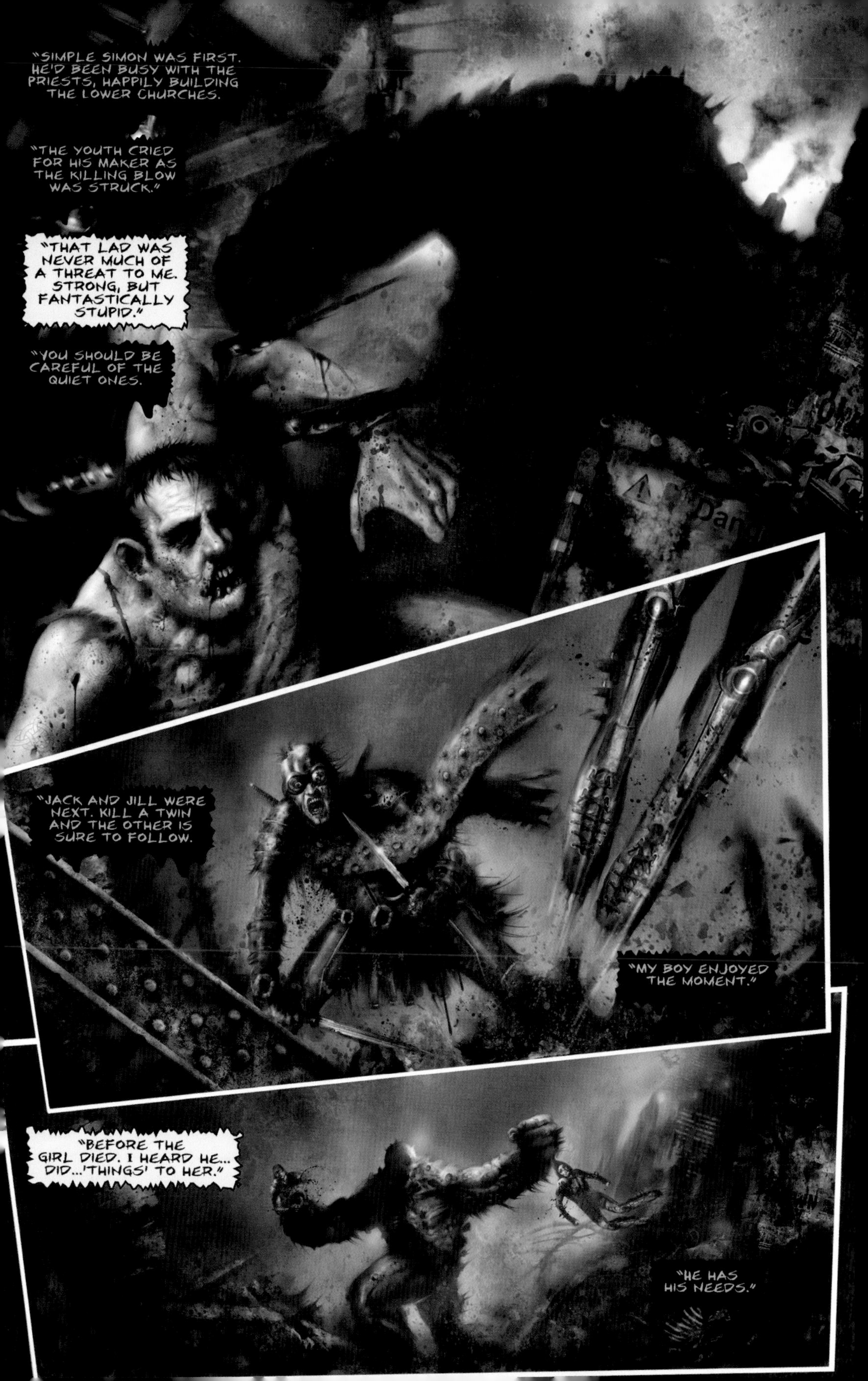
"SIMPLE SIMON WAS FIRST. HE'D BEEN BUSY WITH THE PRIESTS, HAPPILY BUILDING THE LOWER CHURCHES.
"THE YOUTH CRIED FOR HIS MAKER AS THE KILLING BLOW WAS STRUCK."
"THAT LAD WAS NEVER MUCH OF A THREAT TO ME. STRONG, BUT FANTASTICALLY STUPID."
"YOU SHOULD BE CAREFUL OF THE QUIET ONES.
"JACK AND JILL WERE NEXT. KILL A TWIN AND THE OTHER IS SURE TO FOLLOW.
"MY BOY ENJOYED THE MOMENT."
"BEFORE THE GIRL DIED. I HEARD HE... DID...'THINGS' TO HER."
"HE HAS HIS NEEDS."

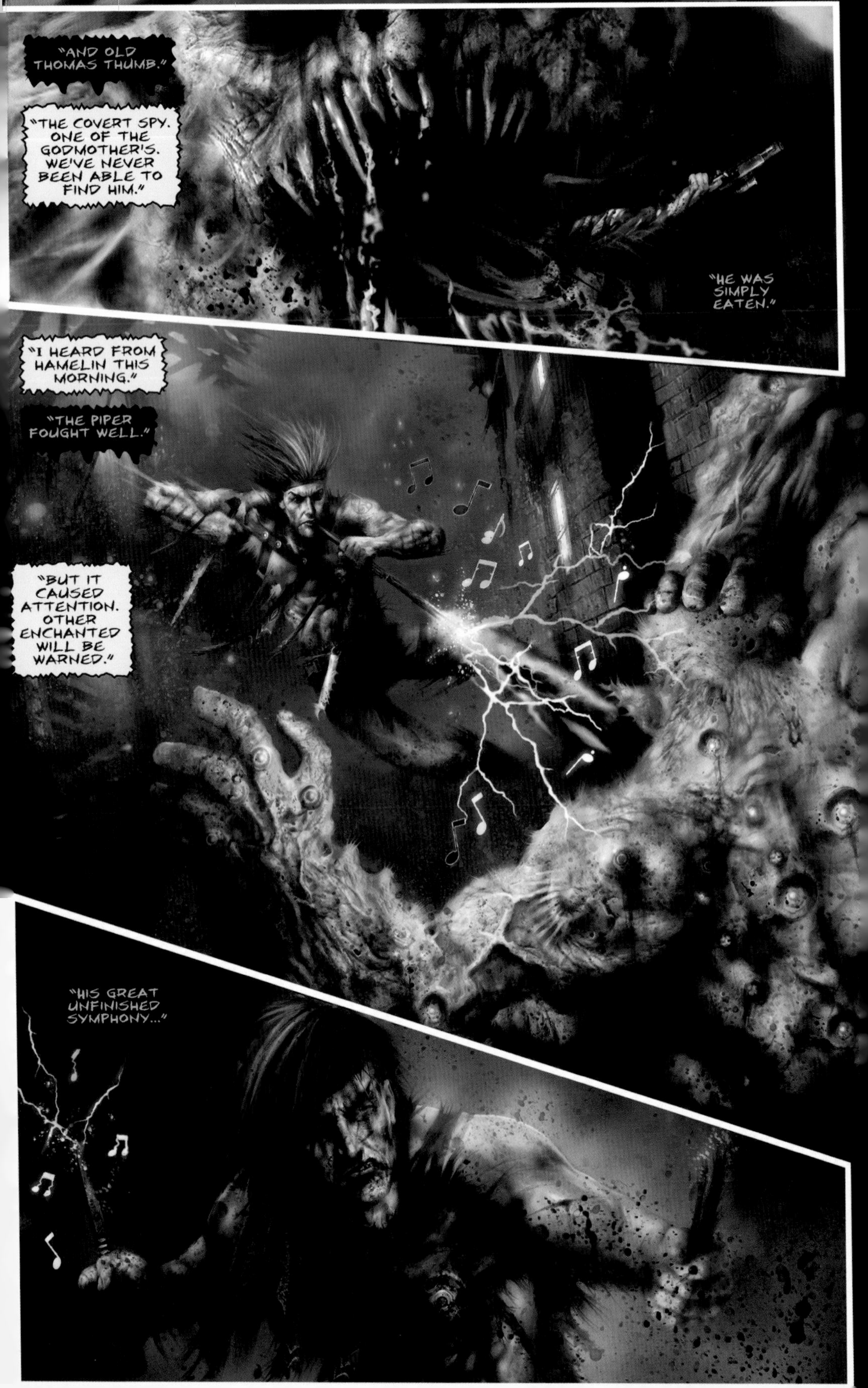
"AND OLD THOMAS THUMB."
"THE COVERT SPY. ONE OF THE GODMOTHER'S. WE'VE NEVER BEEN ABLE TO FIND HIM."
"HE WAS SIMPLY EATEN."
"I HEARD FROM HAMELIN THIS MORNING."
"THE PIPER FOUGHT WELL."
"BUT IT CAUSED ATTENTION. OTHER ENCHANTED WILL BE WARNED."
"HIS GREAT UNFINISHED SYMPHONY..."

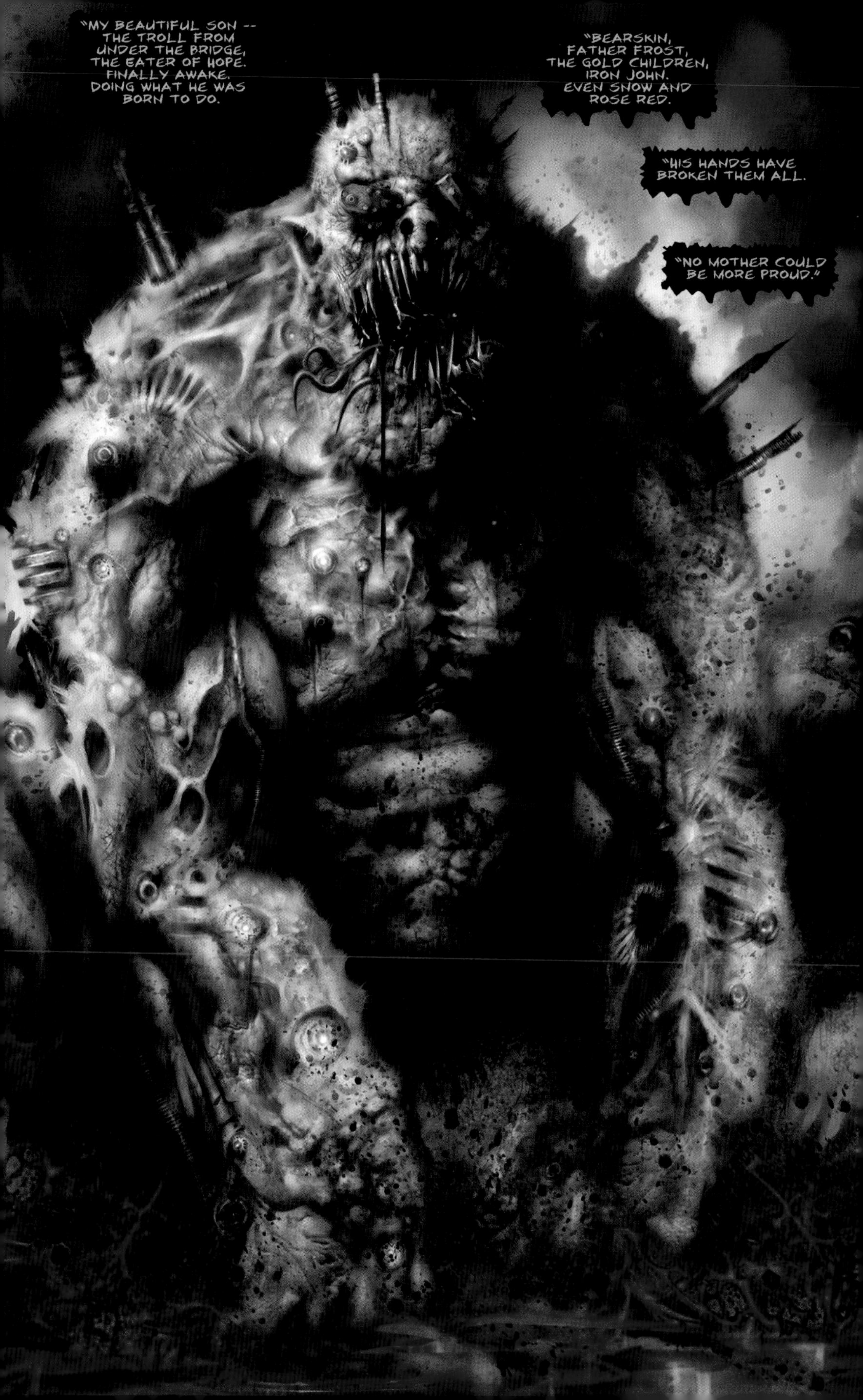
"MY BEAUTIFUL SON -- THE TROLL FROM UNDER THE BRIDGE, THE EATER OF HOPE. FINALLY AWAKE. DOING WHAT HE WAS BORN TO DO.
"BEARSKIN, FATHER FROST, THE GOLD CHILDREN, IRON JOHN. EVEN SNOW AND ROSE RED.
"HIS HANDS HAVE BROKEN THEM ALL.
"NO MOTHER COULD BE MORE PROUD."

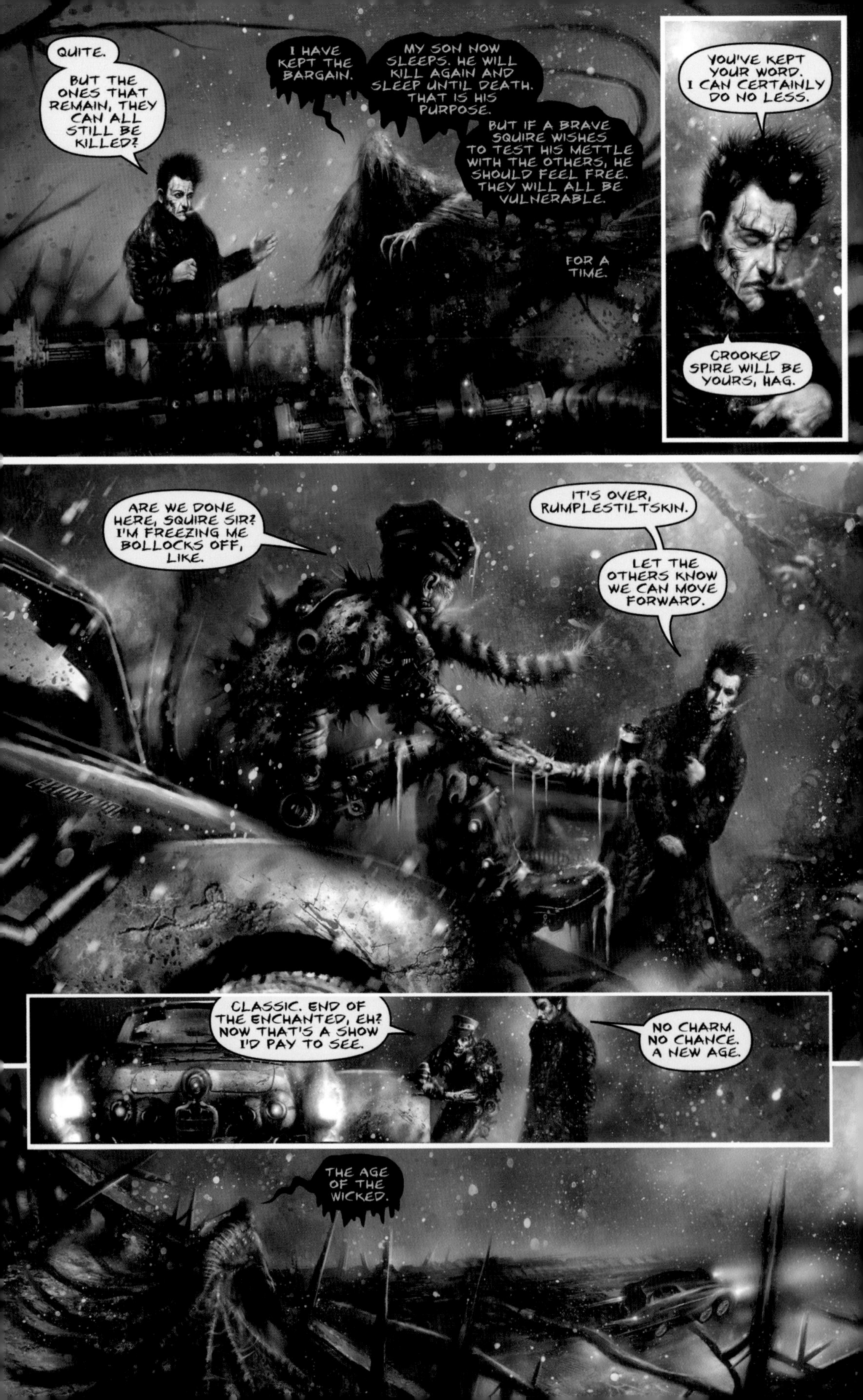
QUITE.
BUT THE ONES THAT REMAIN, THEY CAN ALL STILL BE KILLED?
I HAVE KEPT THE BARGAIN.
MY SON NOW SLEEPS. HE WILL KILL AGAIN AND SLEEP UNTIL DEATH. THAT IS HIS PURPOSE.
BUT IF A BRAVE SQUIRE WISHES TO TEST HIS METTLE WITH THE OTHERS, HE SHOULD FEEL FREE. THEY WILL ALL BE VULNERABLE.
FOR A TIME.
YOU'VE KEPT YOUR WORD. I CAN CERTAINLY DO NO LESS.
CROOKED SPIRE WILL BE YOURS, HAG.
ARE WE DONE HERE, SQUIRE SIR? I'M FREEZING ME BOLLOCKS OFF, LIKE.
IT'S OVER, RUMPLESTILTSKIN.
LET THE OTHERS KNOW WE CAN MOVE FORWARD.
CLASSIC. END OF THE ENCHANTED, EH? NOW THAT'S A SHOW I'D PAY TO SEE.
NO CHARM. NO CHANCE. A NEW AGE.
THE AGE OF THE WICKED.

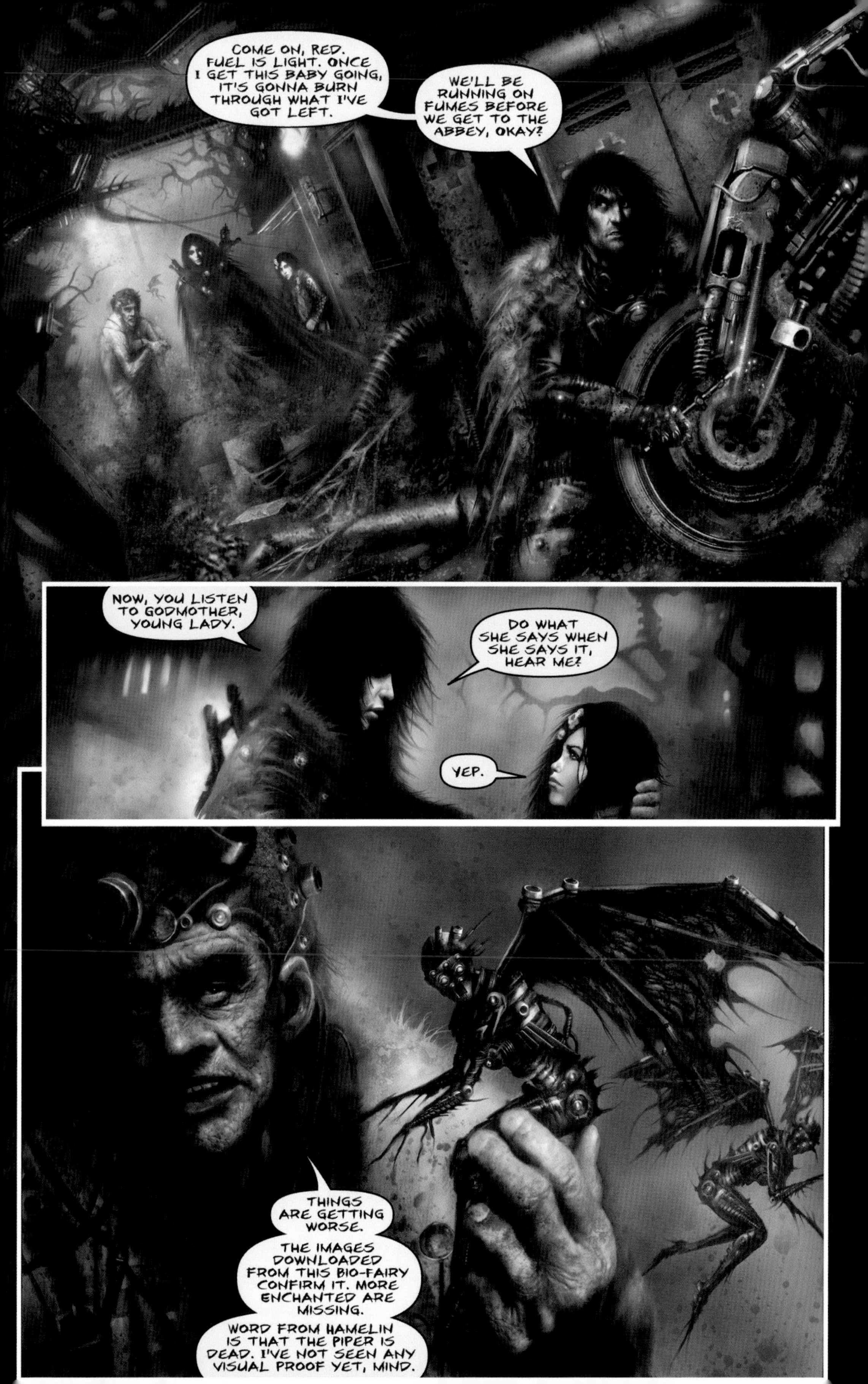
COME ON, RED. FUEL IS LIGHT. ONCE I GET THIS BABY GOING, IT'S GONNA BURN THROUGH WHAT I'VE GOT LEFT.
WE'LL BE RUNNING ON FUMES BEFORE WE GET TO THE ABBEY, OKAY?
NOW, YOU LISTEN TO GODMOTHER, YOUNG LADY.
DO WHAT SHE SAYS WHEN SHE SAYS IT, HEAR ME?
YEP.
THINGS ARE GETTING WORSE.
THE IMAGES DOWNLOADED FROM THIS BIO-FAIRY CONFIRM IT. MORE ENCHANTED ARE MISSING.
WORD FROM HAMELIN IS THAT THE PIPER IS DEAD. I'VE NOT SEEN ANY VISUAL PROOF YET, MIND.

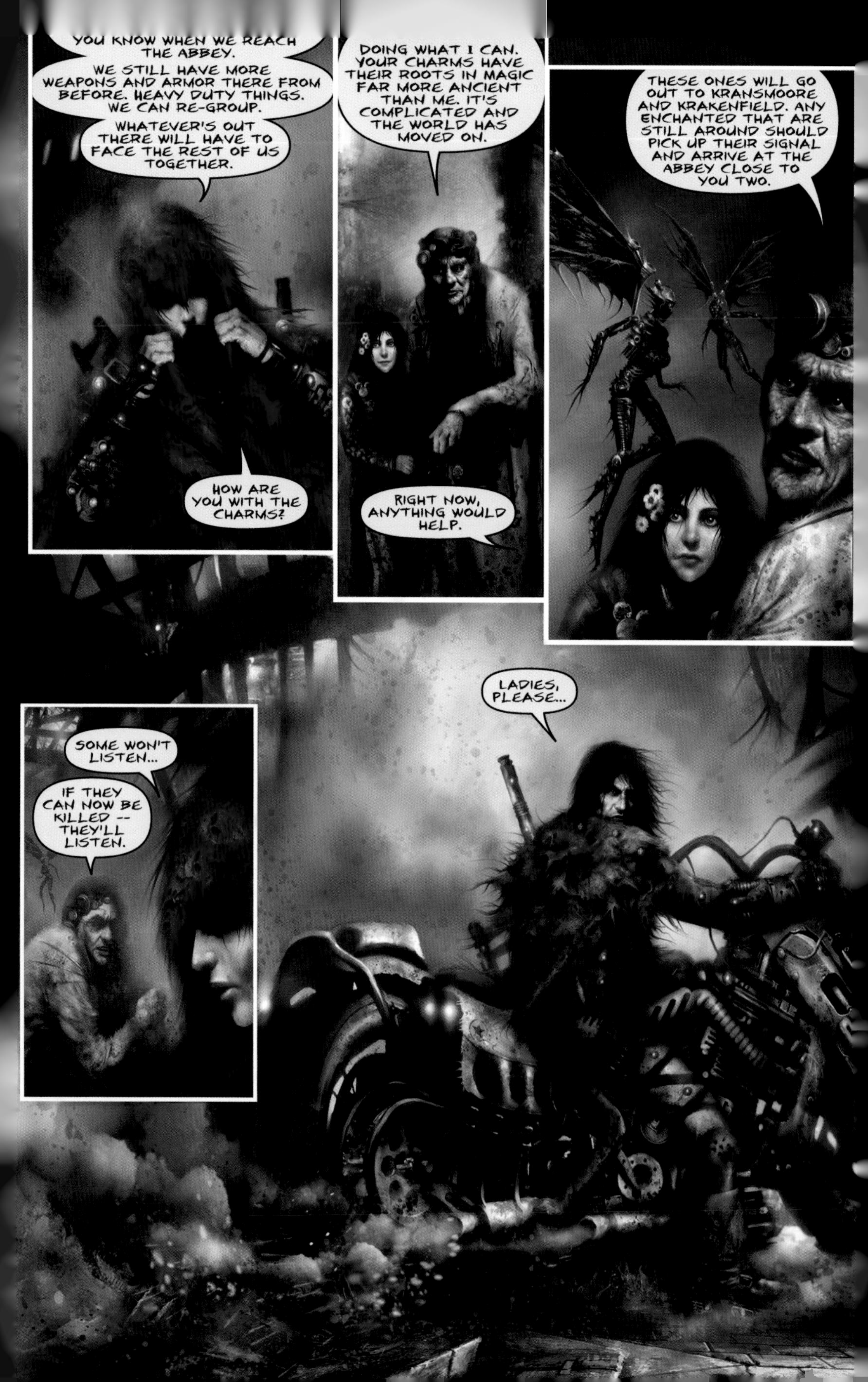
YOU KNOW WHEN WE REACH THE ABBEY.
WE STILL HAVE MORE WEAPONS AND ARMOR THERE FROM BEFORE. HEAVY DUTY THINGS. WE CAN RE-GROUP.
WHATEVER'S OUT THERE WILL HAVE TO FACE THE REST OF US TOGETHER.
HOW ARE YOU WITH THE CHARMS?
DOING WHAT I CAN. YOUR CHARMS HAVE THEIR ROOTS IN MAGIC FAR MORE ANCIENT THAN ME. IT'S COMPLICATED AND THE WORLD HAS MOVED ON.
RIGHT NOW, ANYTHING WOULD HELP.
THESE ONES WILL GO OUT TO KRANSMOORE AND KRAKENFIELD. ANY ENCHANTED THAT ARE STILL AROUND SHOULD PICK UP THEIR SIGNAL AND ARRIVE AT THE ABBEY CLOSE TO YOU TWO.
SOME WON'T LISTEN...
IF THEY CAN NOW BE KILLED -- THEY'LL LISTEN.
LADIES, PLEASE...

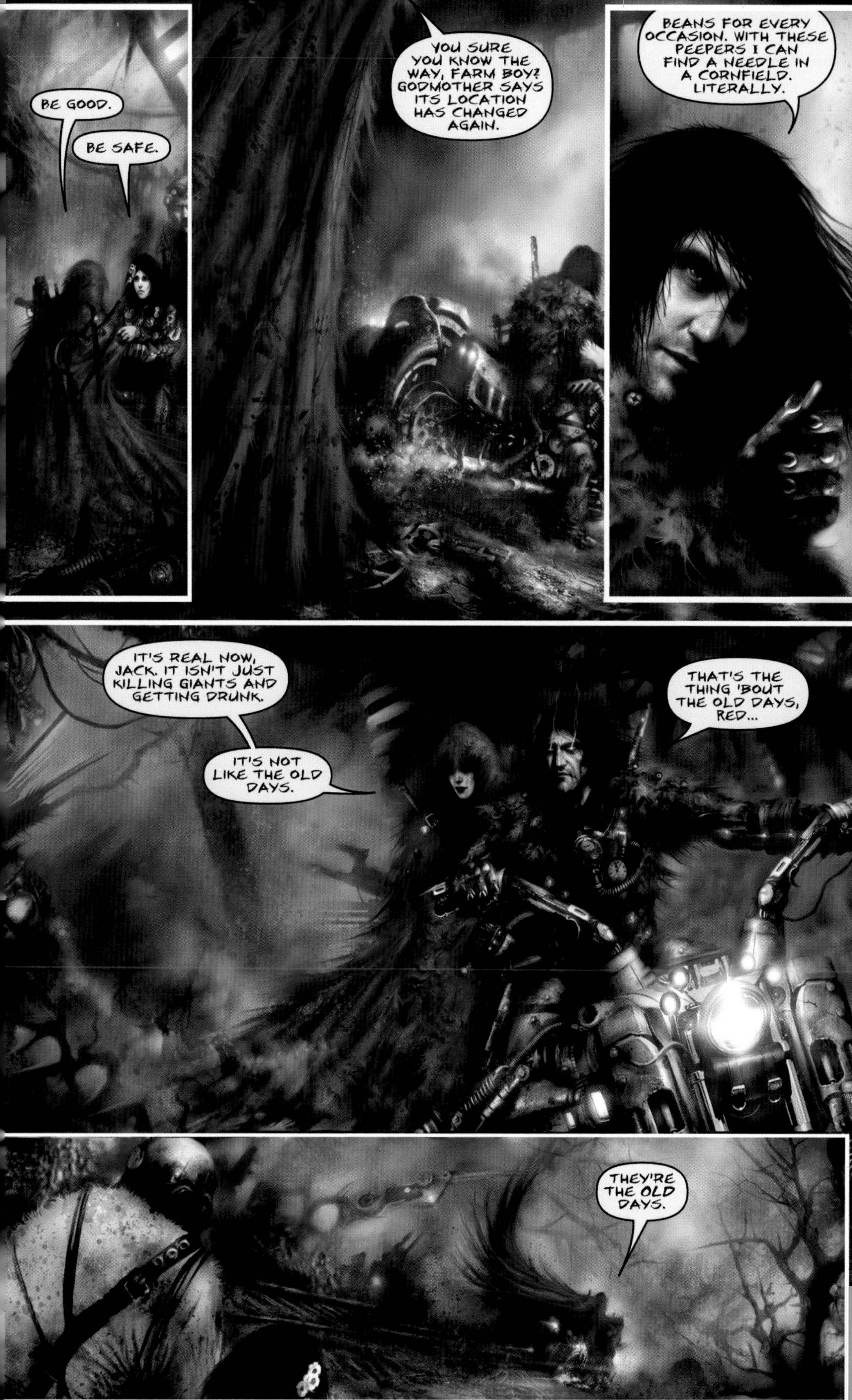
BE GOOD.
BE SAFE.
YOU SURE YOU KNOW THE WAY, FARM BOY? GODMOTHER SAYS ITS LOCATION HAS CHANGED AGAIN.
BEANS FOR EVERY OCCASION. WITH THESE PEEPERS I CAN FIND A NEEDLE IN A CORNFIELD. LITERALLY.
IT'S REAL NOW, JACK. IT ISN'T JUST KILLING GIANTS AND GETTING DRUNK.
IT'S NOT LIKE THE OLD DAYS.
THAT'S THE THING 'BOUT THE OLD DAYS, RED...
THEY'RE THE OLD DAYS.

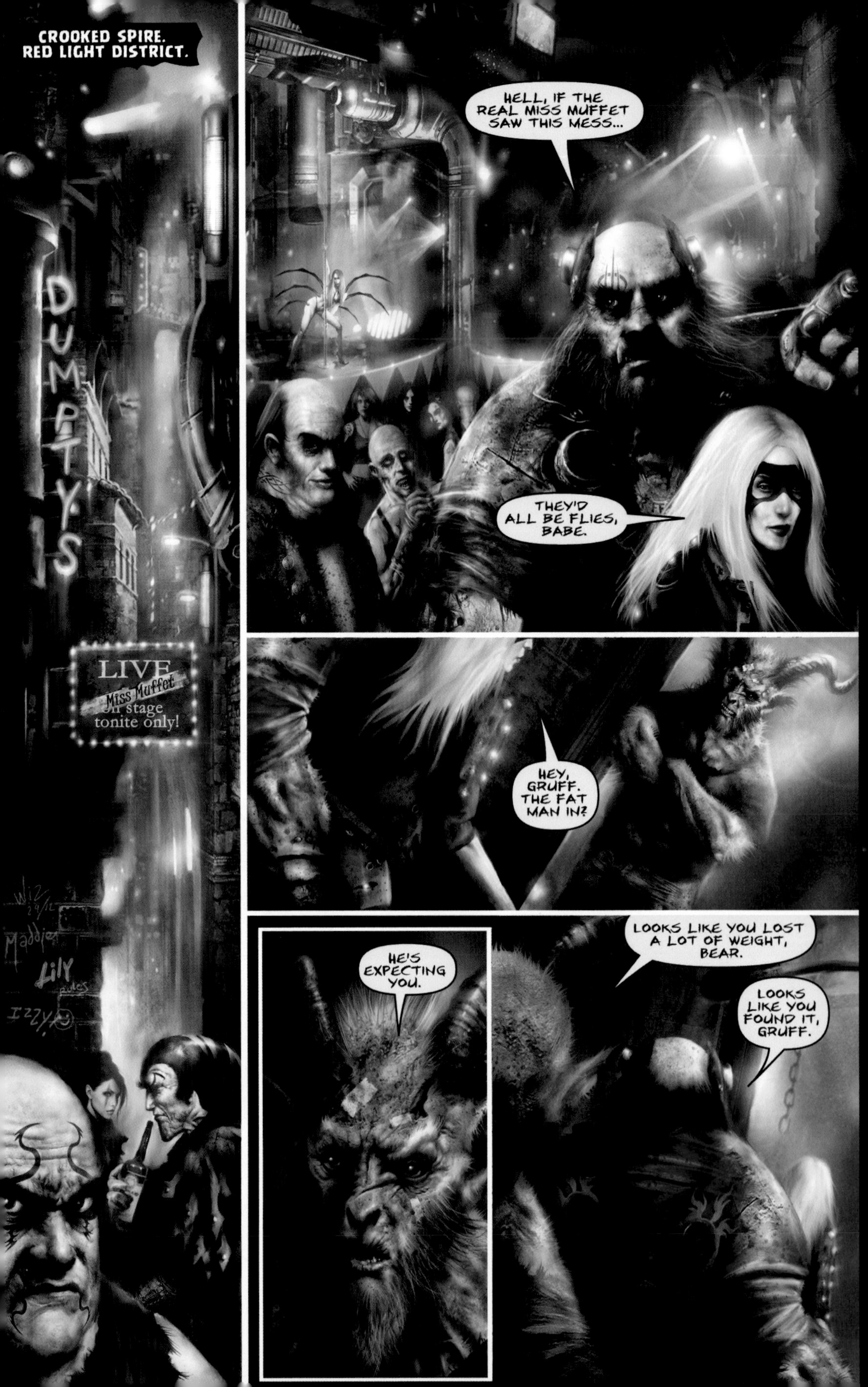
CROOKED SPIRE.
RED LIGHT DISTRICT.
DUMPTYS
LIVE
Miss Muffet
on stage
tonite only!
HELL, IF THE REAL MISS MUFFET SAW THIS MESS...
THEY'D ALL BE FLIES, BABE.
HEY, GRUFF. THE FAT MAN IN?
HE'S EXPECTING YOU.
LOOKS LIKE YOU LOST A LOT OF WEIGHT, BEAR.
LOOKS LIKE YOU FOUND IT, GRUFF.

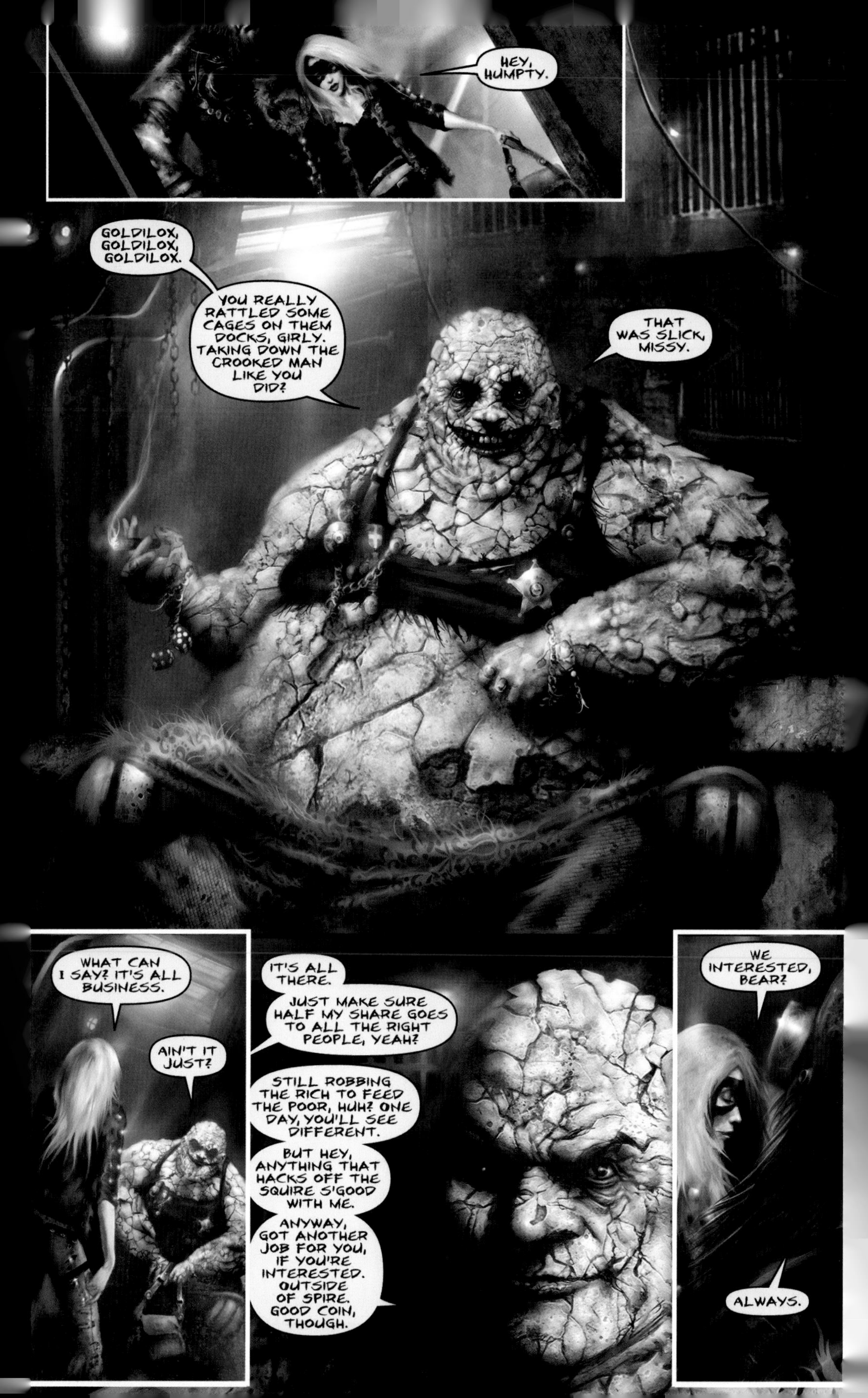
HEY, HUMPTY.
GOLDILOX, GOLDILOX, GOLDILOX.
YOU REALLY RATTLED SOME CAGES ON THEM DOCKS, GIRLY. TAKING DOWN THE CROOKED MAN LIKE YOU DID?
THAT WAS SLICK, MISSY.
WHAT CAN I SAY? IT'S ALL BUSINESS.
AIN'T IT JUST?
IT'S ALL THERE.
JUST MAKE SURE HALF MY SHARE GOES TO ALL THE RIGHT PEOPLE, YEAH?
STILL ROBBING THE RICH TO FEED THE POOR, HUH? ONE DAY, YOU'LL SEE DIFFERENT.
BUT HEY, ANYTHING THAT HACKS OFF THE SQUIRE S'GOOD WITH ME.
ANYWAY, GOT ANOTHER JOB FOR YOU, IF YOU'RE INTERESTED. OUTSIDE OF SPIRE. GOOD COIN, THOUGH.
WE INTERESTED, BEAR?
ALWAYS.

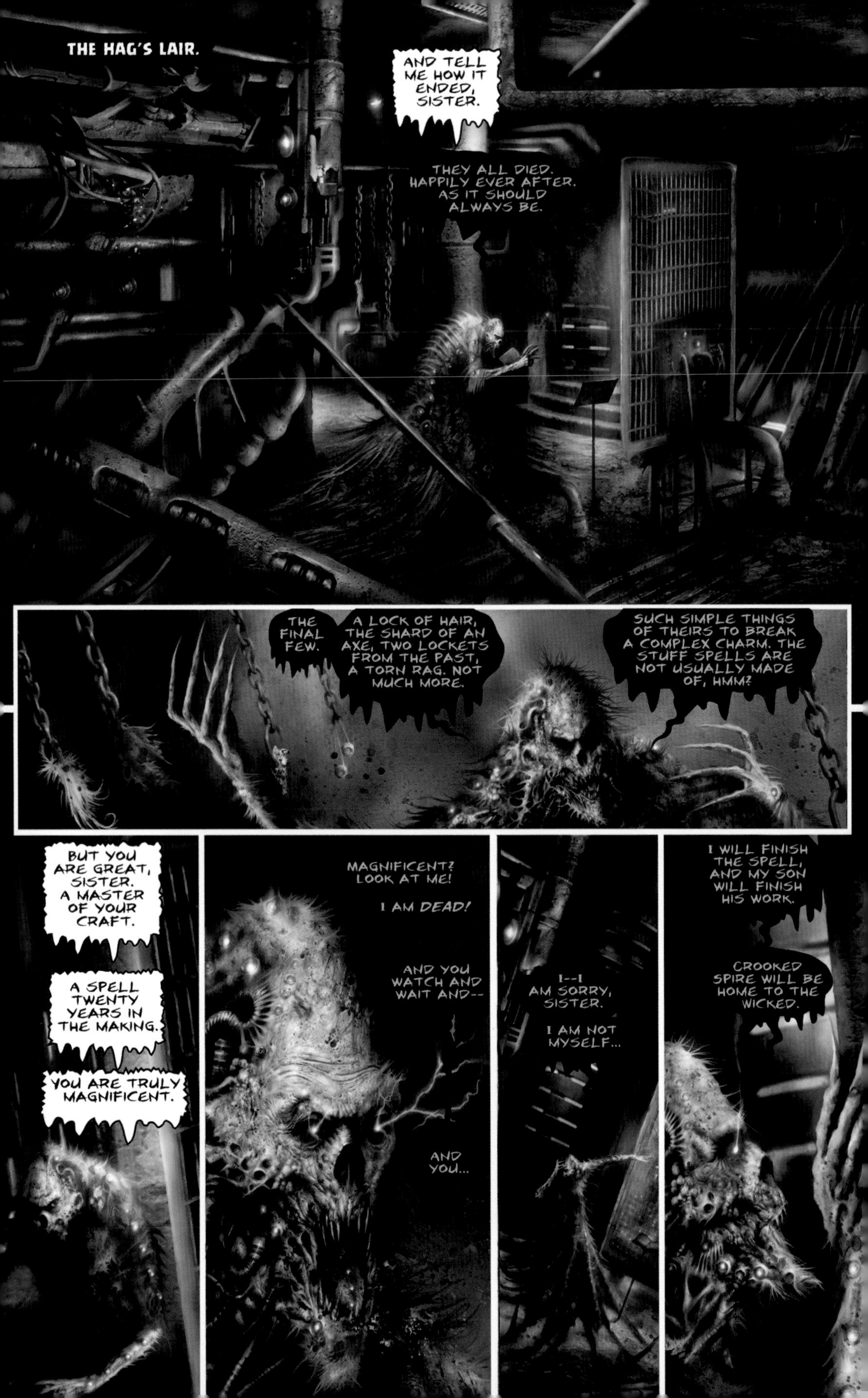
THE HAG'S LAIR.
AND TELL ME HOW IT ENDED, SISTER.
THEY ALL DIED. HAPPILY EVER AFTER. AS IT SHOULD ALWAYS BE.
THE FINAL FEW.
A LOCK OF HAIR, THE SHARD OF AN AXE, TWO LOCKETS FROM THE PAST, A TORN RAG. NOT MUCH MORE.
SUCH SIMPLE THINGS OF THEIRS TO BREAK A COMPLEX CHARM. THE STUFF SPELLS ARE NOT USUALLY MADE OF, HMM?
BUT YOU ARE GREAT, SISTER. A MASTER OF YOUR CRAFT.
A SPELL TWENTY YEARS IN THE MAKING.
YOU ARE TRULY MAGNIFICENT.
MAGNIFICENT? LOOK AT ME!
I AM *DEAD!*
AND YOU WATCH AND WAIT AND--
AND YOU...
I--I AM SORRY, SISTER.
I AM NOT MYSELF...
I WILL FINISH THE SPELL, AND MY SON WILL FINISH HIS WORK.
CROOKED SPIRE WILL BE HOME TO THE WICKED.

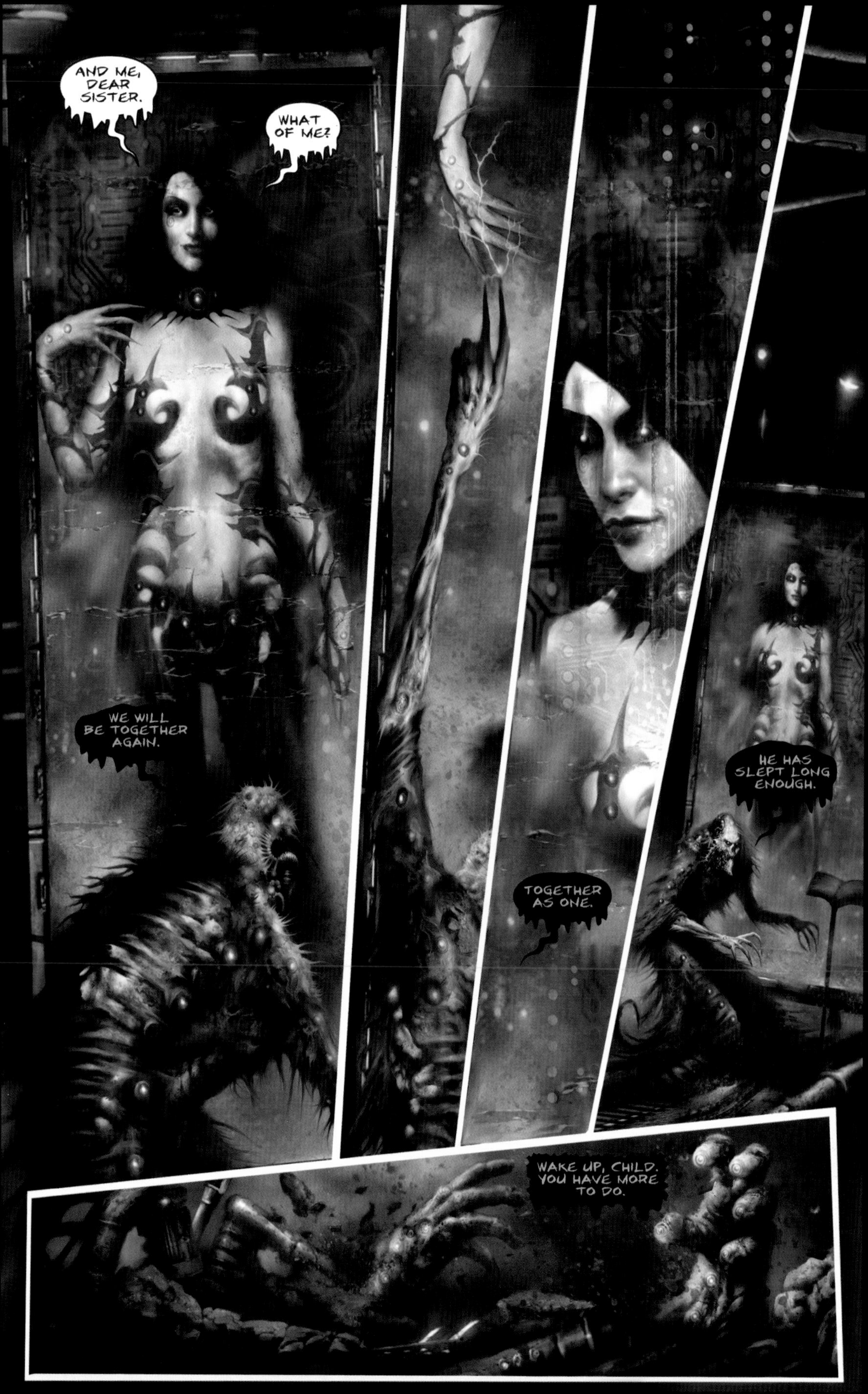

AND ME, DEAR SISTER.
WHAT OF ME?
WE WILL BE TOGETHER AGAIN.
TOGETHER AS ONE.
HE HAS SLEPT LONG ENOUGH.
WAKE UP, CHILD. YOU HAVE MORE TO DO.

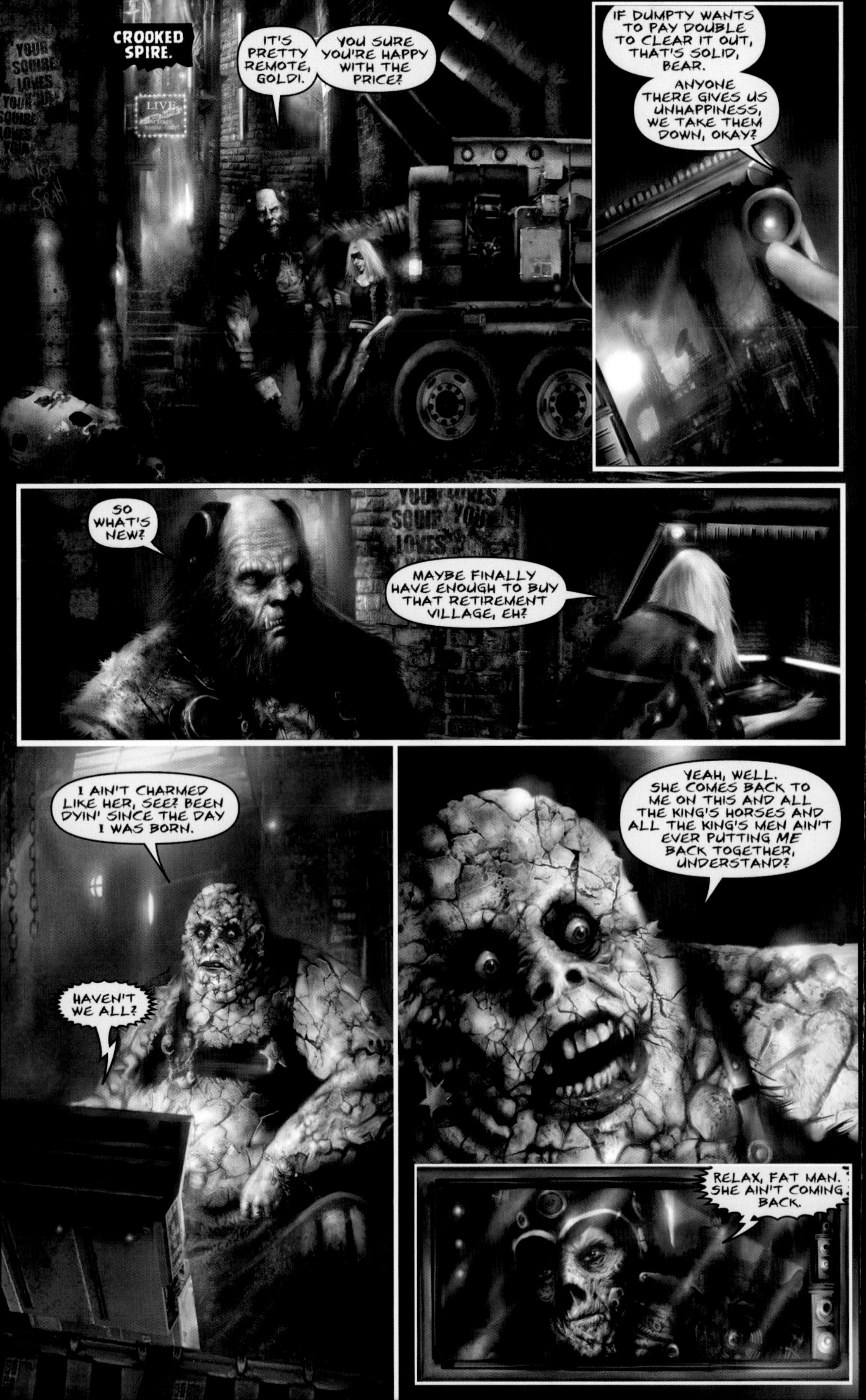
CROOKED SPIRE.
IT'S PRETTY REMOTE, GOLDI.
YOU SURE YOU'RE HAPPY WITH THE PRICE?
IF DUMPTY WANTS TO PAY DOUBLE TO CLEAR IT OUT, THAT'S SOLID, BEAR.
ANYONE THERE GIVES US UNHAPPINESS, WE TAKE THEM DOWN, OKAY?
SO WHAT'S NEW?
MAYBE FINALLY HAVE ENOUGH TO BUY THAT RETIREMENT VILLAGE, EH?
I AIN'T CHARMED LIKE HER, SEE? BEEN DYIN' SINCE THE DAY I WAS BORN.
HAVEN'T WE ALL?
YEAH, WELL. SHE COMES BACK TO ME ON THIS AND ALL THE KING'S HORSES AND ALL THE KING'S MEN AIN'T EVER PUTTING ME BACK TOGETHER, UNDERSTAND?
RELAX, FAT MAN. SHE AIN'T COMING BACK.

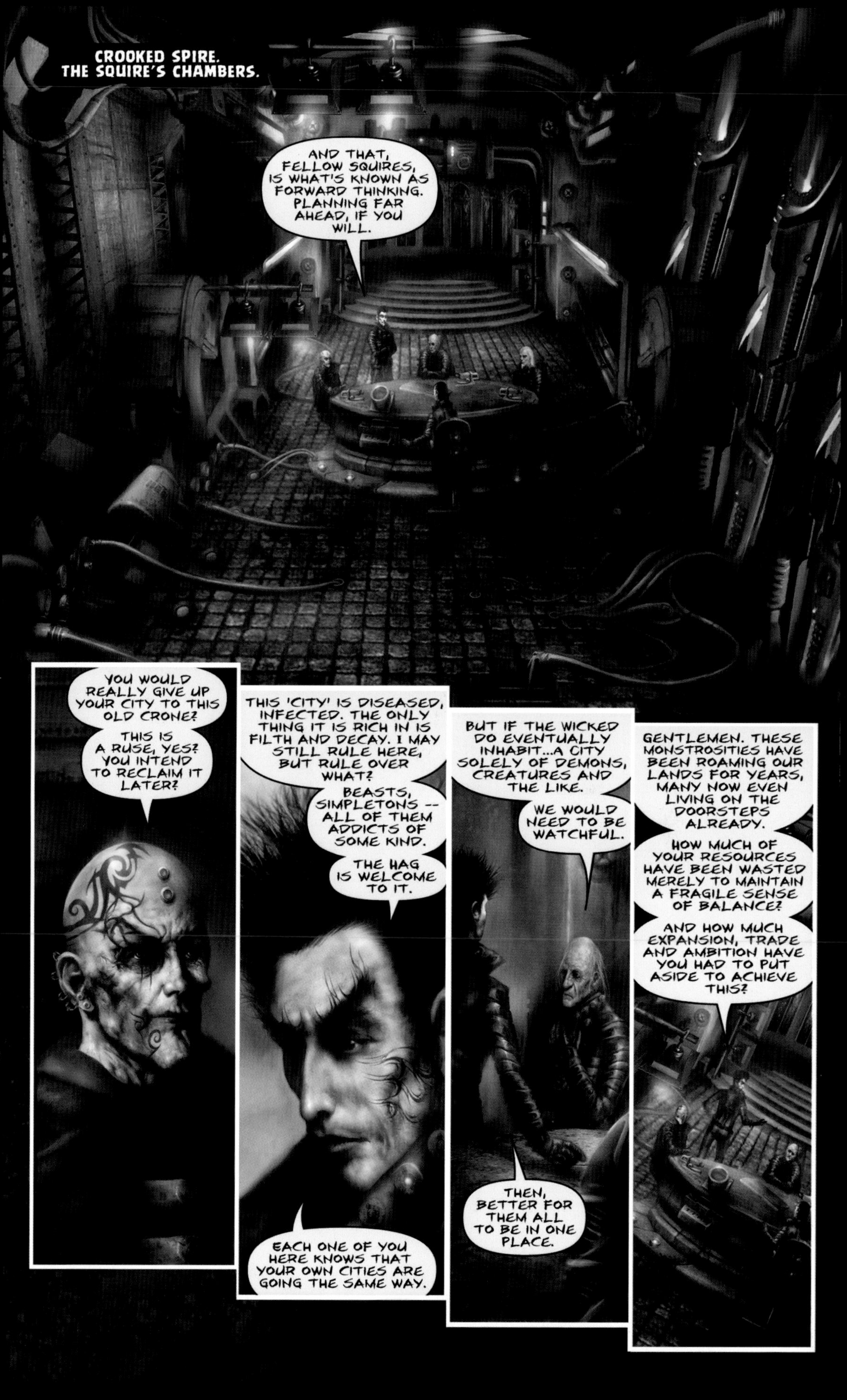
CROOKED SPIRE. THE SQUIRE'S CHAMBERS.
AND THAT, FELLOW SQUIRES, IS WHAT'S KNOWN AS FORWARD THINKING. PLANNING FAR AHEAD, IF YOU WILL.
YOU WOULD REALLY GIVE UP YOUR CITY TO THIS OLD CRONE?
THIS IS A RUSE, YES? YOU INTEND TO RECLAIM IT LATER?
THIS 'CITY' IS DISEASED, INFECTED. THE ONLY THING IT IS RICH IN IS FILTH AND DECAY. I MAY STILL RULE HERE, BUT RULE OVER WHAT?
BEASTS, SIMPLETONS -- ALL OF THEM ADDICTS OF SOME KIND.
THE HAG IS WELCOME TO IT.
EACH ONE OF YOU HERE KNOWS THAT YOUR OWN CITIES ARE GOING THE SAME WAY.
BUT IF THE WICKED DO EVENTUALLY INHABIT...A CITY SOLELY OF DEMONS, CREATURES AND THE LIKE.
WE WOULD NEED TO BE WATCHFUL.
THEN, BETTER FOR THEM ALL TO BE IN ONE PLACE.
GENTLEMEN. THESE MONSTROSITIES HAVE BEEN ROAMING OUR LANDS FOR YEARS, MANY NOW EVEN LIVING ON THE DOORSTEPS ALREADY.
HOW MUCH OF YOUR RESOURCES HAVE BEEN WASTED MERELY TO MAINTAIN A FRAGILE SENSE OF BALANCE?
AND HOW MUCH EXPANSION, TRADE AND AMBITION HAVE YOU HAD TO PUT ASIDE TO ACHIEVE THIS?

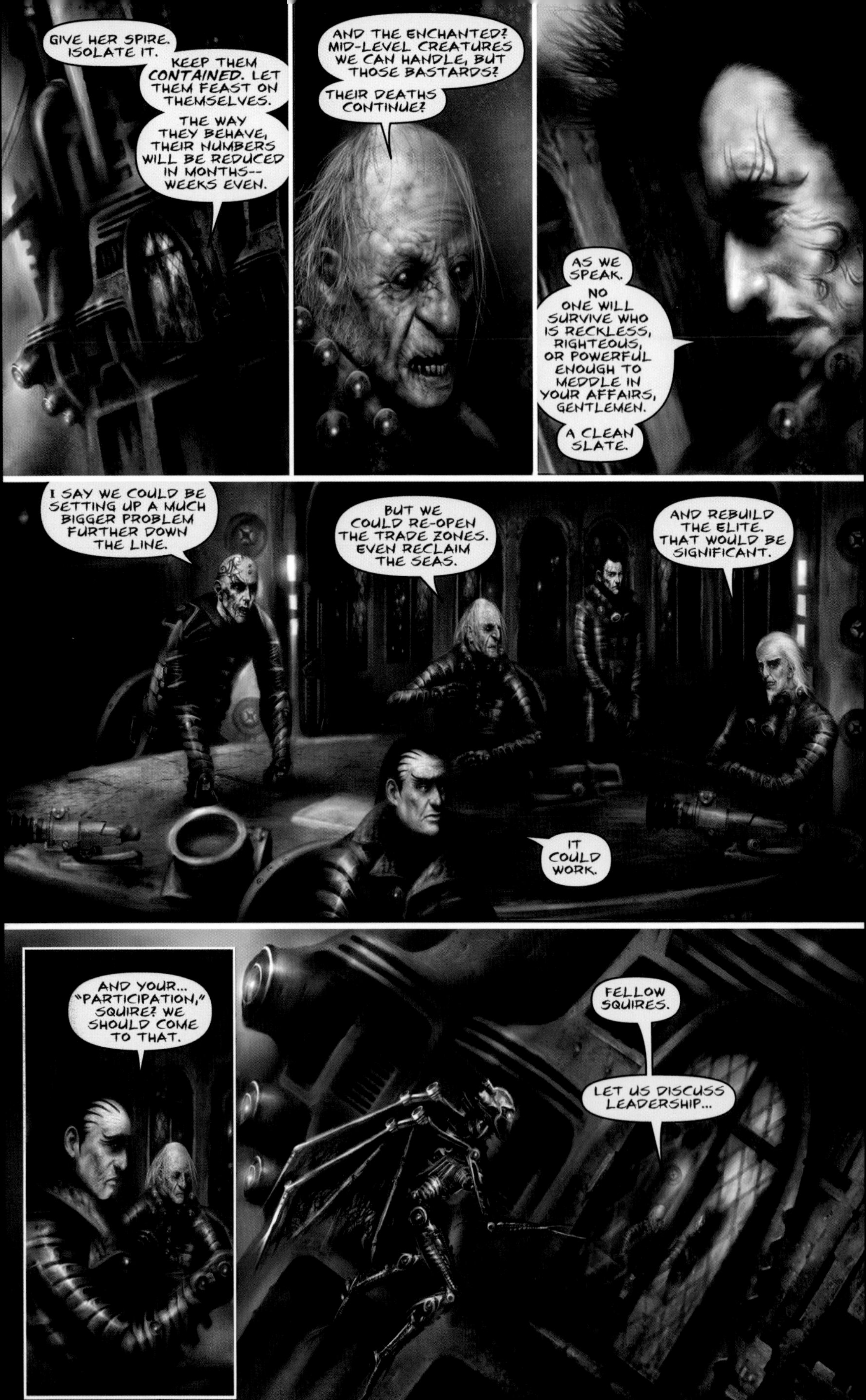
GIVE HER SPIRE. ISOLATE IT.
KEEP THEM *CONTAINED*. LET THEM FEAST ON THEMSELVES.
THE WAY THEY BEHAVE, THEIR NUMBERS WILL BE REDUCED IN MONTHS-- WEEKS EVEN.
AND THE ENCHANTED? MID-LEVEL CREATURES WE CAN HANDLE, BUT THOSE BASTARDS?
THEIR DEATHS CONTINUE?
AS WE SPEAK.
NO ONE WILL SURVIVE WHO IS RECKLESS, RIGHTEOUS, OR POWERFUL ENOUGH TO MEDDLE IN YOUR AFFAIRS, GENTLEMEN.
A CLEAN SLATE.
I SAY WE COULD BE SETTING UP A MUCH BIGGER PROBLEM FURTHER DOWN THE LINE.
BUT WE COULD RE-OPEN THE TRADE ZONES. EVEN RECLAIM THE SEAS.
AND REBUILD THE ELITE. THAT WOULD BE SIGNIFICANT.
IT COULD WORK.
AND YOUR... "PARTICIPATION," SQUIRE? WE SHOULD COME TO THAT.
FELLOW SQUIRES.
LET US DISCUSS LEADERSHIP...

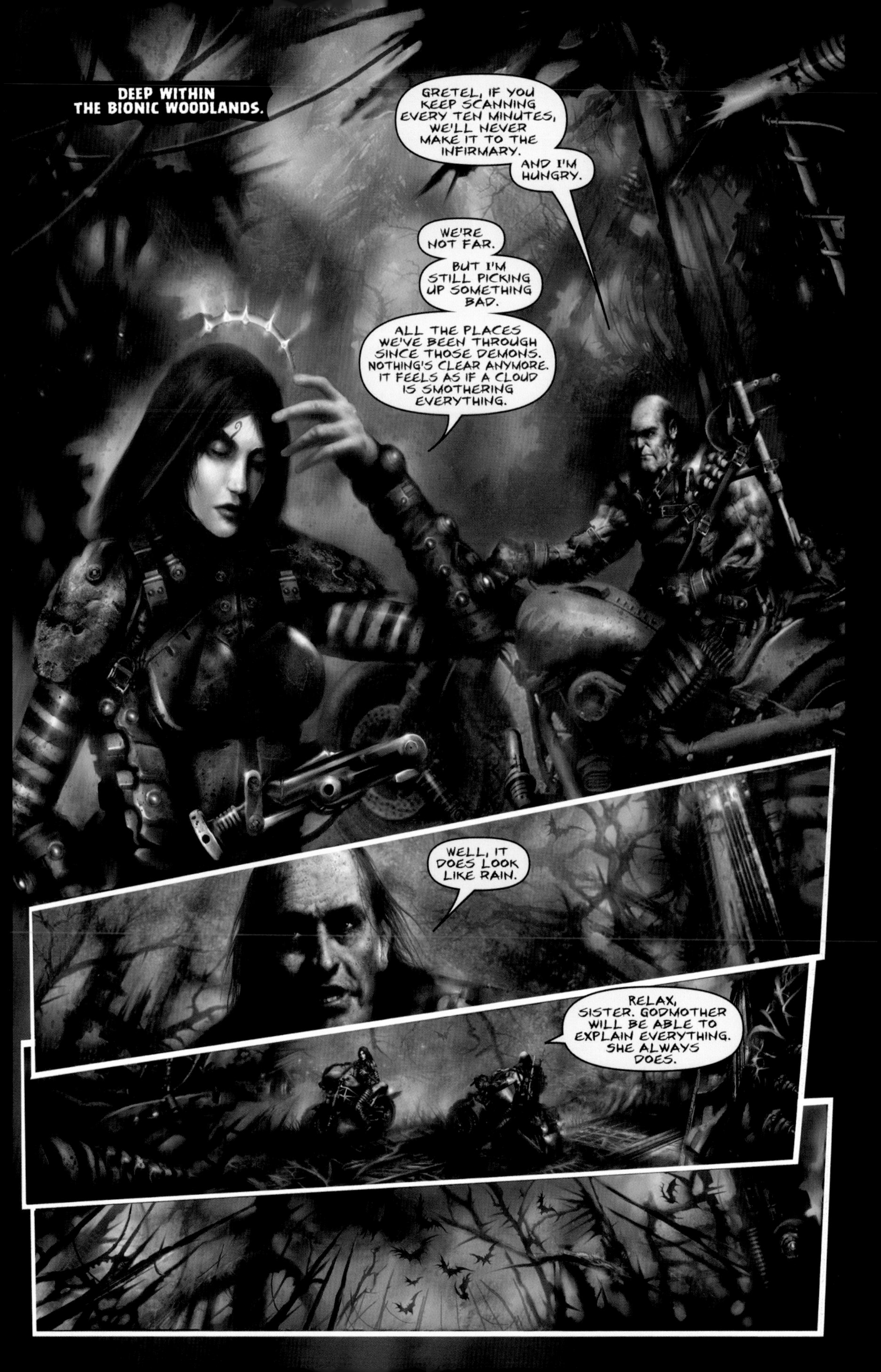
DEEP WITHIN THE BIONIC WOODLANDS.
GRETEL, IF YOU KEEP SCANNING EVERY TEN MINUTES, WE'LL NEVER MAKE IT TO THE INFIRMARY.
AND I'M HUNGRY.
WE'RE NOT FAR.
BUT I'M STILL PICKING UP SOMETHING BAD.
ALL THE PLACES WE'VE BEEN THROUGH SINCE THOSE DEMONS. NOTHING'S CLEAR ANYMORE. IT FEELS AS IF A CLOUD IS SMOTHERING EVERYTHING.
WELL, IT DOES LOOK LIKE RAIN.
RELAX, SISTER. GODMOTHER WILL BE ABLE TO EXPLAIN EVERYTHING. SHE ALWAYS DOES.

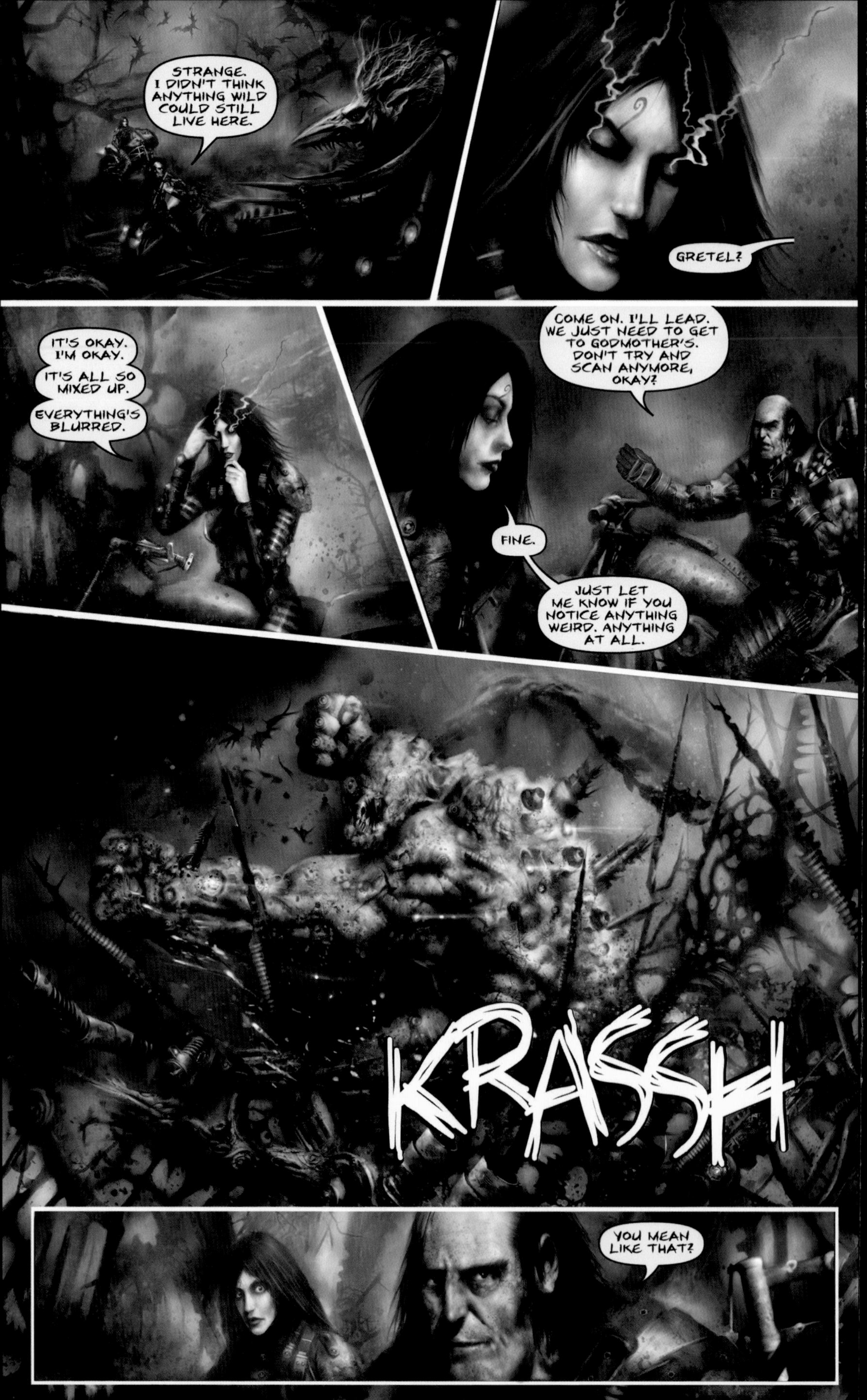
STRANGE. I DIDN'T THINK ANYTHING WILD COULD STILL LIVE HERE.
GRETEL?
IT'S OKAY. I'M OKAY.
IT'S ALL SO MIXED UP.
EVERYTHING'S BLURRED.
COME ON. I'LL LEAD. WE JUST NEED TO GET TO GODMOTHER'S. DON'T TRY AND SCAN ANYMORE, OKAY?
FINE.
JUST LET ME KNOW IF YOU NOTICE ANYTHING WEIRD. ANYTHING AT ALL.
KRASSH
YOU MEAN LIKE THAT?

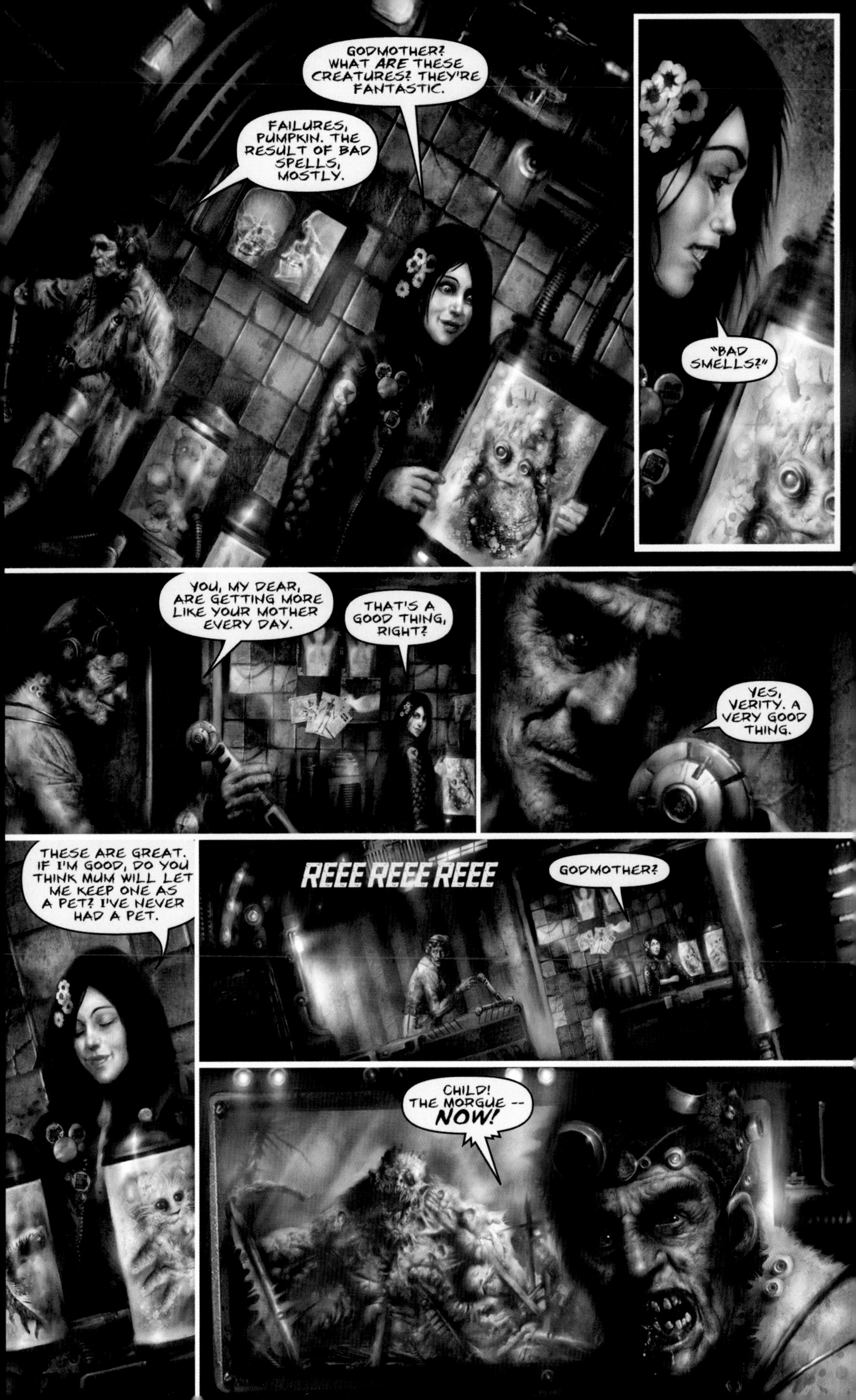
GODMOTHER? WHAT *ARE* THESE CREATURES? THEY'RE FANTASTIC.
FAILURES, PUMPKIN. THE RESULT OF BAD SPELLS, MOSTLY.
"BAD SMELLS?"
YOU, MY DEAR, ARE GETTING MORE LIKE YOUR MOTHER EVERY DAY.
THAT'S A GOOD THING, RIGHT?
YES, VERITY. A VERY GOOD THING.
THESE ARE GREAT. IF I'M GOOD, DO YOU THINK MUM WILL LET ME KEEP ONE AS A PET? I'VE NEVER HAD A PET.
REEE REEE REEE
GODMOTHER?
CHILD! THE MORGUE -- *NOW!*

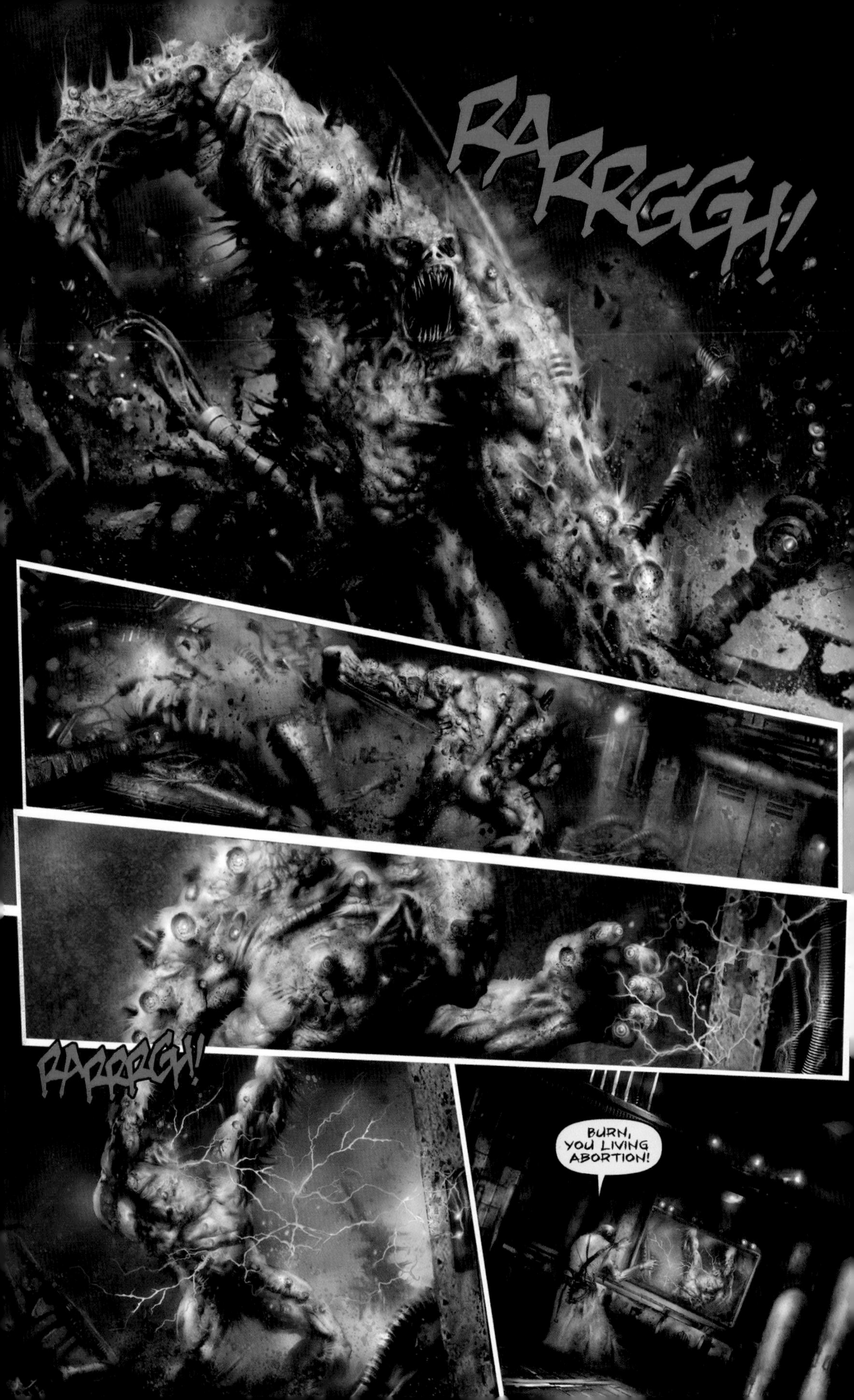
RARRGGH!
RARRRGH!
BURN, YOU LIVING ABORTION!

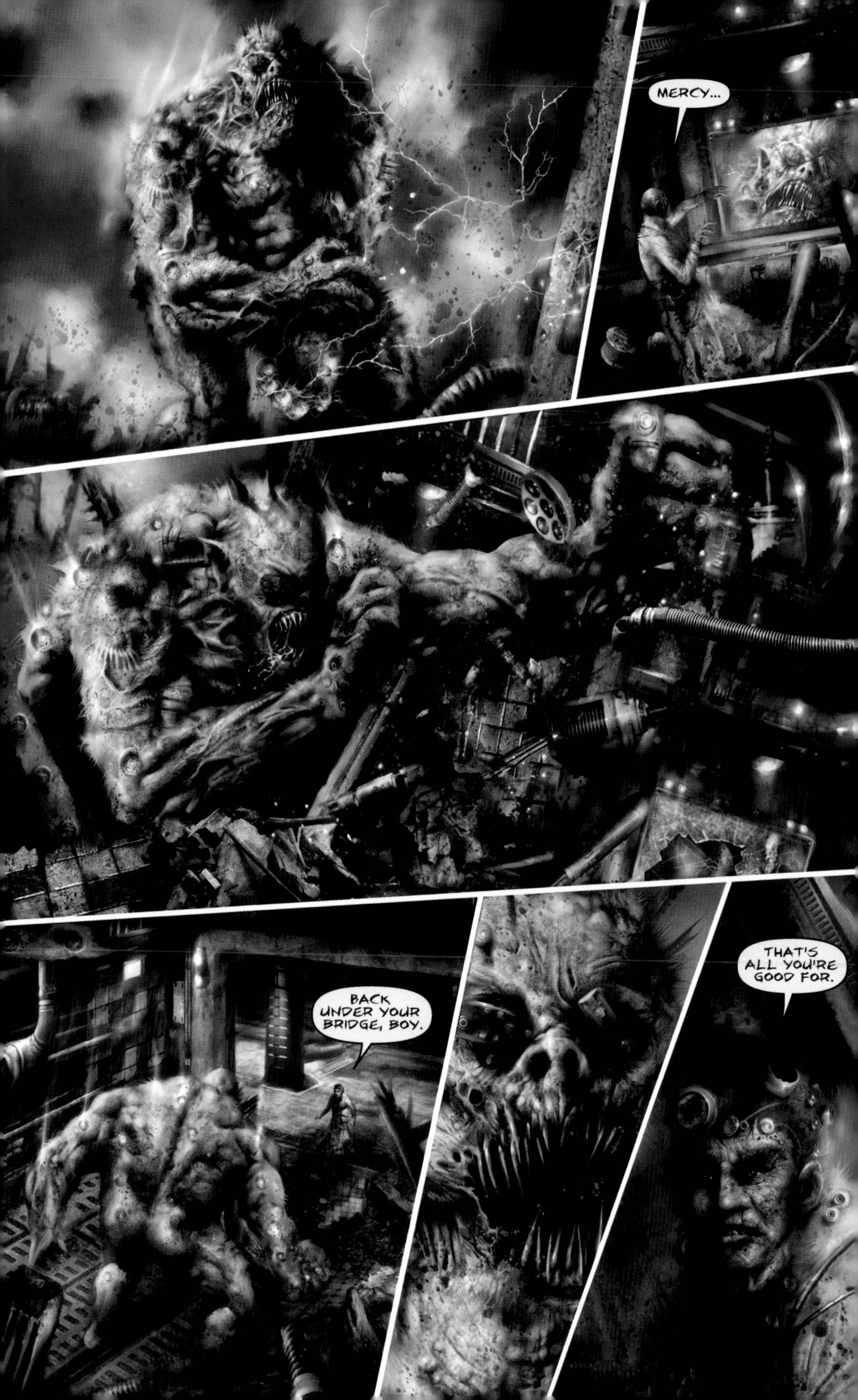
MERCY...
BACK UNDER YOUR BRIDGE, BOY.
THAT'S ALL YOU'RE GOOD FOR.

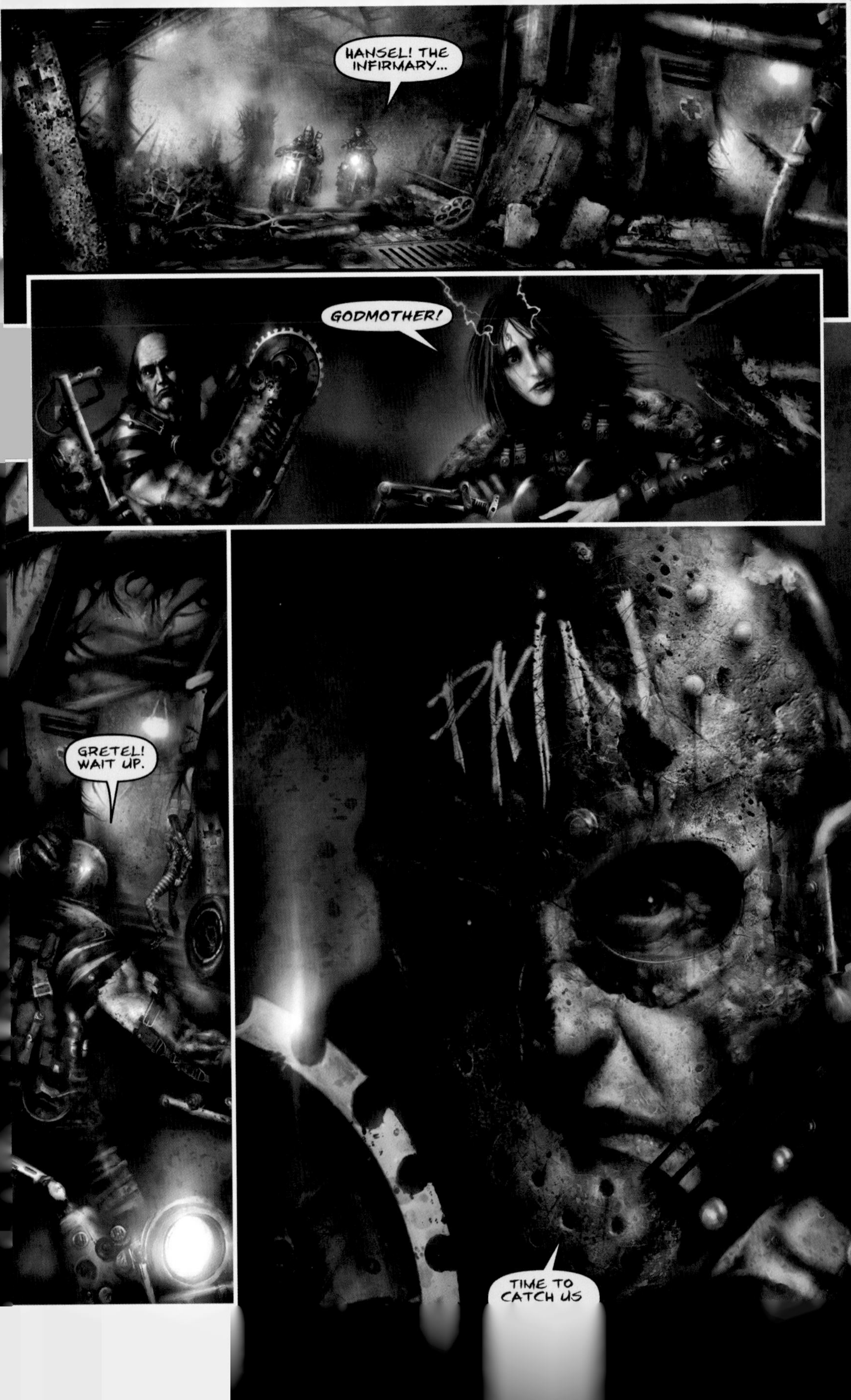
HANSEL! THE INFIRMARY...
GODMOTHER!
GRETEL! WAIT UP.
PAIN
TIME TO CATCH US

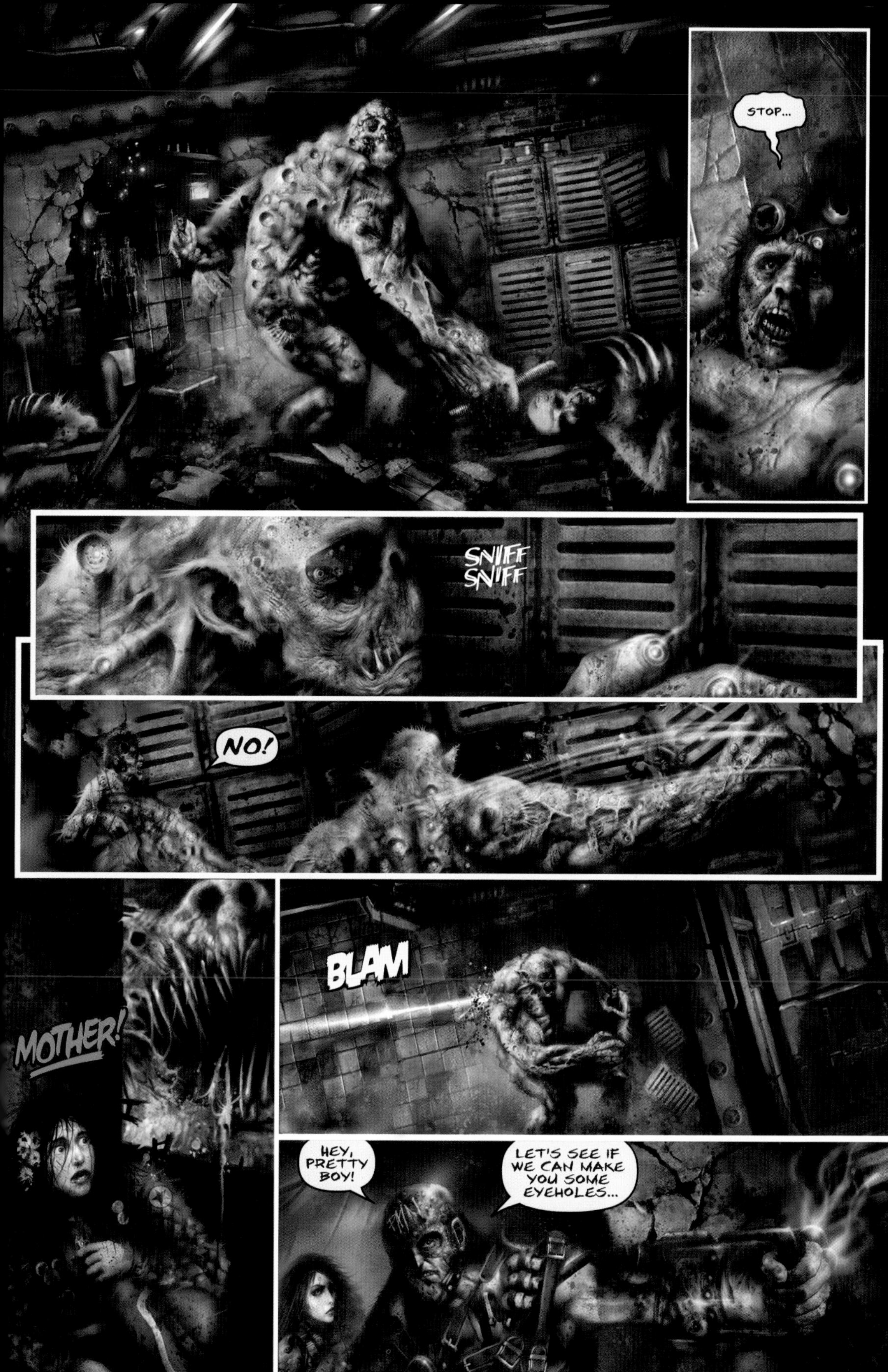
STOP...
SNIFF SNIFF
NO!
MOTHER!
BLAM
HEY, PRETTY BOY!
LET'S SEE IF WE CAN MAKE YOU SOME EYEHOLES...

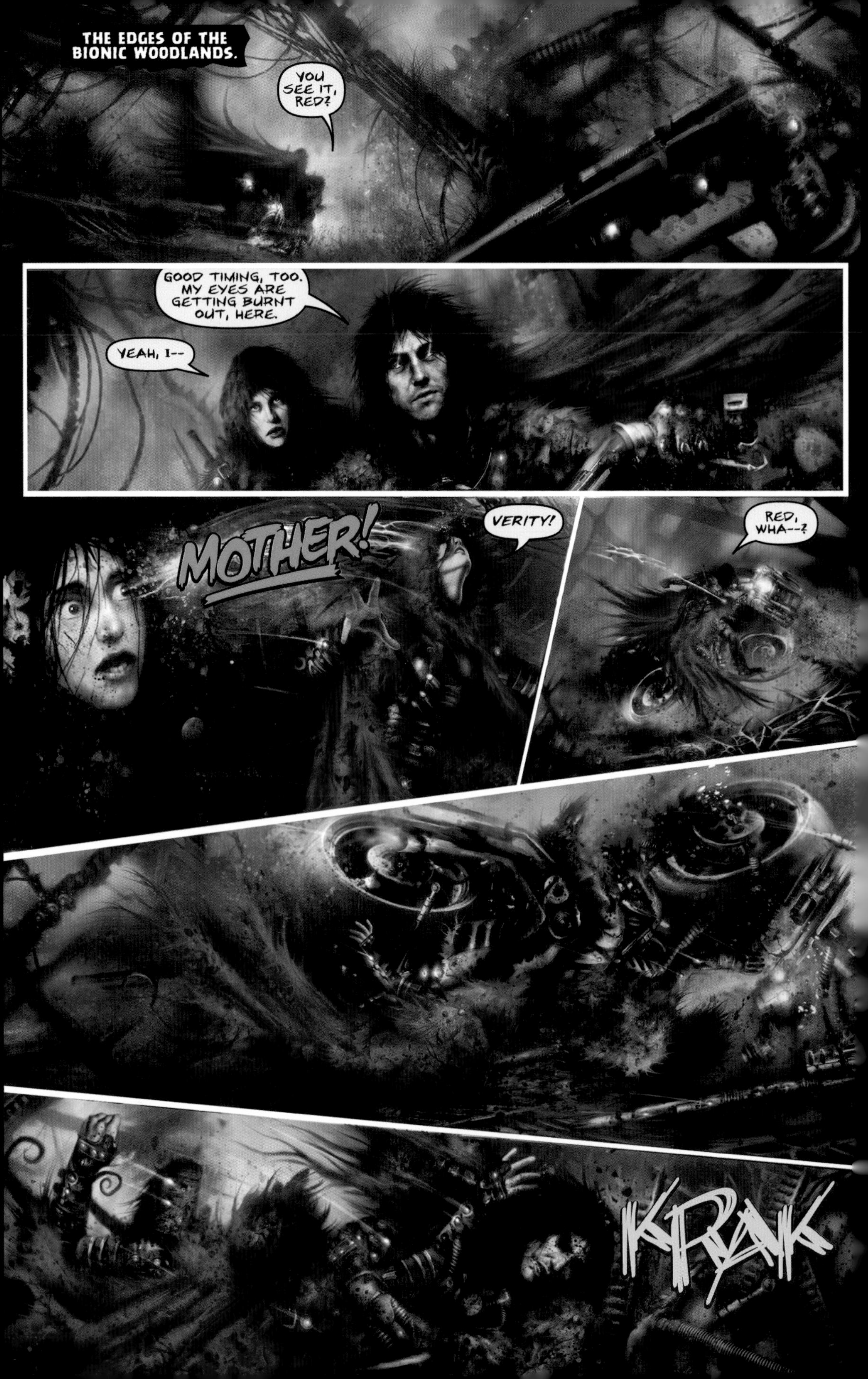
THE EDGES OF THE BIONIC WOODLANDS.
YOU SEE IT, RED?
GOOD TIMING, TOO. MY EYES ARE GETTING BURNT OUT, HERE.
YEAH, I--
MOTHER!
VERITY!
RED, WHA--?
KRAK

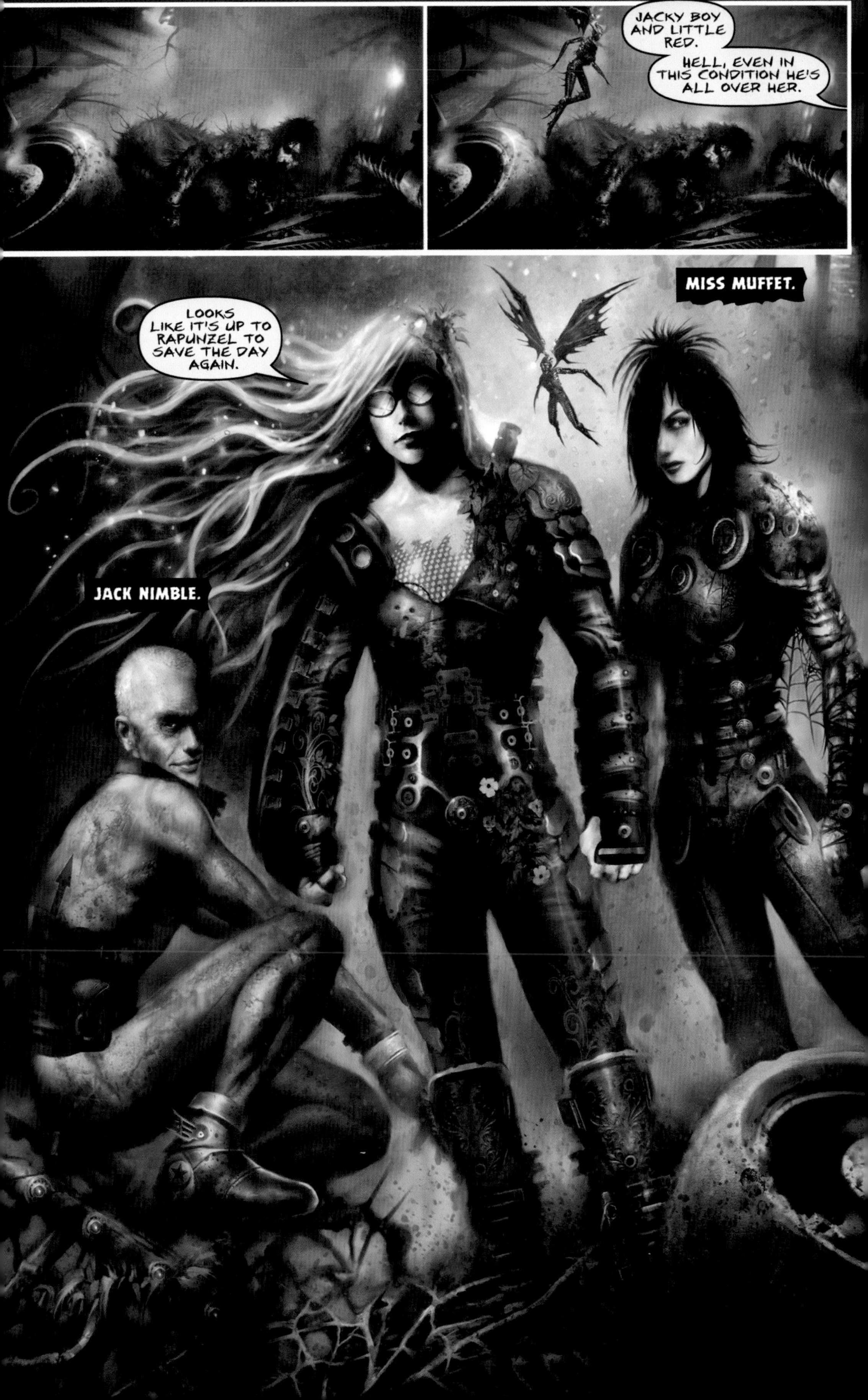
JACKY BOY AND LITTLE RED.
HELL, EVEN IN THIS CONDITION HE'S ALL OVER HER.
MISS MUFFET.
LOOKS LIKE IT'S UP TO RAPUNZEL TO SAVE THE DAY AGAIN.
JACK NIMBLE.

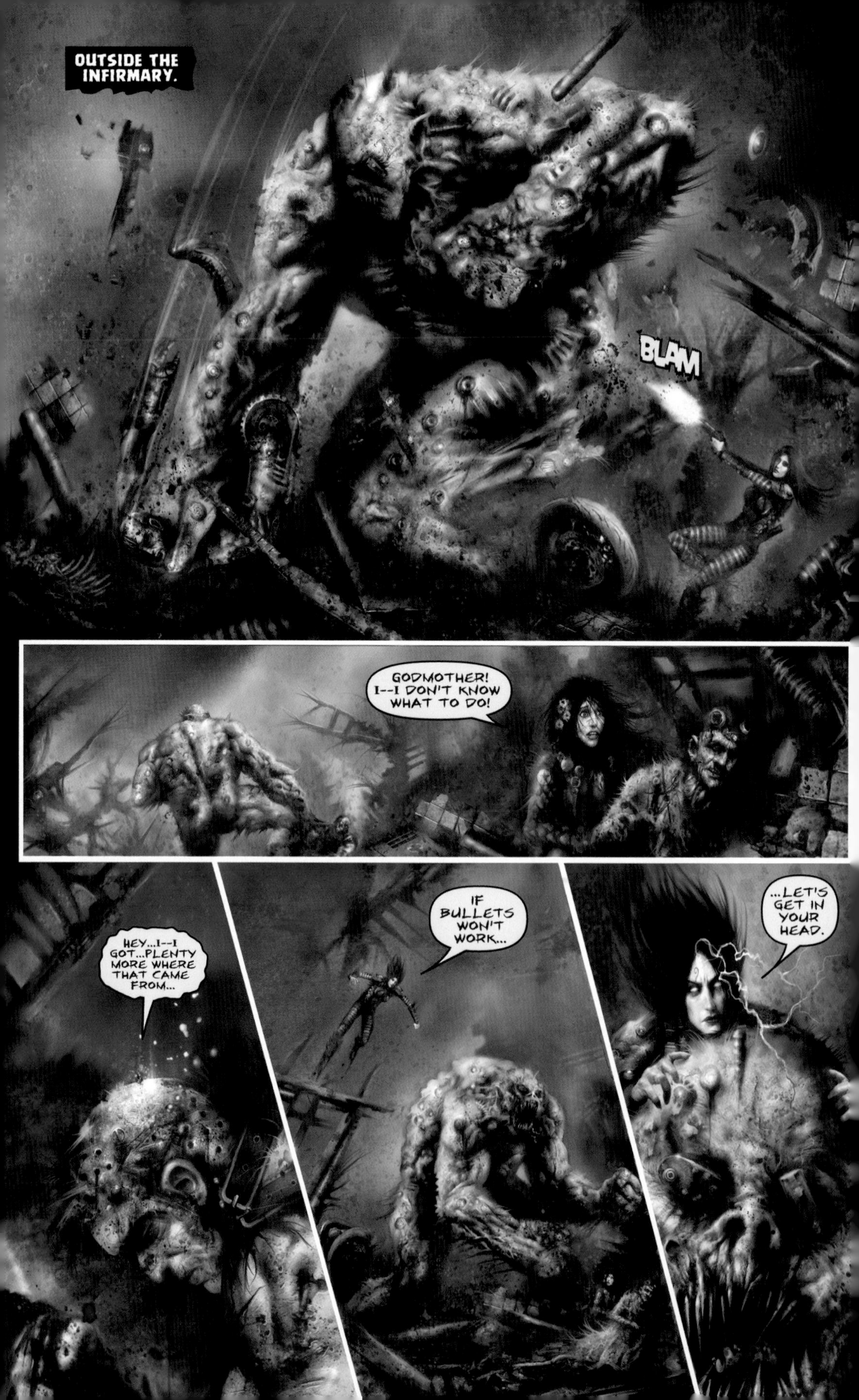
OUTSIDE THE INFIRMARY.
BLAM
GODMOTHER! I--I DON'T KNOW WHAT TO DO!
HEY...I--I GOT...PLENTY MORE WHERE THAT CAME FROM...
IF BULLETS WON'T WORK...
...LET'S GET IN YOUR HEAD.

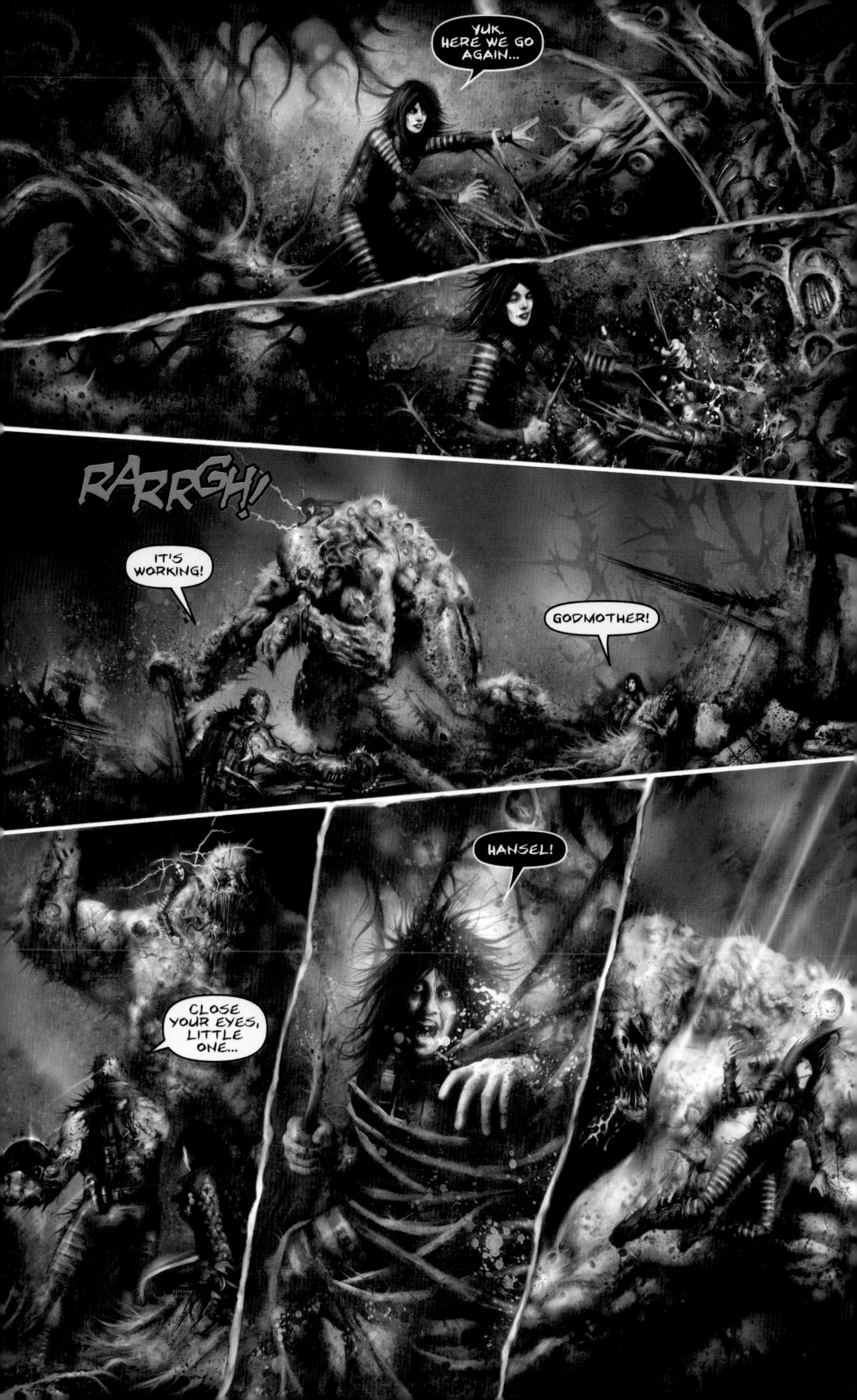
YUK. HERE WE GO AGAIN...
RARRGH!
IT'S WORKING!
GODMOTHER!
CLOSE YOUR EYES, LITTLE ONE...
HANSEL!

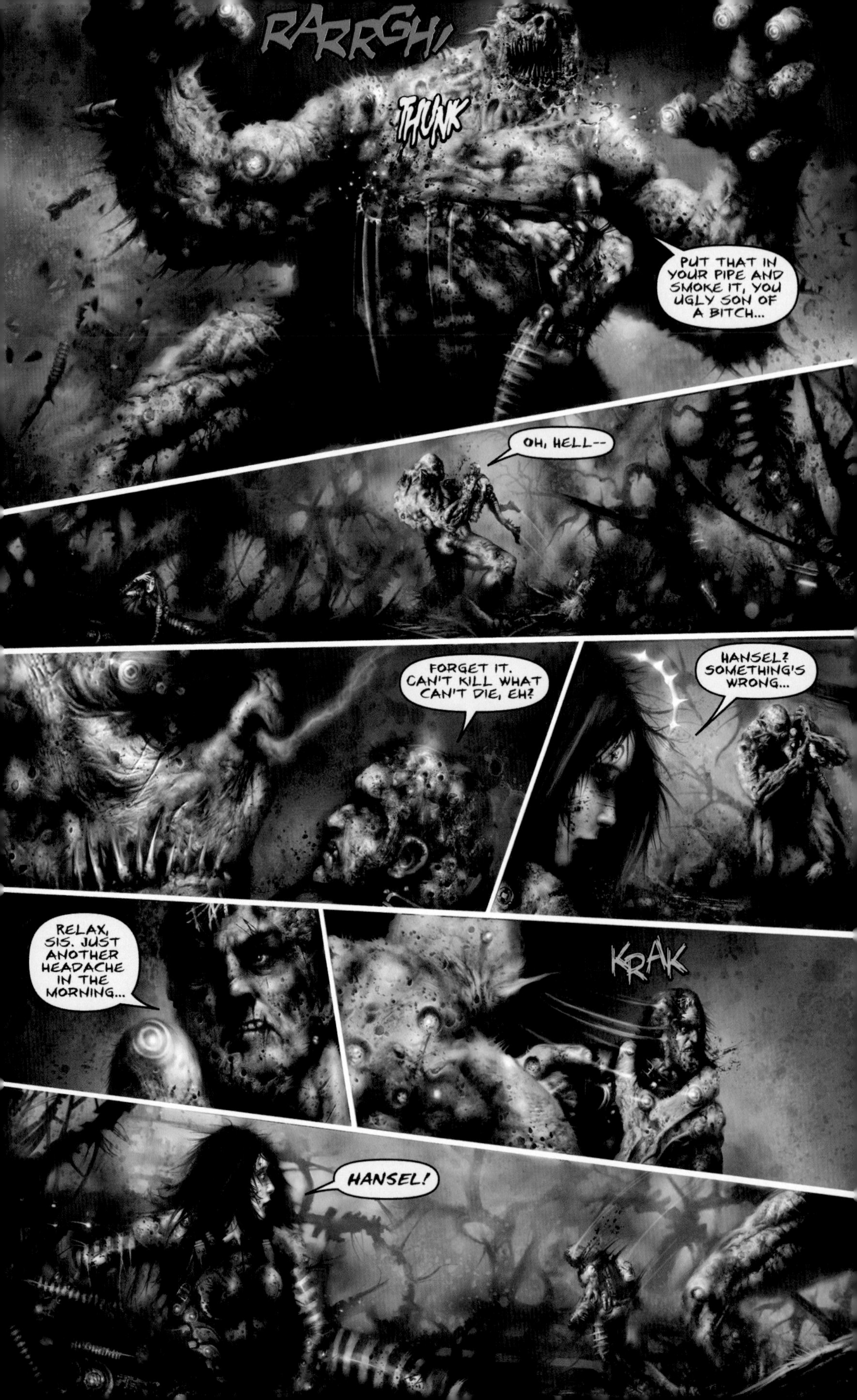
RARRGH!
THUNK
PUT THAT IN YOUR PIPE AND SMOKE IT, YOU UGLY SON OF A BITCH...
OH, HELL--
FORGET IT. CAN'T KILL WHAT CAN'T DIE, EH?
HANSEL? SOMETHING'S WRONG...
RELAX, SIS. JUST ANOTHER HEADACHE IN THE MORNING...
KRAK
HANSEL!

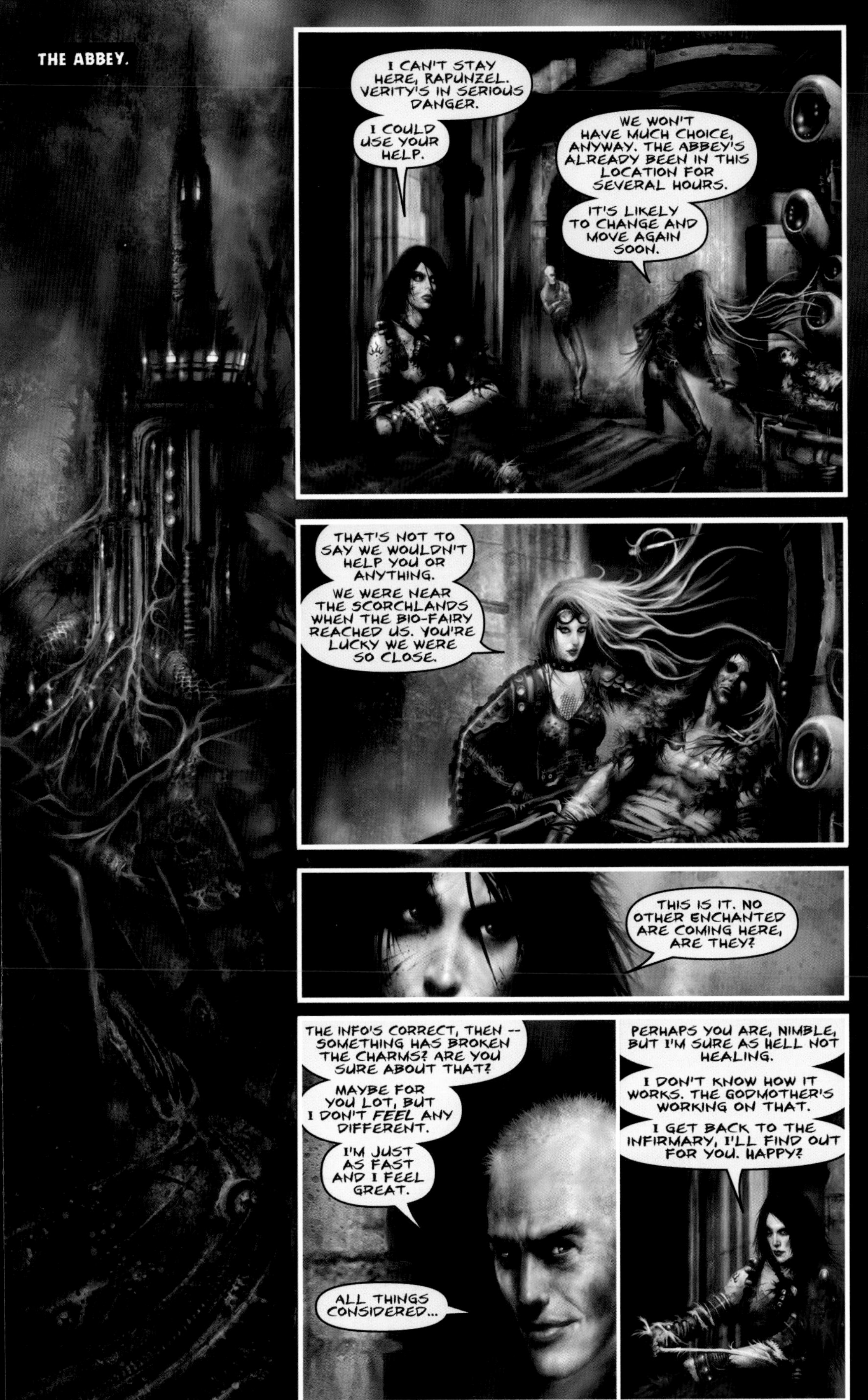
THE ABBEY.
I CAN'T STAY HERE, RAPUNZEL. VERITY'S IN SERIOUS DANGER.
I COULD USE YOUR HELP.
WE WON'T HAVE MUCH CHOICE, ANYWAY. THE ABBEY'S ALREADY BEEN IN THIS LOCATION FOR SEVERAL HOURS.
IT'S LIKELY TO CHANGE AND MOVE AGAIN SOON.
THAT'S NOT TO SAY WE WOULDN'T HELP YOU OR ANYTHING.
WE WERE NEAR THE SCORCHLANDS WHEN THE BIO-FAIRY REACHED US. YOU'RE LUCKY WE WERE SO CLOSE.
THIS IS IT. NO OTHER ENCHANTED ARE COMING HERE, ARE THEY?
THE INFO'S CORRECT, THEN -- SOMETHING HAS BROKEN THE CHARMS? ARE YOU SURE ABOUT THAT?
MAYBE FOR YOU LOT, BUT I DON'T *FEEL* ANY DIFFERENT.
I'M JUST AS FAST AND I FEEL GREAT.
ALL THINGS CONSIDERED...
PERHAPS YOU ARE, NIMBLE, BUT I'M SURE AS HELL NOT HEALING.
I DON'T KNOW HOW IT WORKS. THE GODMOTHER'S WORKING ON THAT.
I GET BACK TO THE INFIRMARY, I'LL FIND OUT FOR YOU. HAPPY?

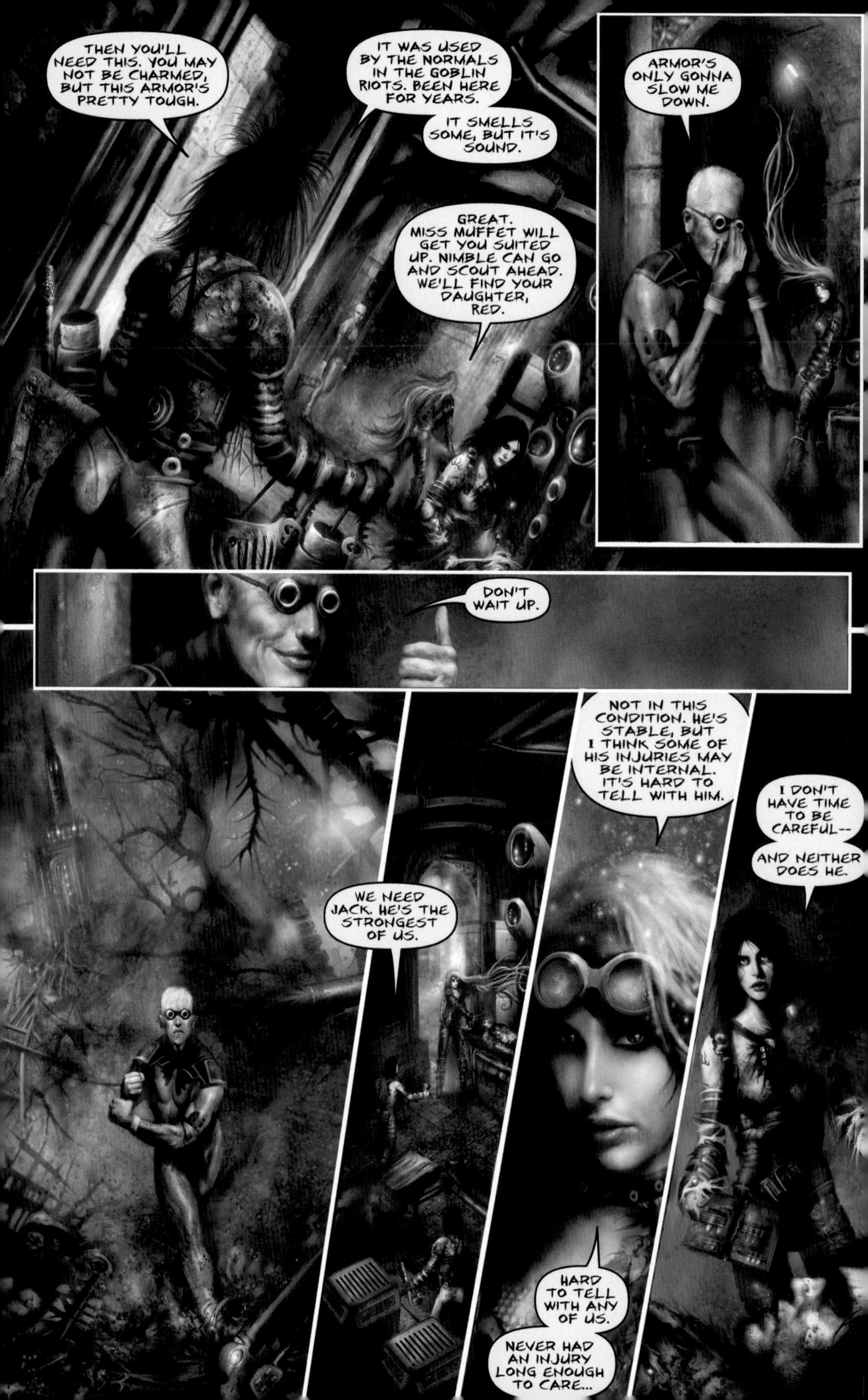
THEN YOU'LL NEED THIS. YOU MAY NOT BE CHARMED, BUT THIS ARMOR'S PRETTY TOUGH.
IT WAS USED BY THE NORMALS IN THE GOBLIN RIOTS. BEEN HERE FOR YEARS.
IT SMELLS SOME, BUT IT'S SOUND.
GREAT. MISS MUFFET WILL GET YOU SUITED UP. NIMBLE CAN GO AND SCOUT AHEAD. WE'LL FIND YOUR DAUGHTER, RED.
ARMOR'S ONLY GONNA SLOW ME DOWN.
DON'T WAIT UP.
WE NEED JACK. HE'S THE STRONGEST OF US.
NOT IN THIS CONDITION. HE'S STABLE, BUT I THINK SOME OF HIS INJURIES MAY BE INTERNAL. IT'S HARD TO TELL WITH HIM.
HARD TO TELL WITH ANY OF US.
NEVER HAD AN INJURY LONG ENOUGH TO CARE...
I DON'T HAVE TIME TO BE CAREFUL--
AND NEITHER DOES HE.

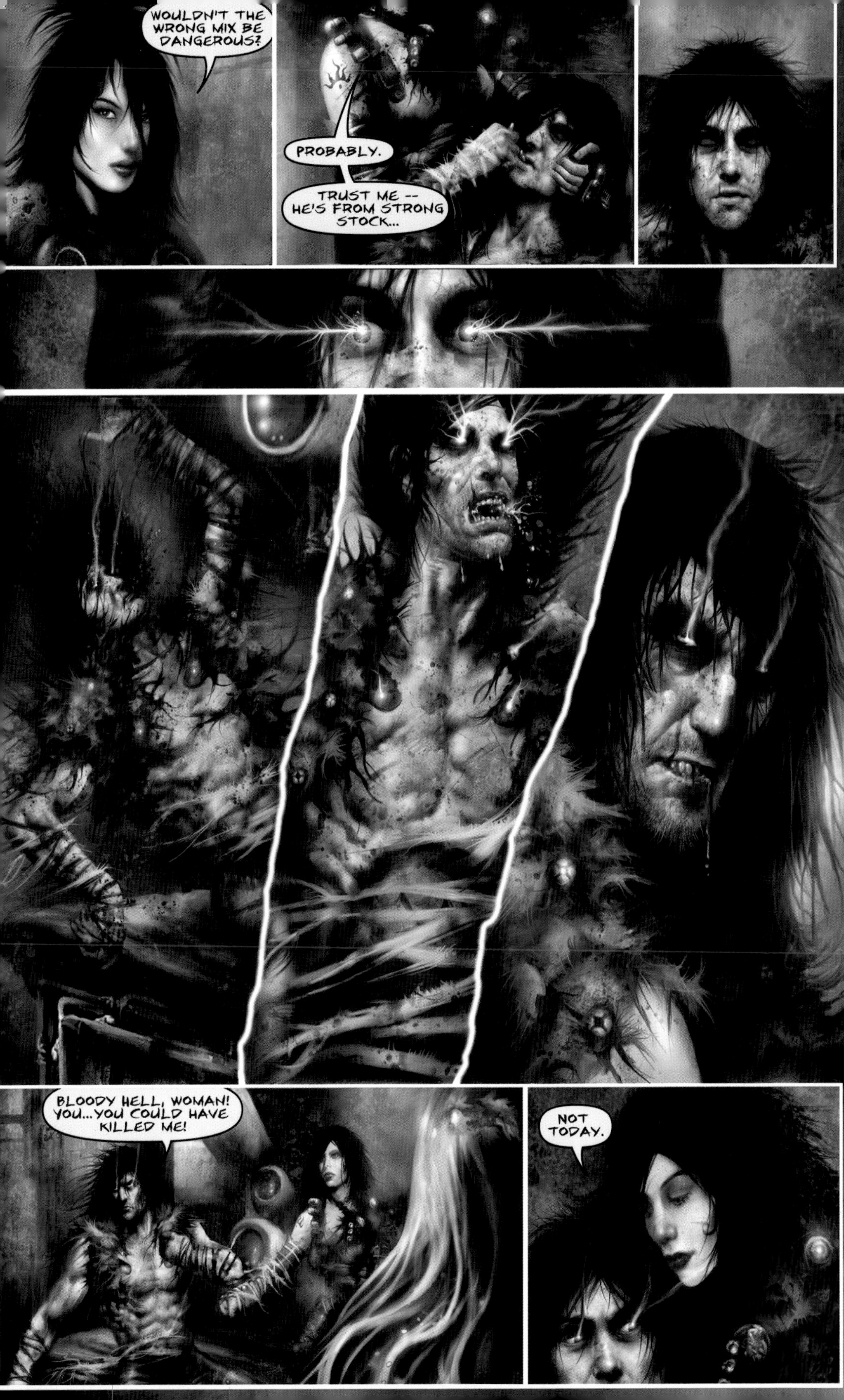
WOULDN'T THE WRONG MIX BE DANGEROUS?
PROBABLY.
TRUST ME -- HE'S FROM STRONG STOCK...
BLOODY HELL, WOMAN! YOU...YOU COULD HAVE KILLED ME!
NOT TODAY.

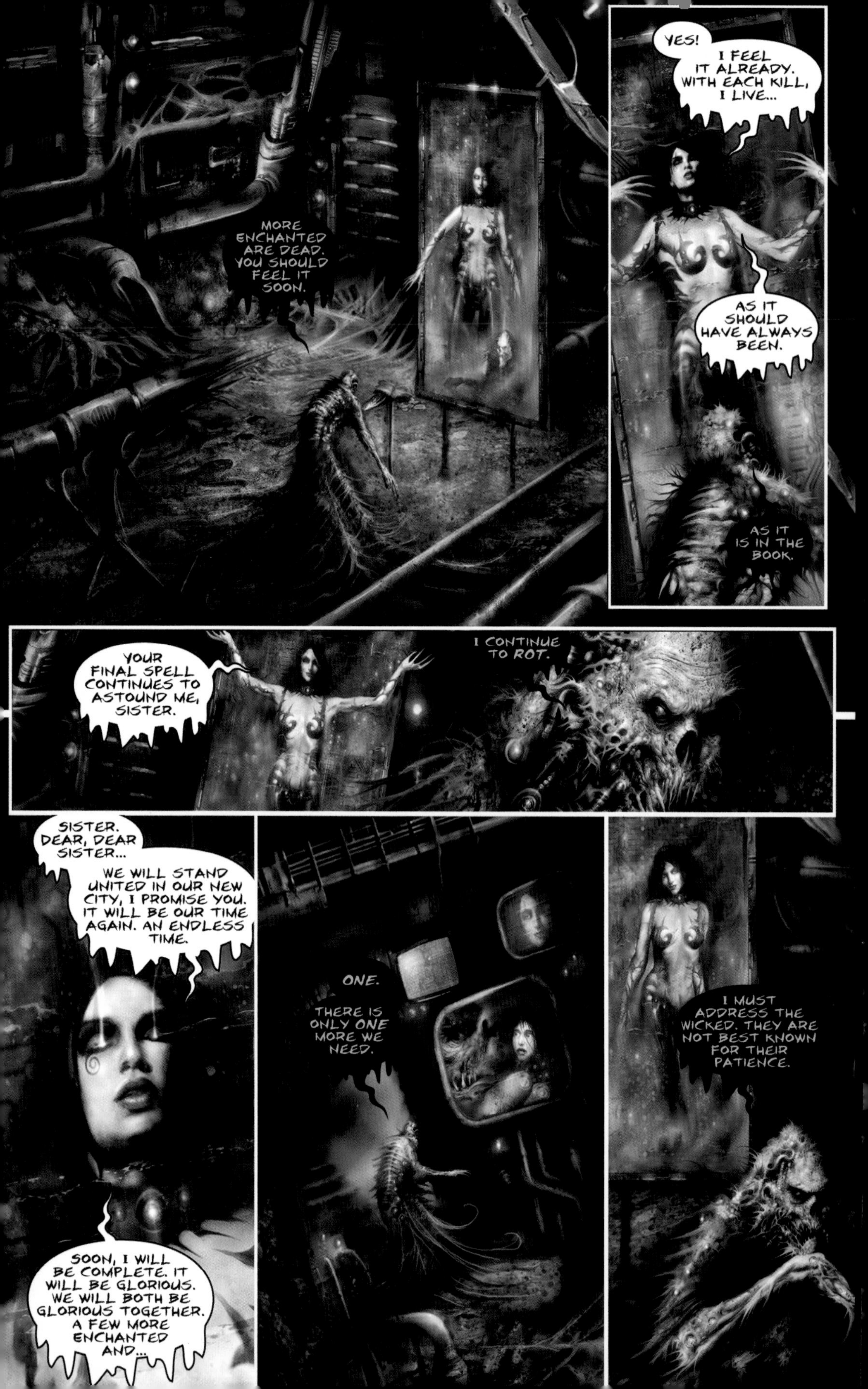
MORE ENCHANTED ARE DEAD. YOU SHOULD FEEL IT SOON.
YES! I FEEL IT ALREADY. WITH EACH KILL, I LIVE...
AS IT SHOULD HAVE ALWAYS BEEN.
AS IT IS IN THE BOOK.
YOUR FINAL SPELL CONTINUES TO ASTOUND ME, SISTER.
I CONTINUE TO ROT.
SISTER. DEAR, DEAR SISTER...
WE WILL STAND UNITED IN OUR NEW CITY, I PROMISE YOU. IT WILL BE OUR TIME AGAIN. AN ENDLESS TIME.
SOON, I WILL BE COMPLETE. IT WILL BE GLORIOUS. WE WILL BOTH BE GLORIOUS TOGETHER. A FEW MORE ENCHANTED AND...
ONE.
THERE IS ONLY ONE MORE WE NEED.
I MUST ADDRESS THE WICKED. THEY ARE NOT BEST KNOWN FOR THEIR PATIENCE.

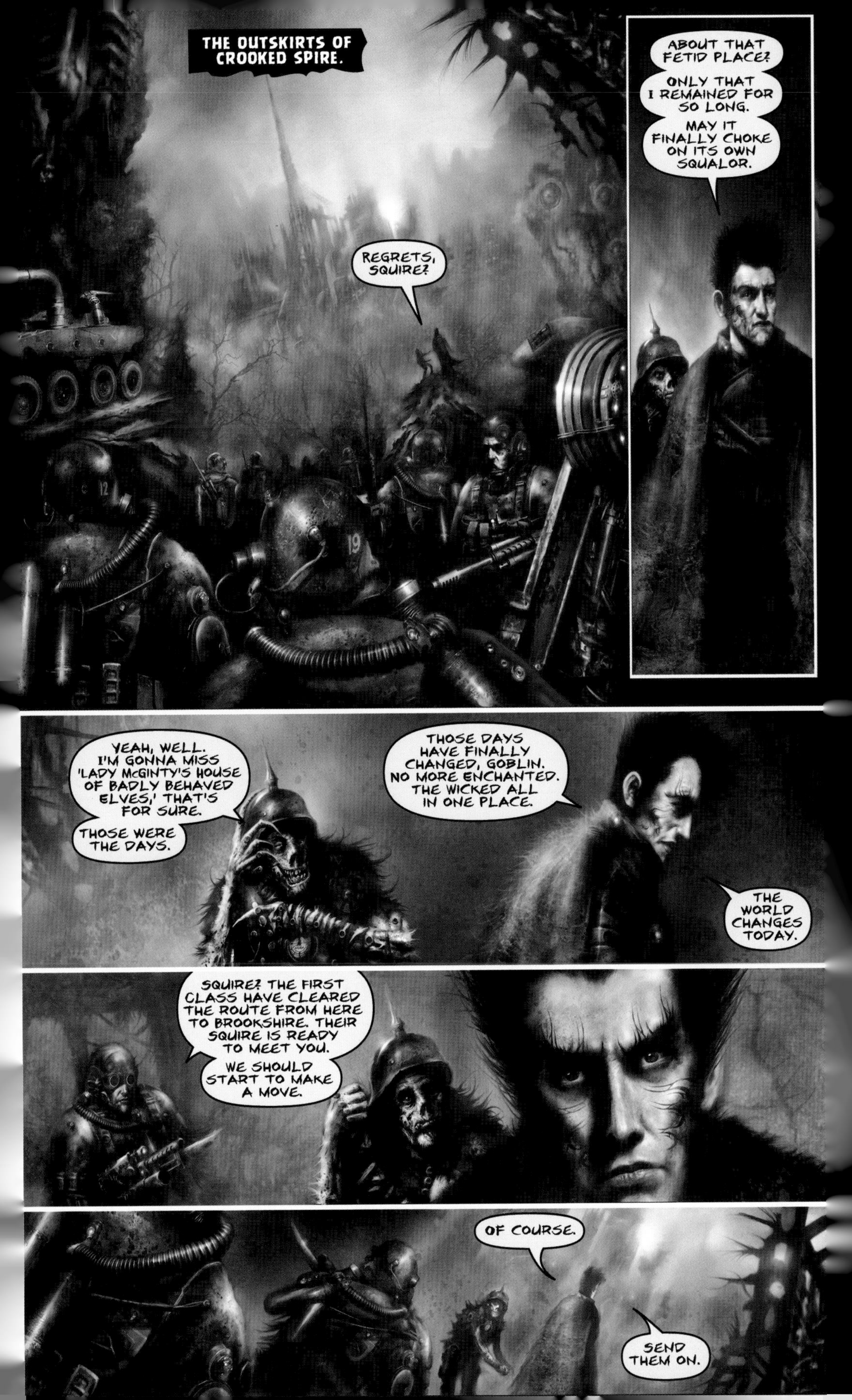
THE OUTSKIRTS OF CROOKED SPIRE.
REGRETS, SQUIRE?
ABOUT THAT FETID PLACE?
ONLY THAT I REMAINED FOR SO LONG.
MAY IT FINALLY CHOKE ON ITS OWN SQUALOR.
YEAH, WELL. I'M GONNA MISS 'LADY McGINTY'S HOUSE OF BADLY BEHAVED ELVES,' THAT'S FOR SURE.
THOSE WERE THE DAYS.
THOSE DAYS HAVE FINALLY CHANGED, GOBLIN. NO MORE ENCHANTED. THE WICKED ALL IN ONE PLACE.
THE WORLD CHANGES TODAY.
SQUIRE? THE FIRST CLASS HAVE CLEARED THE ROUTE FROM HERE TO BROOKSHIRE. THEIR SQUIRE IS READY TO MEET YOU.
WE SHOULD START TO MAKE A MOVE.
OF COURSE.
SEND THEM ON.

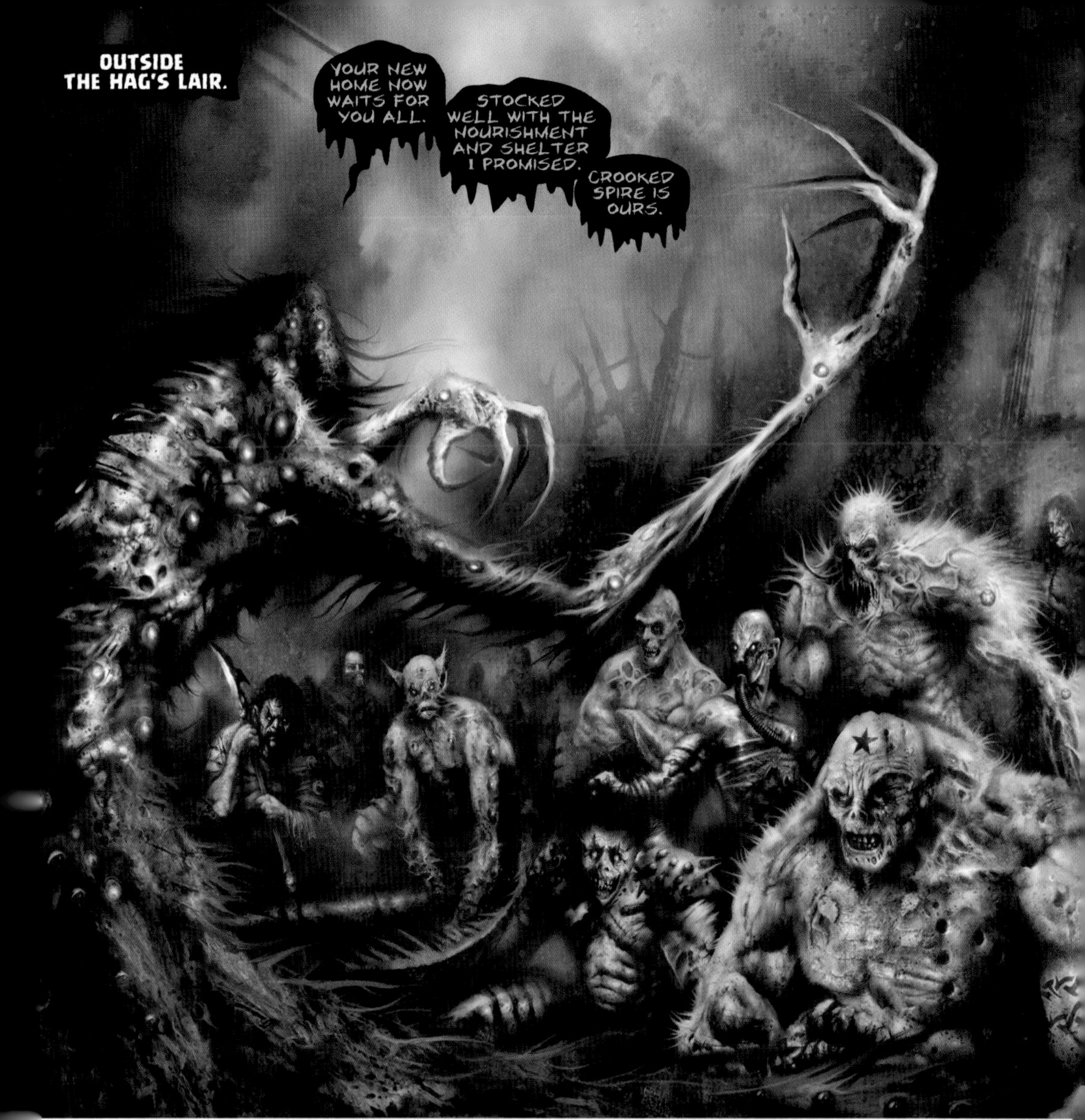
OUTSIDE THE HAG'S LAIR.
YOUR NEW HOME NOW WAITS FOR YOU ALL.
STOCKED WELL WITH THE NOURISHMENT AND SHELTER I PROMISED.
CROOKED SPIRE IS OURS.

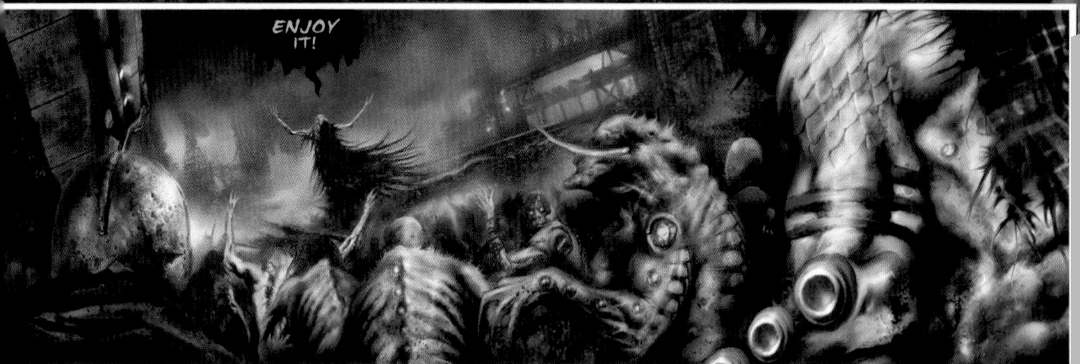
ENJOY IT!

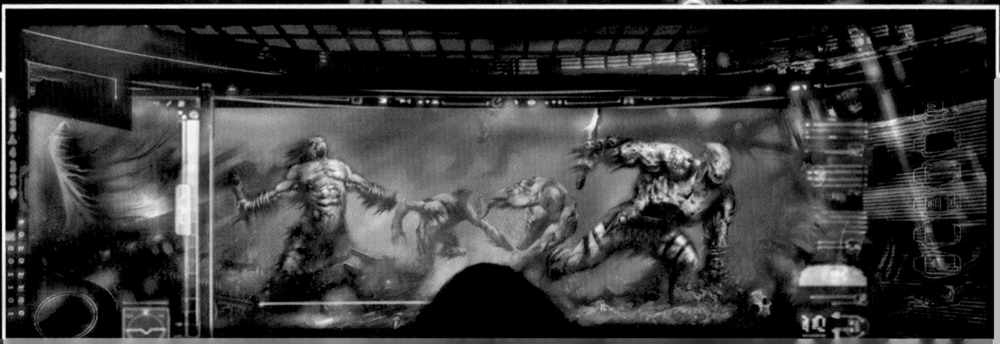

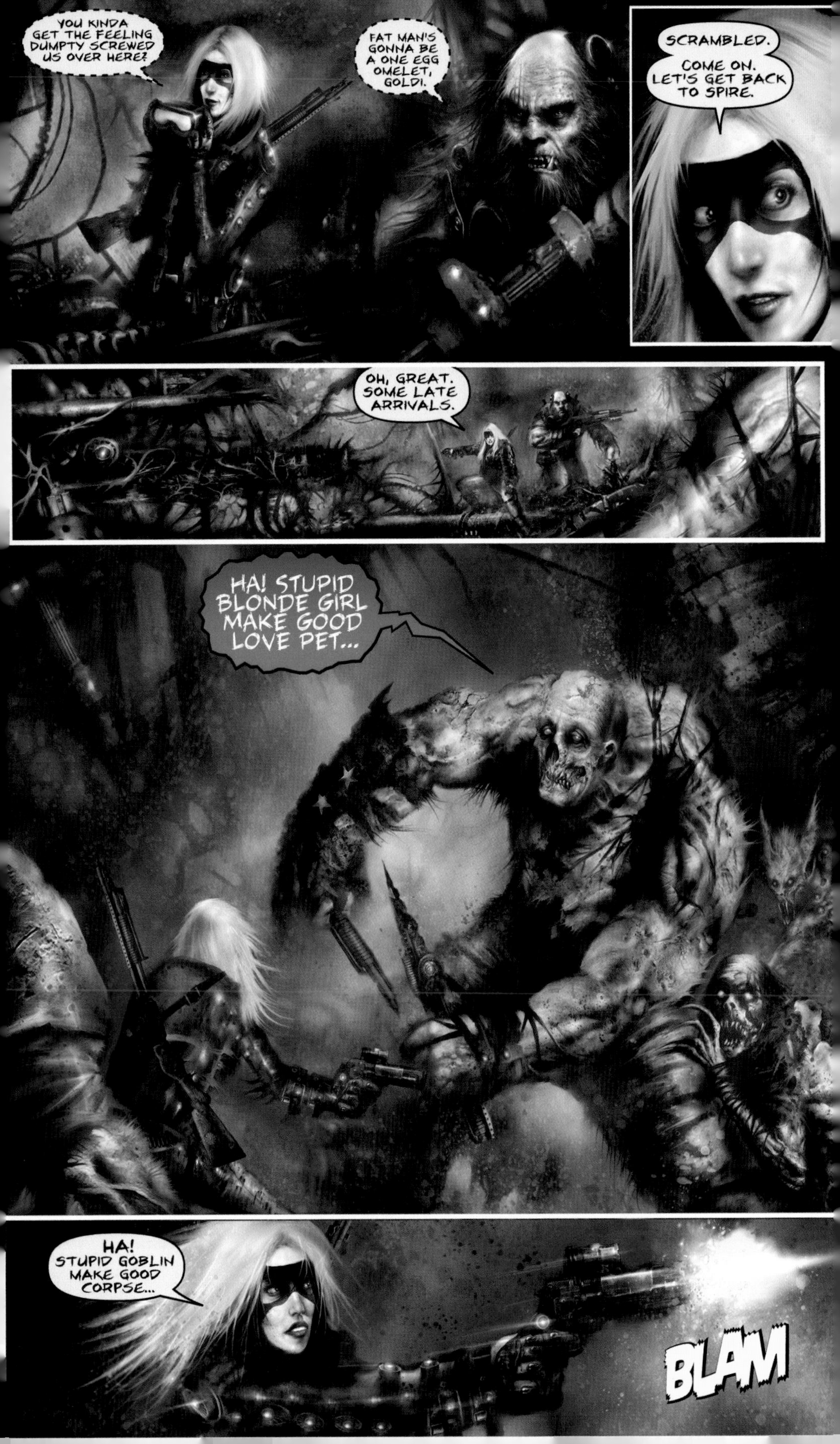
YOU KINDA GET THE FEELING DUMPTY SCREWED US OVER HERE?
FAT MAN'S GONNA BE A ONE EGG OMELET, GOLDI.
SCRAMBLED.
COME ON. LET'S GET BACK TO SPIRE.
OH, GREAT. SOME LATE ARRIVALS.
HA! STUPID BLONDE GIRL MAKE GOOD LOVE PET...
HA! STUPID GOBLIN MAKE GOOD CORPSE...
BLAM

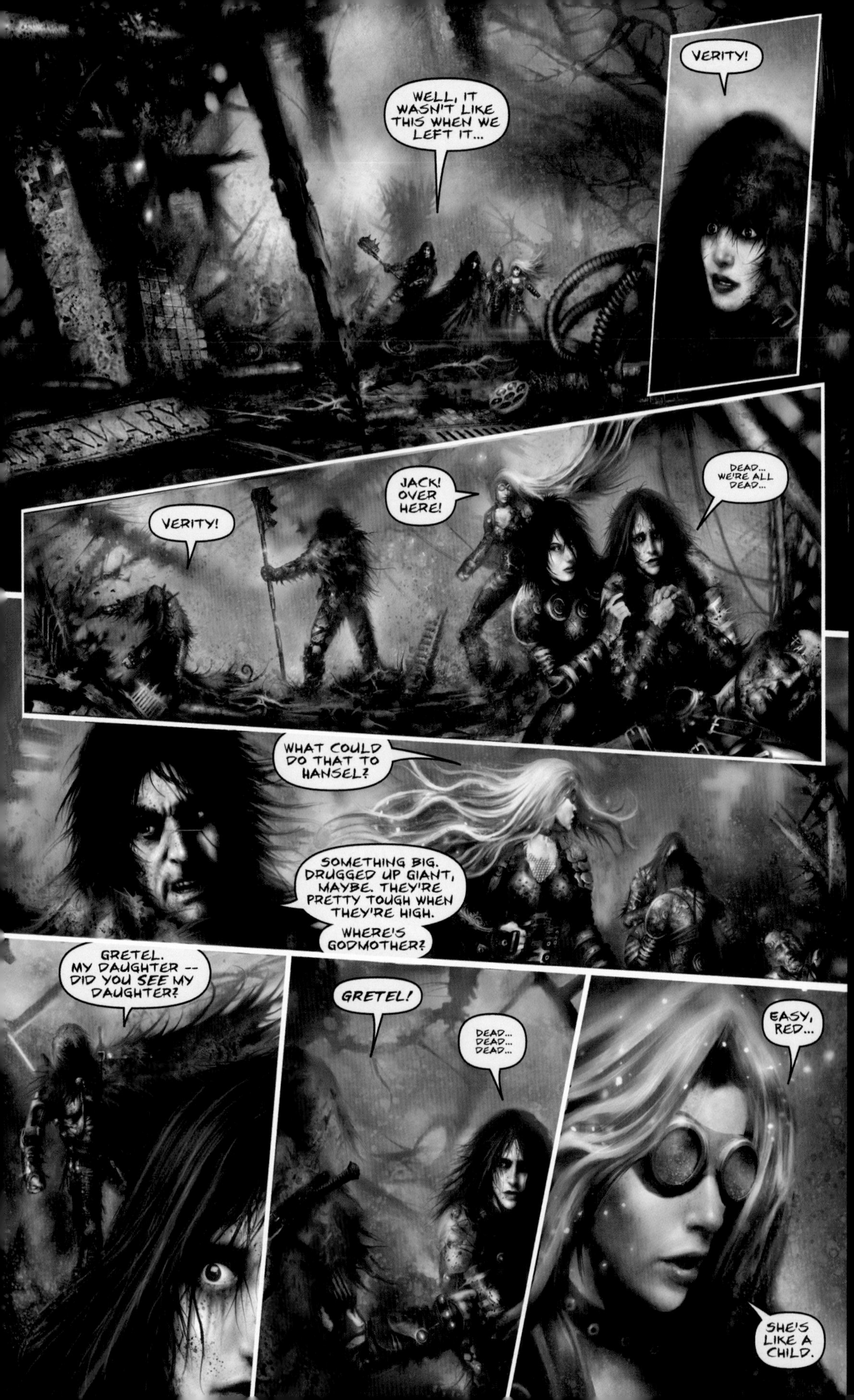

WELL, IT WASN'T LIKE THIS WHEN WE LEFT IT...
VERITY!
VERITY!
JACK! OVER HERE!
DEAD... WE'RE ALL DEAD...
WHAT COULD DO THAT TO HANSEL?
SOMETHING BIG. DRUGGED UP GIANT, MAYBE. THEY'RE PRETTY TOUGH WHEN THEY'RE HIGH.
WHERE'S GODMOTHER?
GRETEL. MY DAUGHTER -- DID YOU SEE MY DAUGHTER?
GRETEL!
DEAD... DEAD... DEAD...
EASY, RED...
SHE'S LIKE A CHILD.

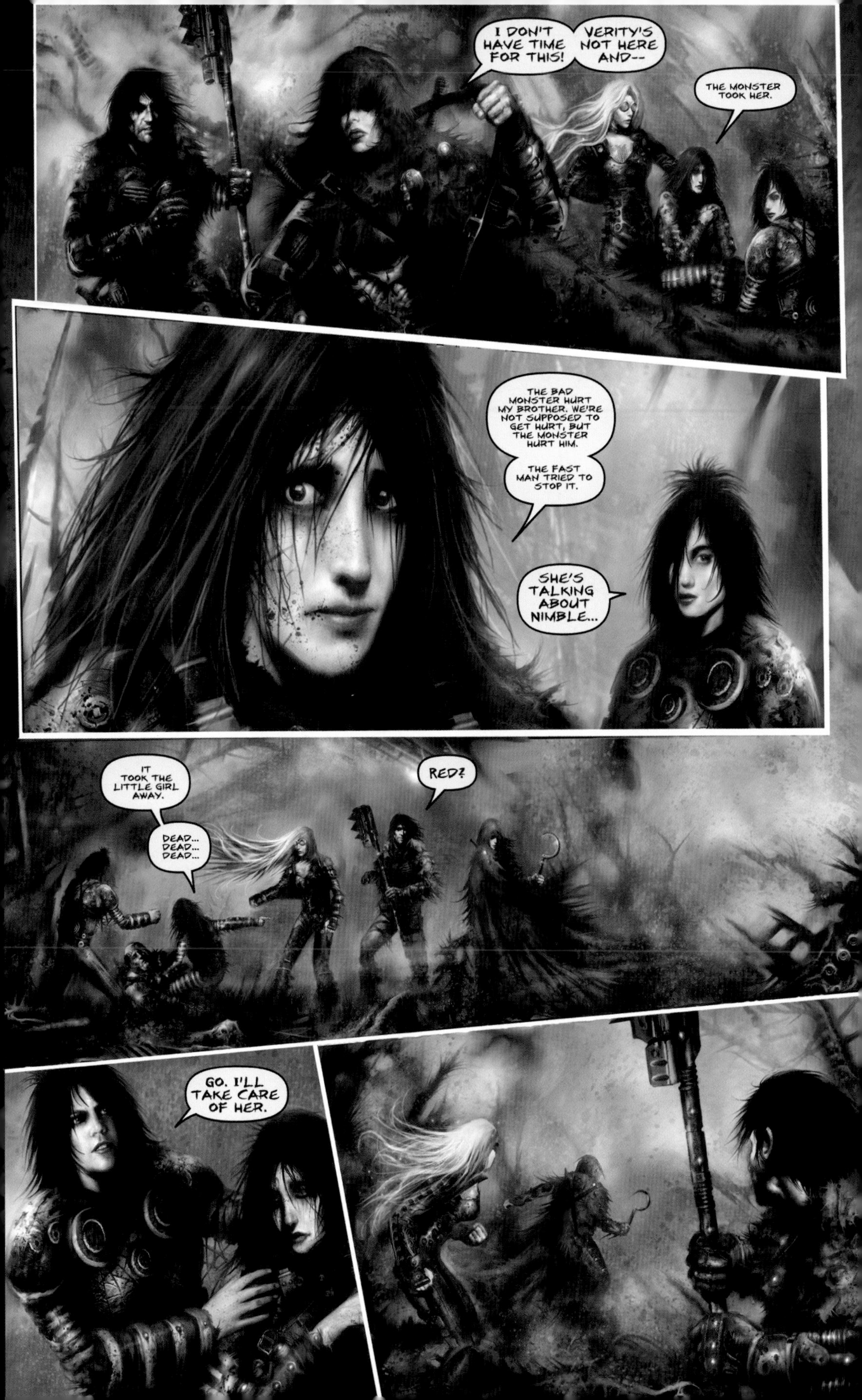
I DON'T HAVE TIME FOR THIS!
VERITY'S NOT HERE AND--
THE MONSTER TOOK HER.
THE BAD MONSTER HURT MY BROTHER. WE'RE NOT SUPPOSED TO GET HURT, BUT THE MONSTER HURT HIM.
THE FAST MAN TRIED TO STOP IT.
SHE'S TALKING ABOUT NIMBLE...
IT TOOK THE LITTLE GIRL AWAY.
DEAD... DEAD... DEAD...
RED?
GO. I'LL TAKE CARE OF HER.

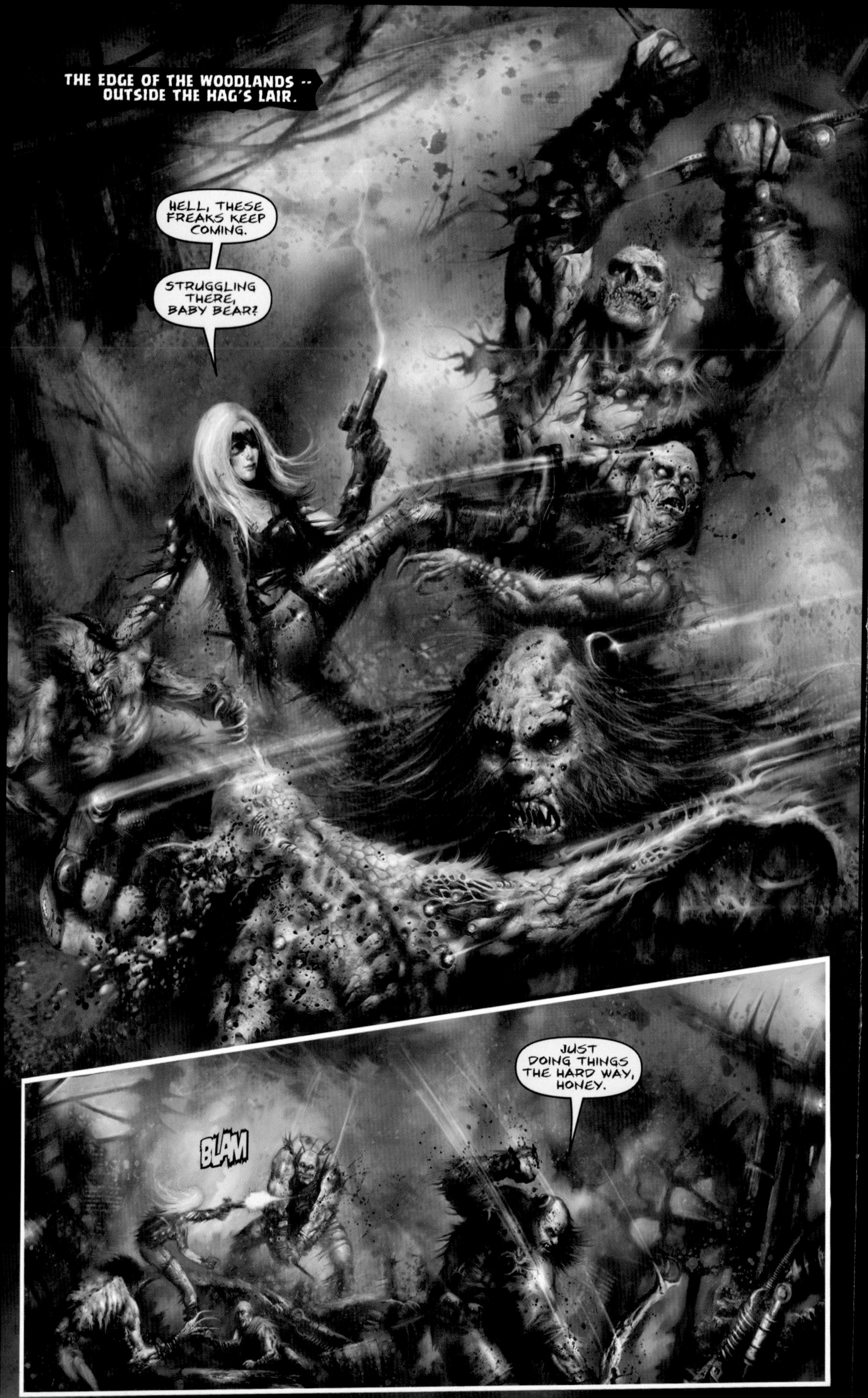
THE EDGE OF THE WOODLANDS -- OUTSIDE THE HAG'S LAIR.
HELL, THESE FREAKS KEEP COMING.
STRUGGLING THERE, BABY BEAR?
JUST DOING THINGS THE HARD WAY, HONEY.
BLAM

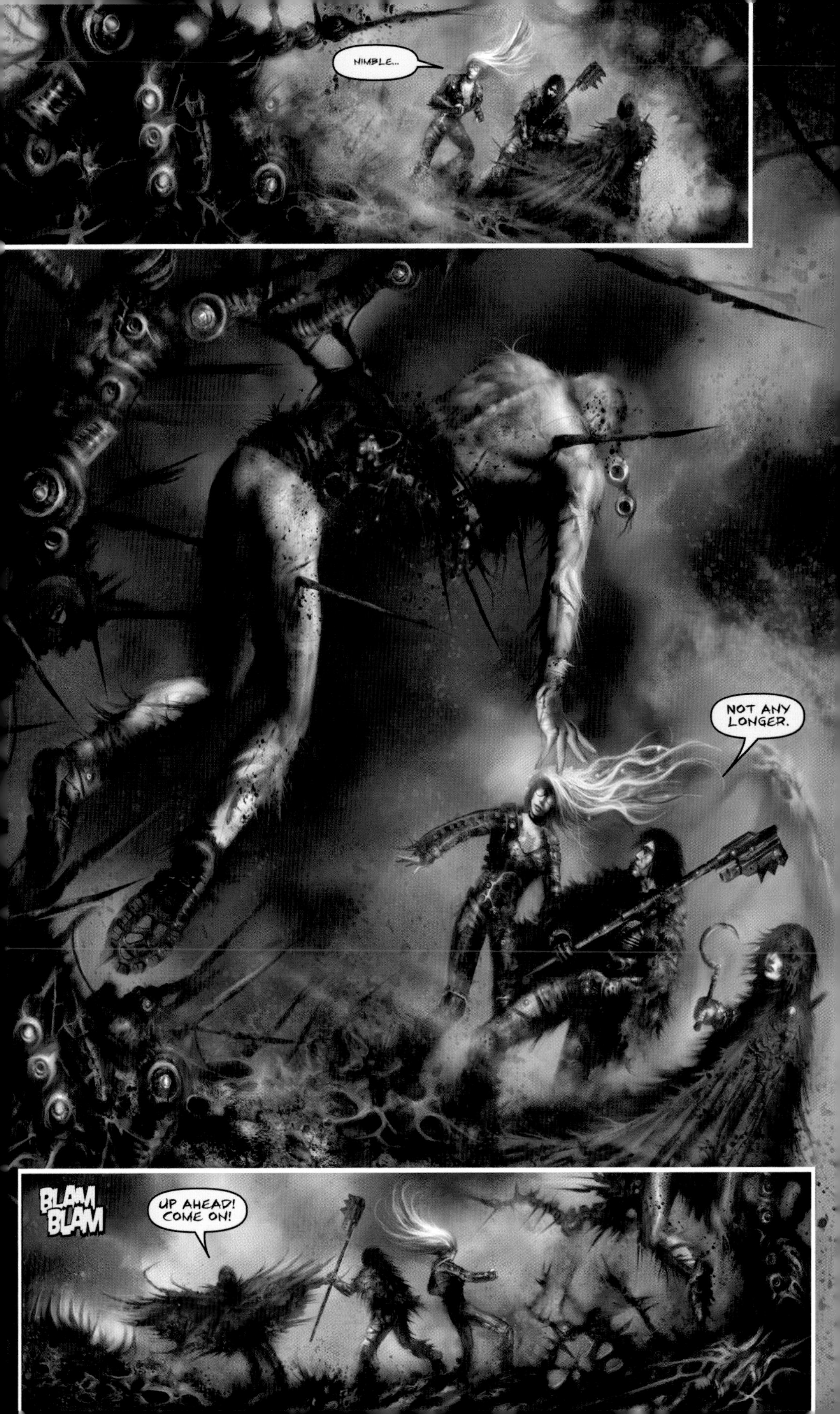
NIMBLE...
NOT ANY LONGER.
BLAM BLAM
UP AHEAD! COME ON!

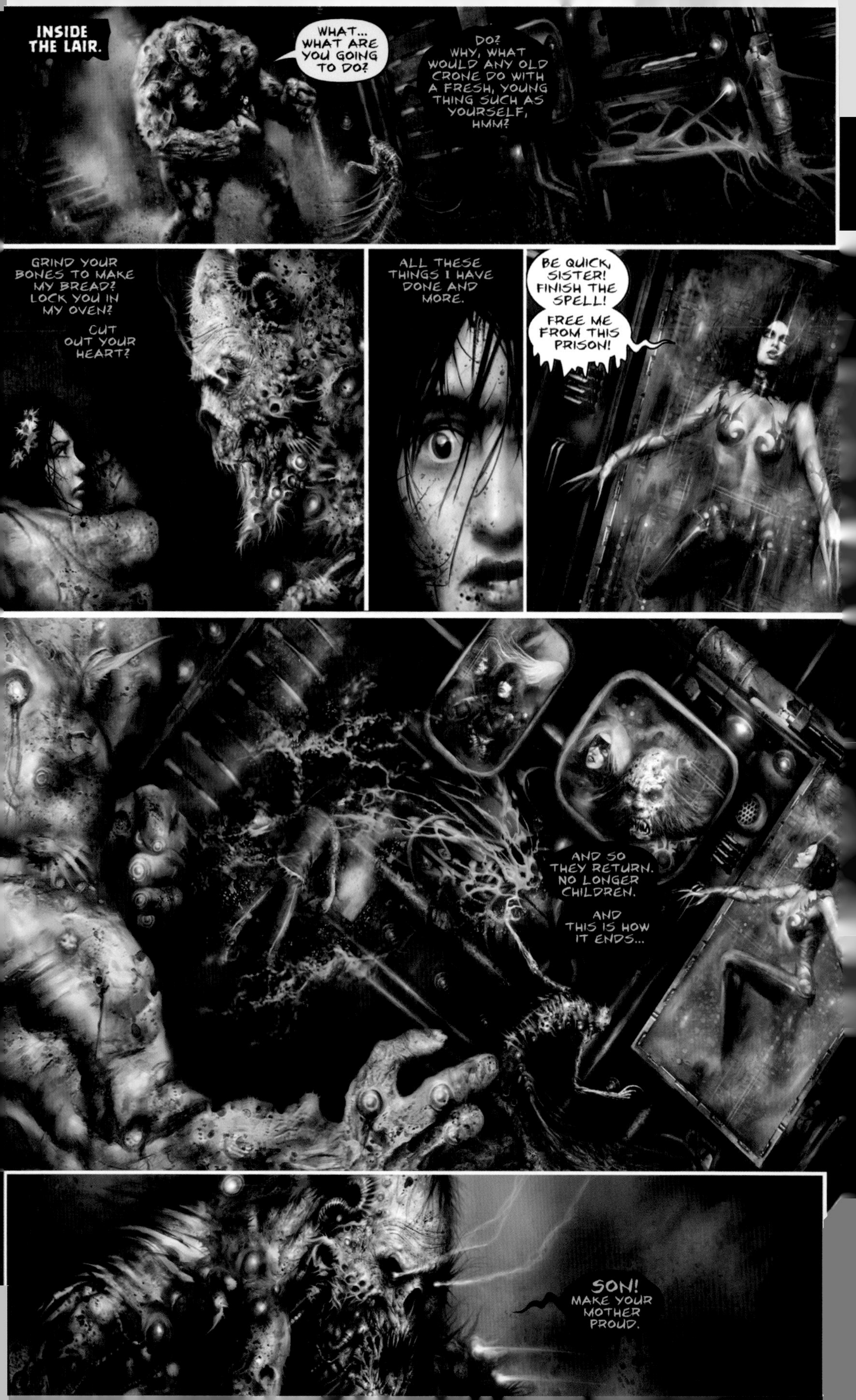
INSIDE THE LAIR.
WHAT... WHAT ARE YOU GOING TO DO?
DO? WHY, WHAT WOULD ANY OLD CRONE DO WITH A FRESH, YOUNG THING SUCH AS YOURSELF, HMM?
GRIND YOUR BONES TO MAKE MY BREAD? LOCK YOU IN MY OVEN?
CUT OUT YOUR HEART?
ALL THESE THINGS I HAVE DONE AND MORE.
BE QUICK, SISTER! FINISH THE SPELL!
FREE ME FROM THIS PRISON!
AND SO THEY RETURN. NO LONGER CHILDREN.
AND THIS IS HOW IT ENDS...
SON! MAKE YOUR MOTHER PROUD.

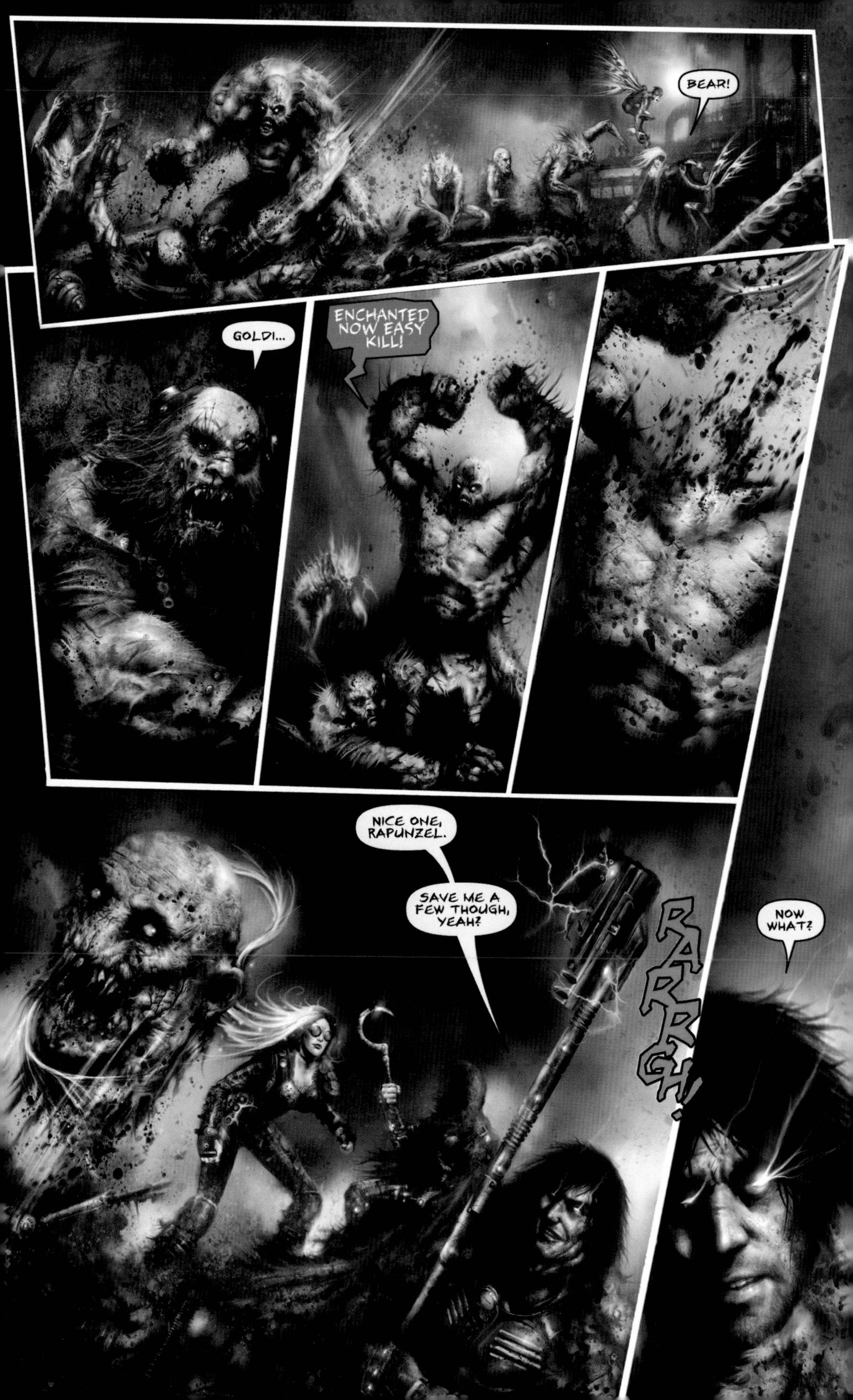
BEAR!
GOLDI...
ENCHANTED NOW EASY KILL!
NICE ONE, RAPUNZEL.
SAVE ME A FEW THOUGH, YEAH?
RARRGH!
NOW WHAT?

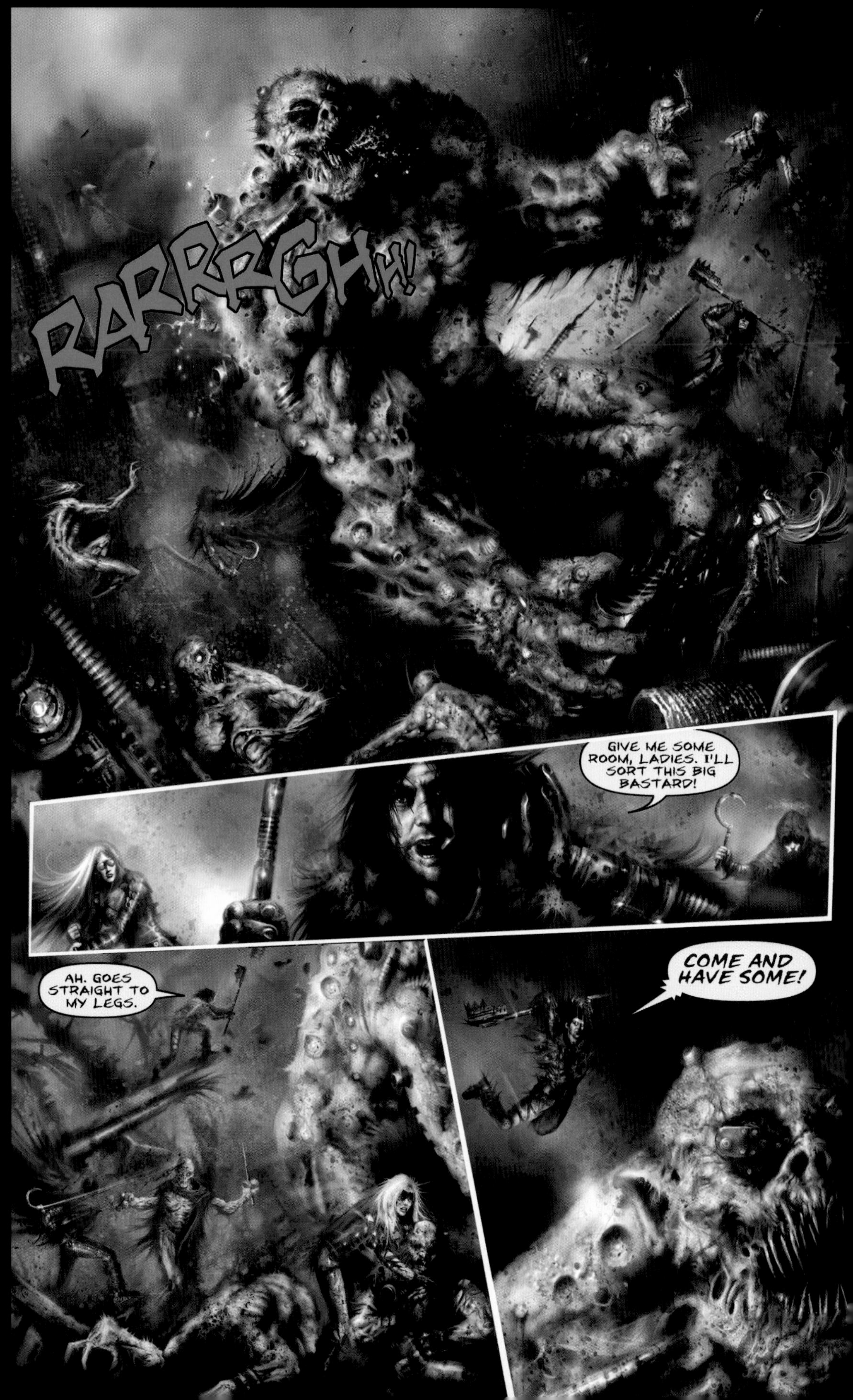
RARRRGHH!
GIVE ME SOME ROOM, LADIES. I'LL SORT THIS BIG BASTARD!
AH. GOES STRAIGHT TO MY LEGS.
COME AND HAVE SOME!

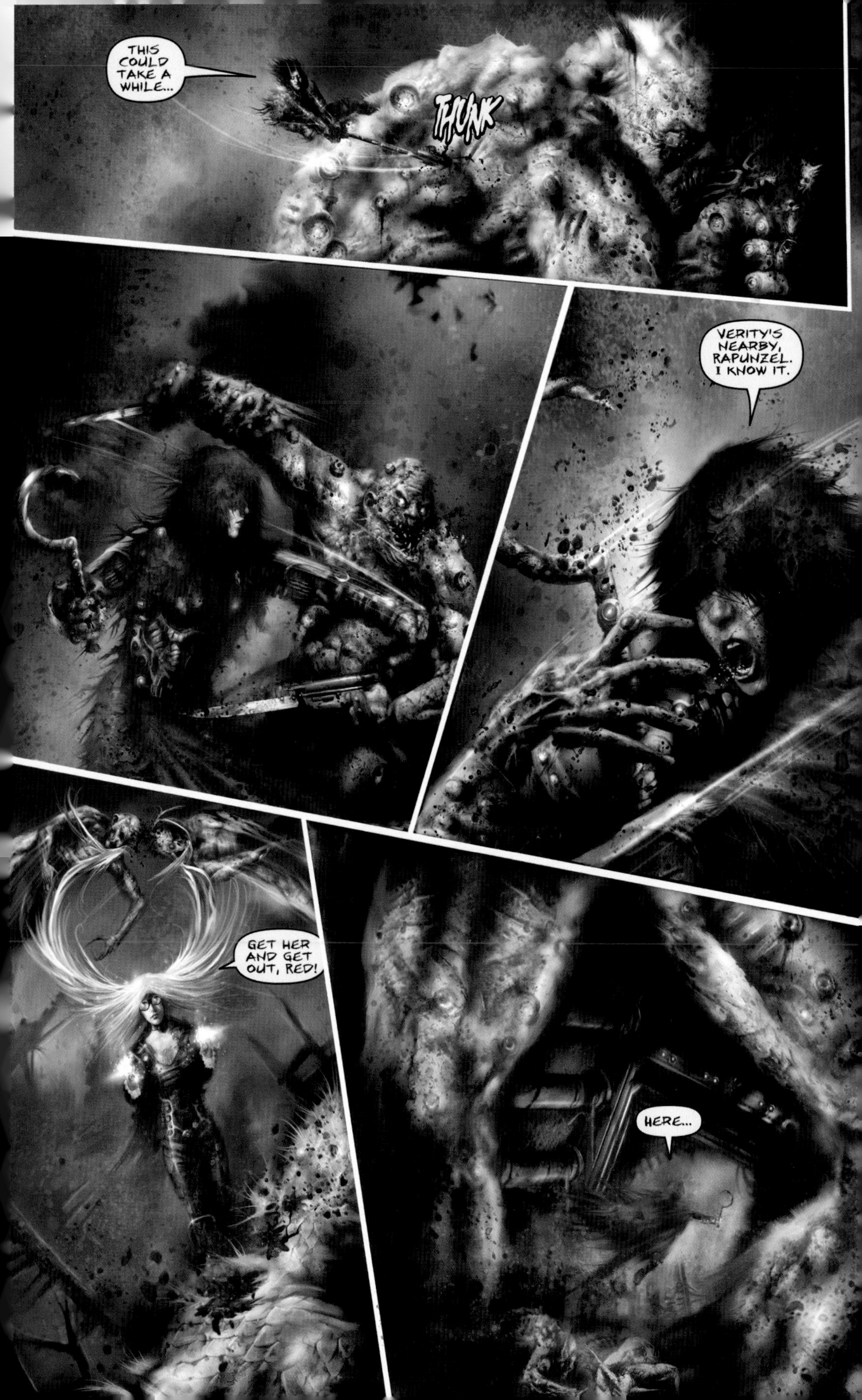
THIS COULD TAKE A WHILE...
THUNK
VERITY'S NEARBY, RAPUNZEL. I KNOW IT.
GET HER AND GET OUT, RED!
HERE...

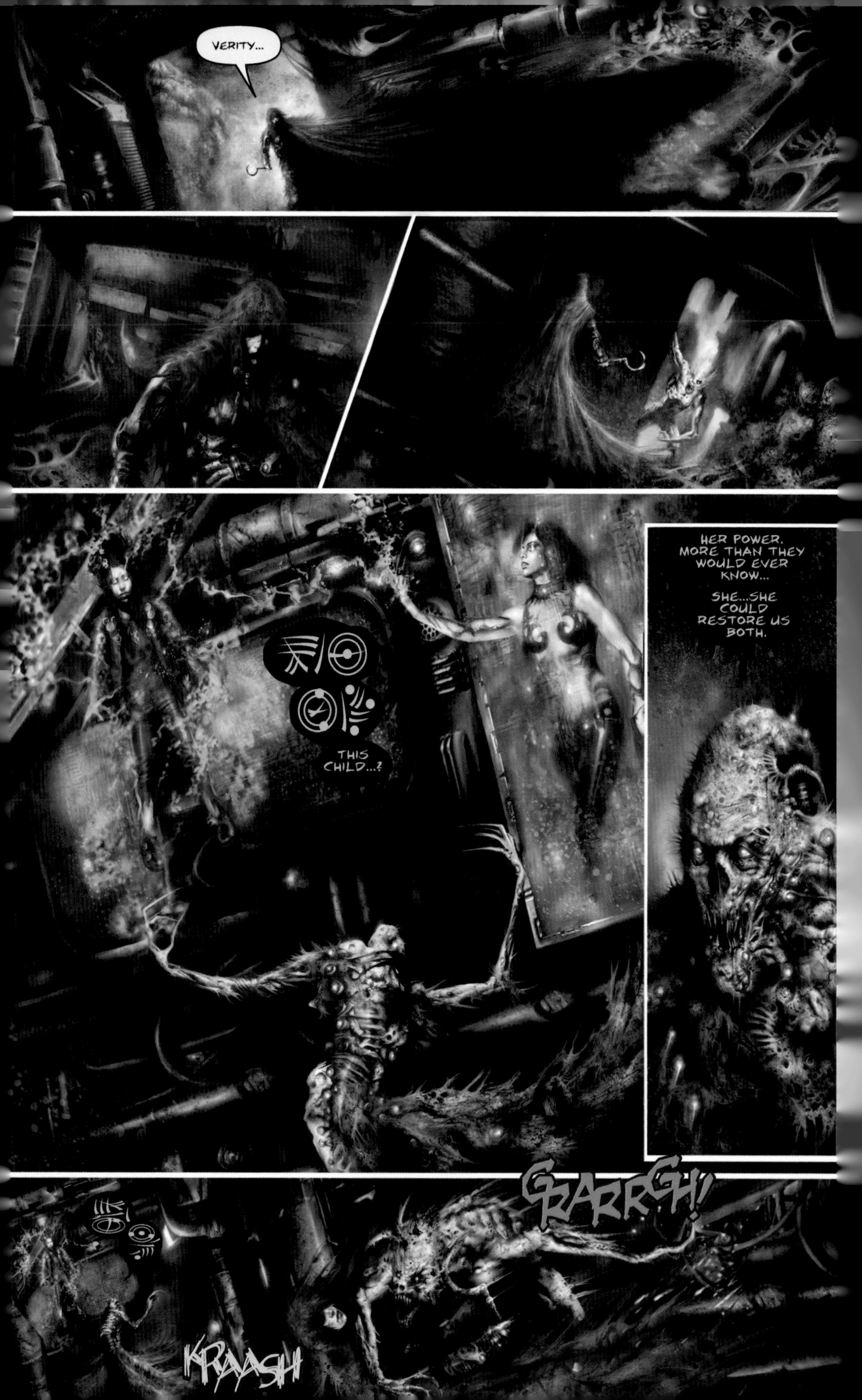
VERITY...
HER POWER. MORE THAN THEY WOULD EVER KNOW...
SHE...SHE COULD RESTORE US BOTH.
THIS CHILD...?
GRARRGH!
KRAASH

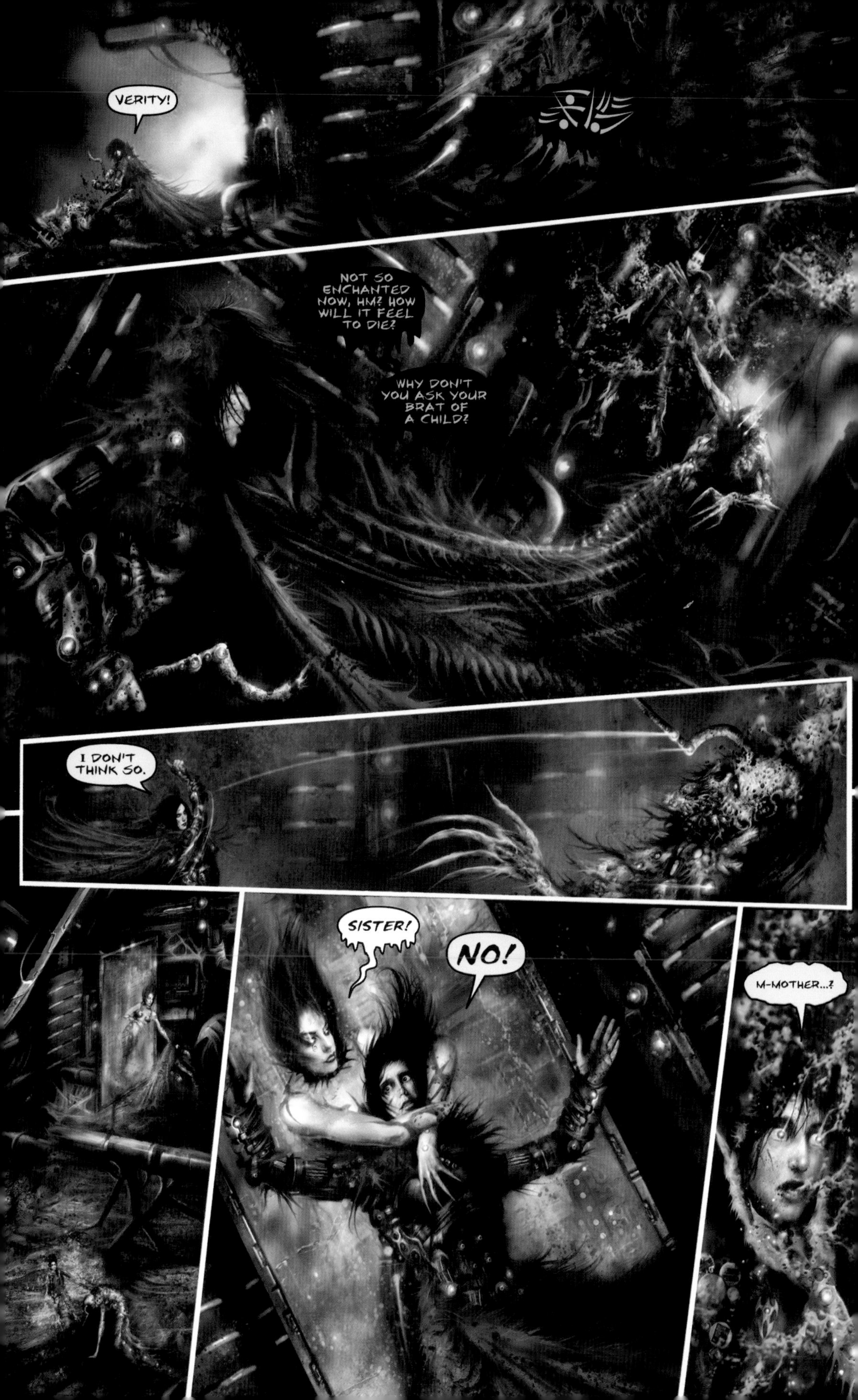
VERITY!
NOT SO ENCHANTED NOW, HM? HOW WILL IT FEEL TO DIE?
WHY DON'T YOU ASK YOUR BRAT OF A CHILD?
I DON'T THINK SO.
SISTER!
NO!
M-MOTHER...?

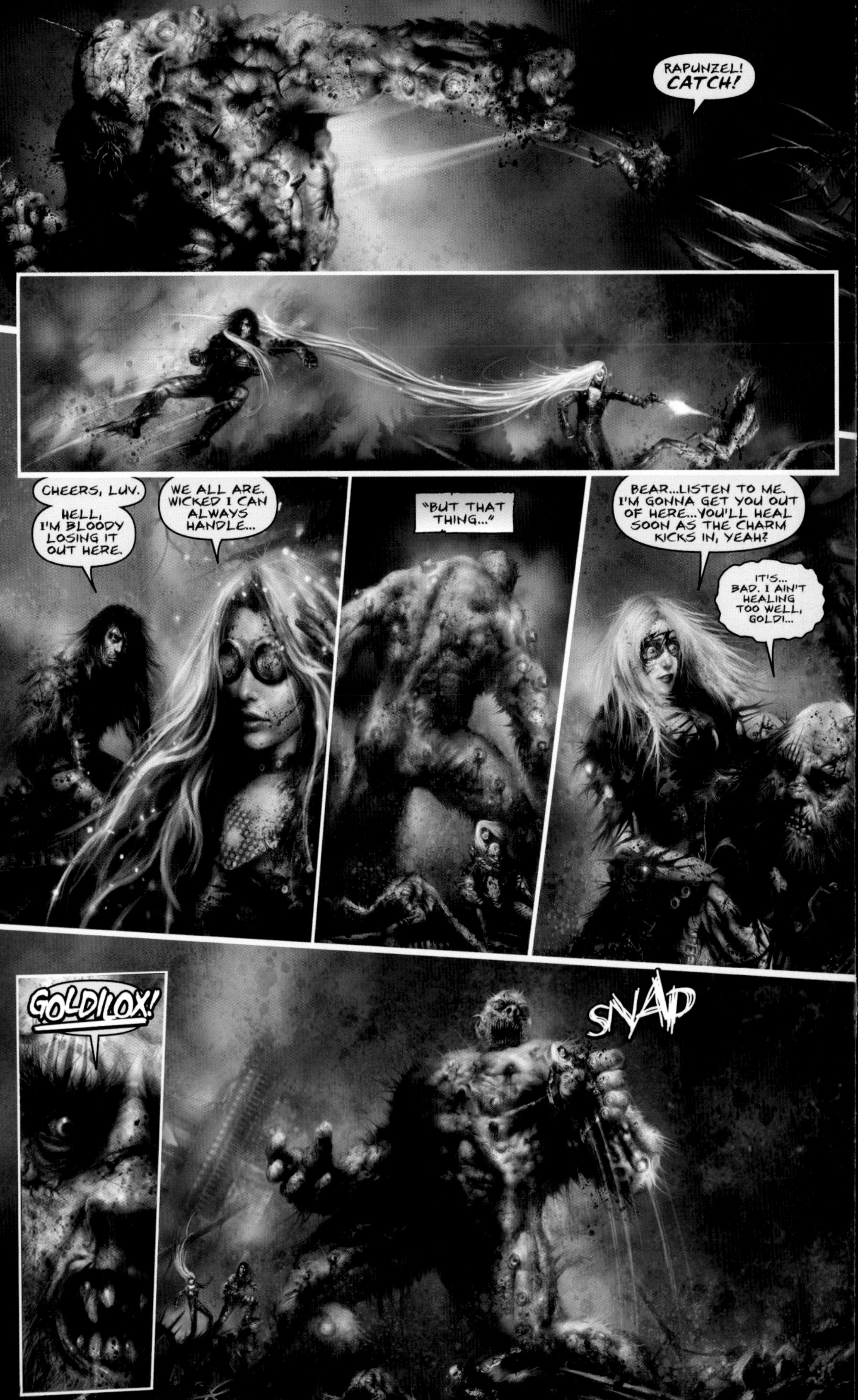
RAPUNZEL! CATCH!
CHEERS, LUV.
HELL, I'M BLOODY LOSING IT OUT HERE.
WE ALL ARE. WICKED I CAN ALWAYS HANDLE...
"BUT THAT THING..."
BEAR...LISTEN TO ME. I'M GONNA GET YOU OUT OF HERE...YOU'LL HEAL SOON AS THE CHARM KICKS IN, YEAH?
IT'S... BAD. I AIN'T HEALING TOO WELL, GOLDI...
GOLDILOX!
SNAP

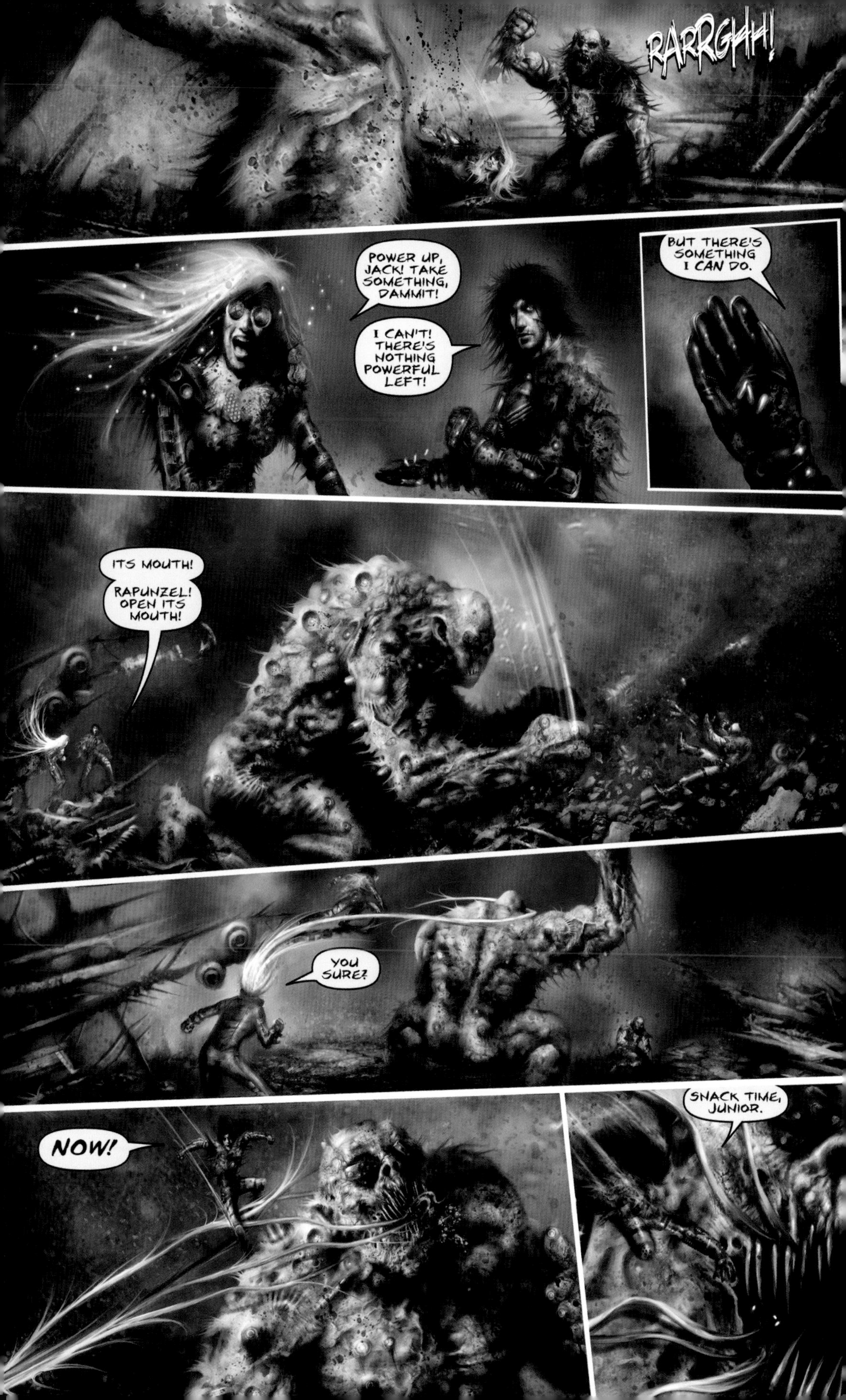
RARRGHH!
POWER UP, JACK! TAKE SOMETHING, DAMMIT!
I CAN'T! THERE'S NOTHING POWERFUL LEFT!
BUT THERE'S SOMETHING I CAN DO.
ITS MOUTH!
RAPUNZEL! OPEN ITS MOUTH!
YOU SURE?
NOW!
SNACK TIME, JUNIOR.

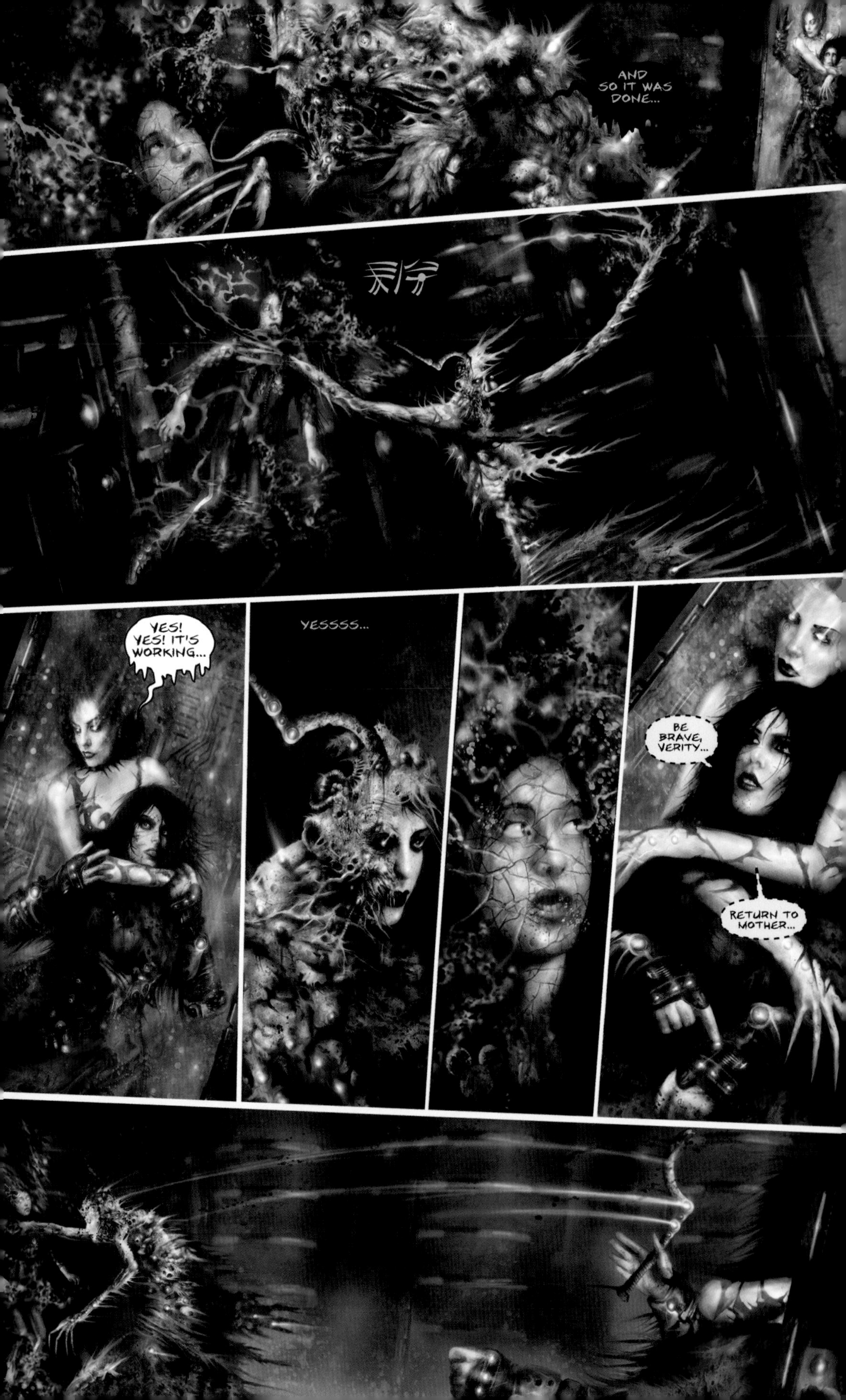
AND SO IT WAS DONE...
YES! YES! IT'S WORKING...
YESSSS...
BE BRAVE, VERITY...
RETURN TO MOTHER...

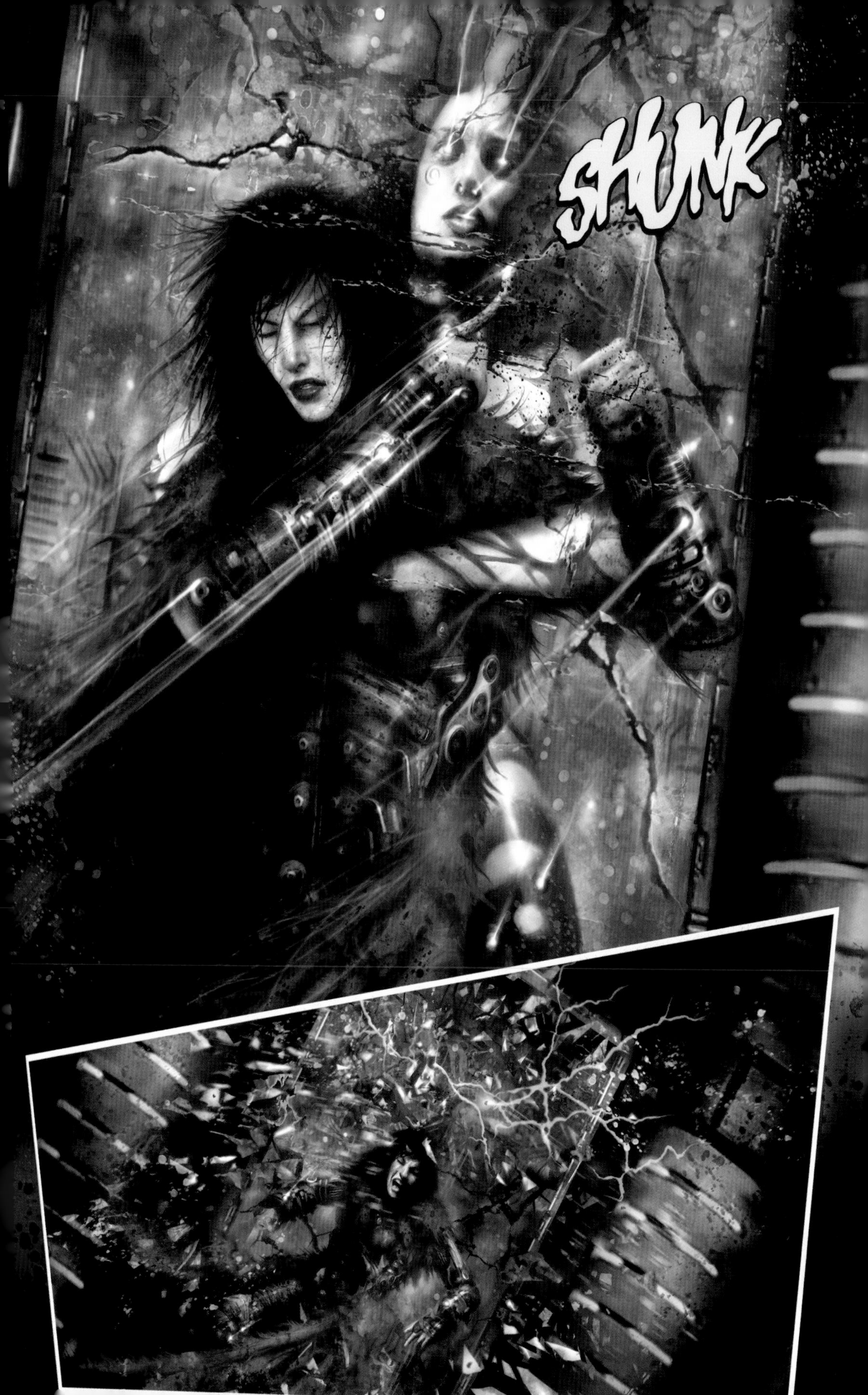
SHUNK

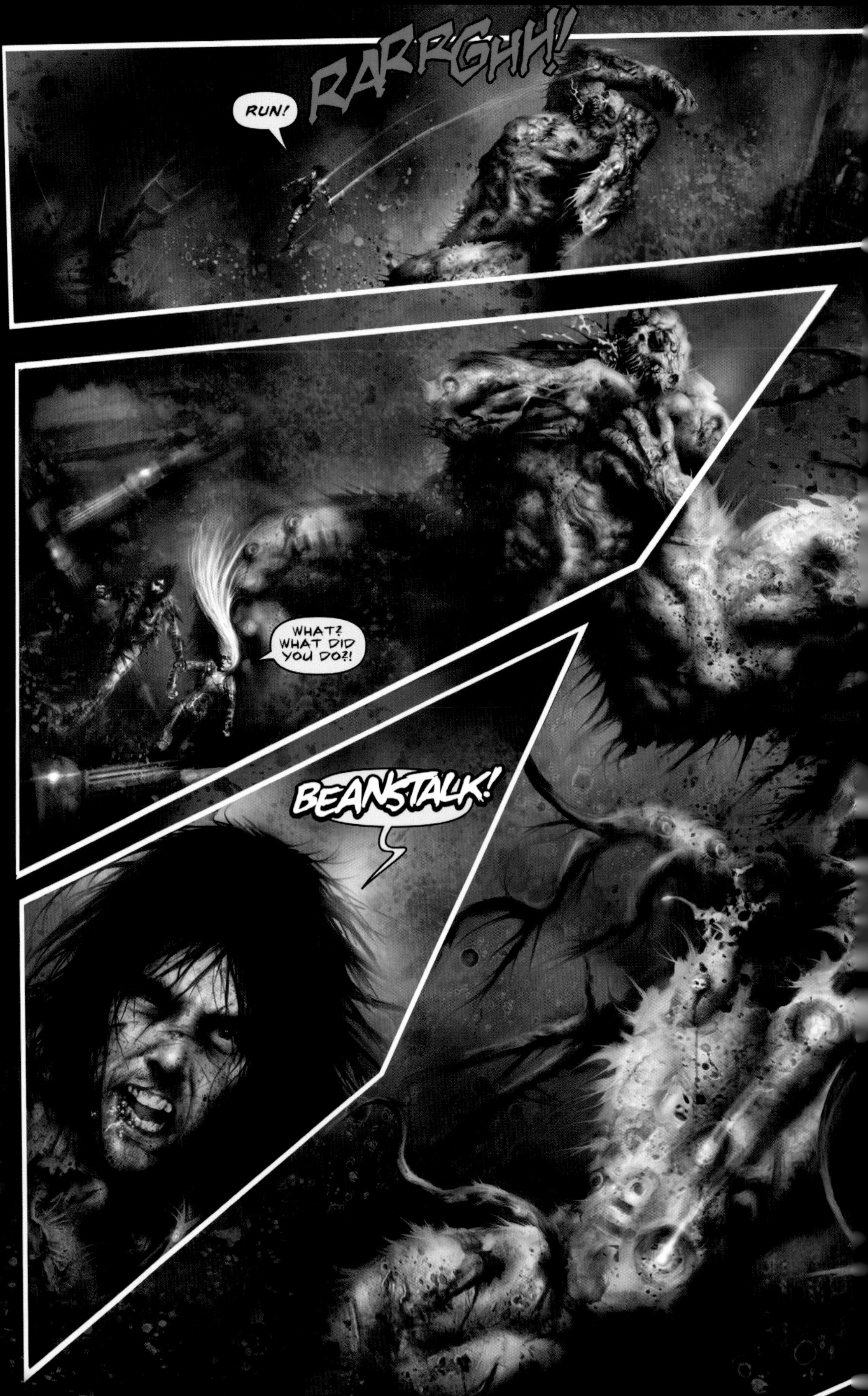
RUN!
RARRGHH!
WHAT? WHAT DID YOU DO?!
BEANSTALK!

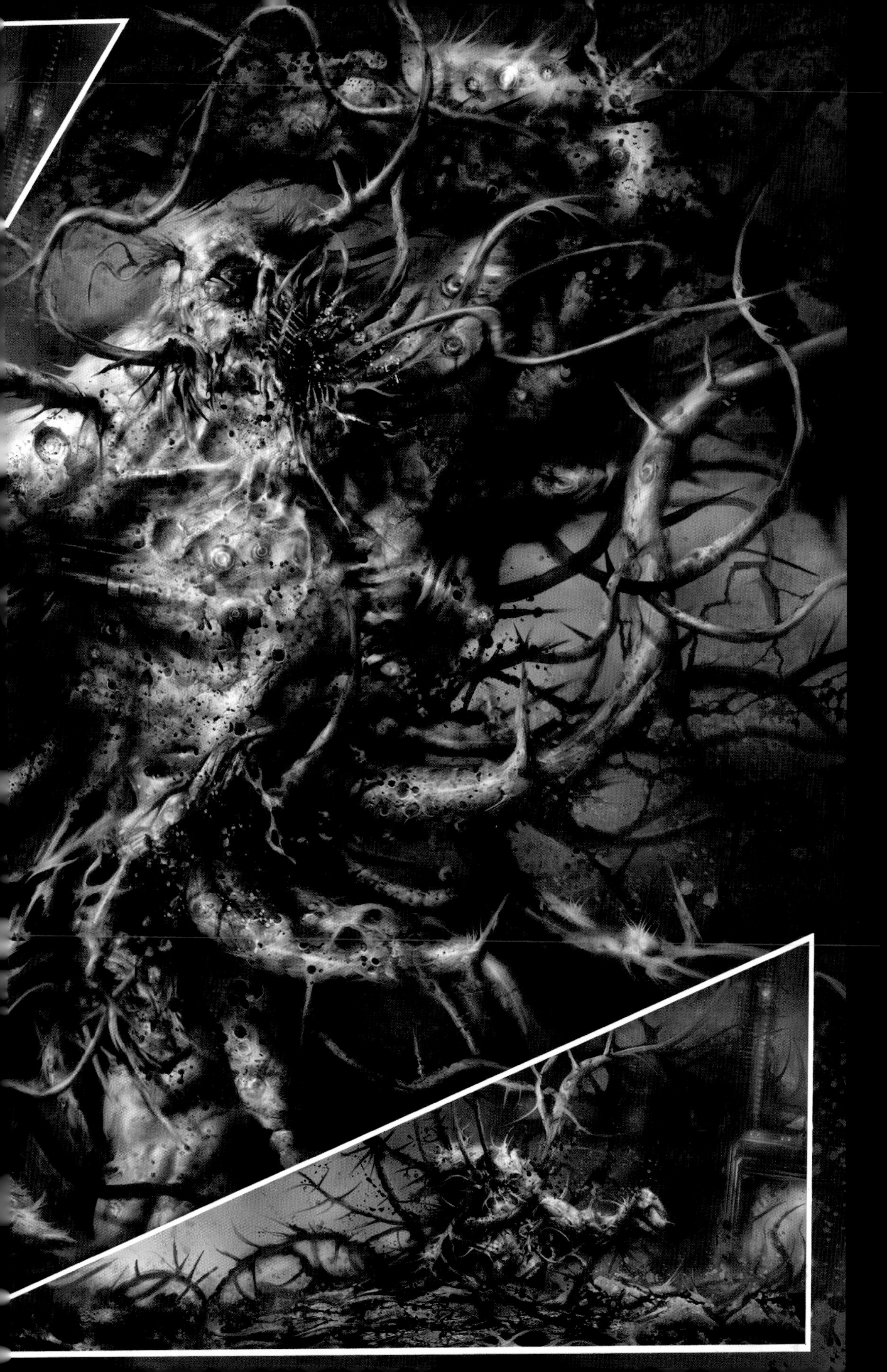

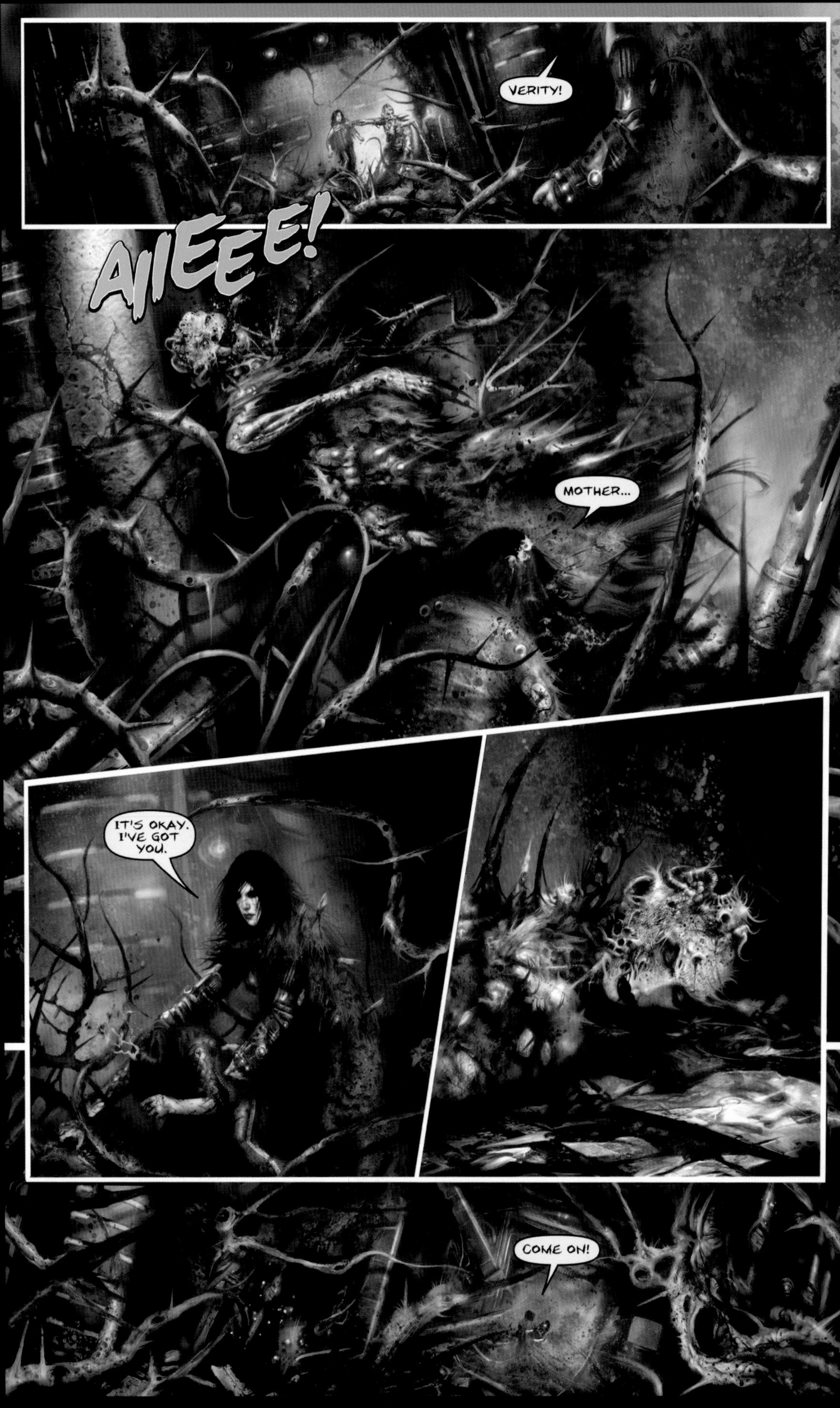
VERITY!
AIIEEE!
MOTHER...
IT'S OKAY. I'VE GOT YOU.
COME ON!

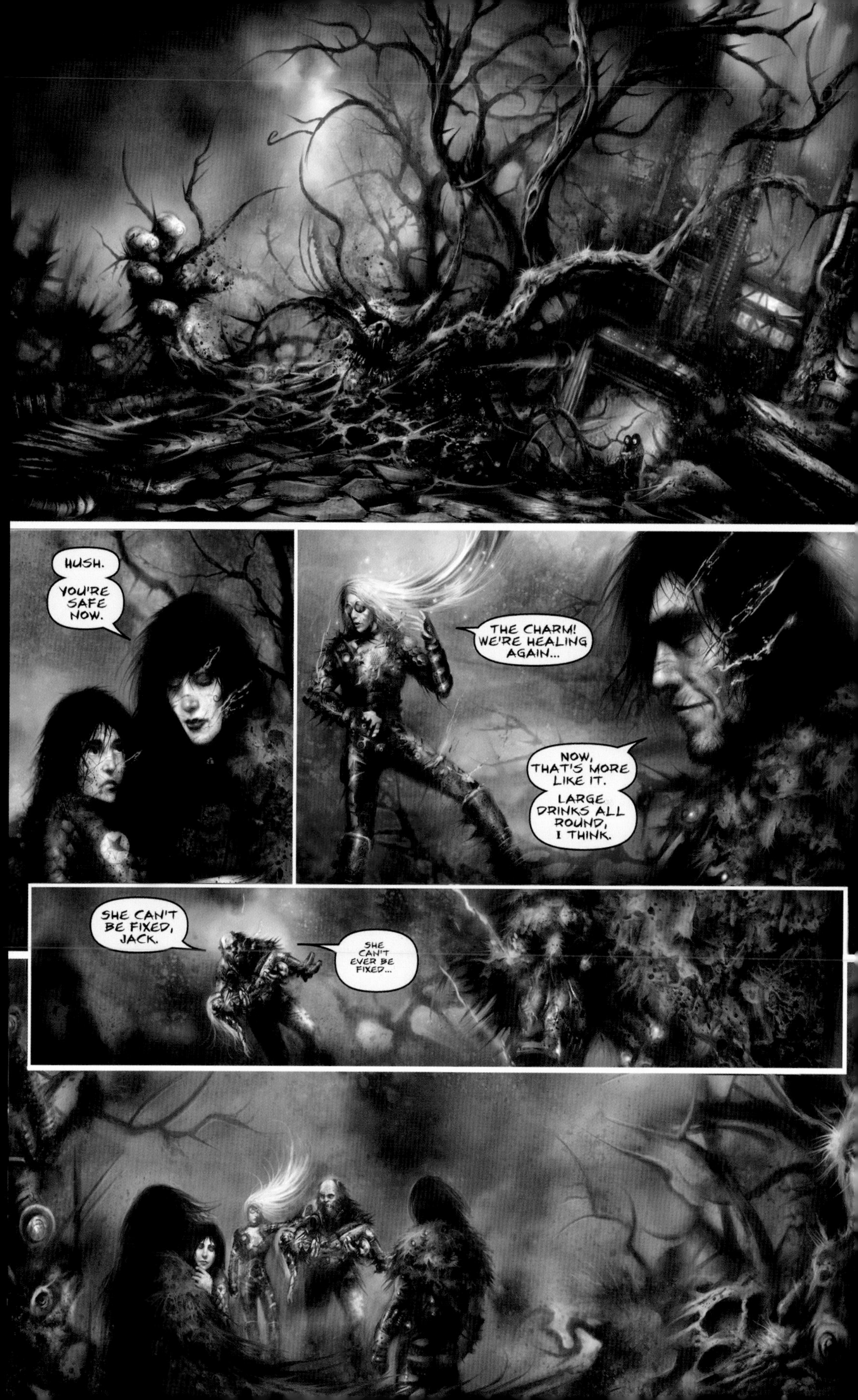
HUSH.
YOU'RE SAFE NOW.
THE CHARM! WE'RE HEALING AGAIN...
NOW, THAT'S MORE LIKE IT.
LARGE DRINKS ALL ROUND, I THINK.
SHE CAN'T BE FIXED, JACK.
SHE CAN'T EVER BE FIXED...

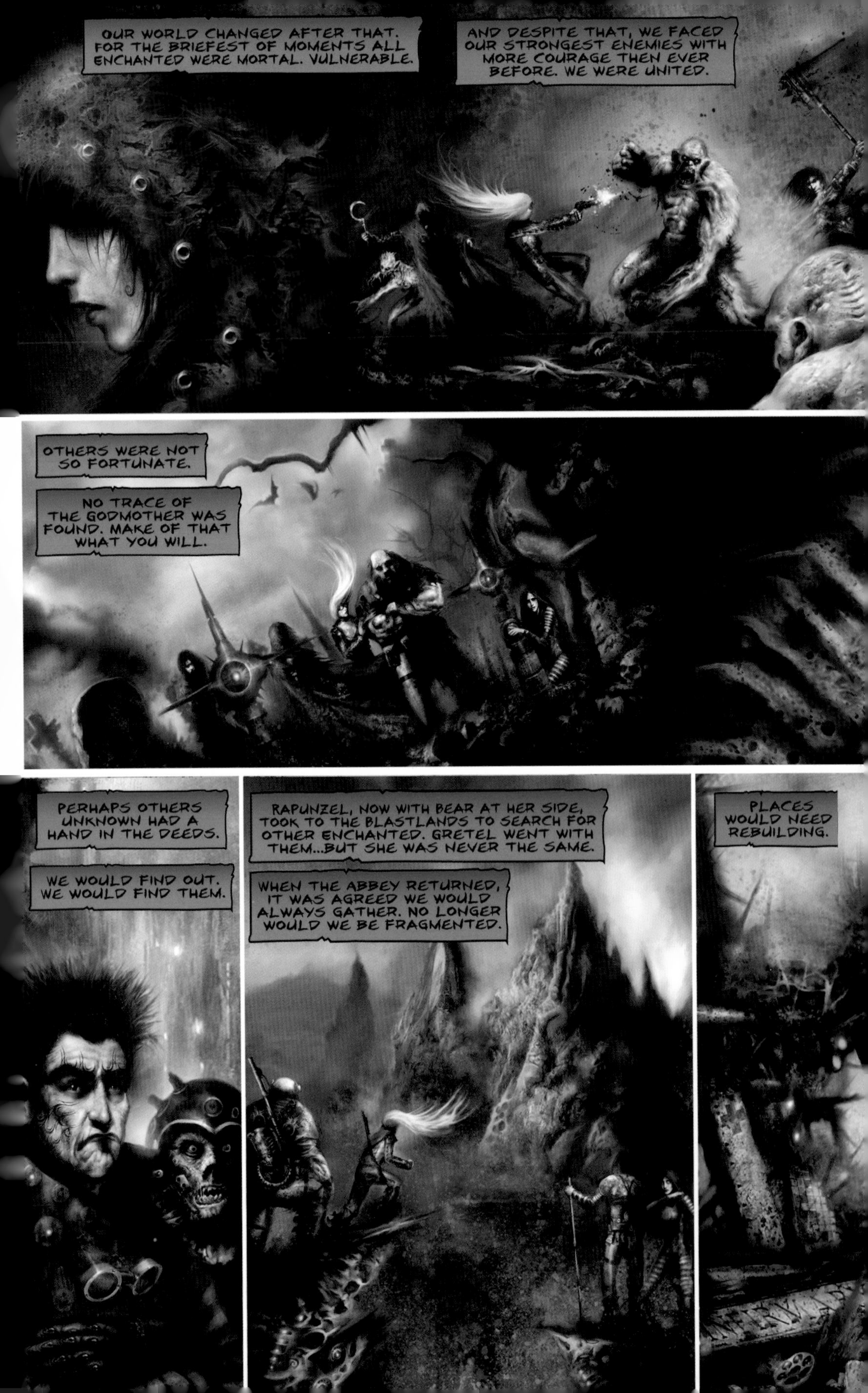
OUR WORLD CHANGED AFTER THAT. FOR THE BRIEFEST OF MOMENTS ALL ENCHANTED WERE MORTAL. VULNERABLE.
AND DESPITE THAT, WE FACED OUR STRONGEST ENEMIES WITH MORE COURAGE THEN EVER BEFORE. WE WERE UNITED.
OTHERS WERE NOT SO FORTUNATE.
NO TRACE OF THE GODMOTHER WAS FOUND. MAKE OF THAT WHAT YOU WILL.
PERHAPS OTHERS UNKNOWN HAD A HAND IN THE DEEDS.
WE WOULD FIND OUT. WE WOULD FIND THEM.
RAPUNZEL, NOW WITH BEAR AT HER SIDE, TOOK TO THE BLASTLANDS TO SEARCH FOR OTHER ENCHANTED. GRETEL WENT WITH THEM...BUT SHE WAS NEVER THE SAME.
WHEN THE ABBEY RETURNED, IT WAS AGREED WE WOULD ALWAYS GATHER. NO LONGER WOULD WE BE FRAGMENTED.
PLACES WOULD NEED REBUILDING.

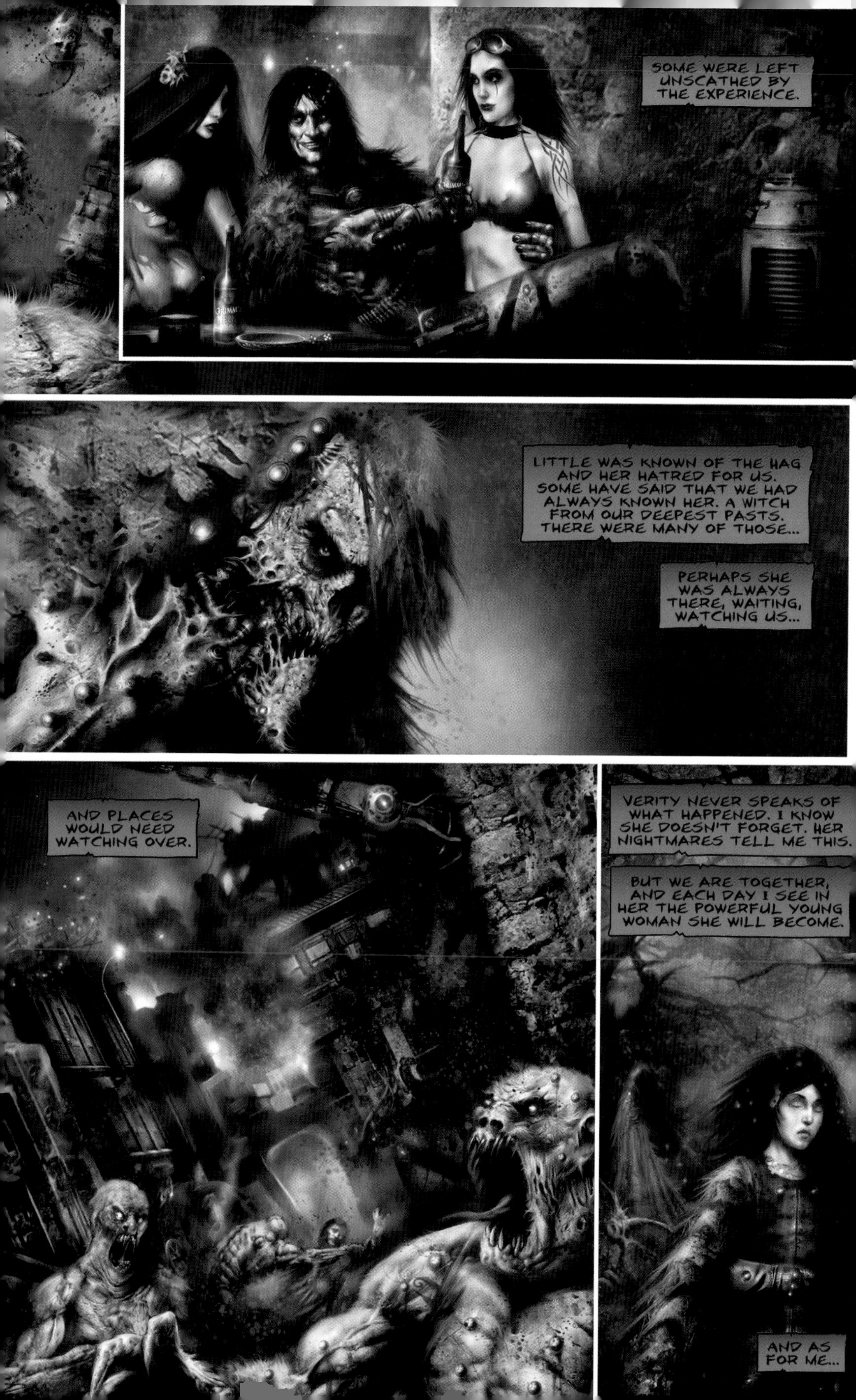
SOME WERE LEFT UNSCATHED BY THE EXPERIENCE.
LITTLE WAS KNOWN OF THE HAG AND HER HATRED FOR US. SOME HAVE SAID THAT WE HAD ALWAYS KNOWN HER. A WITCH FROM OUR DEEPEST PASTS. THERE WERE MANY OF THOSE...
PERHAPS SHE WAS ALWAYS THERE, WAITING, WATCHING US...
AND PLACES WOULD NEED WATCHING OVER.
VERITY NEVER SPEAKS OF WHAT HAPPENED. I KNOW SHE DOESN'T FORGET. HER NIGHTMARES TELL ME THIS.
BUT WE ARE TOGETHER, AND EACH DAY I SEE IN HER THE POWERFUL YOUNG WOMAN SHE WILL BECOME.
AND AS FOR ME...

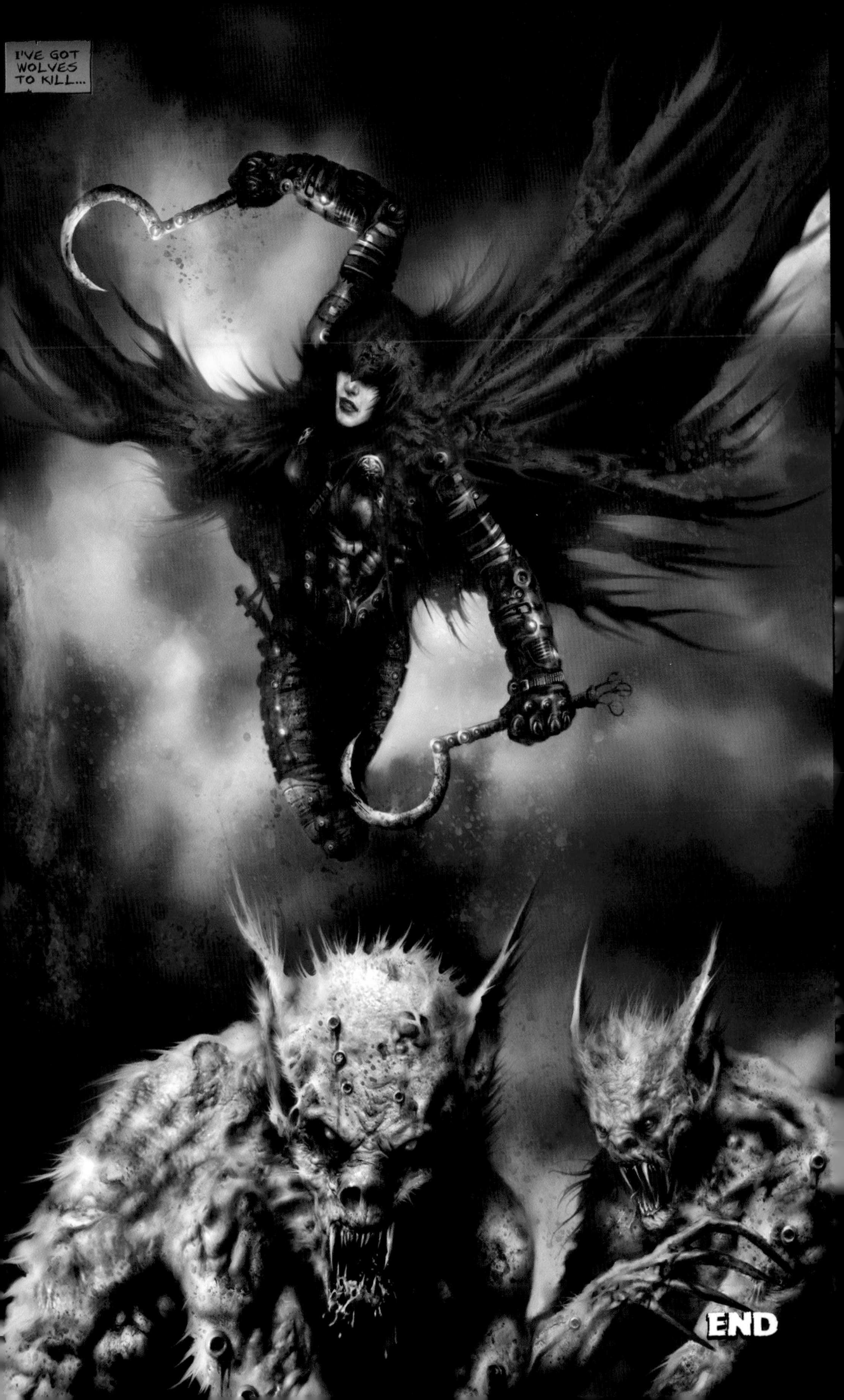
I'VE GOT WOLVES TO KILL...
END

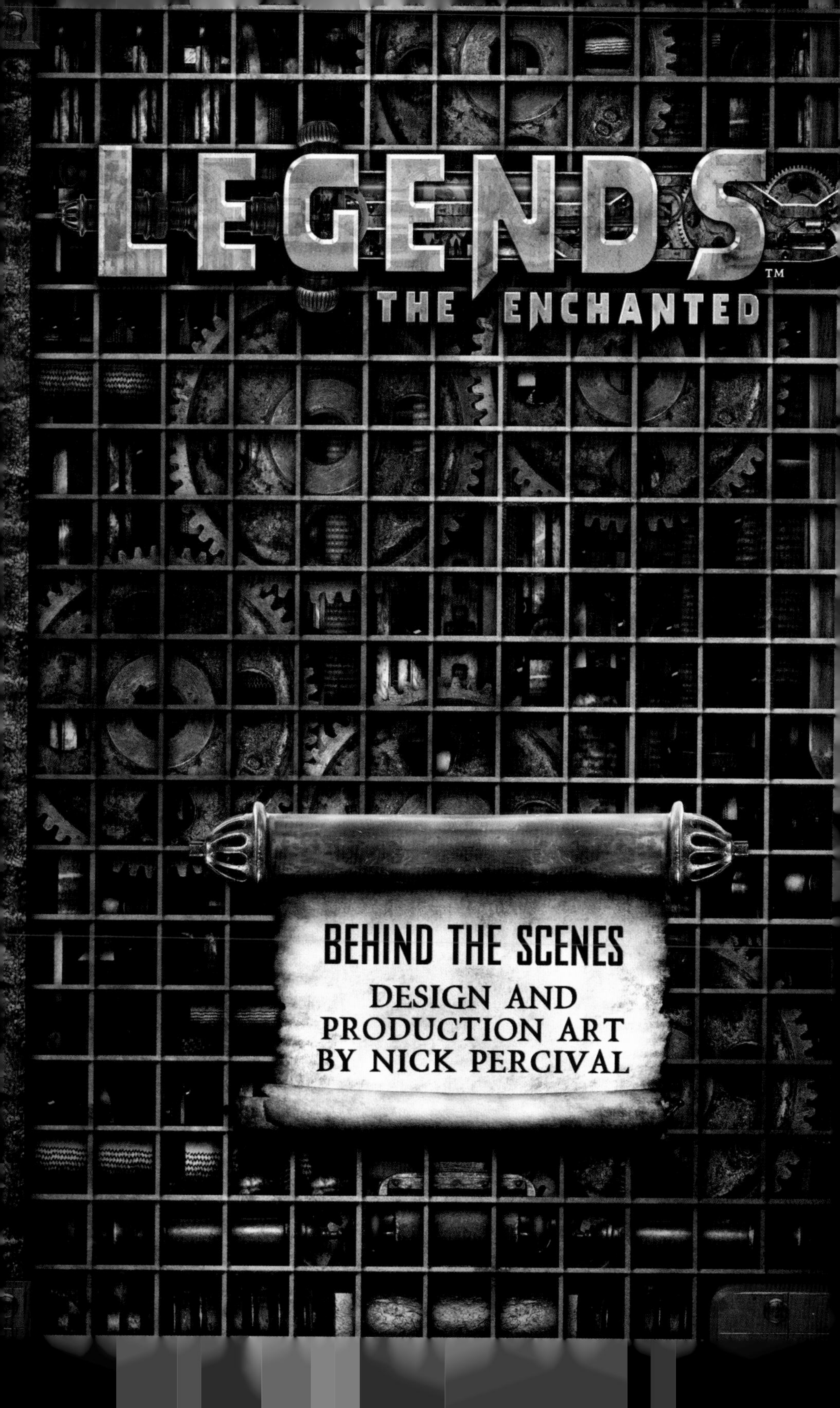
LEGENDS™
THE ENCHANTED
BEHIND THE SCENES
DESIGN AND
PRODUCTION ART
BY NICK PERCIVAL

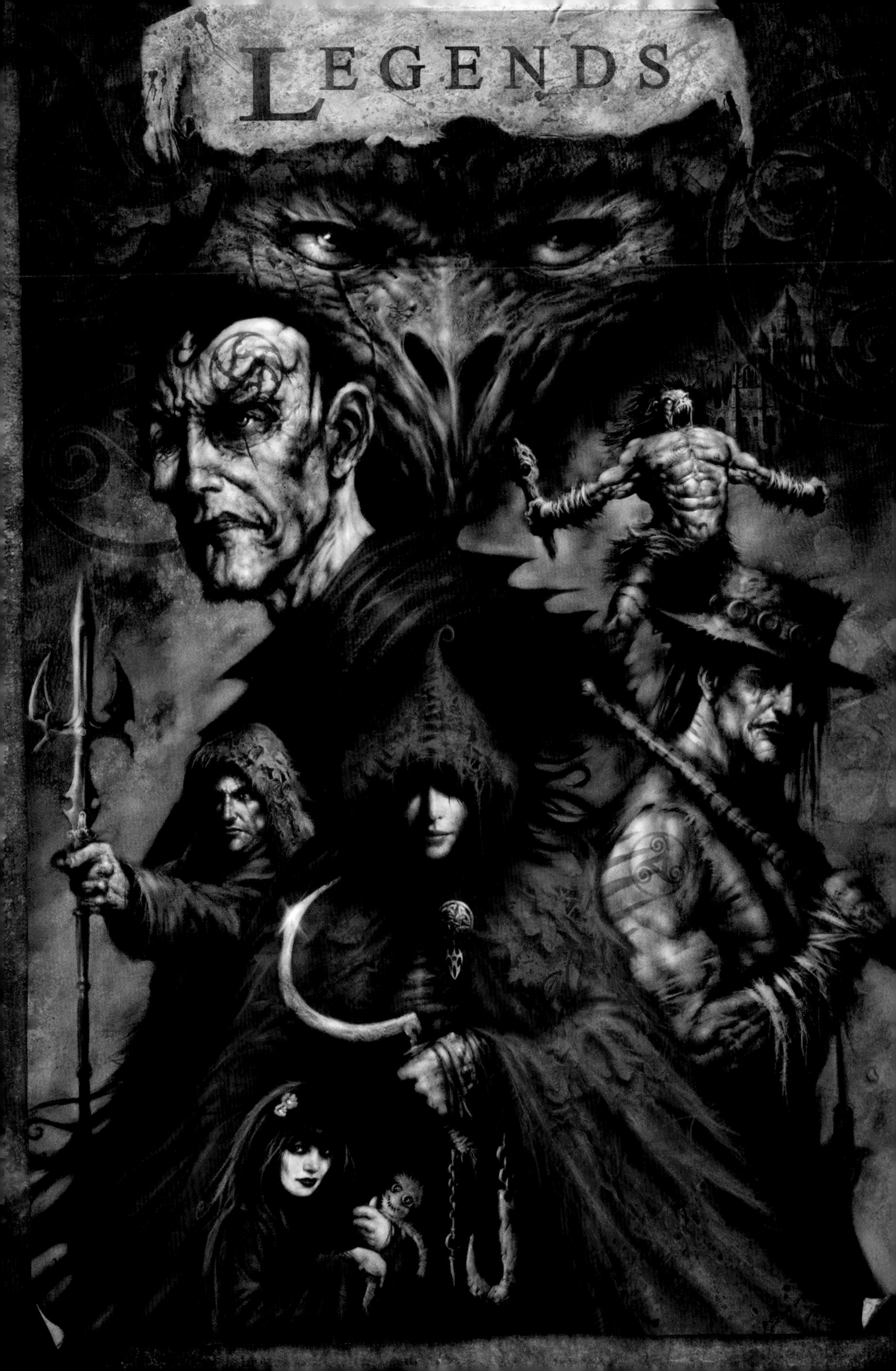
LEGENDS

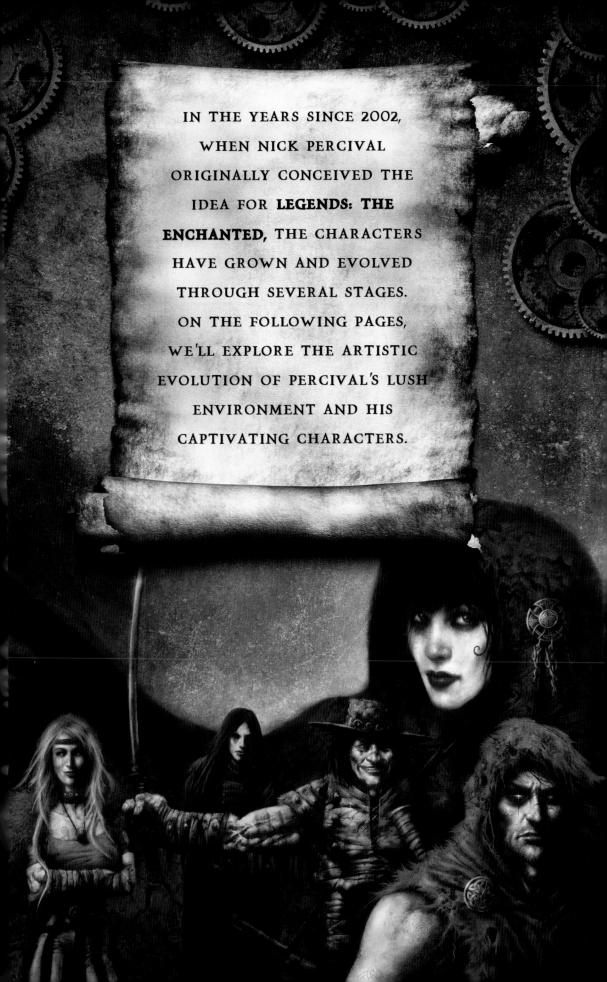

IN THE YEARS SINCE 2002, WHEN NICK PERCIVAL ORIGINALLY CONCEIVED THE IDEA FOR **LEGENDS: THE ENCHANTED,** THE CHARACTERS HAVE GROWN AND EVOLVED THROUGH SEVERAL STAGES. ON THE FOLLOWING PAGES, WE'LL EXPLORE THE ARTISTIC EVOLUTION OF PERCIVAL'S LUSH ENVIRONMENT AND HIS CAPTIVATING CHARACTERS.

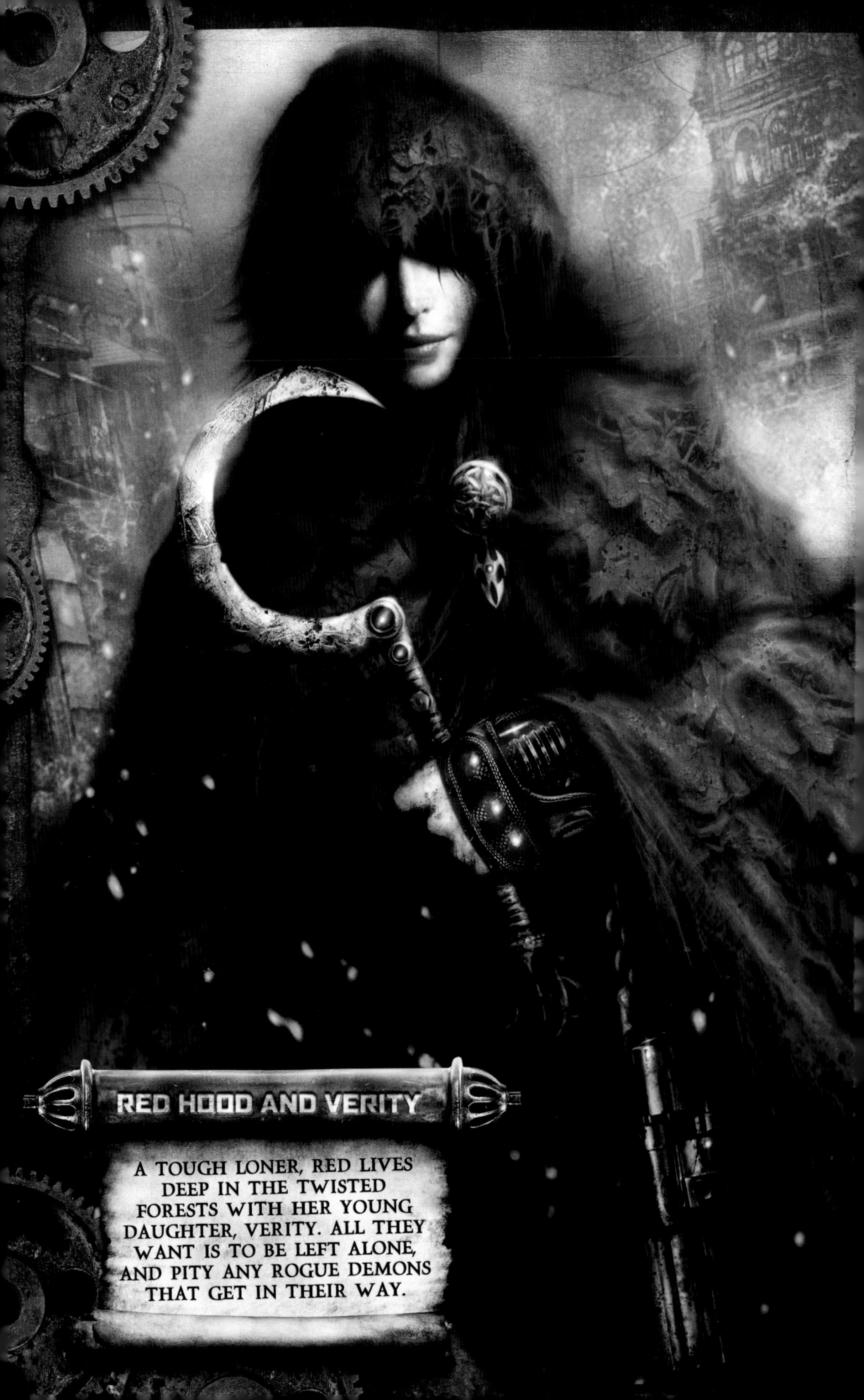
RED HOOD AND VERITY
A TOUGH LONER, RED LIVES DEEP IN THE TWISTED FORESTS WITH HER YOUNG DAUGHTER, VERITY. ALL THEY WANT IS TO BE LEFT ALONE, AND PITY ANY ROGUE DEMONS THAT GET IN THEIR WAY.

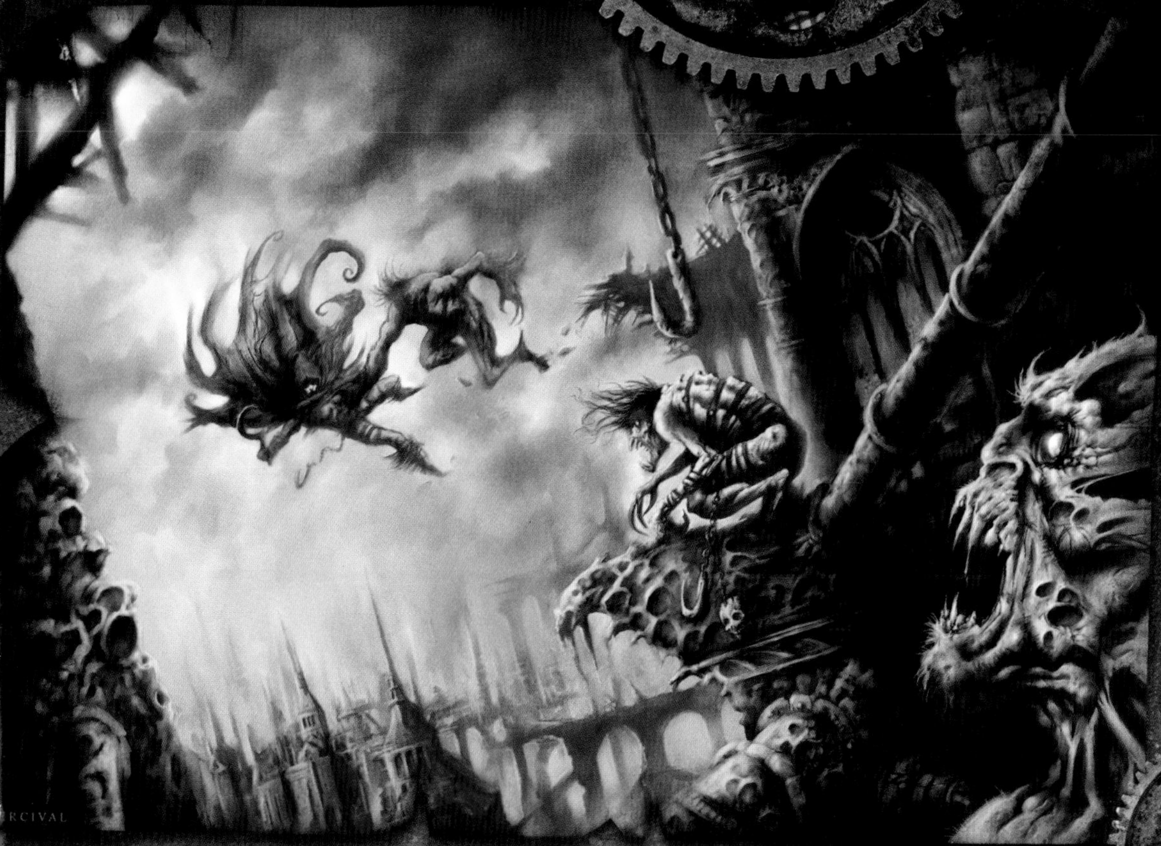

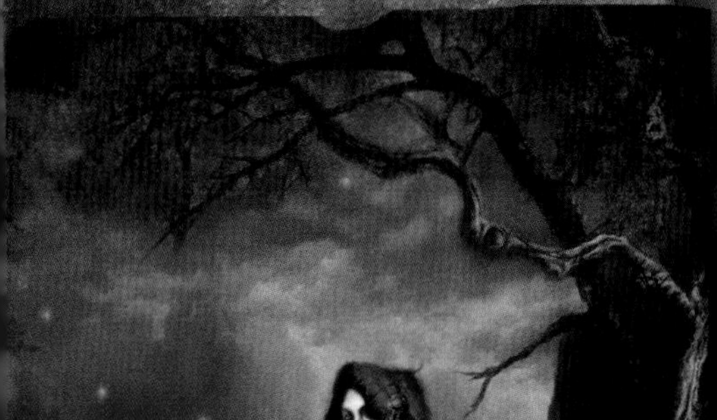

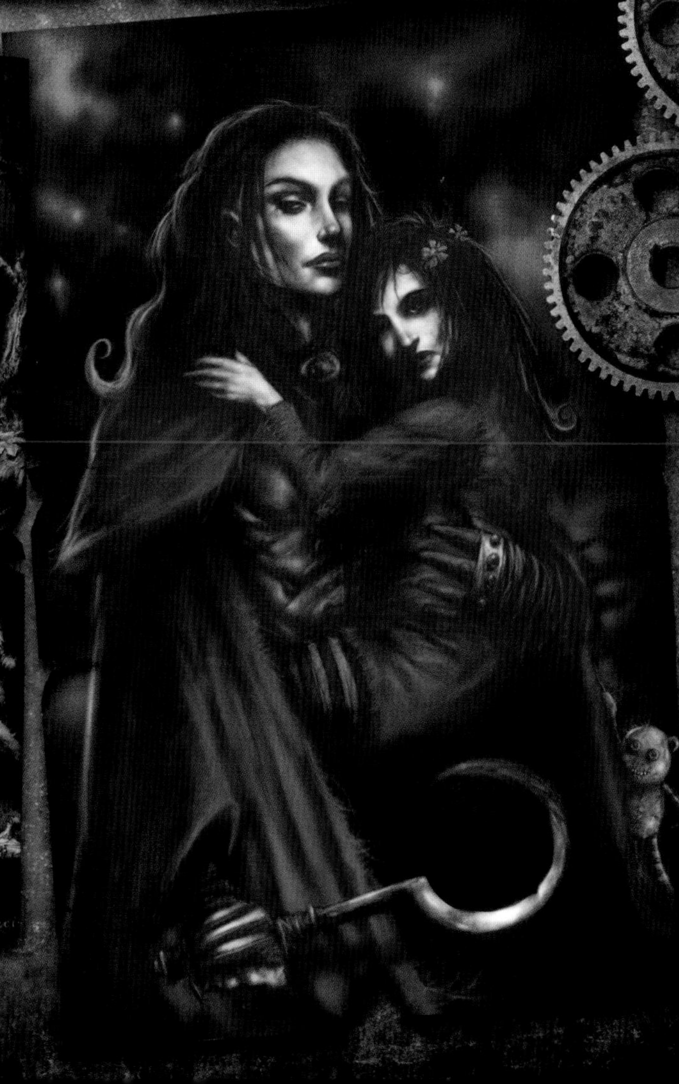

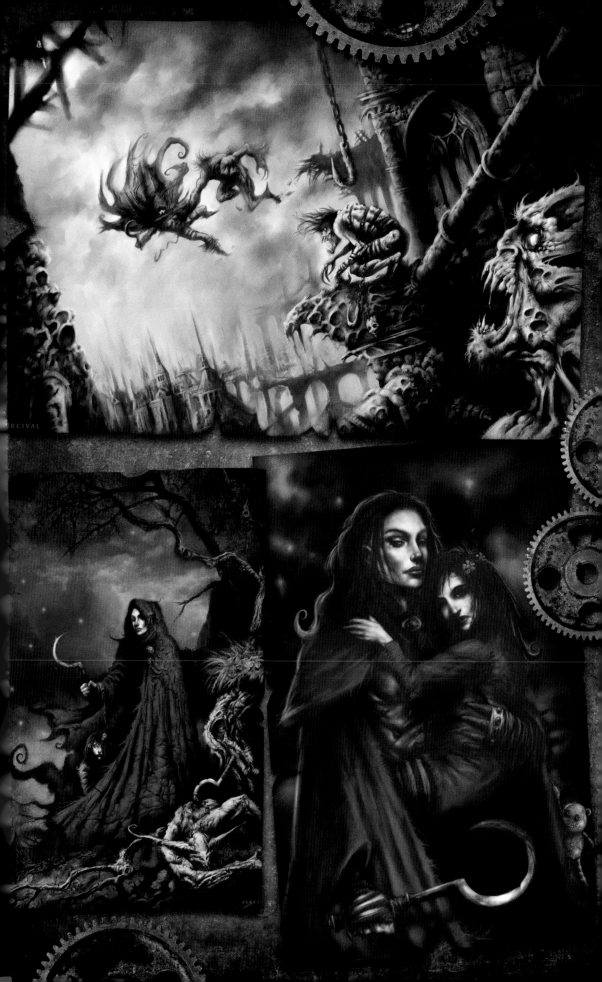

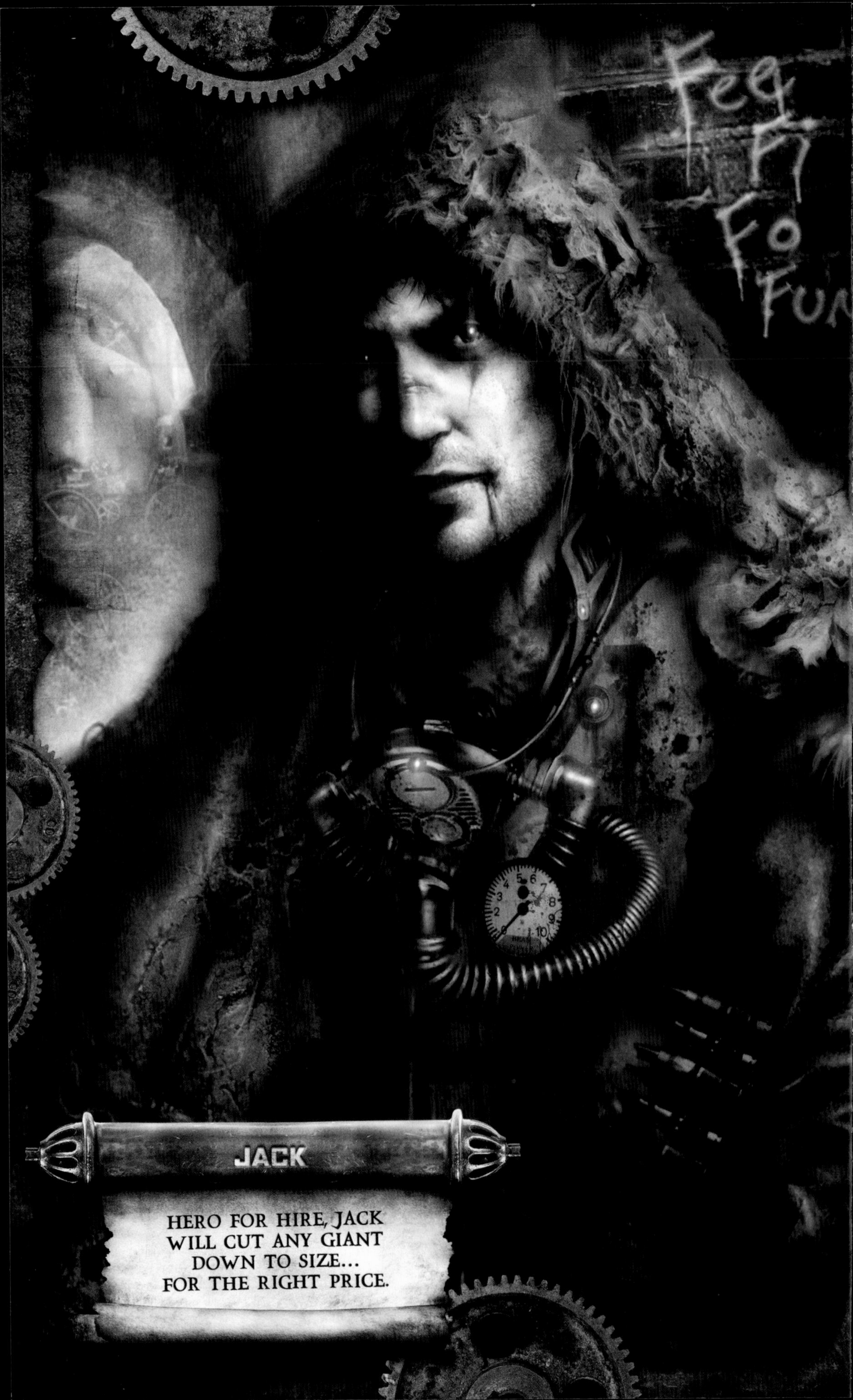
Fee
Fi
Fo
Fun
JACK
HERO FOR HIRE, JACK
WILL CUT ANY GIANT
DOWN TO SIZE...
FOR THE RIGHT PRICE.

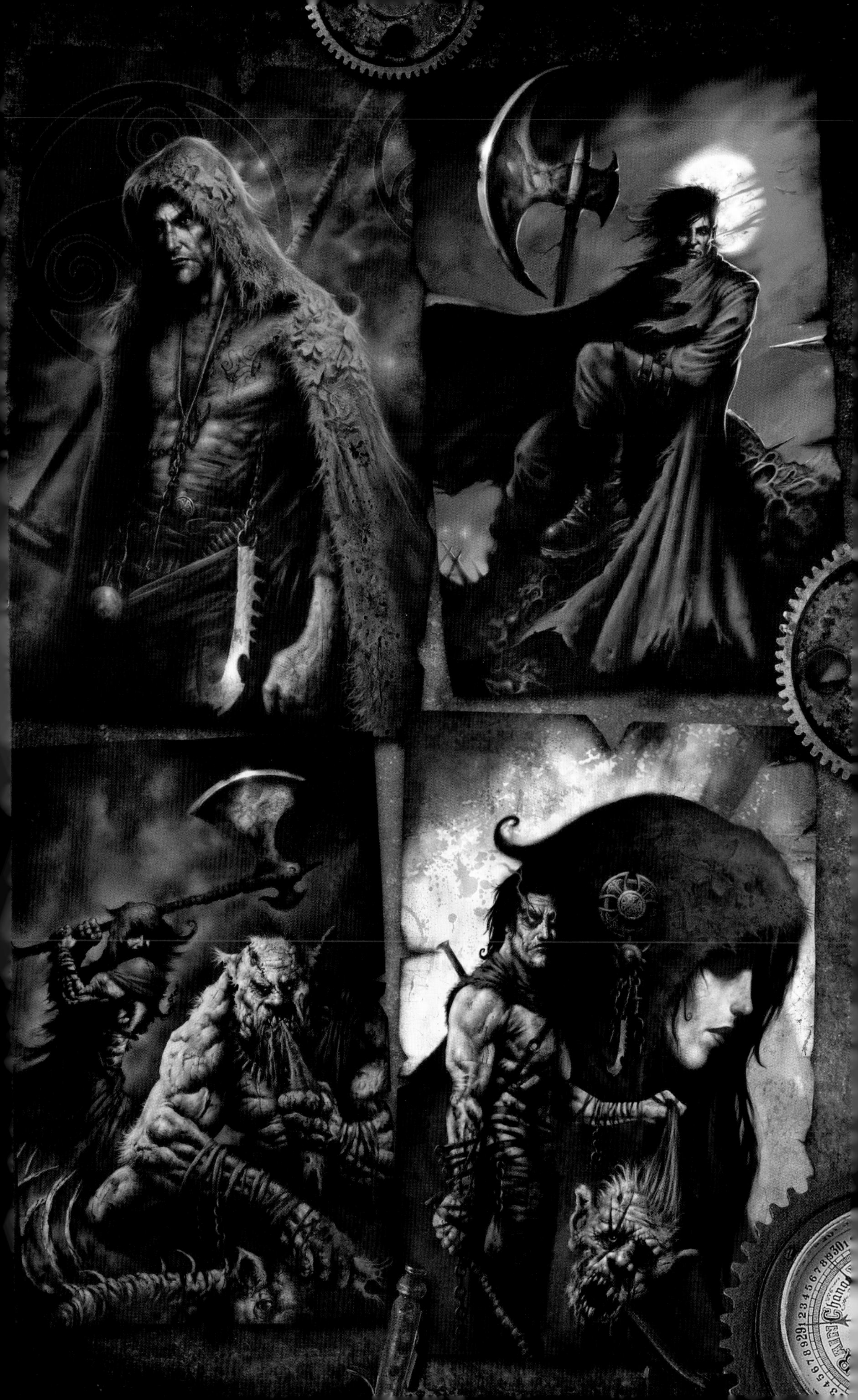

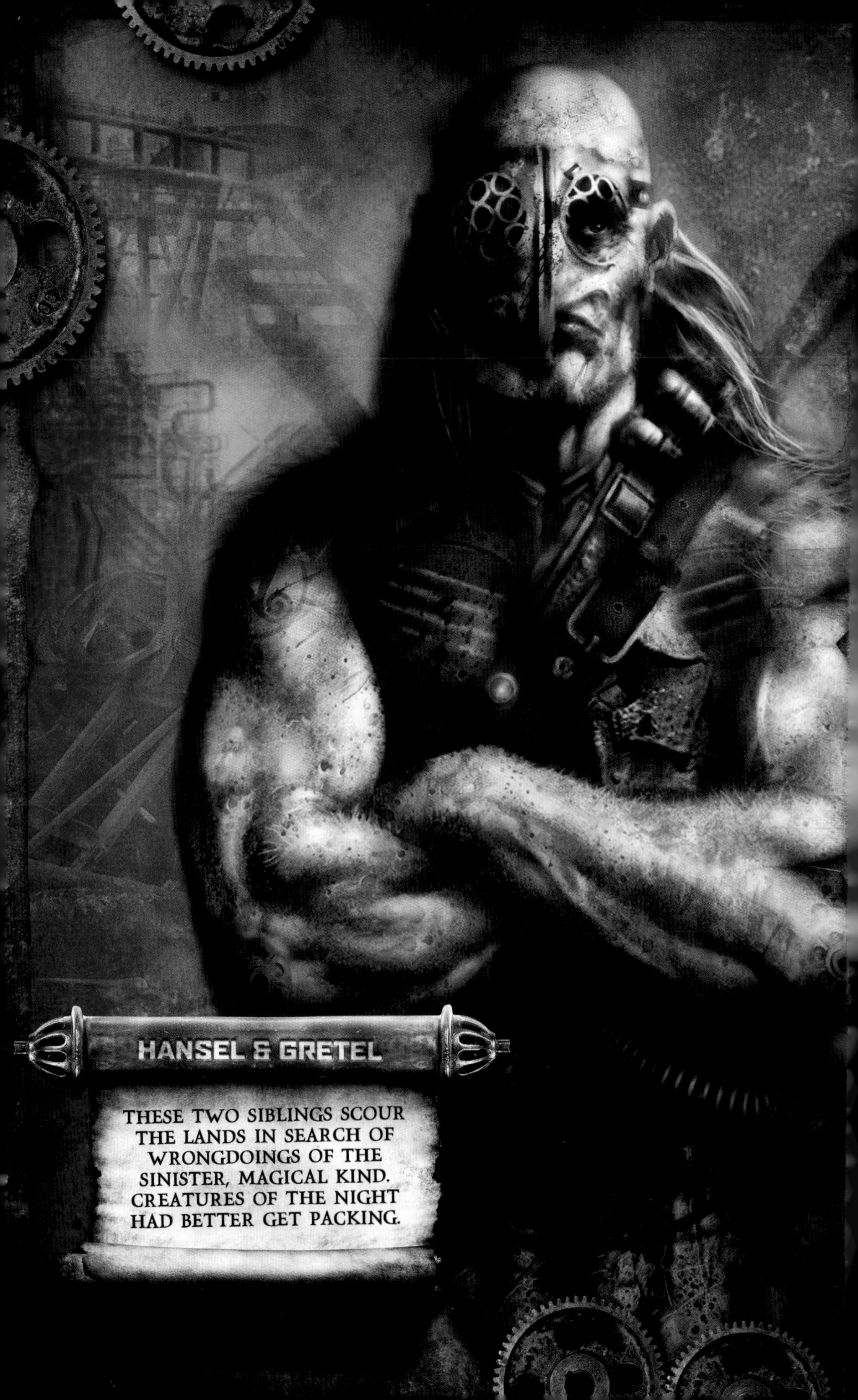
HANSEL & GRETEL
THESE TWO SIBLINGS SCOUR THE LANDS IN SEARCH OF WRONGDOINGS OF THE SINISTER, MAGICAL KIND. CREATURES OF THE NIGHT HAD BETTER GET PACKING.

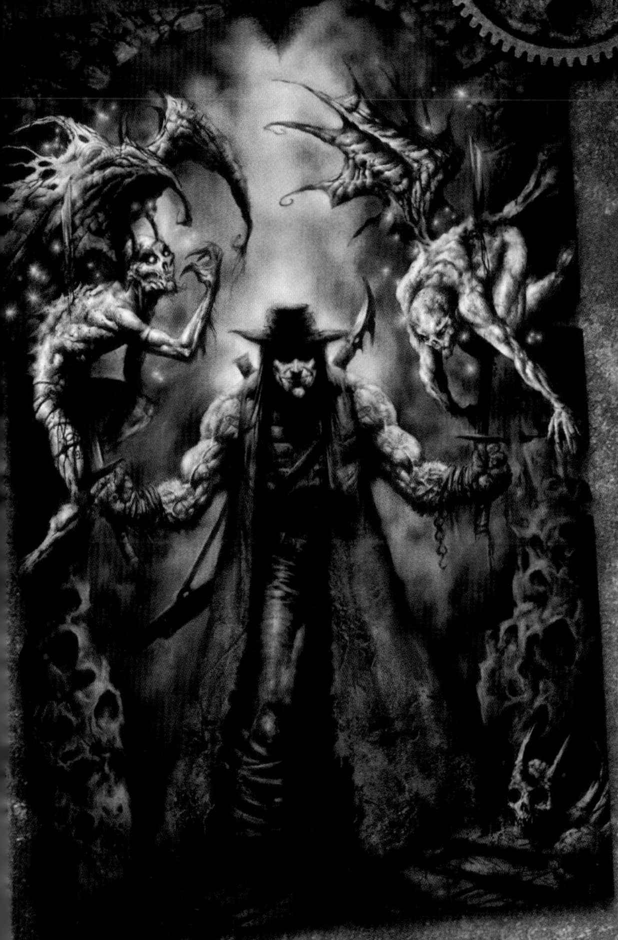

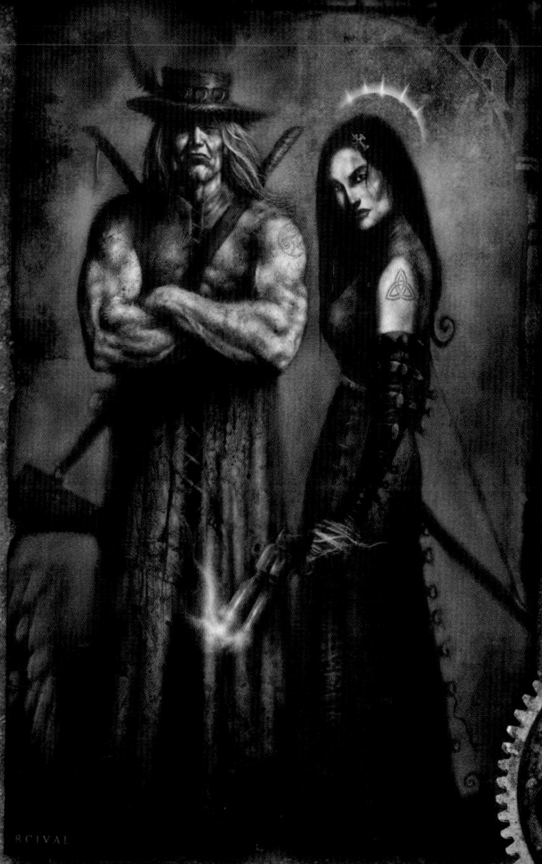
RCIVAL

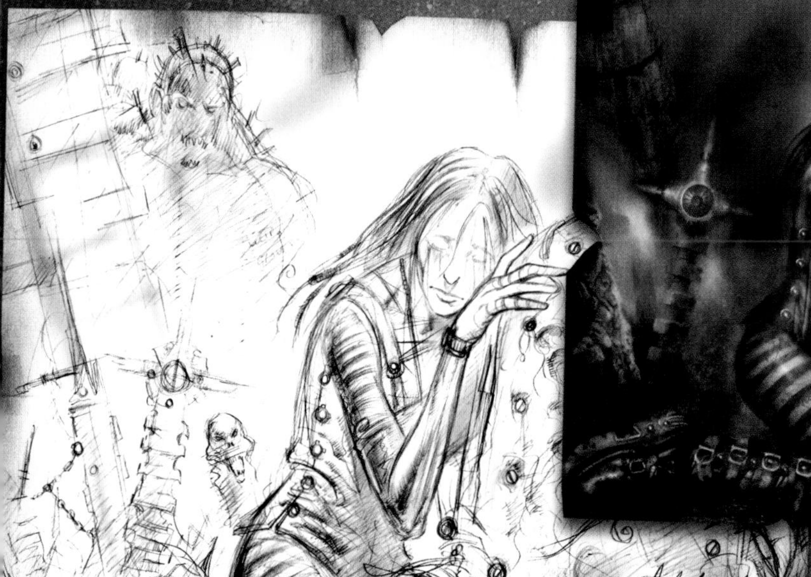

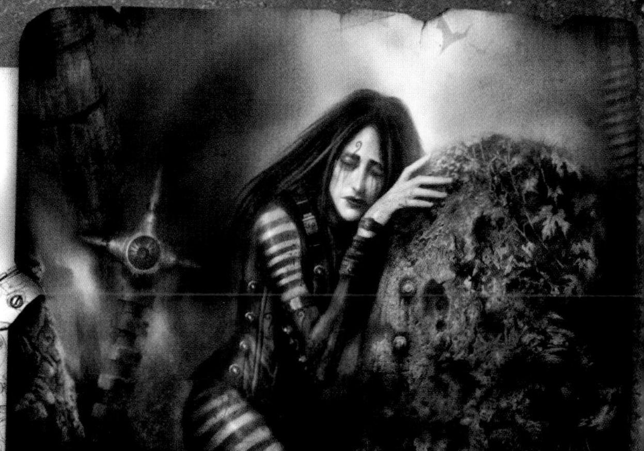

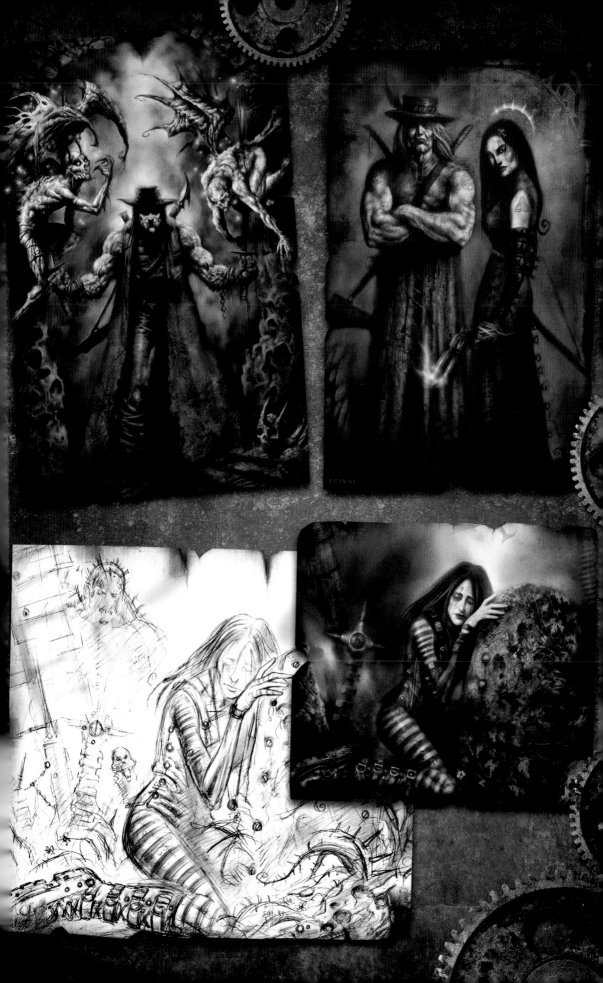

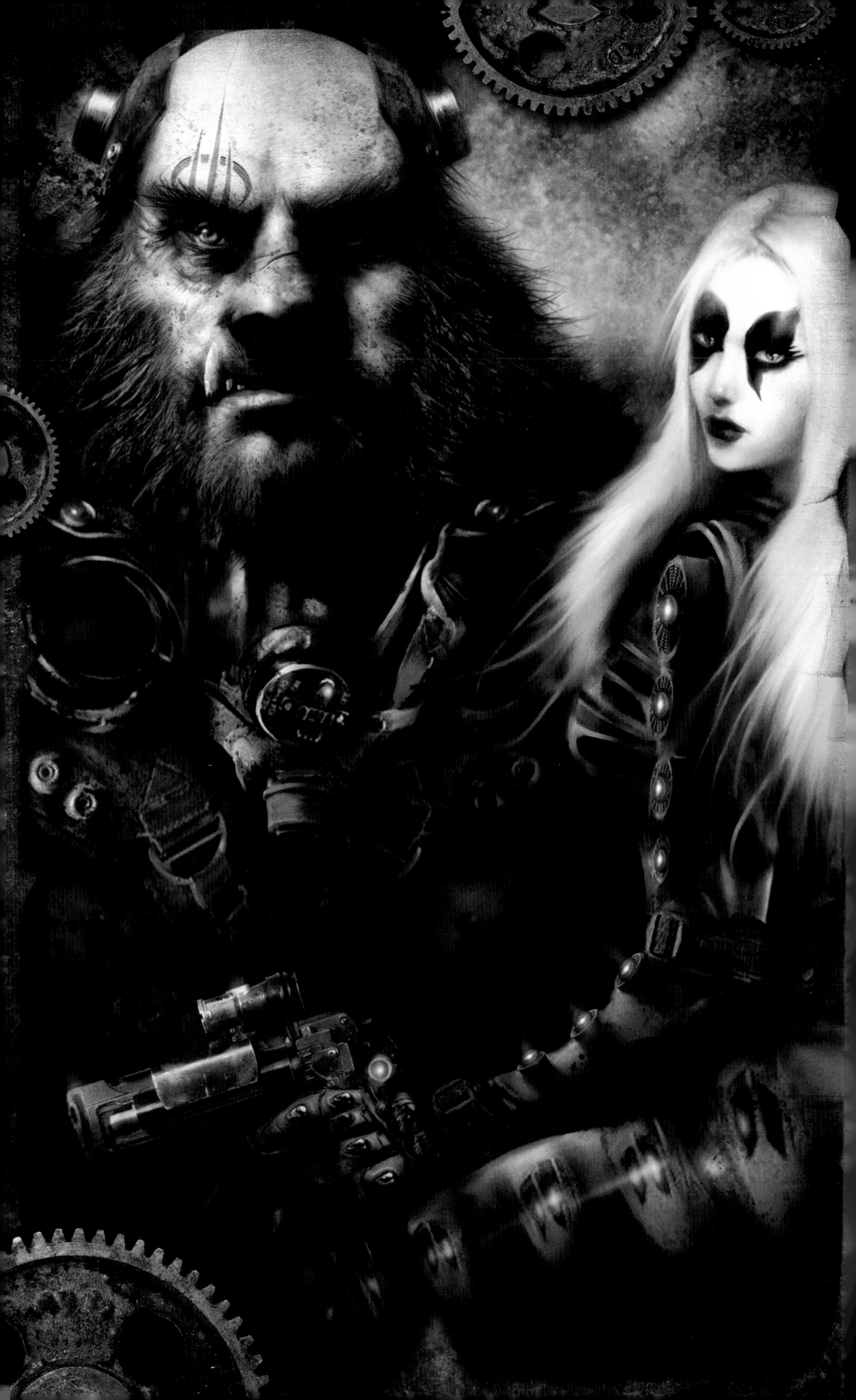

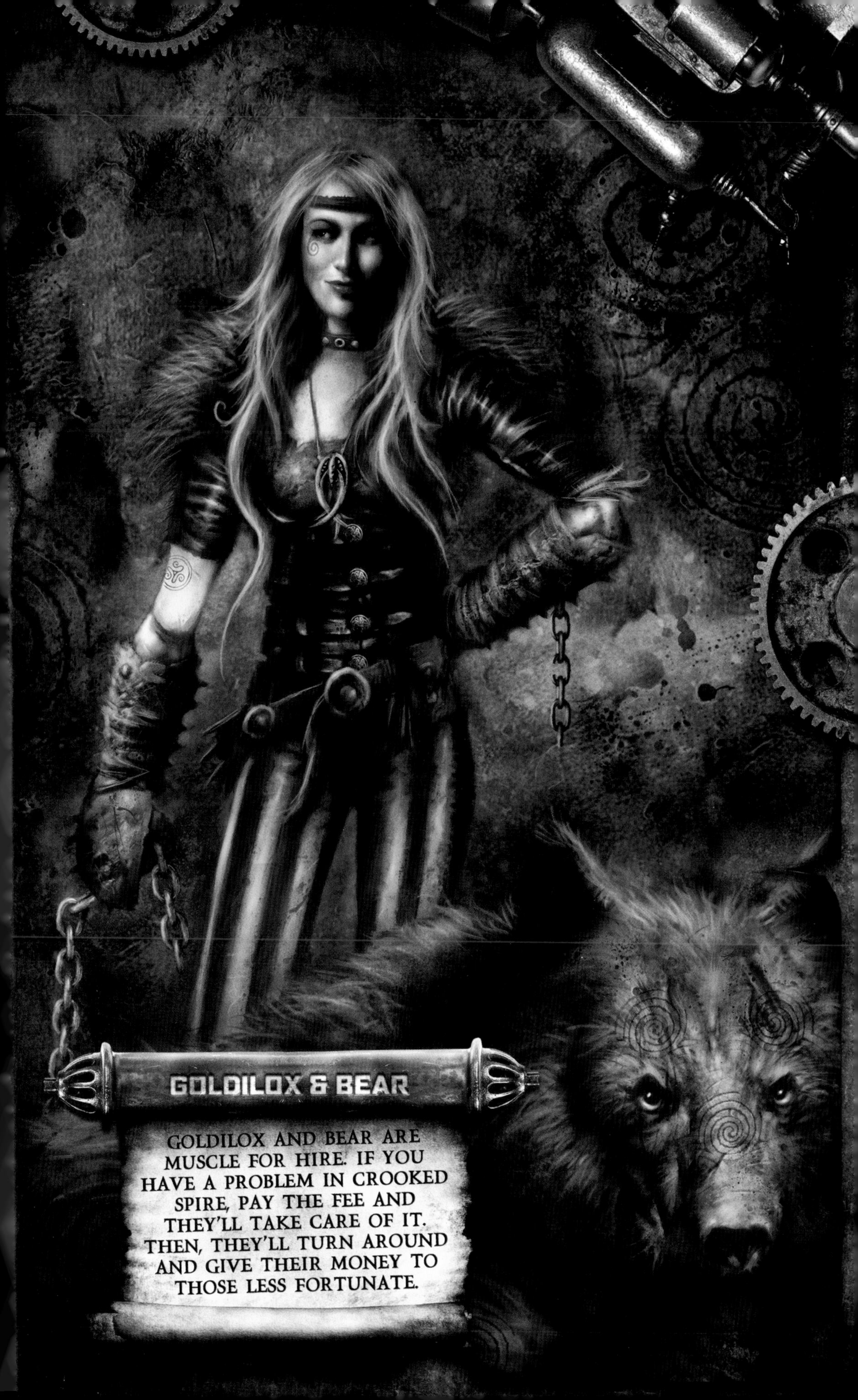
GOLDILOX & BEAR
GOLDILOX AND BEAR ARE MUSCLE FOR HIRE. IF YOU HAVE A PROBLEM IN CROOKED SPIRE, PAY THE FEE AND THEY'LL TAKE CARE OF IT. THEN, THEY'LL TURN AROUND AND GIVE THEIR MONEY TO THOSE LESS FORTUNATE.

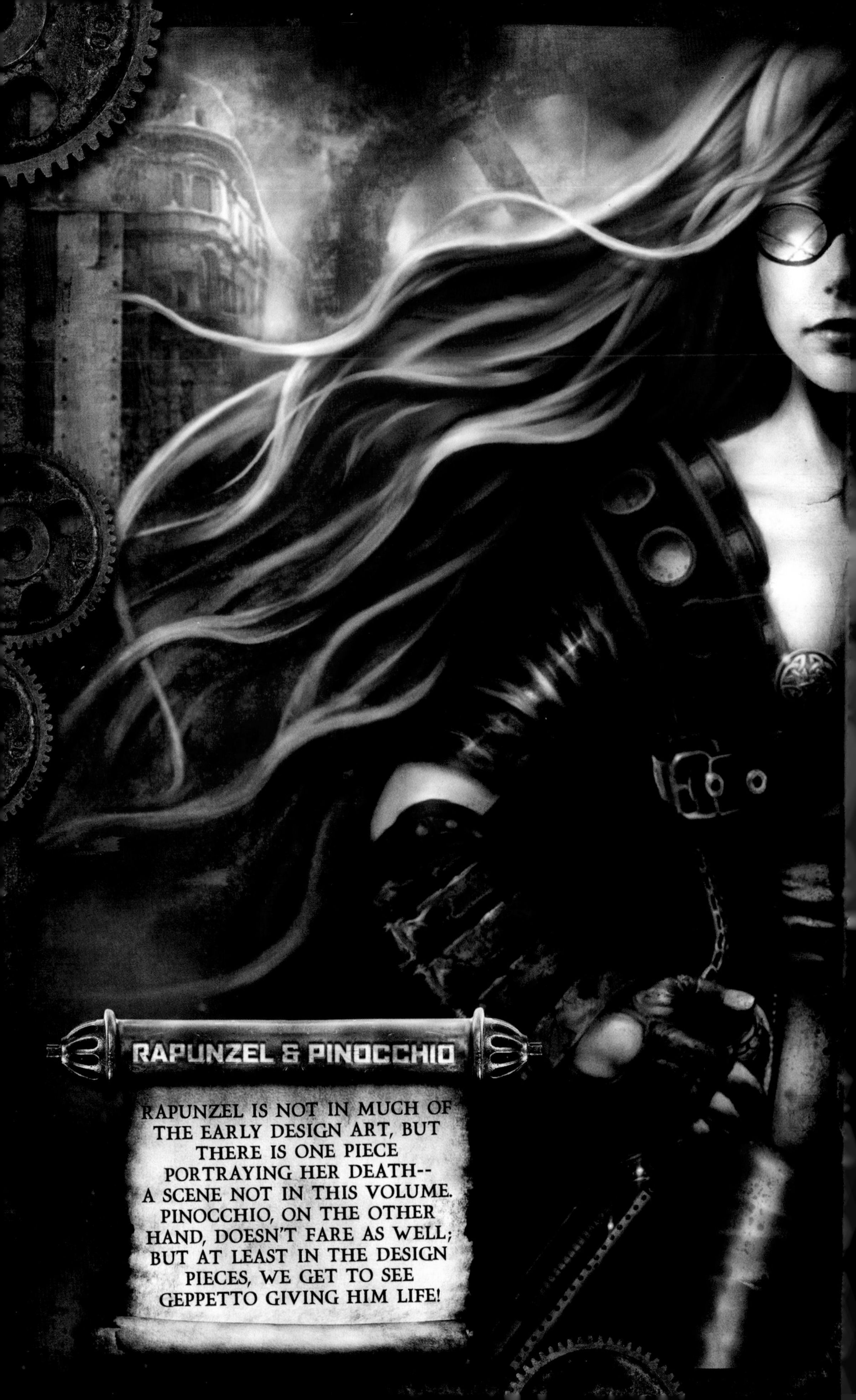

RAPUNZEL & PINOCCHIO

RAPUNZEL IS NOT IN MUCH OF THE EARLY DESIGN ART, BUT THERE IS ONE PIECE PORTRAYING HER DEATH-- A SCENE NOT IN THIS VOLUME. PINOCCHIO, ON THE OTHER HAND, DOESN'T FARE AS WELL; BUT AT LEAST IN THE DESIGN PIECES, WE GET TO SEE GEPPETTO GIVING HIM LIFE!

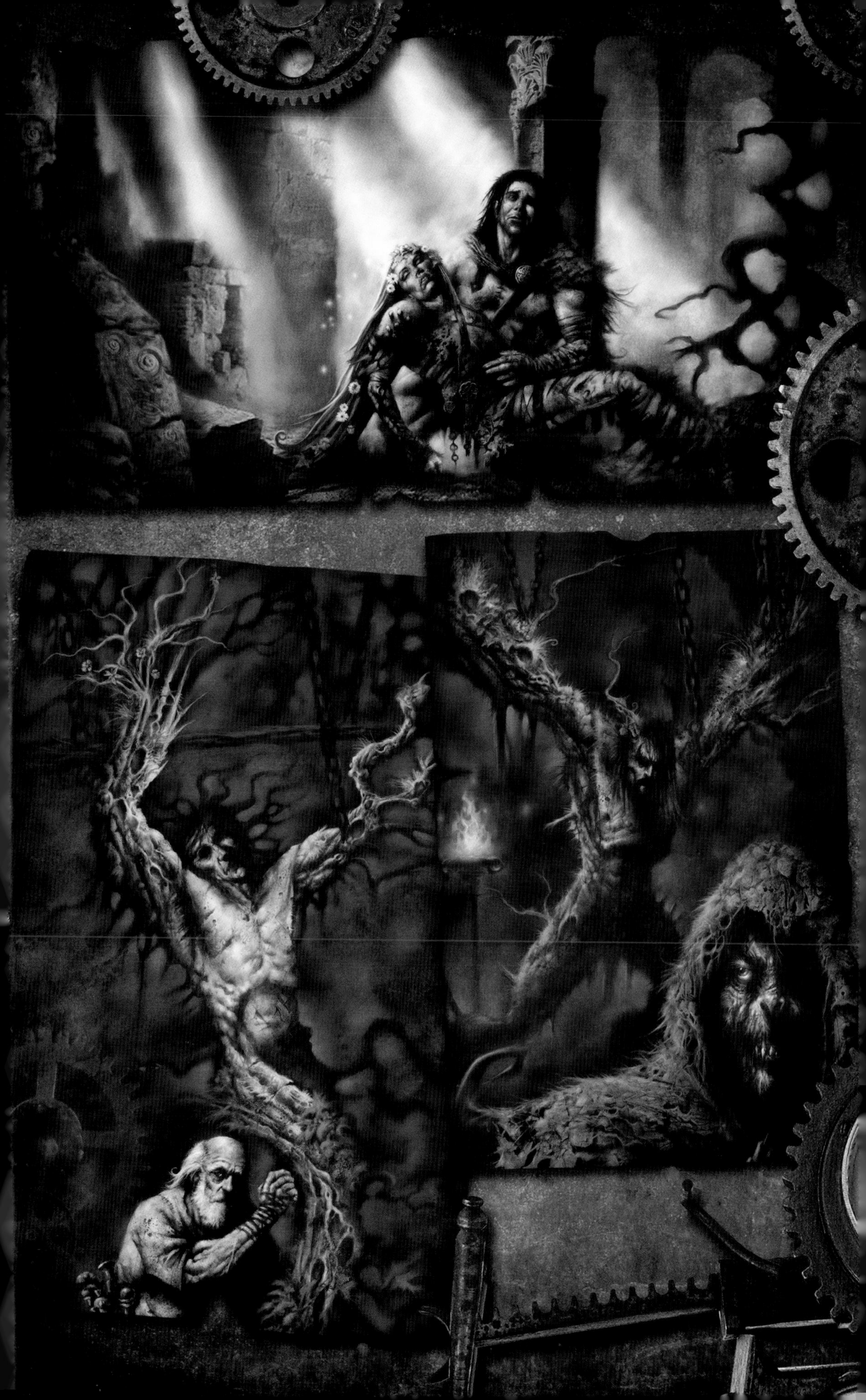

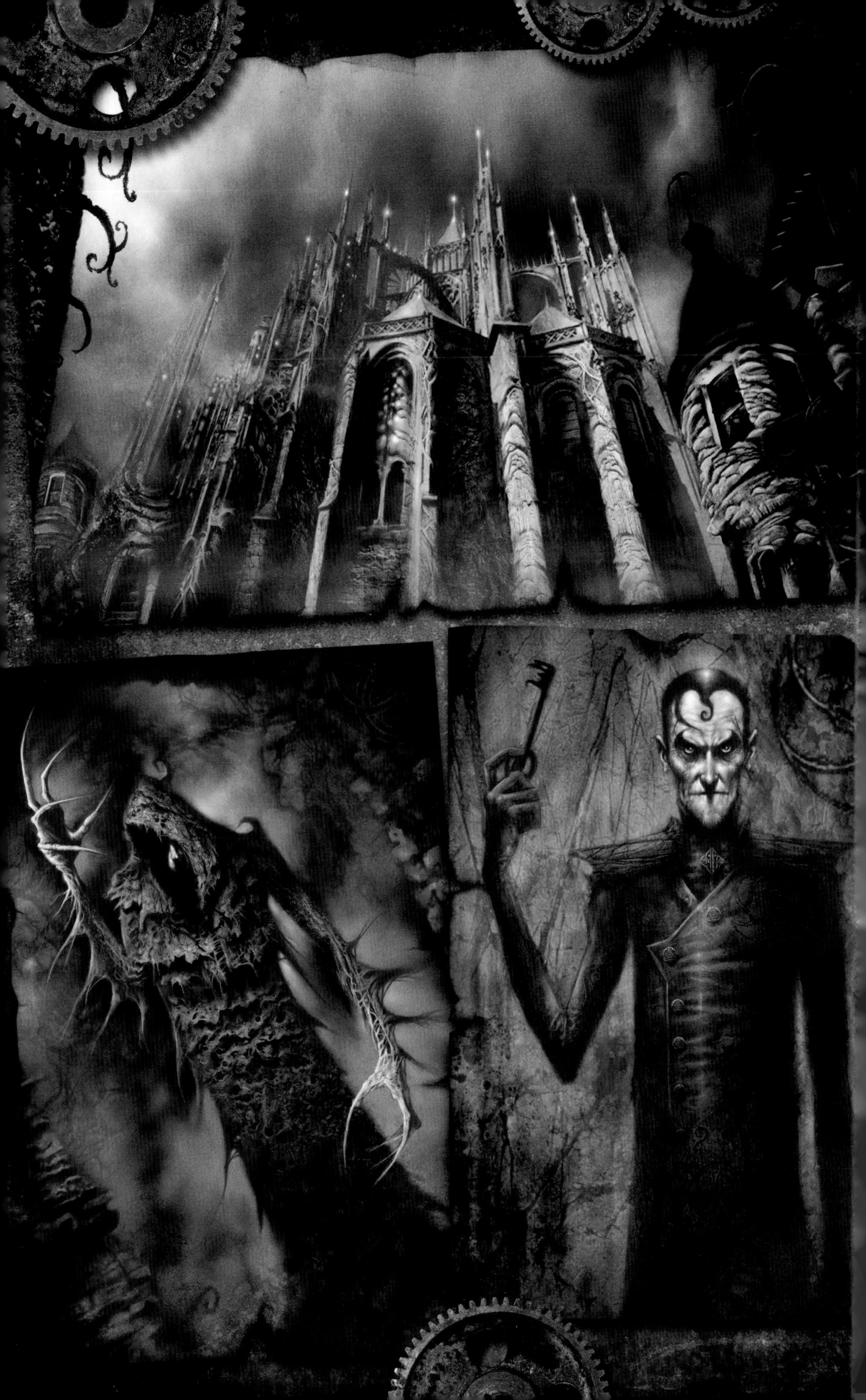

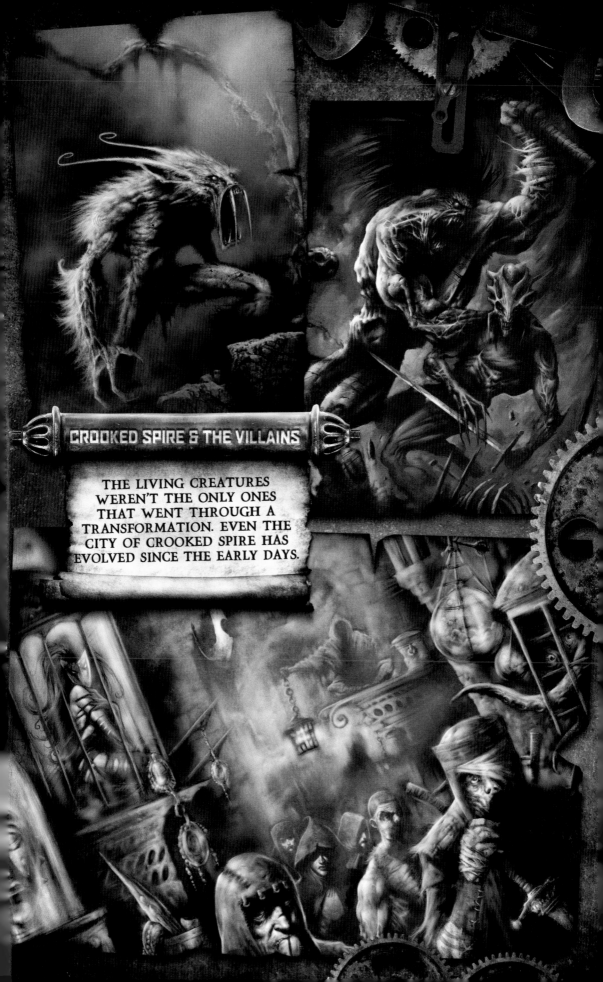

CROOKED SPIRE & THE VILLAINS

THE LIVING CREATURES WEREN'T THE ONLY ONES THAT WENT THROUGH A TRANSFORMATION. EVEN THE CITY OF CROOKED SPIRE HAS EVOLVED SINCE THE EARLY DAYS.

THE TROLL

THE SON OF THE HAG, THE TROLL LIVES MOST OF HIS YEARS ASLEEP UNDER THE BRIDGE. BUT WHEN MOTHER CALLS... WHO SAYS A MINDLESS KILLING MACHINE CAN'T STILL BE A MAMA'S BOY?

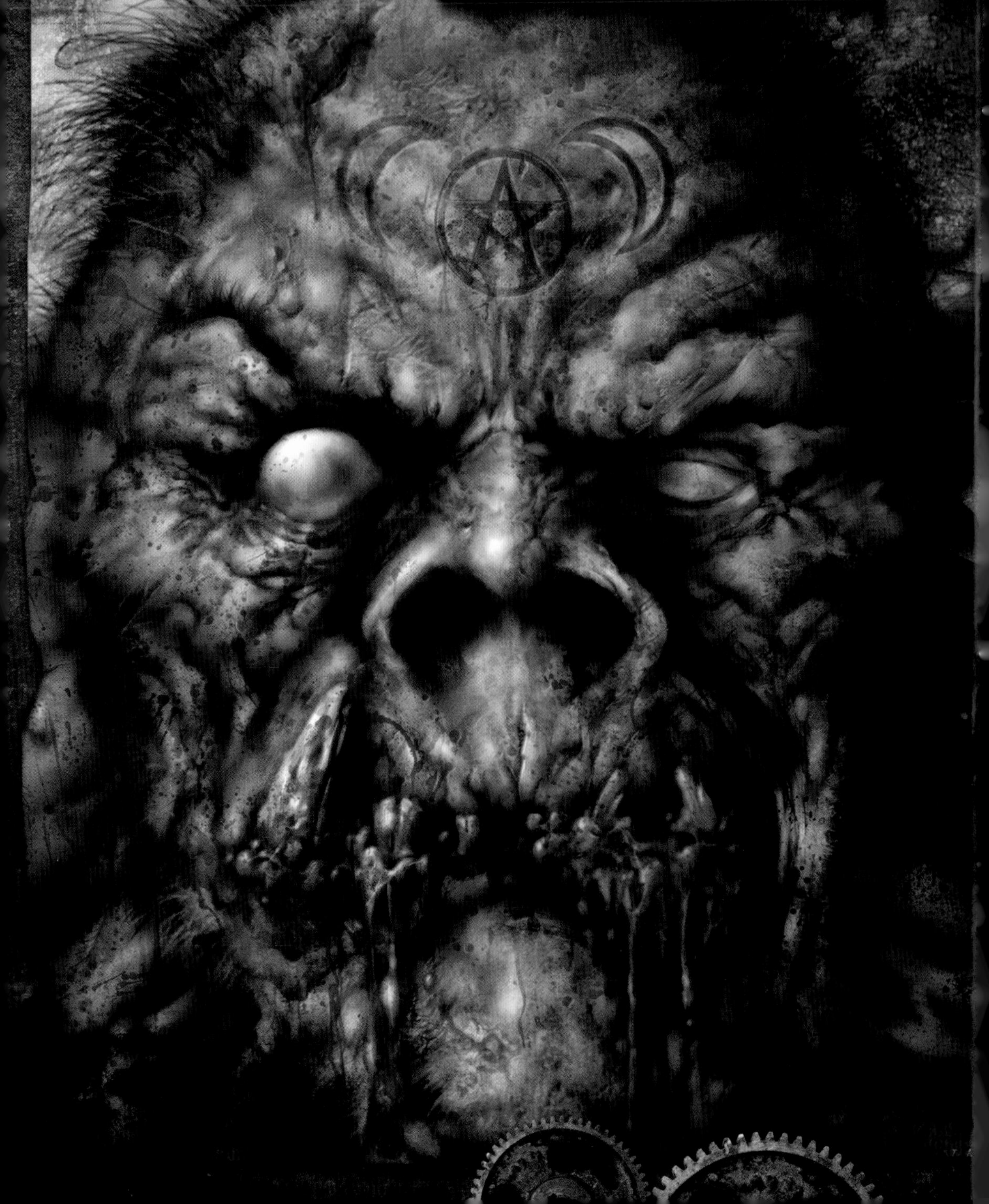

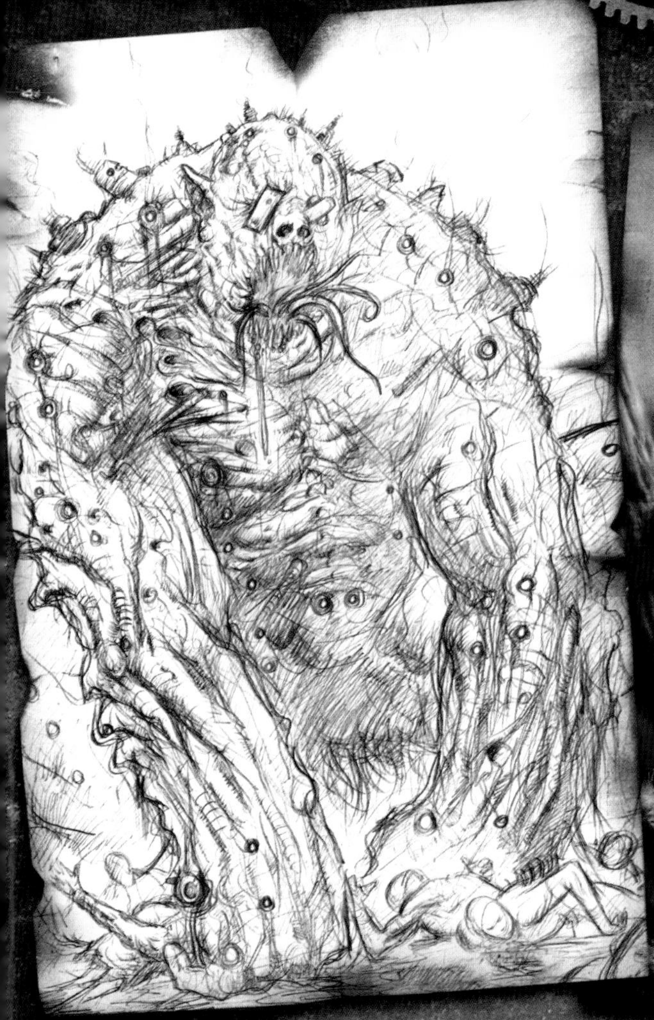

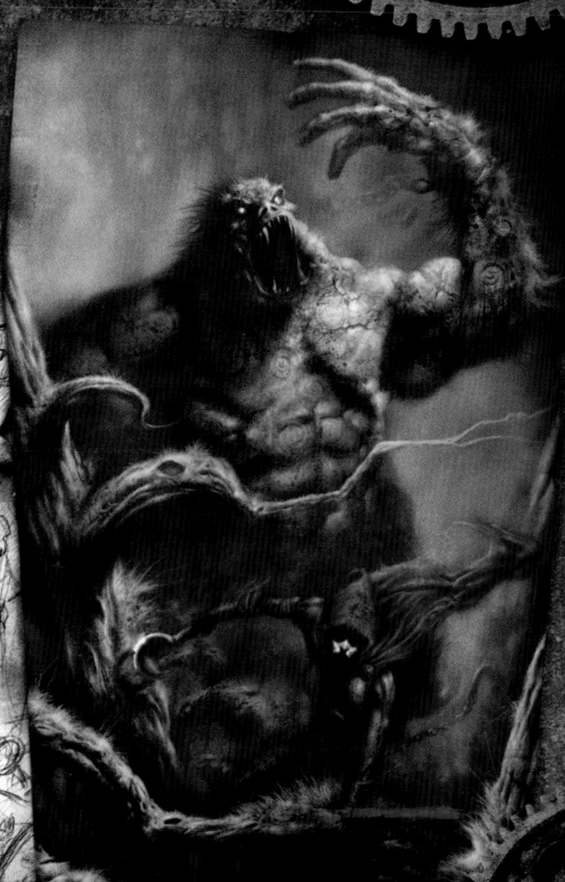

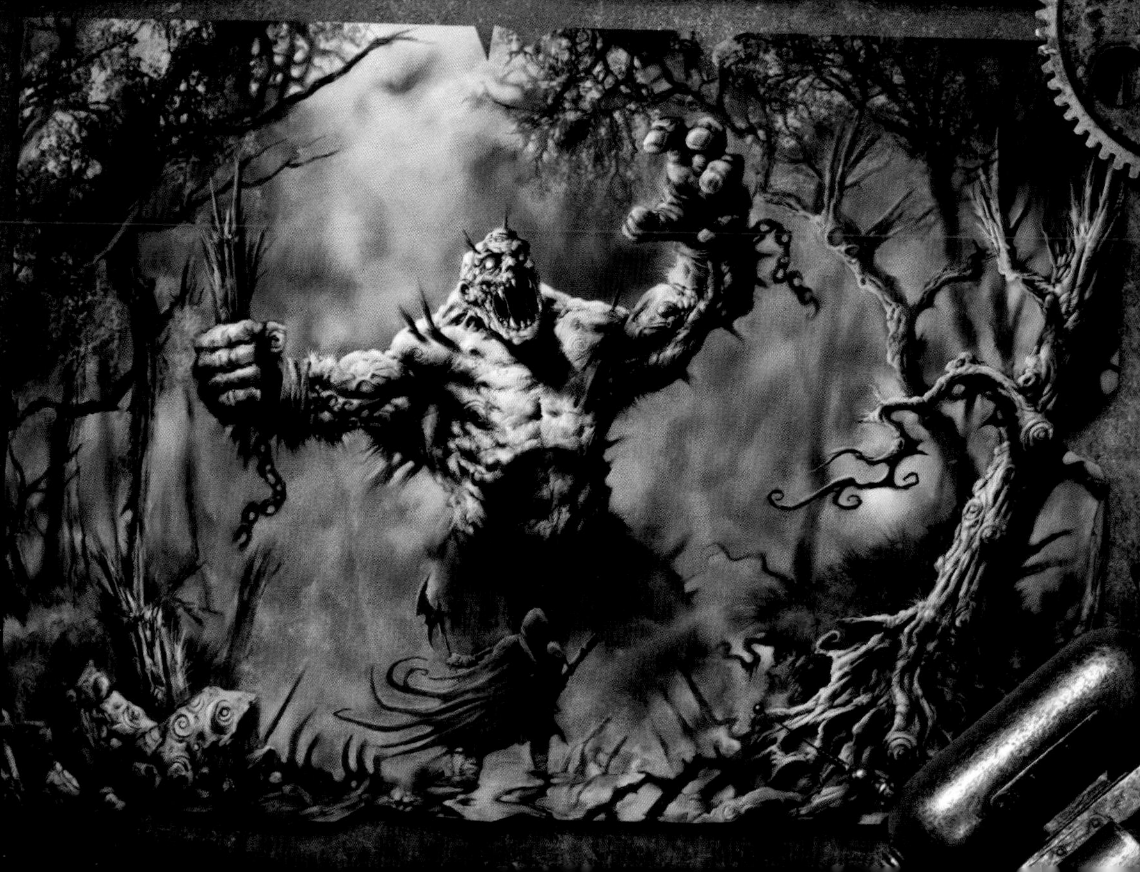

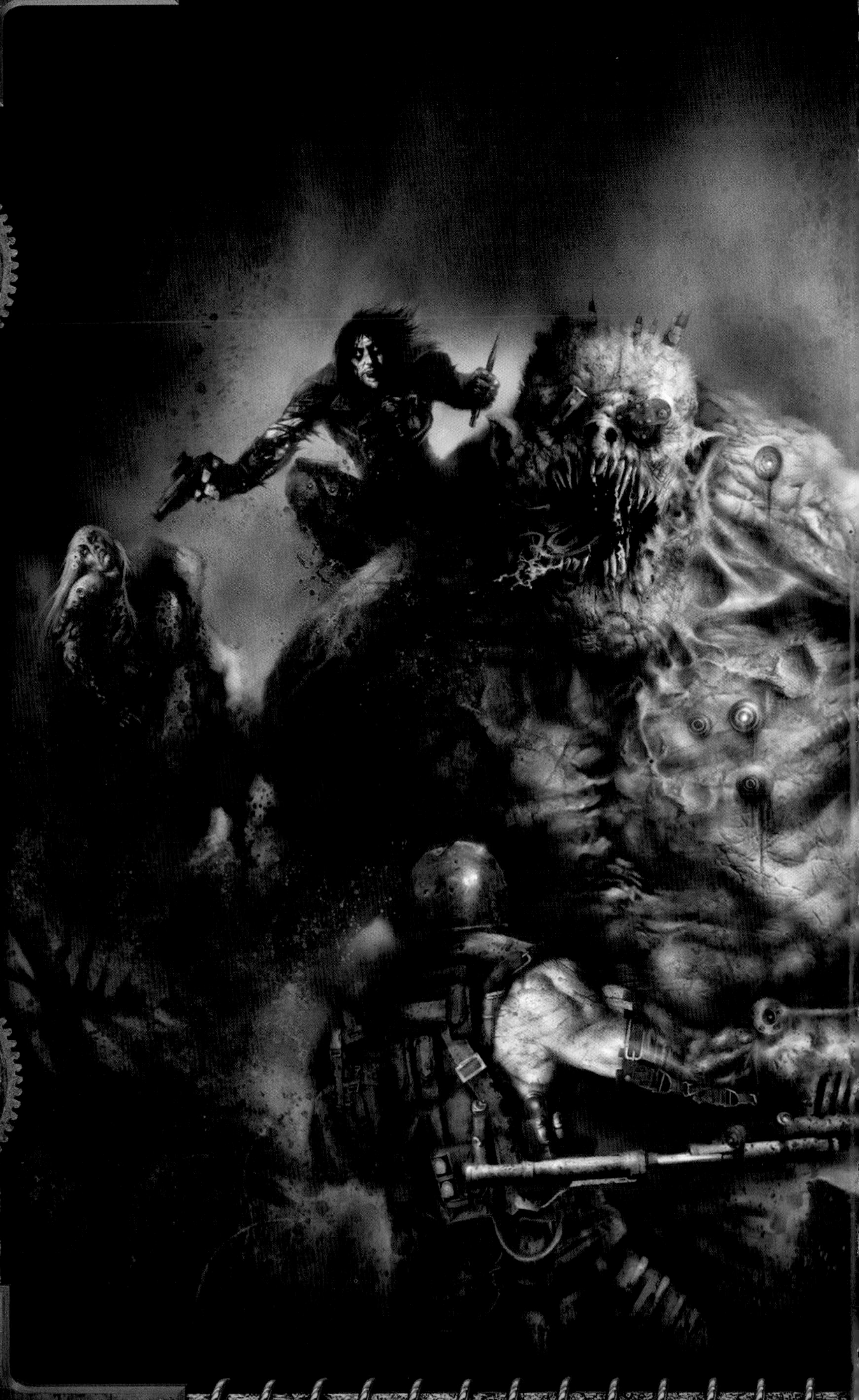

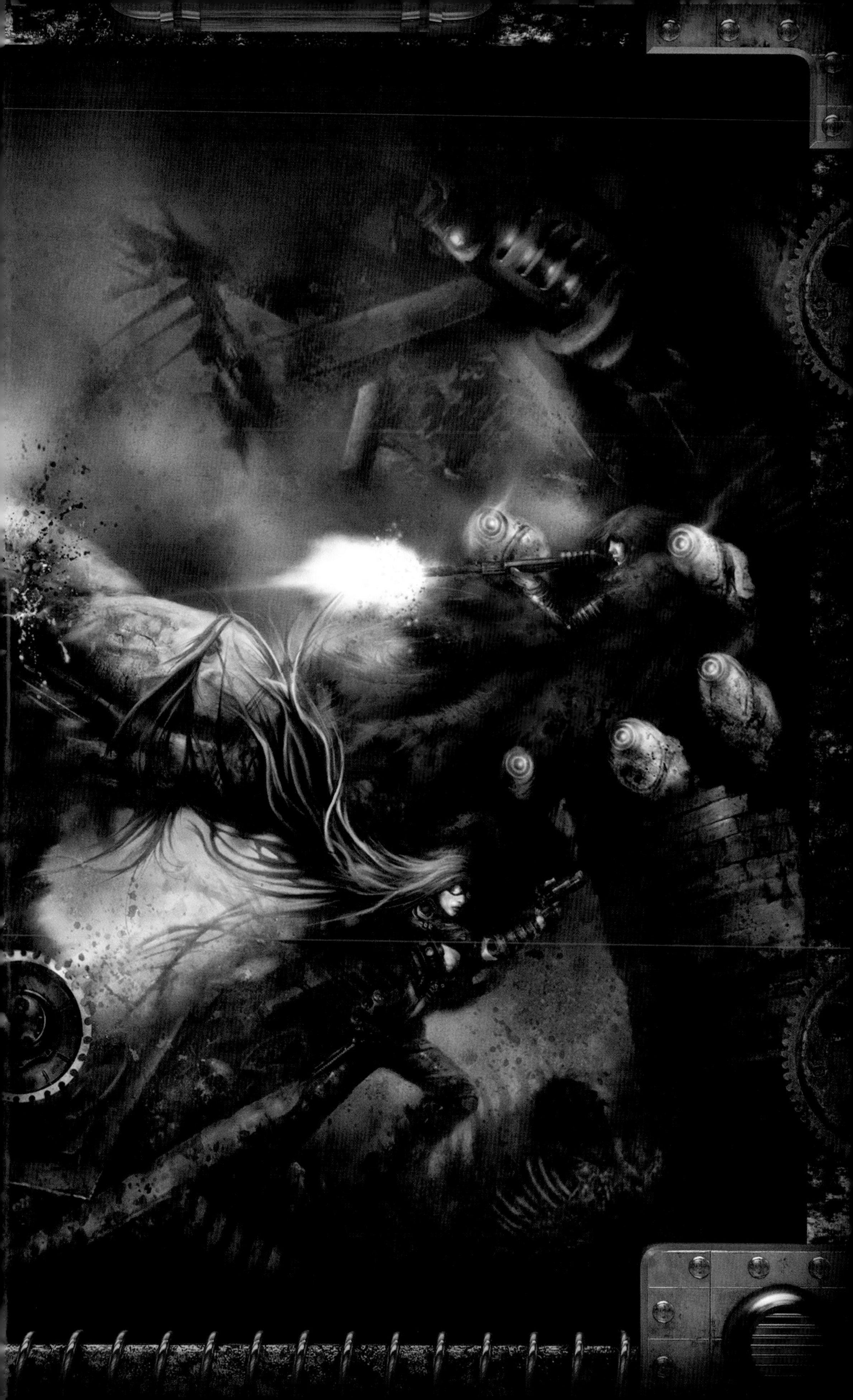

Aladdin™

LEGACY OF THE LOST

WRITTEN BY
IAN EDGINTON
ILLUSTRATED BY
STJEPAN SEJIC & PATRICK REILLY

EDGINTON ◆ SEJIC ◆ REILLY
RADICAL
Aladdin
LEGACY OF THE LOST
RADICAL BOOKS

TRADE PAPERBACK

152 PAGES | FULL COLOR | $14.95

"ALADDIN IS YET ANOTHER TITLE THAT MAKES A STRONG CASE FOR RADICAL BEING THE FUTURE OF COMICS."
PHILADELPHIA DAILY NEWS

ON SALE JULY 2010

From the mystical city of Shambhalla to the ends of the Earth comes a tale of magic, mystery and the motivations of power. It is the world of Ala ad-Din, better known as ALADDIN.

This new deluxe trade paperback collects the full miniseries from multi-Eisner nominated writer **Ian Edginton** (*Stormwatch: PHD*) with illustrators **Stjepan Sejic** (*Witchblade*) and **Patrick Reilly**. Extras include an in-depth interview with writer Ian Edginton, never-before-seen production renderings and a gallery of artwork featuring international talents such as **Luis Royo** (*Heavy Metal*), **Marko Djurdjevic** (*Thor*), **Arthur Suydam** (*Marvel Zombies*), **Clayton Crain** (*X-Force*) and more.

WWW.RADICALPUBLISHING.COM

RADICAL BOOKS

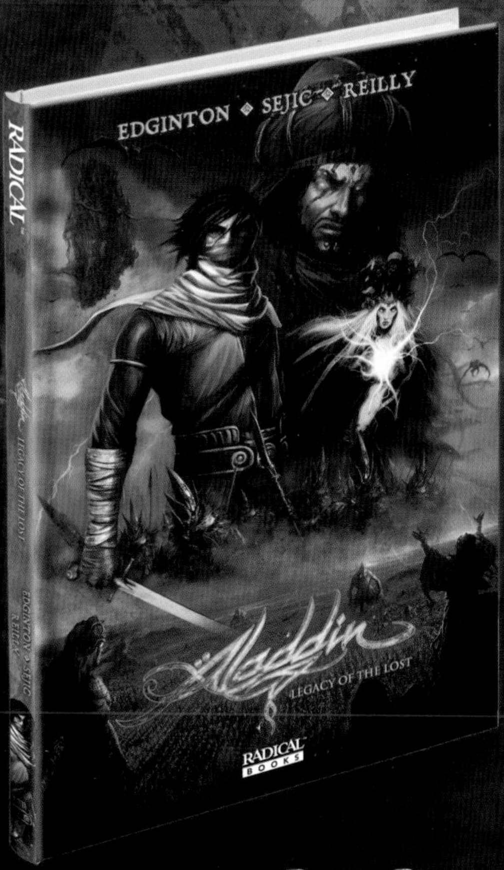